ALSO BY MARK T. BARNES

The Echoes of Empire series

Book One: The Garden of Stones

THE OBSIDIAN HEART

Book Two of
THE ECHOES OF EMPIRE

MARK T. BARNES

Text copyright © 2013 Mark Barnes

All rights reserved.

Printed in the United States of America.

No part of this book may be reproduced, or stored in a retrieval system, or transmitted in any form or by any means, electronic, mechanical, photocopying, recording, or otherwise, without express written permission of the publisher.

Published by 47North – Seattle, Washington

www.apub.com

ISBN-13: 9781477807606
ISBN-10: 1477807608
Library of Congress Control Number: 2013936768

Cover illustrated by Stephan Martiniere

To the family and friends who never questioned that this was what I should do. To the storytellers, past and present, who lit the way.

SOUTHEASTERN ĪA

YEAR 495 OF THE SHRÍANESE FEDERATION

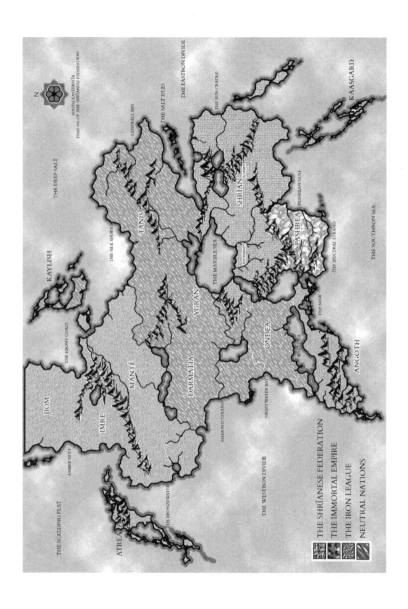

SHRĪAN

YEAR 495 OF THE SHRÍANESE FEDERATION

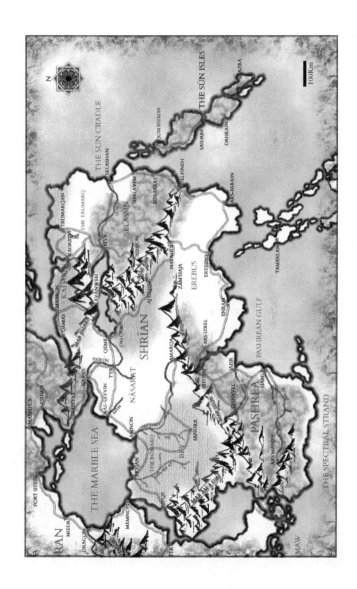

THE OBSIDIAN HEART

BEFORE

"THERE ARE THREE GREAT RIVERS: THE PAST, THE PRESENT,
AND THE FUTURE. NEITHER THE PASSAGE OF TIME, NOR OURSELVES,
ARE CONSTANT. WE, LIKE TIME, ARE SUBJECTIVE AND VIEWED WITH AS
MANY LENSES AS THERE ARE PEOPLE TO SEE. WE, WITHIN TIME, ARE AT
ONCE THE INITIATOR AND OBSERVER OF PASSING EVENTS, SAILORS ON A
RIVER OF CAUSE AND EFFECT: THE MOMENT WE HAVE CAUSED AN EVENT,
OR WITNESSED ITS EFFECTS, WE ARE SWEPT BY THEM AND LEFT ONLY
WITH IMPERFECT MEMORIES OF THE SMALL PART OF THE WHOLE WE HAVE
SEEN. NO MATTER HOW MUCH WE TRY, THERE IS NO GOING BACK, AND
THERE IS NO SEEING EVERYTHING THERE IS TO SEE. NOR CAN WE BUT
GUESS AT WHAT IS TO COME."

—From *The Three Rivers*, by Ahwe, scholar, philosopher, and explorer
(First Year of the Awakened Empire)

It has been almost five centuries since the formation of the Shrīanese Federation, an alliance of the surviving six Great Houses and the Hundred Families of the Avān, who fled the fall of the Awakened Empire and its monarch, Mahj-Nāsarat fe Malde-ran, as the result of the Human Insurrection.

The land within and around Shrīan is littered with the detritus of past empires, echoes of glory and the high watermark of civilisations lost to time, internecine war, and blind ambition. Set against Shrīanese imperialism and the return to days of glory, is the Human governed Iron League, an alliance of nations set on ensuring no new empire rises to seize control. The Humans, also known as the Starborn, remember their days of servitude and are unwilling to bend their necks again.

Rahn-Erebus fa Corajidin, the leader of the Great House of Erebus, and leader of the Imperialist political faction, is dying, his body failing from the poison in his soul. Neither the powers of his Angothic Witch, Wolfram, nor the cures available to him have brought relief. Shrinking from the thought of dying before he has achieved the heights expected of a leader of his family, Corajidin begins secret excavations of the Rōmarq—a place rich in the ancient and powerful artefacts of ages past, where Corajidin is sure the answers to his illness can be found in the lost works of Sedefke, the greatest inventor, explorer and scholar in history.

To provide better access to the treasures he wants, Corajidin persuades his people to follow a course of civil war against his peer, Far-ad-din, whose prefecture borders the Rōmarq. It becomes clear Far-ad-din's forces can not win against the might of the Great Houses and the Hundred Families. Indris, former Sēq Knight turned mercenary, is both Far-ad-din's general and son-in-law. Driven to serve his father-in-law's cause through the guilt he feels at the loss of his wife, Anj, Indris urges Far-ad-din to flee for his life, leaving his city of Amnon forever. Once Far-ad-din is safely away, Indris surrenders to the invaders.

While Indris is kept alive for questioning, he sees that many of those who supported Far-ad-din are executed quickly, and in secret, by Corajidin's forces. On the verge of losing his own life, Indris is saved by his uncle, Rahn-Näsarat fa Ariskander: the Asrahn-Elect and the Arbiter of the Change, set to oversee the course of the war against Far-ad-din.

Indris is surprised when both himself and his comrade, Shar-fer-rayn, are pardoned for their part in the civil war. His relief is short lived, as he suspects Asrahn-Vashne, leader of the Federationist political faction, will want Indris to repay the debt of his pardon. That night, overcome by the nearness of death, Indris becomes involved in a tryst with an unknown woman and, after a single night of passion, wakes to find her gone.

Mari, Corajidin's warrior-poet daughter and a senior member of the Feyassin—the Asrahn's elite personal guard—is shocked that her father wants to continue his ransacking of the nearby wetlands. The glow she felt after her assignation with a nameless lover the night before fades rapidly, as she listens to her father's schemes to rise to even greater heights of power. She is even more shocked by how sick and aged her father has become, as well as his obsession with the words spoken to him by the oracles: that Corajidin is destined to become the father of the empire, and the leader of his people. Despite Mari's urging him to find another way to cure his ailment, Corajidin renews his efforts in the Rōmarq to the find the answers he needs, as well as the weapons of past civilisations that may aid him in fulfilling his destiny. Corajidin's young wife, Yashamin—of an age with Mari—is one of Corajidin's most vocal supporters, wanting to see her husband as the most powerful man in Shrīan. Corajidin's sons, the witch-trained Kasraman, and the deadly swordsman Belamandris, are enlisted more fully in his plans.

Hesitant to become drawn into Shrīanese politics and the vendettas of the Great Houses, Indris plans to leave Amnon—the city filled with nothing but painful memories. It is his friends Shar, Hayden and the Wraith Knight, Omen, who convince him to stay long enough to pass on what they know about Corajidin's activities in the nearby Rōmarq. Before leaving Amnon, Indris speaks with his uncle, Ariskander, and the Asrahn-Vashne. He reveals that he and his comrades had been investigating the illegal excavations in the Rōmarq and their belief that it was forces working for the Erebus who were responsible. Vashne and Ariskander ask Indris's help to locate and return Far-ad-din, so the truth of Corajidin's falsehood and corruption can be more fully understood.

Though initially prepared to allow events to unravel as they would, Corajidin is thwarted when he is informed that, rather than Vashne stepping down from his post as Asrahn at the end of the year—the Magistratum is considering allowing the well-loved monarch to remain as Asrahn indefinitely. Corajidin is furious, yet it is his Master of Assassins, Thufan, as well as Wolfram and Yashamin, who convince Corajidin to take matters into his own hands and to seize power before it is too late.

Mari is drawn deeper into her father's schemes when she is asked to help in Vashne's assassination. She is surprised to discover Indris, the man she had a one-night romance with and the child of the Great House of Näsarat she had been taught to despise, would be present during the proposed attacks.

Yet she questions what she had been taught, as well as her father's ambitions. During the assassination attempt, Mari decides to distance herself from her family's grab for power, and takes no further part in it. Her inaction leads to her brother, Belamandris, being badly wounded in a battle with Indris, and causes her father and his colours to reveal themselves to Vashne and Ariskander. Though Vashne, his wife, his daughter and one of his sons are killed, and Ariskander and another of Vashne's sons are kidnapped, Indris and his comrades manage to escape. Mari seeks to absolve her guilt by presenting herself to the Feyassin she betrayed, taking responsibility for Vashne's death. She knows it is something she may not survive, and is beaten almost to death in retribution.

Indris, badly wounded in the assassination of Vashne but saved by Shar and Ekko, wakes to find his old Sēq teacher, Femensetri, has healed him of his wounds. She, like Vashne before her, tries to remind Indris of his duty to his people, as well as to himself. It is at a place of peace, in the heart of troubled Amnon, that Indris and Mari are once more reacquainted.

Indris's and Mari's feelings grow, despite the enmity both have been taught to feel for each other's Houses, and despite the guilt he feels over his long missing wife. Driven by a sense of obligation and duty, Indris goes into the streets of Amnon to see what kind of place Corajidin and those who fly his colours would make of the world. Seeing the harsh truth, and unable to deny what he must do, Indris and his friends agree to help find Ariskander—the man intended to take Vashne's place as leader of Shrīan, as much as Corajidin would have it otherwise. He also agrees to try and find Far-ad-din and bring him back, to further thwart Corajidin's play for the highest office in the land.

As Corajidin continues his drive for power, Mari and Indris work together to find and return Ariskander: Indris, motivated by a deep sense of what he secretly feels is his failed obligation, as well as admiration for his missing uncle; Mari, because she wants to save her father from the doom she clearly sees coming. Indris and his comrades set out into the monster-infested Rōmarq, the marshlands that hold the ancient ruins of lost civilizations, to rescue Ariskander. Mari remains in Amnon—a spy in her father's own household—with newfound allies who fight to maintain order. Mari finally realises her father will not be stopped: his obsession with survival justifying his callous actions, time and again. When he talks of allying himself with the exiled covens of the witches, she knows she cannot save him. She allies herself irrevocably with Indris.

While spying on her father and those closest to him, Mari finds an unexpected ally in Thufan's son, Armal. It is Armal who reveals that Vahineh, Vashne's daughter, managed to escape the purge on her House and was later captured. Though Armal dies in an ambush in the streets of Amnon—he and Mari killing their attackers—Mari frees Vahineh and guides her to safety with their allies.

Indris and his friends trek through the Rōmarq, the haunted lands of the vanished Time Masters; survive dangerous battles with malegangers, the hideous marsh-puppeteers and the rat-folk Fenling. During their trek they fight off a party of Fenling who have joined with Thufan and Belamandris. Indris shoots and critically wounds Thufan, and uses his mystic abilities to thwart Belamandris and the Fenling from their pursuit, sending Belamandris and Thufan back to Amnon. Indris and his comrades arrive in Fiandahariat, a Time Master ruin, soon after but fail to save Ariskander from Corajidin's spite: Ariskander is executed and has his soul bound into an Angothic Spirit Casque. Indris manages to recover the casque, but Corajidin escapes. Indris rushes back to Amnon where he, his friends, and his allies defy Corajidin's ambitions.

Vahineh, knowing of Mari's involvement in the death of her father, mother and brothers, tries to recruit Mari to enact vengeance on Corajidin. Mari refuses, but a maddened Vahineh decides instead to have her revenge by killing Yashamin, and tells the recovering Thufan that it was Corajidin who was ultimately responsible for the death of his son Armal.

Seeing his plans falling apart around him, Corajidin attempts to flee Amnon. Refusing to admit defeat, he formulates a plan to gather his colours and to make a stand elsewhere. Betrayed by Thufan, his own Master of Assassins, Corajidin is nearly killed, but not before he sees his beloved son, Belamandris, mortally wounded.

Though Indris, Mari and their allies are victorious, it is not without cost. Mari is outcast from her own family. There is no clear candidate to lead

Shrīan, and the Iron League now sees a weaker Shrīan, easy to conquer. The Great Houses and the Hundred Families know their struggle has only begun.

Camped far from Amnon, recovering from his near-mortal wounds, Corajidin's supporters swear their loyalty as Wolfram makes good on his promise to find Corajidin the allies he needs to make his future a reality. As the storm clouds gather, Corajidin broods over his dying son as he is introduced to the Emissary, a servant of powerful and enigmatic masters. The Emissary promises Corajidin much: power, majesty and long life. He accepts it all, wants it all, though part of him wonders how the Emissary came to be, for though now she is the servant of dark forces, she once was Anj-el-din, Indris's missing and presumed dead wife.

And now . . .

1

"WHILE I MAY CALL MY MISTAKES OPPORTUNITIES, TO OTHERS THEY MAY BE SEEN AS DISASTERS."

From *The Darkness Without* by Sedefke, inventor, explorer, and philosopher (751st Year of the Awakened Empire)

DAY 347 OF THE 495TH YEAR OF

THE SHRĪANESE FEDERATION

Indris sat in the shade of a faded awning on the balcony of the Iron Dog, eyes narrowed against the glare from the sun-seared granite of the Caleph-Avānweh. The dark borders of the balcony and flapping awning became a picture frame around a frenetic, colorful world. The city of Avānweh, cupped in the meshed fingers of hills and valleys between snow-capped mountains and the shimmering mirror of the Lakes of the Sky, teemed with people. Visitors had gathered from over land and sea in the vivid hues of a fistful of nations for the New Year's Festival with its troupers, dramatists, martial tournaments, sporting events and the famous Näsiré Flying Carnival.

He smiled at the procession of people, the colour and shape of the crowd, even as he relished the solitude of his seat. It was like watching the world perform, with thousands of interwoven stories he could watch if only he went out amongst the crowd. But here, in the shade and comfort, he could just . . . be.

Sipping the last of his sharbat, Indris stretched his legs out under the table. The chipped old glass was cool and rough in his hand, bubbles and small cracks floating in the translucency. The flavours of yellow lotus petals, orange and pineapple were refreshing.

The Iron Dog was mostly empty during the day, patronised by a few hard-bitten nahdi in quiet conversation with their silk-draped factor, a tall man who talked his clients through a handful of letters of offer. One or another would glance up at Indris curiously before returning his attention to where his next employment was coming from.

Indris rubbed a worn corner of his tanj board. Unfolded it was almost a metre wide, with seven hundred and sixty-nine hexagonal tiles laid out like a large six-petalled lotus flower. With twenty-seven pieces per player and up to six players a game, tanj was not for the faint hearted. The pieces from this morning's game remained where they had been abandoned, little effigies caught mid drama before their story had been fully told. The game had been interrupted when Mari had to keep an appointment with an armorer. Shar, Hayden, Ekko, and Omen had left too. He suspected they were looking for any excuse to do something other than play a game invented as not only a metaphor for the rules of sende, but the complex and fluid relationships between the Great Houses and as a tool for strategic thinking. His friends got annoyed when he won, and even more annoyed when he played badly to make the game, and their time together in peace, last longer. So now he had time alone, a rare and precious gift neither to be overlooked, nor wasted.

Rummaging around in his satchel, Indris took out his journal, brush and ink, and a few small pieces of wood and precious metals. He caught the attention of the housekeep and ordered another sharbat, and bread and vanush—a ground paste of eggplant, herbs and spices. Opening his journal he looked at his most recent sketches of things he wanted to build, or improve. Rough sketches of a new Tempest Wheel, made more efficient by the placement of different metals in a long screw, rather than a series of platters. Some half thought out formulae to make travel along the outer edges of the Drear safer. Even the designs for a new one-person wind-boat he had named the *Skylark*—an agile clockwork eagle, powered by disentropy. There were a few older projects, discarded as too hard at the time, which he had not looked at in a long while. One in particular, a Drearjammer, piqued his interest again as pieces of the puzzle around his original design fell into place. *So many things to do*, he thought, *but where to start?*

A figure took the seat opposite him, head covered by the deep hood of an over-robe. Indris's hand dropped to the hilt of his dragon-tooth knife, the move hidden by the table. She, for he took the stranger to be a woman from the long slender fingers and softness of her hands with their shadows of blue veins raising the pale skin, was tall. Her over-robe was toned dark sand, patterned with brown vines and tiny yellow flowers. The hooded head was tilted down, a thick braid of dark hair coiling free of the obscuring hood.

"Mari's game plan is Ancestors awful for a warrior-poet," the woman said in a sharp voice, which Indris recognised with shock. "Hayden is waiting to get the game over, knowing he can't win. Ekko plays like he's hammering nails and Shar's game is elegant and beautiful, as I'd expect. I've no idea what Omen thinks he's doing. But, he's dead and the dead don't make so much sense when they've lingered so long."

"Femensetri." Indris looked around to ensure nobody had overheard. She folded her hood back to reveal fine features, dominated by the brilliance of her opal-coloured eyes. Her mindstone was covered by what passed for a fringe, though it was more the artless hang of hair that needed to be trimmed.

Femensetri casually swept most of the wooden tanj pieces into a box. "You don't mind? I assume you remember where all the pieces were." She looked up, a rahn piece in one hand, Sēq Knight and warrior-poet pieces in the other. Years of use had flaked some of the paint from the wooden statues.

Indris waved his hand for her to continue what she was doing. Femensetri set the board for two players, each with an ally to make it more interesting. Fifty-four pieces each with meaning, strengths and weaknesses. Tanj had its own vocabulary. Every set of moves, countermoves, and feints a sentence. Femensetri started by moving her Sēq Master from amongst the ranks in a long straight line to the edge of her territory. Indris responded by moving his Poet Master so it could support the warrior-poets and nearby rahn.

He glanced across the board, then at his former sahai. Though it had been years since she had been his teacher, sitting together at a tanj board brought back many memories, some of which were pleasant.

"You look different," he ventured, gesturing at her hair and clothes.

"Can't just wander here to see you dressed like a Sēq Master now, can I, boy?" She scooped up some of Indris's yanush with two long fingers. He noticed with some distaste the crescents of dirt under her fingernails. After an uninvited sip of his sharbat, she ordered one of her own and a platter of warm bread and grilled meats. He slid the glass across the table, insisting she finish the one he had not had the chance to touch.

The two scholars spoke of nothings. The real message lay in the rapid placement of tiny wooden statues, complex moves and countermoves. Sacrifices and bold heroics, leading to victory or downfall. Move by move, Femensetri's story unfolded for Tanj had been used by Sēq spies to share secret messages and intelligence for centuries, the fate of nations hidden amongst the subtle manoeuvring of figurines. Femensetri was replaying the historical invasion by the Avānese of Eidelbon, an ancient city in the Golden Kingdom of Manté. It was a city wealthy in culture, history and money, invaded during the celebrations of its new monarch being crowned. It took Indris a few moves before he realized what Femensetri was doing, then he fell into the rhythms of trying to change history; without about as much luck.

"There are easier and less obscure ways to talk," Indris said between small bites of his bread.

"And every way can be overheard." Her tone was conversational. After moving a piece she noticed she had left a smear of yanush on it. She licked it off and set the piece down again. "Don't be so naïve as to think otherwise, especially here in Avānweh."

"Are your brothers and sisters under the mountain listening now?" Amer-Mahjin, the Sēq Chapterhouse, was deep inside Ïajen-mar, one of the three peaks into which Avānweh was built. A sprawling warren of natural and artificial chambers, it had been home to the Sēq in Avānweh since the rise of the Awakened Empire. Larger than the fortress of Irabiyat, Amer-Mahjin was still just a rural outpost when compared to Amarqa-in-the-Snows, the Sēq's great fortress in the Mar Silin.

"Always and especially those. We've more to fear from family than anybody else."

Your family, he thought, *not mine*.

Tanj moves unfolded thoughts and strategies, one after the other, though soon enough Femensetri was telling a different story from history. The way she replaced the Mahj piece with her Sēq Master. The way the Mahj was then contested by its ally. The use of nahdi reinforcements claimed from additional pieces in neutral territory. These nahdi pieces faced outward from the other pieces indicating they were honorless, criminals or in some other way could not be trusted. The figures had the heads of dogs, showing they were held in low esteem. In truth it was an accurate depiction: in High Avān the word nahdi meant 'iron dog.' The bases of these figures were painted with a gold dot, saying they had once been people of influence. These nahdi replaced the more traditional pieces supporting and protecting the rahn. A radical shift in power. Alliances made with traitors.

The division of her Sēq pieces—some with the rahn, some moving towards the unoccupied centre where the Mahj or Asrahn piece would reside and some remaining aloof—was enough to give him pause. He looked down at the placement of the pieces on the board, reading the message.

"Can you prove any of this?" He sipped at his cool sharbat, wishing it was something stronger. The drink did not stop the sweat that prickled his spine and lower back.

"It's happening now." Femensetri picked at her teeth with a chipped nail.

"What are you doing about it?" He hated the tension in his voice.

"What I can, which is three-quarters of sod-all," she said bitterly. "Our brothers and sisters are divided. The Suret has decreed none of us are to involve ourselves in external matters until a unified direction is agreed. Some want to become more involved in politics. Others want to maintain a distance. There are those who want to assume absolute power, hungering for a return to the old times. Few seem to remember why we were formed in the first place."

"Are we talking about another Scholar War?" he asked tensely.

"More like an esoteric rebellion. We've amongst our number some who want to see how comfortable a throne and crown are. And if the hat fits . . ."

"Sweet Näsarat," he whispered. The other pieces on the board came clearly into focus. "All this during the Assembly? It's not as if there's not enough to worry about, with the elections for Asrahn so soon."

"Which won't be as simple a victory as Nazarafine is expecting, if Corajidin manages to rally enough support."

"So I see." He nodded towards the nahdi pieces on the board. Seeing them so close to the rahn, who in turn was on his journey to the centre of power, was alarming. "Do we have names for these unexpected guests?"

Femensetri withdrew a scroll from her over-robe. She rolled it across the table, scattering pieces left and right. Indris wondered how much of the gesture was metaphor versus how much was frustration. He cracked the seal, then read the names.

"How many different kinds of trouble will this be?" Indris asked.

"How many commanders do you count on the list?"

"Fifteen or so."

"Which is about fifteen or so different kinds of trouble we don't need." Femensetri sipped at her sharbat then spat it on the floor. She grimaced at the taste of the drink now that it had warmed. "And not all the trouble we're going to get."

There had been almost thirty sayfs of the Hundred Families Indris knew of who had been Exiled under Vashne's rule. Some had died in foreign wars. Others had settled for more peaceful lives, never to be heard from again. Then there were those who had made names for themselves, relishing in blood and war and the wealth it brought them. Imperialists, they too were exiled by Vashne for various reasons over the earlier years of his reign.

"All Corajidin's Imperialist friends," Femensetri said with mock excitement, "with armies hardened in foreign service and coffers lined with gold and jewels. Like you said: trouble."

Indris looked out across the Caleph-Avānweh. There were hundreds of people meandering in the early afternoon sun. Summer was almost over. Avān, Humans and the Seethe in their pastel colors and *serill*, the drake-fired glass shining bright. He even saw three of the slender Y'arrow-te-yi, no larger than adolescents, sapling slender and wood hued with leaves and tiny flowers growing in the fronds they had for hair. A pride of Tau-se lion folk strolled amongst them. Shorter maned females in felt vests and breeches decorated with fortune coins walked with a small number of males with one larger, black-maned male as their alpha. They tried, laughing-purring, to herd their excitable and energetic cubs. The young Tau-se sped around the market square. Pounced on each other. Tumbled like clawed balls of fur and muscle, until their mothers scolded them. The cubs would be still for a while, dusting off their felt tunics, before gradually and inexorably returning to their frenetic rampage. A lone figure, nose improbably long and pointed between wide eyes and cheeks so sharp Indris could slice bread with them, stalked through the crowd. It may have looked like a person in a Festival costume, but Indris knew better. The soft-looking leather mask with its swirls of colour and deep tribal lines were its skin. The feathered cloak its folded wings. The Iku was dressed in shades of weather-stained grey like a travelling daikajé—the various orders of warrior-ascetics—a wide sash with hundreds of coloured knots around its waist. A folding fan made of feathers with steel veins was thrust through its sash, and the Iku carried a sturdy walking stick, a weapon dented and bleached from use. Indris doubted any-body knew the lone creature for what it was. The Iku were mystics, thinkers and teachers, and the enigmatic watchers of the world. And often harbingers of strife. Indris rested his hand on Changeling, remembering years of tute-lage at Amarqa-in-the-Snows, under the black bead eyes of an Iku weapon master who had made not only what was in Indris's hands deadly, but made weapons of his body and mind also. And here one was, alone, so far from home. *Are you here to watch, to teach, or to destroy? Perhaps a measure of all three?*

Indris's attention was diverted by a beaten old wind-galley that hummed over the square, misaligned Tempest Wheels clattering. The Disentropy Spools wobbled, grinding against their mountings. Faint veins, like spinning heat-haze, distorted the air as it passed by towards the lakes, looking for a place to land. Above it all a flight of gryphons powered across the sky, riders' armor and spear points glittering as the enormous beasts turned in forma-tion. Indris wished he were up there with them, aboard the *Wanderer* with Mari and his other friends. There was a sense of freedom in being able to soar above the problems of the world. To let the prow turn in whatever direction the wind was heading and simply drift along. Seeing everything gave the world perspective, putting into context the importance of the ones he loved.

Femensetri snapped her fingers to get his attention. She had an expectant look on her face. Indris knew he had the option of walking away. Or sitting there and ignoring her. He also knew she would eventually get her way because she knew he cared.

"I suppose you want me to do something about this, since you can't?"

"You and yours are the only ones I trust," Femensetri said. Her gaze softened as she stood. "Tread lightly, Indris. You drew attention to yourself at Amnon. The Sēq released you from public service, but not from the Order. Some of our brothers and sisters see a chance for a scholar to sit the throne again. And here you are, the scholar son of one of the most ancient and respected bloodlines in the country."

"When are you and the Sēq going to leave me be? There are other people who can assist with these little dramas, you know."

"You're the one who agrees to help when asked." Femensetri shrugged. "I can't see you losing your conscience, ethics or morality any time soon."

"How inconvenient for me," Indris said. He did not try to match Femensetri's toothy smile with one of his own, it being too disheartening to even fake enthusiasm.

❀ ❀ ❀

"We're not going to have those quiet few weeks you promised, are we?" Shar said, poking Indris in the chest with a stiffened finger. The lotus wine had stained her blue lips a deep indigo. Her light inebriation caused the warchanter's skin to shine softly, like it was backlit by candles. "Whose brilliant idea was it to come here?"

"We had to get Omen his new body and you, Shar, said you wanted to see Avānweh," Indris reminder her. "And yes, we'll get our quiet time. I doubt it'll be here, though . . . or now."

"I'd rather work almost anywhere than relax in the same place as them Exiles." Hayden ran a finger and thumb along his drooping brassy moustache, eyes narrowed in his weathered face. "I figure nothin' good'll come of them being here."

"We need to tell Rosha," Indris muttered.

Mari's brows curved in a frown. The breeze snagged at her blonde locks, the sun making sapphires of her eyes. "Surely her own spies will tell her what she needs to know?"

"Can't take the chance." Shar shook her head. "Look what happened last time we didn't own up to what we knew. I'd rather not experience another Amnon, or the likes of our little wander through that *faruq-ta* Rōmarq."

"Point taken," Hayden winced, his expression betraying his memories. Then his weathered face brightened, his colour improving a little. "What's one more jaunt before I head home? I suppose the meadows of Ondea can wait a few days more for me."

Indris's lips almost managed a smile at the thought of losing Hayden. They had fought together in the Brave Companions, then again after Indris had escaped from Sorochel while on his quest to find his missing wife, Anj. But Hayden's days of adventuring had run their course, and the old drover accepted it with good grace. Indris envied Hayden his coming peace.

"Amonindris?" Ekko's voice was pitched low, in the rumble-purr of what passed for a Tau-se whisper. "May we talk privately, you and I?"

"Of course." Indris excused himself as his friends listened to Hayden's plans of how he intended to rebuild his homestead, raise horses, and drink home-brewed beer on his verandah as he watched the sun come down. With Ekko a looming presence at his side, Indris wandered to one side of the balcony where he could see scores of people in brightly coloured and fantastical costumes in the market square below. A handful of children were running around the central fountain and its obelisk, kites in the shapes of eagles, dragons and shields wheeling on the ends of knotted strings clutched in their hands.

Ekko leaned on the balcony rail, his eyes narrowed with pleasure, nostrils flaring as he inhaled the stories the world told him. Indris almost did not want to intrude.

"What's bothering you, Ekko?"

"It is Sassomon-Omen," Ekko replied. "I am not a long time friend of the Wraith Knight—indeed, his kind I find . . . disturbing, in much the same way as do you Avān. But I've noticed his lapses. He seems to lose awareness of what transpires around him, and I have my misgivings about travelling with a companion in whom I do not have complete trust."

Indris turned to look back at Omen, who was lurking amongst long streaks of shadow, as motionless as a roof gargoyle and silent, despite the chatter around him. Hayden going home. Omen fading away. Anj. Losing friends was always painful, and tolerable only in the company of the ones who remained.

"I understand, Ekko." Indris patted the giant lion-man on the shoulder. "And thanks for your honesty. Keep your eyes open. If we don't take care of each other, who'll do it for us?"

❈ ❈ ❈

The Qadir Näsarat was cut into a crevice on the Caleph-Rahn on Mar-Silamari, called by its less poetic name of Star Crown Mountain in modern times. Tall phoenix-capped columns of blue marble and gold leaf marked the entrance. Balconied galleries and tall windows with stained glass dotted the red stone face of the mountain. Apple blossoms grew amidst natural ponds, ferns and native violets growing between moss-covered rocks exposed to the jagged circle of sky high above. There were several heavy-looking doors of iron-banded wood. Small covered balconies with fretwork screens looked inward amidst long tear tracks of water on the ruddy stone.

Mari had declined to come, feeling uncomfortable being caught in the palace of her ancestral enemy. Indris did not blame her. Though she and Roshana had seen eye to eye at Amnon, it was far from being a friendship. More a cessation of hostilities.

They were escorted inside, then up a seemingly endless flight of stairs to a solarium. From there the Mar Jihara was a saw-backed mountain wall almost close enough to touch. Clouds swirled like lazy sea foam around the mountaintops, darkened and swollen with rain. High above the qadir, the peaks of the Iajen-mar reared like a fistful of bloodied sword blades, capped in snow. Beyond World Blood stood the last of the three sisters, towering Mar-Asrafah, the Skyspear.

They waited for an hour. Hayden stood with his back to a carved metal column, sunlight making a brassy halo of his bobbed hair. His face was in shadow, save for pale scores of light across his nose, temple, cheek and jaw. The elderly man cradled his long-barrelled storm-rifle to his chest, eyes distant. His complexion seemed ashen under the tan; eyes washed out and skin slack. Ekko loomed large beside him, tail twitching. Indris understood Ekko's nervousness: Roshana had been displeased when her Knight-Colonel of the Lion Guard had resigned his commission to travel with Indris. Omen had paused by the railing, staring southward over the diamond-strewn blanket of the Lakes of the Sky. The glaze on his new ceramic body was either blue or green, depending on the angle it was viewed from. His joints were polished brass. His nails whorled onyx. The Seethe crafters who had made the body had given him the face of Tyen-to-wo, the Laughing Wind spirit of the Seethe: sharp featured with a long pointed nose and chin, and faceted emerald crystals for eyes. It was a departure from his previous face, which had been devoid of all features. Indris had not decided whether he preferred Omen's new visage or not. It was at once more and less than the face of a man in touch with the world around him.

"Our trip to Avānweh not quite turning out the way you'd expected?" Shar said. She was perched on the balcony rail at Indris's side, a bowl of bitter-smelling green lotus tea in her hands.

"Not so much, no." He winced at a lancing pain behind his eyes.

"You've been having headaches ever since Amnon," Shar whispered. "You never had them before."

"I think all the disentropy I used, plus my Awakening, has—"

The sound of the glass doors opening caught Indris's attention. He looked over his shoulder as a bound-caste servant in a short sleeveless tunic approached him. The young woman would not meet his eyes, though with quiet words and a small gesture indicated he should join Rahn-Roshana in the Phoenix Room. As the others made their moves to join him, the servant politely interceded. Indris was to come alone.

The stone walls of the Phoenix Room had been carved with the images of hundreds of phoenixes in different shapes and sizes, flocking within a churning maelstrom of flame. Blue and gold ceramic tiles covered the floor. The outer screens that sheltered the Phoenix Room from the elements were flung wide, turning the round room into something of an eyrie.

Rosha sat tall in her chair, square-shouldered and square-jawed, her dark hair drawn back from even features. Her clothing was simple: a sleeveless blue leather jerkin bezainted with bronze, loose-legged trousers and high supple boots. She looked like a woman of gentle summer. Of olive groves, sun-dappled fields and lakes that shone as sharp as sword edges. Roshana smiled broadly, rising from her seat to take him in a warm embrace. Her companions likewise rose from their chairs: the elderly Poet Master Bensaharēn, layers of clothing elegantly arrayed on his slender frame, his high ponytail and braids plaited with the gold and gems of his commendations; the bookish Knight-General Maselane, scarred hands at odds with his gentle, soft features; and Danyūn, with his lamb's wool hair and blue eyes, the southerner all hard planes of muscle in common warrior-caste clothing. Young for his post, the Näsarat's Master of Spies was an accomplished operative of the Ishahayans, the Gnostic Assassins from the mountains beyond the Rōmarq. Only Mauntro, her commander of the Lion Guard, was absent. No doubt keeping the qadir secure.

"This is an unexpected pleasure," Rosha said, gesturing for Indris to take a seat. He cast a casual glance around the room. Several maps lay on a nearby table, curled edges fluttering in the breeze. A large sheaf of parchments was weighed down by the small bust of Kohar, a general from antiquity who had helped develop some of the cavalry tactics still used today. Close by on a small writing table was more parchment, a scratched old inkwell and a ragged-looking ink brush. One of the maps had several sets of figures on it, representing troop movements across Shrīan.

"I'm afraid this is more about business," he said. "How are you settling in as the Rahn-Näsarat?"

"Well enough," she said, bravado masking uncertainty. She tapped her temple with two fingers. "Still coming to terms with everything my father is—was. Though you prepare for it, nobody ever tells you Awakening is so . . ."

"Breathtaking?"

"Violent." She crossed her legs and sat back in the chair, more his cousin than the monarch of a Great House. "The imposition of so many thoughts. Aspirations, hopes, victories, defeats. Everything. It's like several lives trying to fit with mine. Or take mine over."

"You've survived the storm. Now you need to wait for the waters to settle." He leaned forward to rest his elbows on his knees. "How are the household taking it?"

"Like they have a choice?" Rosha smiled to take the sting from her words. Bensaharēn and Maselane smiled small smiles, while Danyūn cocked an eyebrow. "My staff will be much as Father left it. Maselane will be my Master of Arms. Our relationship with the Gnostic Assassins of the Ishahayan is a long one, so Danyūn will stay on. Hopefully the conversations I'm having with Sayf-Ajomandyan will net me a new Sky Master, now that Far-ad-din and his Seethe aren't with us."

"And I'm looking to retire," Bensaharēn said. The sun flared from his long white hair and short white beard. "But I will serve as Poet Master until we can appoint somebody new. "

"You always said Mari was your greatest—"

"Indris!" Rosha growled. "An Erebus as the Poet Master of the Lament? Be serious."

"I suggested the same," Bensaharēn pointed at Rosha. "See! She is the perfect choice. One of the best I have ever trained, now even more famous after her heroism at Amnon."

"Not now, Bensa. Besides, what I really need at the moment is a Lore Master!" Rosha's expression was frustrated. "The Sēq have not responded to my request." She looked at Indris critically. "You served my father, Indris, and I'd have you with me."

"I advised Ariskander as and when I could, Rosha," Indris said gently. "But my path is elsewhere."

"You're family and you have an obligation." Her voice was hard, with echoes of older rahns long dead. *Family.* Was he, though? Indris was reminded of Ariskander's words. *My sister was a vessel, one who willingly accepted her great burden. Your mother risked all when she sent you forward . . .* Rosha continued, "As your rahn I expect you to serve the Näsarat, in whatever capacity I deem best."

Indris ignored this, and instead took Femensetri's list from his satchel. He gave it to Rosha, who did not so much as glance at it. "Has your Master of Spies told you the Imperialist Exiles have returned to Avānweh?"

"Old news," Danyūn said. "They returned today, via wind-frigates from Tanis."

Indris pointed to the list. "The real leaders, the ones you need to worry most about, arrived via faster wind-skiffs over the last couple of days, no doubt to make their plans in secret."

"What makes you so certain?" Maselane raised a ceramic teacup to his lips and sipped. The sea-patterned glaze shone against his dark fingers and rough nails.

"It's what I'd do. If the key leaders of the Exiles haven't been seen yet, it's because they don't want to be. Were I them, I'd be in talks with fellow Imperialists to stake my claim before the others can. Corajidin will be looking for new friends."

Rosha pursed her lips for a moment, then nodded to Danyūn. The man shrugged and, without a word, left the room. Indris studied the feline way the man walked, the fluid grace, as he seemed to glide soundlessly from the room.

"Indris," Rosha began tentatively, "myself and the other Federationists have been discussing our options. After the events at Amnon, Shrīan is in something of a predicament. We lost many experienced leaders, my father and Far-ad-din of the Din-ma Troupe notwithstanding. We need help stabilising the country."

"I'll do what I can." Indris said.

Rosha sat straight in her chair. The cousin was gone. The rahn remained. "The Federationists agree we need your talents. Shrīan is divided. The Iron League threatens more war. We risk losing the Conflicted Cities. We need to reward you for past services so you have the authority to do some real good."

Indris bowed his head to hide his apprehension. "I appreciate the gesture but I've done more for less on Shrīan's behalf over the years. I help from conscience, not coercion."

"Title," Maselane began, "lands, money, influence—"

Indris shook his head. "Have some. Don't need more. There're plenty of people who could do some real good with what you offer."

"And we're finding places for them," she said, frustrated. "They want it. You don't. You respect power and I know first hand you'd not abuse it. You know what's going on here!"

Indris took a deep breath as Rosha talked. He listened with part of his mind as his eyes lost their focus. The branches of the Possibility Tree were blurred at first. Shadowy images, like watercolor brushstrokes across his vision. Soon enough, individual branches began to take on shape. Causes illuminated effects as specific branches were limned in pallid light in his mind's eye. Faction fighting between the Federationists and the Imperialists leading to more civil unrest; Far-ad-din deposed; Ariskander's death; Vashne's death and the return of the Exiles; a weakening of the Avān presence in the Conflicted Cities as the Exiles departed; the potential fall of Tanis to the Iron League; the greater probability the Iron League would turn their military might on Shrīan; the Imperialists using the threat of foreign invasion as leverage for their agendas—

"Indris?" Rosha asked. "Did you hear anything I just said?"

He blinked his eyes slowly. Allowed the room to come into focus as he scanned his recent memory. "You were offering me the estate of Irabiyat, on the borders of Tanis. You think a scholar ensconced there as its governor will be a deterrent. You also want me to keep an eye on the Sēq, expecting they'll cooperate with me. I don't think it'd make a lick of difference, one way or the other. If anything, the Sēq will not react well to me at all."

"I also want you as the Lore Master of the Nāsarat," Rosha added. "Or you could become my Poet Master."

"Not the perfect choice, but far from a bad one," Bensaharēn said.

"I'm not that good a swordsman." Indris shook his head. "And we return to the Sēq. They'd have a collective stroke if I revealed their techniques to outsiders."

"Once you were appointed the Sayf-Irabiyat—something I'll do here and now—you could start your own Family." Rosha strode across the room to her desk and sat. She took ink brush in hand.

"Rahn-Ariskander wanted Rahn-Roshana to marry Yago of the Nāsaré, to strengthen your ties with your distant relations." Maselane drummed his fingertips on his tea cup. "That's out of the question now."

"But"—Rosha added—"you could just as easily marry his older sister, Neva—"

"The lady I'm with is just fine." Indris said with an embarrassed laugh. He remembered Neva from when they were children. A precocious tomboy, defiant and headstrong, always getting herself into trouble. Indris had liked her. He had heard she had grown to become a remarkable woman, the heir to

Sayf-Ajomandyan—old Uncle Ajo—of Avānweh and the commander of his Sky Knights.

"Surely you don't think your relationship with Mari has a future?" Rosha's voice was harsh. "That she survived at Amnon was unexpected, some may say remarkable, but there's no way the Teshri will allow a formal union between the two of you."

"Neither Mari nor I are going to inherit anything meaningful." His voice was calm, masking the anger that flared within. Rosha's eyes narrowed at his tone. "An alliance between the Nāsarat and the Erebus would strengthen our nation with no risk to the bloodlines. Quite the opposite. It might lessen some of the internecine friction between our Great Houses."

Rosha shook her head. "You'd both become outcasts if you even tried. I won't allow you to throw a beneficial alliance with the Sky Lord away, so you can play with your forbidden princess. Woo her, bed her, and then abandon her. There are better options for you."

Indris took a deep breath in his search for patience. "Rosha, I'll help you as best I can, but there are limits. I've been down that road with the Sēq, the Crown, and the State, and it didn't work out well for anybody, least of all me. Leaving Shrīan again wouldn't be such a hardship."

"Would you make an exile of Mari as well?" Maselane asked, surprised. "The woman almost died to regain our trust. You need to respect what she did to remain part of what we're trying to build."

"There are plans for her future as much as there are plans for yours." Rosha rubbed her hands together, as if her saying it made it so. "Easier for you both to end it now, before it cuts too deep. Trust me. I know."

Mari. Would she want to be part of the life being offered him, or the one he wanted for himself? She was the daughter of a Great House, only recently come into her independence. Indris would not have been surprised if she had been offered lands and titles of her own, given her very public display of heroism in Amnon. He could not make any choice that impacted her, without talking to her about it first. To work out their future was one of the reasons he was here.

Thinking of Mari brought back memories. Tenderness. Peace. Passion gladly given and just as gladly shared. The beginning of something Indris had not thought he would experience again, or at least certainly had not planned on experiencing more than once.

Indris turned to look through the glass doors to where his friends waited. A smile quirked his lips at seeing Hayden throw his hands up, no doubt at something Omen said. Shar and Ekko almost doubled over with laughter.

"Well?" Rosha snapped. "Are you going to do what we need of you?"

Indris paused for a moment before he replied.

"What you want and what you need are two very different things. If Mari, my other friends, or I can't enjoy a place without your threats and agendas, then you've nothing to offer. Let me know when you're willing to listen, rather than talk."

He had his hand on the door when there came a swirl of used disentropy across his soul, like inhaling old smoke. It was followed by the sound of a colossal explosion somewhere in the city below.

2

"BEGINNINGS AND ENDINGS ARE INEXTRICABLE. WE BEGIN SOMETHING
NEW, BECAUSE SOMETHING HAS ENDED WE EITHER NO LONGER NEED,
OR IT NO LONGER NEEDS US. OFTEN, WE NEED TO EMPTY THE CUP OF
OUR BELIEFS TO SEE HOW NECESSARY CHANGE IS."

From *Climbing From the Top of the Mountain,* by Kobaqaru,
Zienni Magnate to the Serpent Princes of Kaylish (490th Year of
the Shrīanese Federation)

DAY 347 OF THE 495TH YEAR OF

THE SHRĪANESE FEDERATION

As Mari leaned against the rooftop balcony rail of Nanjidasé, the
fortress of the Feyassin in Avānweh, she looked down at the sheaf of canvas
flapping in the breeze. It had been a while since she had drawn anything.
Slender lengths of charcoal, pointed, chisel-edged, and blunt lay in an old
box, the varnish on the edges worn pale with use. The box—once her
mother's—sat alongside old jars of pigment, used brushes, and a small bowl
of water and a pestle for mixing. She knew the same nervous thrill she
remembered when about to embark on a new project, wondering how her
hands would render what her eyes saw and heart felt.

Mari mixed the pigments and water to make her ink. Took a brush in her hand, closed her eyes. Exhaled. When she opened them again the image was beautiful and clear, which she rendered in sure strokes on the canvas.

The mass of World Blood Mountain seemed to lean over her in the gathering dusk. Silhouettes bustled along nearby streets, past the lantern-lit windows of artisans and vendors. Students from the Habron-sûk, the Heron School of warrior-poets, walked in a small group, long spears across their shoulders, swords at their hip and shields slung on their backs. Memories of her training at The Lament tugged at her. Of long days, short nights, pleasure, pain, and dreams. Always the dreams. Of greatness and glory. Of being a name to ring true amongst the line of heroes who had come before.

The long held breath of the day was preternaturally deep as it exhaled into evening. Mountain shadows were razor edged, vermillion hued, and sharp against an indigo sky marbled with streaks of yellow cloud. It was as if the light had been frozen, reflected from the red orange stones of the city and the mountains into which it was carved. Hard shadows framed townhouses that seemed to thrust themselves from the terraced rock, or pooled around the base of the city where it rose and fell in valleys and foothills.

Mari set down her brush as the sun rolled behind the mountain, and shadows fell in a silent avalanche. The tiny sparks of lanterns ignited across Avānweh. It was if somebody had scattered bright chips of amber, sapphire, and diamond across a rumpled charcoal quilt. The temperature dropped sharply. Mari folded her arms across her chest, shivering. In thirteen days autumn would come. It would be a new year. With a new Asrahn and the relentless anvil of summer only a vaguely remembered nostalgia as the new world turned and hopefully both tempers and the country cooled with autumn.

It seemed an age since she had last been at Nanjidasé. Some of the greatest warriors of her people had lived within these walls. Had trained in its wide courtyard. Meditated under its arched colonnades, in its sculpted gardens, or under its domes with their mosaic ceilings.

So much history. Her affair with Indris. Vashne's death. Her defiance of her Great House and its legacy. Estrangement from her father and brother. Nazarafine's offer to command the Feyassin. Indris had spoken to her of his encounter with Belam, how Thufan had taken revenge. Indris did not know whether Belam had survived, though Mari was sure if her brother had died the world would have known of it. History. What was it Indris had said to her? *The ripples of today were stones in the waters of yesterday. We form our truths from the facts of what's gone before. You can't separate what was from what is. You can only change what will be.*

So here she was. Ready to try for a new tomorrow where her yesterdays did not matter so much. Today was her new beginning. Too many pebbles had been cast into the pond for her to see clearly. Everything was ripples, the mirror of her life distorted—

Danger lashed her senses.

Mari threw herself sideways. Sparks flew as the blade meant for her back struck the railing where she had stood. She let momentum carry her. Rolled smoothly to her feet.

There were three cowled figures. They wore dark, tight-fitting short coats over trousers bound with cord about the legs. Their exposed skin had been blackened, as had the blades of their long curved knives. Spread out, they approached on silent feet.

"You've some stones on you," she admitted. "But no brains."

The assassin on the left sped forward. A blur in the gloom. Mari stepped within the arc of her enemy's arm. Grasped the wrist. Twisted savagely. Smashed an elbow into the assassin's jaw. Caught the knife, which fell from their hand before it hit the ground. The assassin came again. Using his momentum, Mari blocked; folded her hand down. Grasped the assassin's wrist and elbow. Spun. Propelled the assassin over the high railing into the empty air. The assassin tumbled soundlessly into the darkness.

"Look what you've done." Mari tapped the long-knife against her thigh. Smiled lopsidedly. "Now I've got a knife, too."

The assassin to the right approached more cautiously, one knife extended before them, the other obscured behind. After the first frenetic pass of steel, Mari danced back. Weapons rang against each other. Steel scraped. She kept her assailant between herself and the third assassin, who tried to circle behind her. Pride warred with common sense and lost.

"Assassins on the rooftop!" Mari bellowed as a knife scored her ribs. Hopefully somebody heard her shout. She bared her fangs in a snarl. Her own blade bounced from some kind of armor beneath the assassin's hooded robe. The shudder in her wrist and forearm told her it was metal. All she had was a sleeveless jerkin and kilt.

Mari found herself forced back to the railing. Knives flashed in the jade-tinted moonlight. Fists pummelled. Feet lashed. Knees struck. Shins and forearms slammed against each other. She focussed on her breathing. On remaining calm. On moving. Always moving, to face one opponent at a time.

She found her opening. Swung low. Mari felt the burn as the assassin's knife arced over her shoulder to open her back. Her dagger punched through armor. Pierced the assassin's inner thigh. The knife came out followed by a torrent of blood. A bit-down curse. The assassin stumbled backward. Mari's blade opened the assassin's chin, rather than the throat as she had intended.

Blood trickled down her back. Her ribs. The final assassin came on. Flowed from foot to foot. It seemed as if his body swayed, an illusion of movement. At the last minute he leaped forward, knife a blur. Mari bent aside. Felt the horrific force of the blow as fist, not steel, hammered into her.

The assassin she had wounded rushed forward. She sheathed her knife behind his collarbone.

Yet her footing was off. There was too much blood on the ground. The assassin's body, driven by momentum, crashed into her. Mari was forced back. Bent painfully over the rail.

She expected it would not have been hard for the last assassin to kick her feet out from under her. To push on his fallen comrade. To spill them both over the railing, into the gulf beyond.

History, the word echoed in her mind. What was becomes is. Makes what is, what will be. The ripples of her past struck the riverbanks.

✳ ✳ ✳

Falling.

Impact drove the air from her lungs. Cold, wet stone. Sliding. She may have imagined the sound of her ribs creaking, though not the pain. The pain was very real.

Mari flung her arms out. Grabbed a handful of the bougainvillea that climbed the arched aqueduct, some ten metres below Nanjidasé. She tried to settle her mind into the lelhem—the meditative state where the warrior-poet could ignore pain, or fatigue. It failed miserably.

Her body an aching mass, Mari clambered down the vine-wreathed arch that held the viaduct aloft. Had she been flung even a meter further, there would have been nothing to stop her descent into the lantern-bright radiance of the city below. She tried not to think about it. One hand after the other. Find her footing. Get down to solid ground.

Above her the heavens opened up. Rain poured down.

Eyes narrowed, she stared up at Nanjidasé. It was too dangerous to return, in case more assassins waited. Indris was too far away, the *Wanderer* out in the Shoals. Head down, Mari forced her tired, aching body through the rain to somebody she knew would help.

❊ ❊ ❊

"Don't you have any other friends?" Ziaire joked as Mari cracked open her eyes. "Why does it feel like I'm the one you always come to when you need your sorry hide patched up?"

Mari tenderly pushed herself up in bed. The pain was a lot less than she had expected. She prodded at the dressing on the wound on her flank. Ziaire was reading from a thick stack of parchments in her hand. Other houreh came and went, adding to or reducing the stack one by one.

"Actually, it was Femensetri who healed me the first time at Samyala and Indris the second time at the Healer's Garden. You just happened to be there," Mari gestured to her healed wounds. "Who did the honors this time?"

"A lot of Pearl Courtesans have come to Avānweh for the New Year's Festival." Ziaire handed Mari a bowl of watered apple juice. The famous courtesan was radiant in her layers of pearl-gray silk. Hers was the kind of beauty other women did not find threatening, any more than one did extraordinary art. "One of our houreh from Tanis studied with the Nilvedic Scholars. He's quite a gifted healer. In time he'll go on to replace his father as the Prime of Tanjipé, governing the House of Pearl's interests there, as I do here. But you were lucky this time. Your wounds weren't so bad."

"Maybe I'm not trying hard enough?"

"Oh, no. You're quite trying." Ziaire grinned. "You had some cuts that looked worse than they were and bruises that will heal. Otherwise you're fine, you poor baby. But now it's time for you to get up. It's a beautiful day and I've an assignation. Come with me. We need to talk."

Ziaire showed Mari to a room where she could bathe and change. She stared at herself in the mirror, noting the hardness around her eyes and mouth. As memories from last night shot across her mind, she started to tremble violently. Her breath came in short gasps. Sweat prickled her hairline and upper lip. She grasped the edges of the mirror, knuckles white. Forced her breathing into a regular rhythm. Caught and locked her reflected gaze until the trembling ceased. She washed and dried her face, startled at Ziaire's voice at the door.

Joining her friend, Mari's face relaxed into a smile. Ziaire threaded her arm through hers as they took to the streets. Neither said much of consequence as they wove through the midmorning crowd. The two women passed beneath the shadow of an aqueduct. Flowering ivy had crept up the arches that supported the old waterway, red buds like drops of blood amongst the leaves. In the distance, over the background hum of city life, Mari heard the basso groan of waterwheels and the dull twang and creak of gondola cables. Green-coated kherife walked past, nodding their heads politely. Nanjidasé was nearby as well as the Habron-sûk. Whether in recognition of sende, or simple respect, courtesy was a safe course to take. Mari could not help but to flick her gaze around, searching for killers in the shadows.

Ziaire stopped near a shaded well, tiled with a mosaic of vividly coloured birds and flowers. She took a ewer from a hook, wiped it with a bandanna she had folded in her sleeve. With casual elegance, the courtesan held back her sleeve as she dipped the ewer, then took a deep drink. She offered the vessel to Mari, who finished off what remained. The water was cold and clean on her tongue. Ziaire took Mari's arm again and they walked on.

"What happened?" the other woman asked quietly.

"I cut myself knitting," Mari muttered sourly. Ziaire laughed even as she squeezed Mari's arm hard enough to hurt. "What? Alright. Assassins tried to kill me in Nanjidasé."

"Assassins?" Ziaire's expression flowed into worried lines. "Why do you think they came for you?"

"My list of sins is long and colourful," she mocked, then sobered at Ziaire's glare. "Erebus's balls, you've no sense of humour today. And no, I don't actually find it too funny myself. If I think too much about it . . . I didn't escape, so much as avoided being killed. As for why? Ziaire, it could've been for anything. My part in Vashne's death? My betrayal of my House? The chance I may command the Feyassin? A jilted lover, of which there've been more than—"

"Are you going to do it?" Ziaire asked abruptly. "Command the Feyassin, I mean? Nazarafine needs to know, Mari."

"It's a lot of work and I don't know if I'm ready to exchange my father's yoke for Nazarafine's so quickly." Mari struck a pose, one fist on her hip, the other held palm upward as if balancing the world in her hand. "*Make them as great as they were in the days of the Awakened Empire, Mari*'. I don't know that the Speaker for the People appreciates how difficult that will be."

"Probably not. But that's *your* problem," Ziaire eyed Mari shrewdly. "Or not."

"The Poet Master's Schools aren't what they used to be. Where elitism hasn't culled numbers, the soaring costs of training have. I've been here ten days and haven't made the progress I'd hoped. If Nazarafine wants the Feyassin to be what they were in the old days, I'll need to recruit outside the warrior-poet schools. Some of the other academies have students with real talent. They can be given the additional training they need."

"How many Feyassin does she want?"

"During the Awakened Empire, each of the twelve Great Houses sponsored a company from their own Prefecture. They also trained new recruits. Even if I could get the six remaining Great Houses—"

"Five at the moment, with Far-ad-din gone."

"Siamak will replace him, I'm sure. Even with six companies, that's only six hundred Feyassin. More than we've had, but less than she wants. The golden age of the warrior-poet is long past."

Gone were the days when being a warrior-poet was a call to service. These days most warrior-poets graduated, then took on contracts with foreign nobles. Or become pampered teachers to entitled students with more money than skill. Worse, her father's agenda against Far-ad-din had made the rahns and the sayfs nervous. They wanted to keep as many warriors as they could to defend their own interests.

"But you're not bitter." Ziaire's lips twitched in a smile. Mari rolled her eyes in response. "Nazarafine chose you for a reason."

"Her sense of humour?"

"She's likely to be Asrahn, Mari," Ziaire said bluntly. "You've walked away from your Great House. What else do you have?"

"A future with Indris," Mari replied. "The luxury of making my own choices? The freedom to go wherever I want?"

"Don't count on it. Roshana plans to arrange a marriage between Indris and the Sky Lord's granddaughter—" She stopped talking suddenly, hand over her mouth. Her laugh sounded forced. She squeezed Mari's arm and bestowed a dazzling smile. "I'm sorry, Mari. I don't know what I'm saying today. Rumour and innuendo as cures for boredom, you know how it is."

You always know what you're saying, Mari thought. Her face flushed. Roshana was trying to arrange a marriage for Indris? Indris had said nothing of the kind.

"What do you know of the explosion yesterday?" Mari asked tersely, simmering anger hardening her tone. Hardly the best question to lighten a mood, though the words were out of her mouth before she could rethink them.

"Not much," Ziaire admitted. "Apparently some Humans, Mantéans from the look, were found dead amongst the rubble near the Arbiter's Tribunal. It answers the questions many have been asking about the Iron League stepping up hostilities . . ."

". . . because my father may become Asrahn. You may as well say it. I wonder whether all the murders and disappearances in the city will be laid at his feet also?" *Whether he orchestrated them or not, which is anybody's guess.* "Some of the deaths I've heard about have been . . ."

"Monstrous?" Ziaire chewed her lip. "I'd heard the same. Bodies mauled, as if by an animal. Throats torn out. Blood missing. That's where there's a body to be found. Some are saying it's the Humans, sending Nomads into the city as part of their effort to disrupt the Assembly and the election."

"Or, somebody who'd find it convenient if Humans were accused of such things."

Ziaire gave Mari an appraising look, seemed about to speak, but remained quiet.

They came to a gallery overlooking the plaza that led to the Iphyrone, the great horse and sports track of Avānweh, which had been carved through ravines in the mountain. Diorite columns shaped into rearing horses supported filigreed bronze arches so fine they seemed spun from sugar. Sunlight streamed down, a syrupy glow thick with lazy motes of dust that flared like golden pinheads. The sounds of hooves, iron-shod wheels, and the roar of the crowd swelled from shadowed stone corridors. Those who loitered there were privileged. Curious heads turned in Mari and Ziaire's direction, faces partially occluded by hoods, parasols or awnings held aloft by bound-caste servants. Ziaire flicked open her steel-veined fan, silk panels painted with cheerful flowers. Mari recognised a few faces, though none belonged to people she was curious enough to approach. She wondered whether the person who wanted her dead was among them.

"It's been a long time since I've been to the races," she said instead of voicing that thought. Memory brought the taste of tobacco, whiskey, and rich over-priced food to Mari's tongue. "And I've never seen the Näsaré Flying Cirq, which I mean to remedy. What's on today at the Iphyrone?"

"Chariots this morning." Ziaire spared a smile for those who sought her attention, expertly weaving herself and Mari away from those who sought conversation. "Then hart mounted archery and rifles this afternoon. The various sûks will be having their competition of the weapons forms. Bensaharēn, your old teacher, is here having some good-natured fun with Nirén of the Habron-sûk. Delfyne of the Grieve arrived this morning and proud young Jarrah of the Saidani-sûk. Only the Beys didn't send their Poet Master: apparently there's more trouble brewing with the Fenling and the marsh-puppeteers in the Rōmarq. There's rumour of a gryphon or wyvern race, too. Neva, the Sky Lord's heir, will no doubt win the gryphon race. She always does. Have you met her? She's quite a woman."

"No, I've not," Mari said tersely.

"I wonder whether your father will be here?" Ziaire scanned the crowd as if oblivious to Mari's tone. "His status is still in question after Amnon."

"It's no more than he deserves," Mari was unsurprised at the sour taste of the words in her mouth. She had tried to save her father from his destructive course. There had been no stopping him. Not then, not now. "I'm tired of being what my father wanted me to be and I've no intention of walking in his shoes. Given what he's done, justice was bound to catch up with him."

Ziaire shrugged. "The Arbiter's Tribunal is still deliberating."

"Did many witnesses from Amnon come forward?"

"Some," Ziaire rested her hand on Mari's. It was soft and dry, the skin unblemished by the sun. Bands of red and yellow gold encircled her fingers and thumbs, shining brightly. "But it's out of your control, Mari. Let it go."

"I could've testified!" she snapped. She had been there, seen her father slice into Vashne's hearts. It had been her most shameful day, the day she had betrayed the man whose life she was sworn to protect. Try as she might to give fate the chance to redress the balance of her crimes, Mari had lived.

Ziaire's look was hard. "Nazarafine didn't want you involved—"

"Wait a—"

"No," Ziaire shook her head. "As a Feyassin you serve the Crown. The Speaker for the People, our monarch until the election, forbade you from testifying. If you testify you become implicated and Nazarafine didn't want that. The Arbiter's Tribunal has all the evidence it needs to make a judgement."

"And my father has enough gold to buy one." Even after everything, people still underestimated her father's influence. "I'd heard my father called all his old allies back from their exile."

Ziaire nodded. "With Vashne gone, many of them have returned to Shrīan."

"All their old titles and positions have been given to new sayfs. It'll be a free-for-all. I wonder how many bodies will wash up in the canals, conveniently opening positions of power?"

Ziaire waved to a plain, somewhat serious-looking man who stood in the shade of a fountain. Mari recognised Selassin fa Martūm, one of Vashne's nephews. He had often called on the Asrahn to intervene in some financial disaster or another, more often than not sourced in an addiction to gambling and courtesans.

"Martūm?" Mari asked.

"It's a favour to Nazarafine," Ziaire said dourly. "With Vahineh sick as she is, they want to present Martūm as the potential new head of the Great

House of Selassin. I'm to take a look and see whether he may be the man for the task."

"His reputation says otherwise."

"They generally do about people who actually want power." The courtesan kissed Mari farewell. "But duty calls and we must be professional about these things. Keep your beautiful head low, Mari. I'm rather fond of where it is."

"You and me both."

Mari remained in the gallery above the plaza after Ziaire left. Blushing orchids, vines of honeysuckle, and leafy ferns swayed in the southerly breeze. The ground was dampened by the fine spray from a small waterfall nearby. She allowed the buzz of voices around her to drift into background noise. For people to become sunlit, shadow-etched shapes, abstract patterns of movement in her periphery.

Until conversation was stilled.

A stream of women and men passed under the southern arch of the plaza. They were a mismatched group. Some were dressed in outdated Shrīanese styles. Others in the vivid silk coats and jewels of Tanis, or the scaled serpent leather of Kaylish. Some wore the flamboyant shirts, breeches, and high boots of the Marble Sea corsairs, while others the supple leather and felt of the Horse Clans of Darmatia. No matter their choice in fashion, from their features and carriage they were clearly upper-caste Avān.

The Exiles. Mari's heart thumped when she caught sight of a face she remembered. Somebody she had not seen in many years. As if sensing her, he looked up to scan the crowd. Saw Mari and smiled.

Nadir was leaner then she remembered in his Tanisian silk coat and trousers. Two gold-washed, sharply curved daggers were thrust through the sash at his waist. A row of small emeralds was affixed above his left eye. He was tall, with a high brow beneath red black waves of shoulder-length hair. His nose had been broken and poorly set since she had seen him last. The pale tracery of old scars, a claw wound perhaps, lined his cheek. His eyes were dark as polished jet. She remembered the way his voice had sounded, smooth and deep when she had rested her head on his chest. Nadir had been a fellow student at The Lament before his parents had taken him from the school in his graduating year.

His sisters, Ravenet and Kimiya, were with him. The two women were a few years younger than Nadir. Ravenet was patrician and aloof, while there was something of the wanton in Kimiya's gaze and bearing. They looked exotic in their Tanisian silks and bracelets of golden bells, hair plaited with amber and emerald beads. They lifted their chins in challenge, smiles knowing.

Jhem of the Family Delfineh, Nadir's father, idled next to them. His dark eyes were ophidian, hooded under the buttress of his brow. Grey-flecked dark hair was swept back from his high, lined forehead. A tall reed of a man, he eyed those around him dispassionately. Mari heard people whisper the man's name, which brought a wry smile to his lips. Jhem. The Blacksnake.

Nadir caught Mari's gaze and held it. Her skin flushed. He smiled. She looked away. The Exiled warrior represented a history she preferred remain in the past.

Mari fled as subtly as she could. She hastened down several flights of stairs, patterned with floral shapes that shone through the nearby wooden screen. Her footsteps echoed hollowly in the quiet places, where only the moist air and the gentle vibration of nearby cataracts kept her company. The stairs exited on a jacaranda-lined street that crossed the shallow cradle of Avānweh. Heading south she reached the bustle of the waterfront promenade known as the Gahn-Markesh. Looking around she saw Nadir in her wake, his hand raised in greeting as she turned, mouth opened to shout something she would never hear over the crowd—or respond to even if she did.

The Gahn-Markesh was a long, wide road with hotels, stores, bright flowering gardens and myriad stairs. The three sisters of Avānweh stabbed at the heavens to the north. The Lakes of the Sky undulated into a blue-grey haze to the east and west, with the tall peaks of the Mar Ejir stretching away from the nearby southern shore. A thicket of ship masts swayed in the warm wind, surrounded by wheeling kestrels and gulls. A small number of wind-galleys, skiffs, and yachts drifted overhead, the toys of the wealthy, searching for a place to put down. Mari watched a wind-galley that had seen better days come to rest in the water. A powerful explosion of steam erupted as water bubbled around the madly rotating Tempest Wheels and the spinning dumbbell of the Disentropy Spool. The water churned for several moments before it eventually settled into a simmer, then a gentle series of ripples that lapped at the weather-beaten hull.

From time to time Mari would pause and look back, sometimes see Nadir searching for her and other times not. She threaded through the ambling crowd. Breathed deeply of spices, weathered timber and sun-warmed water. At the eastern end of the waterside market was a bridge to the Shoals—a series of small islands, little more than sandbars—only fifty metres off shore. Indris's wind-galley, the *Wanderer*, was out there amidst dozens of other vessels.

And there Nadir was, standing between Mari and her goal, in the shade of a fruit vendor's awning, eating raisins he had cupped in his hand. Mari froze at the sight of him, and Nadir smiled and gestured for Mari to eat from his palm. Mari looked Nadir up and down, her chin raised, almost smiling despite herself at the calm assurance of his pose.

"I think the days of me eating anything of yours are long over, Nadir." Mari was surprised at the evenness of her tone, though not at Nadir's relaxed chuckle. "Was a time you'd never say no, Mari," Nadir said. *His voice had sounded so deep when her head had rested on his chest.* She turned, the flush of her cheeks unwelcome. She struggled to find equilibrium. It had been so long, but still his voice sent tingles down her spine.

"Was a time I'd do a lot of things. Sometimes I still do, just not with you. What do you want, Nadir? Why are you here, and why, by Erebus's long cold shadow, did you follow me?"

"Nostalgia?" He stepped forward, rattling the raisins in his hands. Nadir popped one into his mouth, chewing with obvious delight at the taste. "Desire? Regret? Can I have more than one reason? Maybe it's because seeing you brought back memories I thought I'd wanted to forget, only to find I was so very wrong. You sure you don't want a raisin? They're very sweet, juicy, and quite . . . delicious."

A barrage of old emotion welled up in her. She wanted to hug him. Punch him. Kiss him. Kill him. A very rational anger based on old wounds rose like bile. She clenched her fists until the knuckles made a loud cracking sound.

Nadir smiled his familiar smile. Broad. Cheerful. Fangs in the open. Up close his scars gave him a rakish allure. "In all the Ancestors' names, I've missed you. It's been far too long, Mari."

"You disappeared without a word!"

"And I'm sorrier for that than you know."

"No need, I got over you soon enough." Mari gave a look of mock contrition at Nadir's equally false look of hurt. She frowned when he smiled, kicking herself for falling into old habits with him. "It wasn't that you left, Nadir. I could handle that you left. But I'd no idea what happened to you!" *Other than the rumours of your Family being exiled for treason, which is a story in itself. And now you're back, and your father is back, and your father and my father being together can not end well for many people.*

"If you've questions of me, then ask." He emptied his hand of the raisins, then held it out as if to take hers. "Had I the choice, you would've been the last person on Ía I would've left. Please, can't we talk? What harm is there in you hearing me out?"

"No harm, other than the time out of my life I won't get back."

"If you ask, I will tell, and I promise it'll be a tale for the ages."

"Really?" Mari glared at the man from beneath her ragged fringe, suddenly irritated by the way errant strands of hair caught in the corners of her eyes, or the harsh glare of the sun through blonde strands. She warred with her need to express a long-held righteous indignation and moral high ground at being the one left behind, with her need for answers. After several long moments where Nadir's grin withered under her gaze, curiosity won.

"Fine. So long as it's in public." Mari stared at Nadir's hand, still bridging the gap between them. "And not today. Tomorrow. Or the next day. Leave a message for me at Nanjidasé and make sure you'll be where you say you'll be this time."

Nadir bowed his jaunty bow and smiled a gentle smile, the one he knew she had always found hard to resist. Thankfully time had robbed her of that sentiment at least. She looked down at the raisins being trampled under the feet of passersby, becoming little more than dark spots of ruin on the hot street.

She chewed her lip, and breathed against the niggling pain in her ribs from last night's adventure. An assassination attempt. Now the return of the Exiles to bolster her father's power, and a lover from the past dropping back into her life, just at the time Rosha was trying to marry Indris off. *Balls*, she thought. Mari eyed a nearby vendor selling alcohol: horns of Angoth honey mead, jugs of the fiery moonshine made by the Jihari tribes, jars of the dark beer from Narsis Prefecture she had acquired a taste for, plus Seethe wines and all manner of exotic, mind-numbing indulgences from across the Marble Sea.

Mari bought a couple of jars of beer, then some loaves of hot bread and some dips and roasted meats from vendors along the markesh. Nadir had soured Mari's hunger for wanting to see Indris, but not for the safety of company. Tonight she would make sure she had friends with her at Nanjidasé, do some thinking, then do some drinking. Then tomorrow, Indris.

Whatever her father might be planning with the Exiles, she doubted she would want to face the idea of it sober. Then once she sobered up, there were assassins she needed to find . . . and end.

3

"IT IS NOT ENOUGH TO REVEL IN THE MISFORTUNE OF MY ENEMIES. THEY MUST KNOW, BEFORE THE END, IT WAS I WHO WAS THEIR UNDOING."

—From *The Intransigent Winter of Monarchy*, by King Voethe of Angoth, thirteenth year of his reign (493rd Year of the Shrīanese Federation)

DAY 348 OF THE 495TH YEAR OF

THE SHRĪANESE FEDERATION

The din from the race below rattled around Corajidin's private balcony at the Iphyrone. Incense burners scented the rooms with vanilla and orchid. Tinted glass lamps in the shape of horse heads lined the walls, lit by *ilhen* crystals. The air was bone dry with the aftertaste of sand. Sunlight streamed in solid, hard-edged beams across the black marble floor. Dust motes flared, floating sparks of amber drifting in the warmth. Long silk curtains, embroidered with the black rearing stallion of the Erebus, rippled languidly in the breeze.

Corajidin took in the clouds of dust streaming from the hooves of the lead racers as they sped by. Each rider was armoured, their large mountain hart likewise. The lead rider raised her bow. Took an arrow from the quiver at her knee. Drew and aimed. Fired at the gallop. Bullseye! The crowd roared, muffling the thunder of hooves. Corajidin gazed out over the unrestrained mass below, like blended knots of colour in a rug. Tiny beads for eyes. Black dot mouths. Each person a tiny part of a great ravenous beast that needed to be kept controlled and pliant.

Beside him his heir Kasraman raised an eyebrow at the particularly fine shot. Kasraman's ice-blue eyes seemed to shine against his olive complexion, his dark hair casting shadows over his brow. He was a solemn, elegant figure. *So much like his late mother.* Even Kasraman's frightening talent for witch-craft was a gift from Corajidin's first wife.

Corajidin looked over Kasraman's shoulder to where the most wealthy and influential of the returned Exiles enjoyed Erebus hospitality. Rahn-Narseh, the gaunt, iron-haired Knight-Marshall of Shrīan was also there, talking in short, sharp sentences as was her wont. Her grey and green coat and trousers were fine, though plain, with a military cut. Her son, Anankil, loomed nearby, a male version of his mother. The other sayfs already loyal to the Great House of Erebus were scattered in rooms and balconies below. He would speak with them shortly. These Exiles were the ones he needed to convince.

"Is the treacherous mongrel here?" Corajidin's gentle tone belied the way his fingers squeezed the wine bowl in his hand. Like it was somebody's throat.

"He is." Kasraman's smile was wintry. "Do you want him brought in?"

"Yes. It will be instructive."

Kasraman gestured to one of the Anlūki poised by the door. The woman bowed then left the room, returning shortly with two of her armoured breth-ren. The Anlūki had their hands on the hilts of their long shamshirs as they herded a jowly, richly dressed nervous-looking man into the room. The Ex-iles shared curious glances, conversations dwindling.

There came the dry creak of callipers. The limping tread. The clack of a wooden stave against stone. Corajidin stared at Wolfram as he entered the room. Wolfram's expression was closed behind the ragged tangles of his beard, beneath the brindle spears of his fringe. One large-knuckled hand was wrapped around his oft-mended staff, its length held together with rusted coffin nails, bands of metal and straps of knotted leather.

The traitor blanched. He whimpered and struggled. Sweat speckled his brow, eyes widened in fear.

"Corajidin? What is this?" Jhem of the Delfineh, apparently the leader of the Exiles, said. His voice was deep and sibilant, almost lisping. The years had added more grey to the man's receding black hair, yet his hooded eyes in their deep, seamed orbits were still cold and hard as polished stones.

"A demonstration." Corajidin maintained a set expression. He looked to the captive, resisting the urge to strike him.

"Demonstration?" Tahj-Shaheh asked. The Marble Sea corsair was taller than her father had been, slender yet womanly in her faded suede jerkin and wide-legged trousers. The only child of the late Hatoub had inherited her father's good looks. Years of piracy had darkened her skin and sun-bleached her hair. "What kind of demonstration?"

"I did as you asked," the man said, voice quavering. His complexion gone chalky under his tan. "I made sure—"

"This is Maroc of the Family Zam'Haja," Corajidin pointed at the man. "They have been the traditional wardens of the Zam'Haja district, on the northern borders of Erebus Prefecture—"

"Merciful rahn—" Maroc's words ended abruptly as Wolfram struck him in the face with his staff. The jagged flanges of coffin nails tore Maroc's lips. Blood flowed down his chin. The quivering man mewled in pain.

Corajidin nodded his thanks at Wolfram, who leaned on his staff and fixed Maroc with an unblinking stare.

"Despite my generosity, Maroc decided he would ally himself with the Federationists." Corajidin stood before the crumpled man. He could feel his temper rise; try as he might to maintain calm. Pain took seed between his eyes. His chest twinged. "I paid good money for Maroc, yet when it came time for him to deliver on his promises, he forgot who owned him. I am glad you are here to observe in how low esteem I hold those who betray my patronage. Wolfram?"

"Corajidin?" Jhem, the Blacksnake, glided forward on silent feet. "May I? I've no doubt your man here can terrify, but perhaps I've a way that may be more demonstrative to your audience."

Corajidin shrugged his assent. He was interested in seeing what years of Exile had done to Jhem, whose reputation was already so dark.

"My daughter, Kimiya, taught me this," Jhem's tone was light as he stared into Maroc's eyes. "While I'll never be a witch, there are some things I can do."

The Blacksnake stared into Maroc's eyes. The prisoner struggled in the hands of his captors, yet after a few moments began to quiet. Eventually he was still, his eyes half closed, expression slack. Jhem moved his head closer, nostrils flared, as he stared intently at Maroc. Seemingly satisfied he moved back.

"Is it true you betrayed your master?" Jhem asked in a soothing voice.

"Yes," Maroc whispered.

"Why?"

"Because he had gone too far in murdering Vashne and Ariskander. Too far. Empire, too far . . ."

Jhem drew a curved knife from the sleeve of his embroidered silk coat. Its silver blade was filigreed with bronze, the hilt of polished bone. He handed the blade to Maroc, curling the man's fingers around it.

"I want you to cut out one of your hearts and give it to Rahn-Corajidin."

Corajidin's breath caught in surprise. He spared a glance for Kasraman who looked back with distaste.

Maroc paused, hands trembling. Something lurked in his eyes. Some sense of self-preservation, of fear, and terrible knowing. Even so, the prisoner slid his coat off, then sliced the laces of his silk tunic. He opened the tunic to expose his fleshy torso. The knife quavered. Sweat trickled down Maroc's temples.

All the while Jhem stared deep at Maroc with his lifeless gaze.

Ever so slowly the knife curved down. Pressed against loose, hairy skin. A drop of blood welled. It became a trickle, then a stream as the knife bit deep. With a jerk of his hand, Maroc drew the knife up through muscle. He twitched, tears streaming from his eyes. He sawed the blade for a few moments as blood poured from the wound. The knife dropped with a clatter. The man began to shriek, skin ashen, as he rummaged inside his own chest for his left heart.

Before he could draw it out Maroc spasmed. Blood gushed from his mouth and he collapsed. Even as he writhed on the ground, his life ebbing away, the man tried to remove the muscle. He died with his hand still in his own chest.

"And now the Zam'Haja district needs a new warden," Jhem said blithely. He looked down at the body, head cocked to one side. "Pity he did not have the strength to finish. It would have been a more compelling demonstration if he had, do you not think?"

The Exiles looked away, hands nervously touching the hilts of their weapons. Jhem seemed oblivious to them. He looked up at Corajidin and smiled his dead smile. It made Corajidin's blood chill, even though he had been prepared for something atrocious. Jhem reminded him of the cold-hearted bastard, Rayz of the Maladhi, from the days when he had been Corajidin's Master of Assassins, prior to the late Thufan. The son, Nix—born of incest to an insane, cannibal father and the man's own daughter—was even worse. Smarter, meaner and madder than his parents, Nix had been Exiled along with his father during one of Asrahn-Vashne's purges.

Kasraman stepped forward, his hands held wide in a peaceful gesture. An easy smile lit his features. He gestured for the servants, their own faces tinged with nausea yet eyes rigidly downcast, to refill wine bowls. Bound-caste servants moved silently, replenishing drinking bowls from ewers of water and wine. Trays of fresh grilled fish with lemon, buttered wild rice, mint yoghurt, and crisp salad were laid out on tables. Musicians in tanned leather horse masks played sonesette and theorbo, timpani and the long bamboo flute of the Mar Ejir with its low, resonant sound.

"No doubt you've heard how some of my father's sayfs didn't support him as well as they otherwise might. We didn't want you thinking the Great House of Erebus took betrayal lightly." Kasraman gave Jhem a smile that did not reach his eyes.

"And we are thus instructed," the Blacksnake responded in an emotionless voice. "Which begs the question. Rahn-Corajidin, was it you who killed the arbiters yesterday?" he asked pointedly. The other Exiles paused, seemingly eager for the answer. Arbiters were supposedly sacrosanct, killing them bringing terrible retribution from their peers, as well as the kherife who worked with them to uphold the law.

Corajidin pondered whether he should take ownership of the deed, when the truth was he had no idea who had committed it. Some had said the explosion was Alchemists' Fire, released by Human terrorists who had died in the attack. Several arbiters also perished, including Arbiter-Colonel Pashur, the man who had been crusading to ensure Corajidin was cleared of his crimes. Enough silver nobles to loosen tongues had bought a different story: the explosion was caused by a fire elemental, which had been summoned and released. When the Sēq had not responded to the destructive force of the elemental, visiting witches had bound and banished the creature. Unsurprisingly the witches had tried to keep their involvement quiet. Humans from Manté had been blamed, their use of dark witchcraft the source of horror tales for centuries. Such accusations, founded in truth or not, helped Corajidin's cause against the Humans to no end.

Before Corajidin could answer Jhem's question, though, there was a disturbance. From the corner of his eye Corajidin saw the flute-playing musician—a wiry man with long greasy hair shaped into lank spines—step forward. One of the Anlūki moved in the musician's direction, hand on the hilt of their shamshir. The flute hummed through the air in a vicious stroke. It cracked across the back of the Anlūki's hand, splitting skin and breaking bone with a snap. As others descended on him, the man adopted a ludicrous, capering stance, the long bamboo flute waving before him like a sword.

"You've me to thank for yesterday." The flautist's voice was slightly nasal and low pitched. He swept his horse mask off with a flourish. Nix's grin was wild, his eyes shadowed in a pallid complexion. His greasy hair was swept back from a high, shiny forehead. He worked his mouth like he was chewing on something that tasted poorly, and when he spoke his fingers flicked as if he were speaking with them, too. "A gesture on my father's behalf, and out of his profound respect for an old friendship. Consider this our way of saying old ties are hard to break, Rahn-Corajidin."

Corajidin held up his hand for the Anlūki to halt. The musician bowed with an exaggerated flourish, then danced forward on light feet, flute neatly tucked under his arm. Corajidin felt as uncomfortable under Nix's eye, as he had under the father's. They were cold things, those eyes, and Corajidin wondered whether the man might look more suitable with another six, like the spider the Family Maladhi had as their sigil.

"It's been long and long since the Maladhi have served Your Majesty," Nix said. "My august father apologises for not being here in person to offer you our service. He has sent me to serve you in his stead."

"Thought that sick bastard was in his grave," Narseh's gravelly voice carried across the room. A few of the others nodded. "Died a pauper, riddled with syphilis or some such."

"Death wasn't all he'd hoped it'd be." Nix gave her a sidewise glance, mouth working sourly. He ran fingers through his hair. "I'll pass on your regards when next we speak."

"I had it on good authority you were poisoned by a courtesan-assassin in Tanjipé," Jhem said coolly.

"I'd heard you drowned as we withdrew from the siege of Danai," Tahj-Shaheh added. "Then again, I'd also heard you were captured by the Mantéans and executed for excesses even we'd shy away from."

"But I *was* poisoned, and drowned, and captured," Nix said in a conspiratorial whisper, his eyes wide. "And now I'm not."

"Why *are* you here?" Kasraman asked, cutting to the chase, though poorly masking his revulsion.

"Rahn-Corajidin invited my father to return to suckle at his golden teat." The odd man bowed over the chair, bending nearly double, the gesture almost mocking. "Or he would have, we're sure, had he known Father was still about. So return we did, in anticipation of renewing our long and prosperous acquaintance. My father finds the daylight hours taxing so has asked me to speak on his behalf. Thanks to my relationship with the Soul Traders, the little friend I set free from its Dilemma Box yesterday was only a small sample of what I can do for you. We've other surprises, too. You'll find our iron webs aren't so idly blown away."

The thought of the cold-hearted bastard, Rayz, made Corajidin feel light headed. The perverted old assassin had served Corajidin's father. Even as a member of the Great House of Erebus, Corajidin never felt safe in the older man's presence. It was said none escaped the Ironweb's plots. Those whom he trapped were never seen again. There were also widespread tales of the man's perversions—not rumours, for Corajidin knew them to be true even as it had been his job to muddy the truth about the man. Rayz was the dirty, ever-hungry spider, lurking to entrap and consume the young and the innocent. Including his own daughter. It had come as no surprise when the incestuous cannibal had been Exiled. It had been long overdue and managed to resolve the problem of killing the man before he became too much of a liability. Corajidin could still feel the man's breath on the back of his neck, sweet and cloying, and his dry old hands with their long, thin fingers lingering . . . Nothing had ever happened, but that did not stop decades of memories of the one man Corajidin feared more than any other from jolting through him.

And now there was the son—

Within seconds, pain coiled in his bowels. Sweat prickled the backs of his hands. Within the space of heartbeats it felt as if somebody were sitting on his chest. He lurched to a chair, the sediment of his illness lay in tiers upon him: the never ending fatigue; the tidal rise and fall of pain; the bedlam of his Ancestors' fractured voices in his head. All spoke of the infirmity that was killing him.

"Your Majesty." The Angothic Witch's rich tenor coiled like narcotic smoke. He drew a vial from a pouch at his belt.

Corajidin's need battled his revulsion as he eyed the potion in the witch's hand. Distilled from the raw essence of the Font, an almost pure disentropic fluid, the brew had restored a vitality Corajidin had not felt in years. Unfortunately, he felt acutely worse in those hours or days when he did not take it.

Corajidin remembered being introduced to the Emissary, the ambassador from the Drear. Everything she represented should have been wrong to him. Yet when she had produced a promise in a vial he had seen only survival, not consequence.

The fluid in the vial shone like a cobalt cloud with white stars in suspension. Corajidin watched the motes of light ebb, each one a tiny dream in the making. He held it up to his nose. Each time he had expected to smell something, some hint of venom, or decay. Something that alerted what remained of his moral compass what he was doing was wrong.

Nothing.

When the first drop hit his tongue, it was like an explosion of pins and needles wrapped in erotic delight. He felt it in the base of his spine. The taste changed from one side of his tongue to the other. It left a warm sweetness in his mouth: he tasted pure mountain snow melt; a hint of honey; the sweetness of a lover's skin; goat's milk and sugar. It tasted like all these things and more, though was none of them and less. It trickled down his throat, to settle like molasses in his belly. He breathed out an unpleasant aftertaste, acidic as reflux.

After a few moments, his strength returned. Pain faded. Corajidin braced himself on the arms of his chair. Rose slowly, feeling for any infirmity in his legs. They shook, at first. Then the trembling receded. Soon there was only the faintest twinge in his stomach. He gently rested his weight on his feet. Even the shooting pains from the cysts in his heels had eased. He teetered, foal-like on uncertain legs, before he found his balance.

Kasraman followed his father's gaze to where it rested on Nix, who crouched on a chair with his long arms wrapped around his knees. The wiry man was staring out the balcony door, one eye twitching as he chewed on his fingertips. Corajidin looked at his son, then looked back at Nix, hoping the anxiety he felt did not show.

"Should I have him removed, Father?" Kasraman whispered.

Corajidin thought about it for a long moment, and replied as softly, "Tempting, but no. Nix, like his father before him, represents some unique opportunities for us."

"Should he prove unsuitable," Wolfram muttered through his ragged beard, "it'll be an absolute pleasure to make an end of him."

As the silence stretched, almost all of the Exiles seemed intent on looking anywhere save at Corajidin. Jhem, however, stared at Corajidin emotionlessly, while Nix tapped the tips of his fingers together in a rapid tattoo. Nobody spoke. News of Corajidin's illness had been kept to a select few. He was hoping the need to reveal his infirmity would not have been necessary. Such was out of the question now.

"Have no fear, my friends," Corajidin assured them, "it is a passing illness that will not jeopardise my aspirations to the highest office in the country."

"As you say." Narseh waved a glass of beer at the Exiles. "I trust Rahn-Corajidin to see our goals met."

"I'm not so sure," Nix countered. He waggled a finger in a warning gesture, "See, I've read about diseases like this. What if we all get infected? Disease. Nasty business, that."

"Who asked you?" Narseh looked Nix up and down with disdain. "Though from the looks of you, disease is something you would know more than a little about, neh?"

"I'll take Corajidin's word this is a fleeting thing," Jhem said, with the hint of an almost-smile. "We've all come a long way to take back what's ours. I doubt he'd have wasted our time."

Corajidin nodded his agreement. "The sooner we have you with us on our great endeavour, the better."

Kasraman gestured for the Exiles to approach as Wolfram unrolled a large map of Shrīan on the table.

Corajidin gestured to the map as the Exiles gathered round. Each Prefecture of Shrīan had been truthfully rendered with the names of the sayfs who governed each city. Erebus Prefecture had been given the most detail, where the various holdings of each sayf had also been mapped. Some of these holdings were coloured, where others had been left blank.

"I take it the blank holdings are for the taking, Rahn-Corajidin?" Nix pointed at the map. "That one used to be ours."

"And can be again." Wolfram waved his hand across the map. "Coloured holdings are not up for negotiation. Nor are holdings outside of Erebus Prefecture—"

"My father governed Näs-Sayyin, in Näsarat Prefecture," Tahj-Shaheh gestured to a place on the Marble Sea, halfway between Amnon and Narsis.

"We're not in a position to offer you anything outside of Erebus Prefecture." Kasraman's voice was conciliatory. "We believe there may be options for you in Kadarin Prefecture, though you'd need to speak with Rahn-Narseh. We want to do right by you, yet there's only so much we can do."

"I'm a Marble Sea corsair," Tahj-Shaheh said with forced calm. "What bloody good would holdings in the deserts of Kadarin do me?"

"You can piss off then, girl," Narseh said in a voice made gravelly from shouting orders. She looked at Corajidin. "What use is she to you if all she wants is the bloody sea?"

"I've wind-corsairs in my fleet too, old woman," Tahj-Shaheh lifted her chin belligerently. "If you don't want them, you can have a nice tall glass of shut the—"

"There are sea ports in Erebus on offer and Kadarin faces the sea for thousands of kilometres," Jhem lisped indifferently. He included the other Exiles in a sweeping gesture. "Corajidin, we have spent the last couple of days discussing this and we are agreed. Your offers of land and title are most welcome. All we need do is agree on the price."

"What of those of us new to Shrīan?" Pah-Chepherundi op Sanojé was not a Shrīanese Exile, though the powerful princess-turned-witch had arrived with them. She was one of the heirs of a former Great House, their majesty a thing of the distant past. One of what was mockingly called the Bronze Avān, her own government had turned on the princess, banishing her from the Ivory Court of Tanis for her excesses. It was difficult to reconcile her reputation with her appearance. A petite woman with large pale brown eyes in a doll-like face, only her smile hinted at darker truths. "I can match the price offered by my colleagues here."

"You are welcome Pah-Sanojé, otherwise you would not be standing here. As for price? This is not a negotiation, my friends." Corajidin left the table, wine bowl cradled in his hands. He had seen the avarice in their eyes. Though years of foreign service had made them wealthy, they were more than ready to return home.

"Fine: what will your patronage cost us, Rahn-Corajidin?" Feyd's tone was forthright. He was a leader of the Jiharim, the tribes of the Mar Jihara mountains. His skin was seamed and dark as old mahogany, his spade-shaped beard bristly as wire. His old boots with their cracked leather were worn, his wide-legged trousers dusty. The cunning old tribesman had managed to unite many of the fractious, blood happy Jiharim tribes under his banner. His ruthlessness and unconventional approach to warfare were things Corajidin wanted to exploit.

"If you sign your caste patents here, now, it will cost you twenty-five percent of everything you have." Corajidin turned and walked towards the balcony. "For that you get my patronage and a seat on the Teshri, as befits a sayf of Shrīan. Your money will help you buy your own future, and that of the nation."

Silence. Corajidin fought the urge to look back. Though he wanted very much to see the impact his words had, now was a time for strength. Let them think they needed him more than he needed their wealth. He gestured to a nearby servant who spooned spiced lamb with pine nuts and cracked wheat into a lettuce leaf. Wrapped the parcel carefully. The servant handed the food to Corajidin without meeting his gaze. He took a bite and chewed slowly. The contrast of the spiced lamb and crisp lettuce on his tongue was refreshing. *Be calm.*

Corajidin leaned out over the balcony. The noise from the race had lessened somewhat as the riders thundered around the far side of the track. Though he could hear the Exiles talking urgently—arguing, really—he did not want to break his silence. Instead he took a relaxed sip of his wine. Lost himself in the view as the sun tracked colour across the stone outside.

It took several moments for him to realize his name was being called. He turned, expression bland.

"We're aware of what happened in Amnon, great rahn," Feyd's gaze was shrewd. "What's to say our investment will be a good one?"

"Your position isn't as strong as it was," Sanojé said. "One might say Vashne's and Ariskander's deaths were a mistake."

"Destiny!" Corajidin whipped a finger at Sanojé. "Destiny called and I answered. Who are you to ignore it? Amnon was part of a plan. Despite what happened, the Arbiter's Tribunal has neither seen fit to incarcerate me, nor to plague me further with censure. Yesterday's attack will no doubt give them further pause."

"With respect, Rahn-Corajidin," Tahj-Shaheh said as she leaned against the wall, crossing her very long legs at the ankle and her arms across her breasts, "you managed to avoid any censure all those years ago when some of us were—"

"Enough!" Corajidin felt his face flush. It was true, he had managed to distance himself from the scandal that had seen Jhem, Rayz, Tahj-Shaheh, and her father broken from the ranks of the Avān elite. There would never come the time to reveal that he had known of the Arbiter's investigations, or how he had bribed a corrupt investigator to destroy any evidence of Corajidin's wrongdoing. The others had been doomed already, and Corajidin had seen no point in going to any effort or expense for lost causes.

"Kasraman," he continued, "I understand there was quite the influx of Exiles into Avānweh yesterday?"

"We've almost a score of Exiled sayfs and some wealthy expatriate Avān from Tanis and Ygran, all seeking positions here." Kasraman said. "Not to mention Shrīanese women and men of influence who see an opportunity to improve their caste."

Corajidin nodded. "I respect people with vision. People with *commitment*. Leaders who realize swearing loyalty to me is an investment in a mutually assured future."

"You have not changed much, my friend," Jhem said, his dead eyes unreadable. "I can not speak for the others, though I for one want to come home. Twenty-five percent of everything I own is a lot. But the seventy-five percent I keep is more still. Where do I sign?"

Wolfram opened a leather folio. He withdrew several sheets of vellum, marked with the rearing black stallion of the Great House of Erebus. An inkpot and brush were placed beside it.

"Welcome to the future, Jhem," Corajidin breathed. He gestured to the map. "I'm glad to have you back!"

Corajidin waited while the others took their turn after Jhem. His hearts pounded so hard he felt blood pulse in his head.

"Now it is time to speak with the others downstairs," Corajidin said, looking down at the map. There was always room for those lean enough and driven enough to take what they wanted from those weaker than themselves. "There are a few who will need to follow in the late Maroc's footsteps before the day is done."

❈ ❈ ❈

Late afternoon sun streamed through fretwork shutters at the Qadir Erebus, patterning the black onyx sarcophagus with hard-edged diamonds. The air was perfumed with frankincense. The sounds of Avānweh hummed beyond the palace walls: the rattle of cart wheels, the drone of hundreds of almost-understood conversations, the rumble of waterfalls.

The Emissary from the Drear's lithe silhouette was a stain on the dimness about her, difficult to tell where her outline ended and shadows began. Corajidin schooled his features to stillness. He reminded himself Belamandris lay sleeping, his life owed to the Emissary. He had never feared the question *what can we do for you?* until he had met her.

"What do you want?" Corajidin asked gruffly. The sarcophagus was cool under his palms.

"My masters would have something of you," the Emissary's voice was a rusted creak. "A small token of your appreciation—and one in your best interests."

"You have spoken with the leaders of the Covens?"

"The Mother and Father Superiors of the Covens won't speak with you—or of you. A gesture of good faith is required, to bring them into your embrace."

"Such as?"

She stirred in the murk. "They want you to open the Mahsojhin."

Corajidin froze for a moment. "And I am to do this how, exactly?"

The Emissary's voice scraped his nerves. "The Sēq were unable to kill the greatest of the Mahsojhins teachers or students. These were sealed between moments to ensure they never challenged the Sēq again. Locked away in the Rahnbathra is something called the Emphis Mechanism. If you retrieve it, I can open the Mahsojhin—with the help of your son and the Angothic Witch."

"And I am to waltz into the Museum of Antiquities and walk out again with this device?"

"I don't care how you do it. Just ensure it's done. And quickly."

Corajidin peered into the obscuring shade, trying to see her. There came a dry slithering. A faint rasp of flesh with an underlying echo of chittering, high-pitched voices. Other than the faint gleam from her scabrous mindstone and the verdigris pommel of her sword, light was loath to go there. He had heard of the Mahsojhin. Knew, as much as any indifferent student knew, the history of the centuries-old Scholar Wars when the witches had tried to seize control of Shrīan. Some of his Ancestors had fought on both sides of the war, though only the Sēq Erebus fa Zadjinn had survived. For all Corajidin knew the man still lived, hiding away in the Long Shadow beneath World Blood Mountain with his mystic brothers and sisters.

"The Exiles have witches," Corajidin said firmly. "I would expect my plans will succeed without the help of the Covens, or the failures in the Mahsojhin."

The Emissary stepped forward a pace, little more than a spectral outline. "Your handful won't be enough to stand against the Sēq when the time comes, nor to make the kind of war you need to unify all the Avān under your banner. Without their help all you love, all you hope for, will come to ashes and dust."

All he loved. Corajidin placed his brow on Belamandris's resting place. Part of him knew he should have let his son go to be with their Ancestors. Yet Belamandris reminded him of himself when he was young, though so much better.

"I can bring him back to you," the Emissary said, divorcing herself from the enshrouding darkness. The Soul Witch's vest, breeches and split-toed boots were rotten and frayed, tied together with straps of soiled leather. Her face had once been austerely beautiful, but was now the visage of a drowned woman, her brow marred by a balefully glowing green stone, like an infected wound. Blackened veins radiated from it, dark against pallid flesh, across her temples and down her cheeks. A long sword was thrust through mottled steel rings on her belt. The weapon was sheathed in red-flecked, jade-hued *serill*. Its hilt wrapped in old skin. The pommel looked like a carved octopus in blackened green onyx. For a moment Corajidin thought he saw shadows writhe around the Emissary's legs, as if betentacled things writhed in the thunderhead murk of her over-robe. "Though your people find it . . . unwholesome . . . I can restore to you the ones you've lost. The son. The—"

"At what price?" he said, cutting her off. He feared the words: *The wife.* But feared her response more.

"Something smaller than the combined glories of the future my masters will grant you."

"Why do I have trouble believing you?"

"My predecessors have had a long and mutually beneficial relationship with your house, Corajidin." The Emissary stood still, waiting for Corajidin to master his surprise. "Such as your mother, the Dowager-Asrahn."

"Khurshad is a malignant harridan." Even her name left a bad taste in Corajidin's mouth. Winters spent under her eye in the freezing halls of Tamerlan, the cheerless isle buffeted by winds from the Southron Sea. "I prefer to think of her as my father's wife, rather than my mother."

"As you like." A rustling shrug. "But it does not change the fact that we know you of old. And have done well by you. Myself, and my associates, are here to help you and those others like you. And so it is my Masters want a token of recognition for their interest in you."

"What do they want?"

"For now, your cooperation in helping us put you where you want to be. The Obsidian Heart in the Eliom-dei hasn't been occupied since your empire fell. Don't you long to sit the Canon Stone, giving your people the guidance they need, in lieu of an indifferent and ephemeral Empress-in-Shadows?"

"How?" he asked, though his soul screamed, *Yes!*

"Do you want your son saved?" she persisted, her questions now seemingly relentless. "Or, perhaps, have *her* restored—a much more difficult thing but not beyond my ability to deliver. But your son I can give you now, if you agree to do as I ask."

"And again, what will this cost me?" Corajidin allowed hues of anger, fear, and frustration to colour his voice. "Do not talk to me of *for now*. I am not a fish to be lured to your hook!"

"Are you not?" She smiled a black-toothed smile. "You tell me what you want, and I will tell you what it will cost."

"For my son?" *To start. But, to bring* her *back?* Corajidin felt elated at the thought, at the same time as felt bile rise in his throat. There were many things he would do, but to traffic with Nomads, even one whom he loved to obsession, was not so easily done. His people would never understand the breaking of one of their most sacred mores, yet, to have her back, taken as she was before her time—

"I see the working of your mind, Corajidin." The Emissary tapped a finger against her temple. "I can hear the creaking of the checks and balances in your head. Listen to me now. Your beautiful son will not linger forever, so a decision must be made. The price for a man of war, are women and men of knowledge. Help us break the Sēq monopoly on esoteric power. Restore the witch covens, old institutions like the College of Artificers, and the Alchemist's Society—"

"I'm not Asrahn yet and why would I invest in the dusty old arcane cults of yesterday? Does anybody even remember them, swaddled in the decay of centuries as they are?"

"Then support them when you're Asrahn. When you break the Sēq, there will be a void you'll want to control. In their day, the witches, artificers, and alchemists had a strong alliance. And a brisk trade in potions and devices the people want, but the Sēq proscribed."

"But the expense!"

"Have Banker's House extend their credit—soon you'll be rich enough to cover their risks—so your new allies can grow tall, rather than staying as the weeds they are. They'll repay your investment, fear not. You'll control all aspects of power, Corajidin, as opposed to the way things are today. Agree to this, and Belamandris will walk by your side again."

Easier said than done. Now the price had been spoken, the taste of his question seemed somehow rotten, and as elusive as catching tomorrow. Break the Sēq? As much as he would relish the outcome, he had more chance of hiding the moon in his pocket.

"And my"—*wife*—"throne?"

The Emissary laughed, seemingly delighted, though it was a blood curdling sound of rust popping from an old gate and the dry creak of hinges. "A throne for a throne. Or thrones, in this case. Were you to become Asrahn— and I *can* help make this happen—then you can do what you please with the Rōmarq and its mud-caked treasures. There you'll find the weapons you need to unify your people: to take the Jade Throne in Mediin, and to bring the Ivory Court of Tanis under your heel."

Her gaze bored into him from the shadow of her hood. "And yes, the price is a life for a life—or is it, a wife? My people believe that death is a jealous thing, and doesn't let go its hold easily. It needs to be tricked. To be distracted with greater prizes, so it doesn't miss a little thing like a single soul. But one thing at a time, my erstwhile ruler of the world. Let me show you I'm good to my word by reviving the glorious Widowmaker. Then we can discuss how deep your pockets, both physical and spiritual, truly are."

My son! The throne! My wife!... Yes, in hallowed Erebus's name I want it all. Corajidin almost choked on his reply, "Yes."

A single word so filled with hope he felt lighter by giving it breath. He fell to his knees in front of the sarcophagus, fighting back a sob of relief.

She said nothing, only stepped back into the sheltering dark.

There was too much silence now. Too many empty places where people should have been. So many gone. Yashamin, Belamandris, Thufan. Even Mariam, though she did little but test the limits of his patience. The opportunities the Exiles represented should have been a cause for celebration with his loved ones, yet he was alone.

Corajidin held up Yashamin's funerary mask from where he had it in the folds of his over-robe. He ran his fingers tenderly across the amber curves of his late wife's face, a perfect rendering of her near perfect features. Corajidin raised the mask before his own face. Pressed the cool amber against his skin. Stared out through the vacant eye slots.

Did he imagine the flicker of a slender shape in the depths between bright windows? Diaphanous silks, revealing as much as concealing the allure within? He could hear Yashamin's voice, a whisper in his head. He had felt her presence since the day she died. Tears gathered at the corners of his eyes.

Why haven't you found the one who cut my throat? Don't you care who took your queen away from you, my love? You must do whatever it takes to make this right. To see our dream become reality!

Startled, Corajidin took the mask from his face. Surroundings resolved themselves into an exorcised silence. It felt like his hearts smashed against his ribs. He turned the mask around. Fancied, for a moment, the shadowed pits of the eyes were simply night-dark irises. The amber was the soft skin of a face kissed by the glow of candles. Even the dark red-black of his jacket looked like strands of her hair.

"Yashamin," he choked out through a throat clenched with grief. He raised the mask back to his face and remembered the gentleness of her skin against his. Then his eyes turned to the sarcophagus and the son who lay within it. His throat constricted. The heat of tears burned in his eyes, yet they refused to come.

He kissed the mask, then carefully secured it within the folds of his over-robe. The Emissary had wrung his need from him for the return of his golden son, yet Yashamin's death remained unanswered. Even so, vengeance was a far cry from her resurrection, and the condemnation of her people that would be the result. Surely she would not want to return, knowing what she would face?

"Would you have it, my heart of hearts?" Corajidin asked the empty air, afraid of a response. "Can we afford to pay for what I would do, until the end of our days, then have history continue our damnation long after we are gone?"

Nothing.

Which was what sende demanded should be, painful and lonely as it was. *Do not treat with the undying, for the spirits of the departed must return to the Well of Souls, there to await rebirth on the Great Wheel of the World.* The laws of his people, and their society, were clear.

Yashamin's return may be forbidden by everything he had been taught, but he would ensure there was a reckoning, a price in spilled blood and ruined lives, for the loss of love.

❋ ❋ ❋

Selassin fa Martūm was waiting for him in his small dining room. The man's plain face was faintly pink with sunburn and his clothing was expensive, layered silks in the most recent fashion. As Corajidin took a seat, he noticed several pale bands of skin on the man's fingers, where he had worn rings that were now missing.

"What brings you, unannounced, to my qadir, Pah-Martūm?" A servant poured Corajidin some tea, stirring a spoonful of honey into the glass. Martūm looked on, licking his lips, expression hardening when the servant stepped back from the table, taking the teapot and honey with them.

"Your hospitality has waned of late, Rahn-Corajidin," Martūm observed.

"I've not offered you refreshment, am not sharing a meal, so sende does not extend any protections to you. You owe me—and others—vast sums of money, Martūm. With your Uncle Vashne dead and your cousin Vahineh not much better, it seems you may have some serious depredations in your immediate future. Not a good time to be an indebted wastrel with expensive tastes."

"But if you kill me, how then will you recover what I owe?"

"I?" Corajidin shook his head. "I'll have nothing to do with your grievous wounding or death. Nevertheless, they may serve as an example to others, which I'll not rue."

"Which is why I'm here, my rahn." Martūm smiled ingratiatingly. "Examples and debts and all kinds of new beginnings. I appreciate our arrangement is, perhaps, strained and may continue to be so until my circumstances are resolved. It may please you to know, however, that I spent the day with Ziaire—"

"How, by all the names of the hallowed dead, could you afford that?"

"Rahn-Näsarat fe Roshana arranged it. It seems they've come to the conclusion that my simpering cousin needs replacing." Martūm inspected an immaculately polished fingernail. "And it looks like I'm the one they will try to Awaken."

Corajidin hid his smile behind his cup. "So."

"And while their talk of Federation and unity and opening our borders was all very interesting, it wasn't . . . financially advantageous."

"So?"

"So." Martūm leaned back in his chair and crossed his legs. "How interested, and how much would it be worth, for you to have a new Imperialist rahn at your disposal? I don't really care what you do with my vote, or what you want me to vote for. All I want is to be kept in the lifestyle to which I've grown exceedingly fond."

Setting his cup very carefully on the table, Corajidin ordered the servant to bring a light meal and more tea. Martūm smiled, an oily stretch of his lips against pink skin.

"Pah-Martūm, I would be very interested, and it would be worth quite a considerable sum. Let's talk, you and I, about how we are best suited to help each other."

4

"THE EVENTS OF OUR LIVES OFTEN OPEN OUR EYES TO THE UNKNOWN. TO
BE ALIVE IS TO AWAKEN TO A NEW WORLD EACH DAY."

—From *The Manifold Life,* by Teren-karem, Sēq Magnate
(991st Year of the Awakened Empire)

DAY 349 OF THE 495TH YEAR OF

THE SHRĪANESE FEDERATION

The late morning glare scored Indris's eyes when he woke. He groaned then rolled over, covering his head with a pillow. Teetering on the edge of sleep, he found himself abruptly awake as the pillow was removed from over his head.

"It's past time you were up," Shar's voice came from the vaguely head-shaped blur Indris squinted at. It felt as if there was a bubble about to burst behind his eyes. "Mari's been and gone, by the way. Didn't want to wake you, so she'll come back later."

"Give me my pillow," he growled. His feeble attempts to grab the pillow were foiled by Shar's nimbleness. She laughed at his misfortune before hiding behind an expression of insincere contrition. The orange-yellow gems of her eyes narrowed in concern though as Indris rolled on to his back, head in his hands.

"The headaches?"

Indris grimaced at her then rose from the bed. Shar remained, eyes intent as he stripped to wash himself. He cast a glance at his old friend, eyebrows raised. She ignored his silent request for privacy so Indris turned his back as he dressed. Shar snorted.

"You've not told the others about this have you?" she asked.

"How can I when I don't even know what there is to tell?" Indris pulled on a pair of loose trousers and shrugged into a tunic and knee-length hooded coat. His old worn boots, with their frayed stitching, were so comfortable it was if he were barefoot. Shar stood close as Indris buckled on his weapon belt. "I'm finding I can do things I was never trained to do. I don't know what it means or how I can do them. I certainly have precious little control of them."

"What else can you do?" she asked surprised and curious in seemingly equal measure. Shar saw the narrowing of his eyes and swore quietly to herself in exasperation. "Indris, my people have been witches longer than your people have existed. Didn't it occur to you I might be able to help?"

"I don't doubt your sincerity, Shar," he said. "But I've seen nothing in the Seethe studies of the Esoterics that even comes close to explaining what's happening to me."

"If the *Ahnah-woh-te* doesn't have your answers, what about the *Fayaadahat*? Surely there's something, somewhere in the works the Sēq have amassed on mysticism?"

"Not that I know of." He frowned, and pointed at her. "And you're not supposed to talk about the *Fayaadahat*, remember? It's supposed to be this great and mystic secret of the Order—"

"That a lot of people outside the Order know about."

"Fine. Be that way. Almost all of the *Fayaadahat* is based on the foundations of Seethe discoveries. We all use the ahmsah to perceive and influence the ahm, the tidal flow of disentropy that flows across the ahmtesh. Our Esoteric Doctrine articulates how we perceive and stimulate natural energy to supernatural ends. Over the years the Sēq expanded on those teachings, but everything is still dependent upon the cause and effect of formulae and disentropy. Shar, this is something very different from anything I was taught."

She jabbed him in the chest with a blue-nailed finger. "Show me."

Indris calmed his mind. The bubble was still there, a growing pressure with an ebb and flow of discomfort. There was no flexing of his Disentropic Stain. No formulae to calculate energy and effect. He flexed his mind. Visualised what he wanted. He reached out and with a soft pressure in his skull, urged Changeling into his hand.

Changeling trembled slightly where she leaned against the wall. Indris focussed his mind. Imagined the coolness of her *kirion* scabbard in his hand. Her elegant recurved shape, the feel of the scales carved into the hilt and dragon-headed pommel. Her weight.

The scabbard scraped on the floor. She shuddered.

Then shot across the room into Indris's hand.

"*Faruq ayo!*" Shar swore in breathy, backward-sounding Seethe. "*Zhar be yaha dein hem?*"

Changeling purred as Indris slung her across his back. "You've quite the mouth on you, you know that? But to answer your question, I've no idea how I did it. Well, maybe a vague idea."

"It's my language and I can swear in it if I like. More importantly, are you supposed to be able to do that?" Shar asked from where she perched on the back of a chair.

"I doubt it," he murmured. "I can't do it all the time. Not yet."

"What else can you do?" she asked with a shrewd gaze.

"Nothing reliable enough to talk about." He winced under her sudden scowl. "The occasional prophetic dream, though I've had those since I was a child. I think I may be able to hear people's thoughts, but it's more like a faint rumble in my head with a few garbled words thrown in. Sometimes I can sense people's intentions, like they're telling me what they're about to do. I have visions of distant places and people. Some other things. I'm flying blind here thinking of what to try."

Indris gestured for Shar to follow him as he left the cabin, heading for the deck. Summer, its punishing hammer a vivid memory, was almost over. The days were getting cooler, spotted by torrential rains. From the deck of the *Wanderer* Indris could see the kaleidoscopic pattern of people attending the lakeside markets. A vivid, teeming mosaic of colour that changed from moment to moment. The clamour of wagon wheels, boat horns, bells, swearing longshoreman, and yelling merchants rolled over him, blending with the hypnotic gurgling of water against the hulls of nearby boats. Behind it all were the towering forms of the snow-capped and cloud mantled Three Sisters of Avānweh: jagged Mar-Silamari to the east, brooding Īajen-mar in the middle, and tall, bladed Mar-Asrafah to the west. He could smell coffee brewing nearby.

A dozen or so cats looked up from where they lay in the sun, tails raised in greeting, their purring a gentle rumble.

"Everywhere I go, cats . . .," Indris muttered as a few of them came and pressed their faces against his legs. Smiling, he reached down to ruffle their long, silky fur.

"How long have you been able to do," she waggled her fingers, "you know?"

"I've been able to do some unexplained things since my years with the Dragons. But nothing like this. It's gotten more pronounced since Amnon. It feels as if parts of myself are being, I don't know, unlocked? It started slowly, after my missing years on the Spines. But I used the ahmsah a lot when we were in Amnon. A lot more than was wise. It's changed me somehow. And my second Awakening? Ancestors only know what that's opened up."

Shar took Indris's chin in her hand. She stared into his eyes, face immobile, as if looking for something. "I'm serious. You need to speak to somebody about this."

He faked a look of revelation, eyes and mouth open wide. "Why don't I just wander on up to the Sēq Chapterhouse and tell them! I'm sure that'd go well. They'd have me in front of the Suret faster than I could spit. May as well drop my trousers and bend over a barrel now."

She playfully slapped his cheek. "There's no need to be snide. But I see how being dragged before the Sēq Council of Masters wouldn't end well."

Indris walked down the gangway to where Ekko and Omen were seated beneath the broad canopy that made the *Wanderer* the centrepiece of a large pavilion. Rugs had been spread over the sand. Couches, camp chairs, braziers, and tables were scattered about. Hayden crouched near one of the Disentropy Spools, the device half dismantled, exactly how Indris had left it the day before yesterday. Hayden gave Indris a pointed look, then gestured to the dismantled device before returning to work. Indris needed to help the old man with the repairs, sooner rather than later.

The smell of coffee was strong, where a small urn rested on a low table. Indris poured a small cup. "I don't think the Sēq would be as interested in helping me as they'd be in helping themselves. I've tracked down an old friend from the early days of the Immortal Companions. She may have some insights."

"Want company?"

"I wouldn't mind," Indris whispered in Shar's ear as he hugged her goodbye, "but she would. She has a few trust issues."

"Be that way," Shar sniffed with mock indignation, citrine eyes bright with humour. "I'll keep these wild boys company 'til you get back. What if Mari comes past?"

"And what about the Spool?" Hayden said tersely. "Truth be told, I can muddle through repairing guns and the like. But this thing is a world of difference, and I figure me making a mistake, then all of us falling out of the sky because of it, ain't so grand."

"This shouldn't take long," Indris said as he waved farewell to Shar and the others. "I'll be back just after high sun. And Hayden—I'll help just as soon as I get back."

✻ ✻ ✻

It was a short walk through the winding lanes of the Shoals. Across the sun-bleached wood, split bollards, and knotted ropes of the Carnat-Farhi Bridge, then westward along the bustling Jahn-Markesh. He pulled the hood of his coat up, as much to keep out the glare of the sun as for anonymity. The smell of sun-warmed water faded, to be replaced by the competing odour of straw baskets piled with sea salt and pepper, saffron and turmeric, coriander and mint. Grilled fish, bent-necked ducks and thick slices of roast pork hung from hooks. Behind the waterfront stalls were the shadowed doorways of taverns and guest houses. Merchant factors. Traders and shipping companies. There were as many Humans as there were Avān on the streets, with a smattering of the nomadic felt-clad Tau-se, manes bright with polished fortune coins, and Seethe in their sky-toned vests and breeches. There was even a Seethe war-player, tall and lean in his *serill* cuirass and hauberk. His *serill* great sword was deceptively slender, almost as tall as its

wielder, its scabbard hung with strands of red-tinted crystals that chimed
with each step.

After climbing a couple of terraces up Skyspear's sheer face, the crowds
gave way to the cool confines of specialised stores and studios. The blade-like
towers of the War Academy jabbed the air over nearby rooftops, nestled
amongst the flat roofs of the Royal University and the dirty ceramic domes
of the almost defunct Alchemist's Society, and the College of Artificers.
Narrow lanes reeked of damp and urine. The sky narrowed to little more
than a harsh blue-white bar overhead, as the old buildings leaned closer together as if conspiring with the shadows they made. Stairs, slumped in the
middle like old saddles, were spotted with moss. Layers of fresh and faded
graffiti marred the crumbling, psoriatic walls. Narrow windows with dirty
glass and flaking paint squinted down. The occasional window was open,
through which Indris heard students debating philosophy, history, and literature. Babies cried. Couples argued. There came the sounds of energetic sex
on a creaking bed, the bed head rapped against the wall. And there was a
miasma of smoke, refuse, and humidity that clung to everything.

Indris breathed deeply when he emerged into the wider, cleaner streets
of the Naktaja. It was a serpentine district, home to bookstores, stationers,
scribes, sages, and the shops of mercenary librarians who had not fit in with
the scholastic Orders. Most of the stores provided support to the university
and its students. Streets, little more than claustrophobic laneways bordered
by a wall of narrow buildings, formed a coiled maze of moss-edged cobble-
stones, windows dark as mirrors. Indris narrowed his eyes at the strip of
sunlight that glared between the tops of the buildings. The air was musty
with the smell of damp stone from the previous night's rain.

Set between two plain stone frontages was The Unwritten Word. It appeared an unremarkable place; tall windows shuttered more by verdigris
than bronze. Set behind a fretwork cast-iron grill, the old wooden door was
sturdy, scored, and scratched with use. Indris tried the grille to find it unlocked. To be on the safe side he knocked before opening the door.

There was precious little space inside. Bookshelves lined the walls from
floor to ceiling, as well as forming neat rows from front to back. Sandalwood
perfumed the still air. *Ilhen* lamps, which gave clean white light without
heat, hung like incandescent sunflowers by chains from the high ceiling.

"Chaiya?" he asked quietly. "It's Indris. May we talk?"

There was no response for almost a minute. Indris stood alone in the silence and silvered light. Then his skin began to goose pimple from a sudden drop in temperature. Breath streamed from his mouth. Frost formed in tiny drifts around the window frames. It crackled as it blossomed like hundreds of tiny white flowers.

"Indris." The echoes of a feminine voice were everywhere and nowhere. Inside and through him. An involuntary chill trickled down his spine. The hair rose on the back of his neck. It was the effect all Nomads had on the living. Chaiya was one of the ephael—a spirit who took neither living flesh nor a simulacrum as her host. The voice came again, resonant and sepulchral. *"What trouble brings the Ghost Tamer to my door? Though word is you have new names now."*

"Chaiya. It's been a long time. You're not the easiest person in the world to find." Indris looked around though could not see the Nomad. He looked to the lights above, almost as bright as daylight. Indris intoned a canto under his breath. Fingers of shadow stretched from the corners of the room, flowing like clouds reflected in a stream. Within seconds the room had darkened perceptibly.

"I prefer not to be found. Cosmopolitan as the people of Avänweh may be, most still hate Nomads no matter what they say, or how liberal they pretend to be. Yet we were friends, you and I."

Chaiya materialised as the room descended into gloom. She was moonlight and shadows: a diaphanous, flowing sculpture of jade radiance etched in black. It was as if old paint had seeped into every translucent seam, line, and crease of her cassock. Between the self-realized strands of her hair. In the fine lines of her knuckles and the helixes of her ears. The Sēq Librarian from Manté was almost as Indris remembered, before she had died at his side. A triangular face with a pointed chin beneath long straight hair; high, broad cheekbones; large eyes with heavy lids; a small upturned nose. She even remembered her freckles, small black stars that floated on her spectral image.

There were those cultures who said Nomads—ghosts, spectres, phantoms, call them what they did—were the shapes of spirits projected by the light of the ahm. Indris could not say such was the case with any certainty. Or doubt. Yet there was a corona of light that wavered about her as if Chaiya were backlit by scores of candles. Her spectral form was much cleaner than those of vampires and ghuls, refusing to leave their rotting corpses in their desperate, degenerate, hunger for life. Better by far than liches, with their ornate, gem-worked, and scrimshawed skeletons, gifted minds always at work for personal gain at the expense of others.

"Thanks for seeing me, Chaiya. I wouldn't have come, but I'm in need." As a kaj-adept, Indris could speak with Chaiya using the subtle vibrations of soul on soul spirits used to communicate. Her voice was a burr against his disentropic stain. It reminded him of the sound of the wind through pine needles.

"*There are few I'd reveal myself to. Fewer who could hear me,*" the Nomad smiled. The room warmed slightly. "*I owe my existence to you. What is it you need?*"

"Knowledge," he replied honestly.

"*I take it what you're after can't be found in the Naqta-Avānweh?*" Her smile in response to her rhetorical question about the Library of Avānweh was like a swirl of mist.

"I need to know more about what was studied in Khenempûr. Not just the usual Esoteric Doctrines, but a wider view of all fields of study." Indris swallowed at the mention of the name of Khenempûr. Almost three kilometres from end to end, its hyperbolic and elliptic towers, roads, and walls had almost been reclaimed by the jungles of Tanis. It was a rambling, haphazard city of strange angles and unsettling dimensions, built by those known in modern times as The Empty, razed millennia ago by the Time Masters. The Avān had eventually settled it after ousting the Seethe. It was one of the few places Indris knew of that had encouraged the complete study of the Esoteric Doctrines, regardless of ideology, or politics.

"*Khenempûr?*" she asked. "*There are few amongst the living* or *the dead who'd have memories of it. What do you need?*"

Indris chewed his lip. "What I'm looking for won't be in any orthodox canon. I think it would need to be written in Hazhi'shi, or Maladhoring. Only the original, specific language—not a translation—would accurately express the underlying philosophies of the text. Given the source of what I need, I have an awful feeling it might be part of the *Sifr Hazhi.*"

"'The Draconic Dialectics'?" Chaiya floated forward, the hem of her cassock roiling like fine powder over the wooden floor. She reached out to touch him. A mortal gesture. Something many Nomads forgot was useless as they could no longer experience physical contact. Indris reached out to cup slightly chilled air in his hands. Comfort in the myth of touch. Her eyes, lanterns glowing out of, rather than windows in to her soul, seemed sorrowful. When she spoke again, her voiced hummed across the strings of his spirit. *"What are you looking for? Come to think of it, can you even read Hazhi'shi or Maladhoring?"*

Indris shrugged awkwardly. "I never learned the language of the Dragons, or the high language of the Elemental Master mystics, though part of me knows I can read them when I see them—don't ask me how I know that." He continued. "My interest is in the mentalist disciplines, what the Sēq called the Mah-Psésahen."

"I've heard the name. In Maladhoring it's the psukazha, and I can't even pronounce it in Hazhi'shi, though it is supposedly a field of study within the Sifr Hazhi. I don't know how useful that will be to you, given Draconic mysticism is sourced in their dreams, and their perceptions of reality. Gifted you may be, but you're not a dreaming Dragon." She drifted back as if caught by the breeze, her form stuttering for a moment with what Indris took to be anxiety. *"Be careful, Indris. This is old power you're looking for. It isn't like the mental disciplines and controls you learned as a psé-adept. The Ilhennim have searched long and hard for another way to wield metaphysical power. Especially one with no side effects. Nobody has ever found one, and the Sēq still badly hunger for an answer. There were rumours of it being studied at Isenandar—the Pillars of Sand— before the school was destroyed.*

"Indris, there have always been legends of lost powers and new schools of thought. Wouldn't they have been found by now? Have you considered such powers don't exist?"

"I'm pretty confident there's some truth to the legends," he said dryly. "And it was once believed nobody could flex disentropy to change the world around them, until somebody did it. If it was written anywhere, studied anywhere we know of, it had to have been in Khenempûr. Or the Spines, of course, but that would be a last resort."

"Or Isenandar—"

"No, *that* would be my last resort. I think I'd take the Spines over going to the Pillars," Indris said quickly. There were few places that elicited such thoughts of dread in a scholar as the Pillars of Sand, the very first arcane school. The Ascendents of the Great Houses were taught there, given insights into terrifying power, their eyes first opened to the consciousness of Ia. Sedefke and his chief disciples had trained them, and they had all become great—mental and spiritual giants—until they had tapped too deeply, and too quickly, into powers that had destroyed the school in a cataclysm that had become almost mythical. Even the history books did not mark Isenandar's location, for fear of stirring into flame the destructive embers of yesterday. But of course the Sēq knew where it was, for digging amongst the bones of history was one of the things they did best.

"It may take a while to get you an answer. The dead aren't known for their perceptions of time. But there's something you should know. I hear things, Indris. The dreams of the living are emanations of the spirit as much as the mind," her voice part sighed, part echoed, ripples across his Disentropic Stain. *"There're those amongst the Sēq who've become very interested in you after Amnon. You need to be careful. The factions are growing as far apart as their agendas. Some of the scholars dream very dark dreams about you. Avānweh is dangerous."*

Indris was uncomfortably reminded of his earlier conversation with Femensetri. Staying was a chance he would have to take for now. "My old sahai has mentioned as much. The Sēq are . . . uneasy. And that doesn't bode well for anybody."

The ghost's shape flickered, her face betraying her fear. *"The barriers between worlds are collapsing, Indris. Something stirs in the deep, their dreams trouble us all. Even the dead are afraid."*

"What *do* the dead fear?" But Chaiya was silent on the matter, as if to give her thoughts voice might make them real. Rather than probe further, he asked, "Would you please find out what you can about the Psésaren?"

"Tread warily, Indris." She drifted forward, a sculpted cloud, to occupy the same space as he. Indris smiled. Clearly she had not distanced herself from what it had been to be living quite yet. His thoughts turned to Omen. His smile faltered. It was only a matter of time before any Nomad forgot why they lingered in the physical world. Some were closer to such a fugue than

others. He flexed his aura so it hummed across hers. The closest thing he could give her to physical connection.

"Thank you, Chaiya," he whispered. "I'll be in your debt."

"Nomads need very little the living can give, Indris," she replied as her form dimmed. Her next words were barely more than a hum in the gloom. *"When I've an answer, I'll find you. Until then, keep your eyes open and tread softly, if you know how to do such a thing."*

Then she was gone.

Indris banished the shadows he had summoned. The *ilhen* crystals shone bright once more. He left, closing the iron grille behind him.

He turned at the clattering of pigeons to see a lone figure, hooded over-robe snagged by the breeze, standing at the far end of the deserted street. The person was an eclipse against sun-drenched buildings, leaning slightly, almost indolently, one hand on her hip while the other dangled, moving slowly, almost like a cat's tail. He felt a chill in his blood at the sensation of the familiar. A posture he knew well, but should not be seeing here. Not after so long. His hearts seemed heavy in his chest, and it was difficult to catch his breath. Changeling moaned apprehensively.

She stood for a moment before walking around the corner. Indris raced to the end of the street, yet they were gone when he arrived.

5

"DISAPPOINTMENT AND ITS SHADOW, ANGER, ARE OFTEN BORN FROM DISILLUSIONMENT. DISILLUSIONMENT IS BORN OF OUR OWN EXPECTATIONS."

—From *The Nilvedic Maxims*

DAY 348 OF THE 495TH YEAR OF

THE SHRĪANESE FEDERATION

"I sent you letters," Nadir said as he spooned honey into a small cup of coffee. Mari leaned back in her chair so the light from the coffeehouse window was not in her eyes. Nadir became a contour limned in stark white. The other patrons became similarly spectral, anonymous cutouts against a harsh background, voices soft against the clack and clatter of porcelain cups and metallic spoons.

Mari had not wanted to speak to Nadir at first, clinging to a resentment as comfortable as well-worn boots. His note had reached her this morning and she had intended to ignore it. Her mind had turned to the thought of languorous hours in Indris's arms. She had even gone to the *Wanderer*, only to find the man she thought she may be falling in love with still asleep. She had been prepared to go on her way when her hand strayed to Nadir's message in her pocket. Her defences had crumbled, without falling. Curiosity rose. It was a question of closure, she told herself.

"Wouldn't have mattered what you wrote," she said dismissively. "You never told me much anyway. We were convenient. We'd meet—"

"We'd love—"

"We'd use each other, then go our separate ways until we had an itch we needed to scratch," Mari finished. She shrugged off the sense of erotic nostalgia. "I'm as much to blame for the shallowness of what we had. I could've said no."

"Could you?" He blew across his coffee. A brief billow of steam coiled in the air. Nadir sipped, eyes half-closed in a familiar gesture of contentment. He had looked at her the same way a lifetime ago. "I couldn't. I suppose that's why I didn't. But it wasn't my choice to leave Shrīan, Mari. When Vashne exiled us we only had a few days to leave the country."

"You could've gotten word to me, at least to say goodbye." Mari fought down the old resentment that clutched at her chest. It was replaced by a smouldering anger at herself that she still cared.

"My father wasn't willing to risk Vashne's patience," Nadir scowled. "We took what we could and rode as fast as possible to the Ygranian border. Our Family needed money, so we rode to Masripur and signed on to work for the pahavāns in Tanis." The pahavāns—princes and princesses of the Avān—were the successors of the once Great Houses of Chepherundi, Murinder, and Daresh, decimated when the Humans rebelled against the Awakened Empire. Now their descendants and their mercenary armies defended the Conflicted Cities along the Harasesh River and the war torn Tanis-Manté border. Mari had wanted to serve there, though her father had other plans.

"What are they like, the Conflicted Cities?" she asked, trying to change tack.

He frowned into his coffee cup. Took up his spoon, stirred, opened his mouth as if to speak, then stopped. When he looked up his eyes were haunted. The scars on his face were vivid against his tanned skin. Nadir blinked, seemingly to rid himself of the phantoms only he could see, and changed direction just as easily as she had. "I hear you've become quite the hero. Rumour is you'll be the next Knight-Colonel of the Feyassin, no less. Congratulations."

"Thanks." She felt her lips quirk in the crooked smile she remembered he had liked. Mari took a sip of coffee to hide it. "Are you interested in joining?" she said, her tone light. It took a harder edge, though, when she said "Which reminds me: what was it you did after you left the Lament?"

Nadir chuckled as his eyebrows almost met his hairline. "Oh, I can just imagine how popular a choice I'd be in the Feyassin. Nadir, the disgraced son of an Exile, now defending the honour of the highest political posting in the land! You can have that!" He took a sip of his coffee before speaking again. "As for what I did? A little of this here, a little of that, there. Fighting every day to stay alive against enemies who very much wanted me and my comrades dead. But Mari, you know what it's like to have parents like ours. You do as you're told, because you're serving something greater than yourself."

"Whom do you serve now, Nadir?"

Nadir's expression was little more than a vague shifting against his silhouette. "Our fathers."

"What?" she snapped.

"Your father lost his Master of Assassins, who was also his Kherife-General, in Amnon. My father has taken on Thufan's old role, and your father was kind enough to take me on as his adjutant. Apparently his last one—your cousin, Farouk—died under questionable circumstances."

"Pretty much everybody who serves my father does so under questionable circumstances. Some live. Many don't. I wish you the best of it, Nadir." If Mari thought Thufan was a villain, he was nothing compared to Jhem's reputation. Jhem was renowned for his dispassion. In those final months before his exile, he had been described by some as the coldest part of Corajidin's shadow.

"Mari," Nadir urged, "Let me explain."

"What's there to explain?" she said flatly. "Your Family was exiled. My father has offered yours his status back, trading one crooked henchman for another, possibly worse. Though I wonder whose father has more blood to wash from their hands, yours or mine?"

"Your father's going to be the next Asrahn, Mari. My Family will become part of his inner circle. We'll be as close to a Great House as one can get, possibly even becoming one in time. We command an experienced nahdi army, honed in the Conflicted Cities and in service on the Ebony Coast to the Serpent Princes of Kaylish. All the Exiles have similar stories. Cleansing Shrīan of its apathy would be as easy as breathing for us. Then there are our witches, keener to serve our purposes than the scholars are yours."

"Nahdi? Witches?" Mari scowled. "Do you already plan more war, Nadir? Hasn't Shrīan been through enough? Is this what you learned in Tanis? Forget sende and make war on the innocent? Such isn't our way."

"Sende was a luxury we couldn't afford in the Conflicted Cities. Not if we wanted to survive."

"Shrīan needs peace!"

"And peace there'll be. Your father's armies haven't disbanded after Amnon. The Exiles have brought a terrifying strength of arms. Rahn-Narseh as the Knight-Marshall commands one of the deadliest forces of heavy infantry ever assembled. But this is all for a greater, lasting peace! A unified Avān people!

"Let's not fight, Mari. It's *your* father's vision I honor." He leaned forward. One hand reached across the table to rest perilously close to hers. It was so different from Indris's hand. Nadir's was broader. Scarred and calloused. She could never imagine those hands ever holding an ink brush. Or cradling an ancient book with as much tenderness as it caressed her skin. She left Nadir's hand where it was. "Even in Tanis I kept track of your career. I was surprised when I learned you're in a relationship with—"

"How are Kimiya and Ravenet?" Mari asked quickly, face burning. "They look like they've done well for themselves."

"Kimiya was the mistress of a nahdi witch in Tanis," Nadir said with a frown. "A rebel Human from Manté. He would call her his apprentice. Father called her his concubine. She doesn't care much either way. Ravenet took more after father and me. There's no shame in talking about your relationship with—"

"I can't talk to you about—"

"The Nāsarat," he continued. He finished the rest of his coffee, then put the cup down hard on the table. Nadir pursed his lips. "What's the old saying? *News travels fast on the lips of witches.* Indris's reputation is, well, a little hard to credit. Maybe I don't have the right to talk to you about your life. But

I'd like to earn your trust. You know, after we survived their displeasure, our fathers had hoped you and I would marry—"

"Don't remember us as we used to be, Nadir," Mari warned. "The present will only disappoint. I know what both our fathers hoped for. Those days are gone."

"Are they? I was what you wanted of me, regardless of what was set against us."

"Fond as memory may be, we weren't Mirajin and Eshemé," she said, recalling the doomed lovers in the famous tragedy of the same name by Nasri of the Elay-At. Born to warring Great Houses, Mirajin and Eshemé had fallen in love despite their differences. Though they survived assassination, machination, and civil war, their relationship had been doomed from the start and the lovers had died in the end. It was one of Nasri's more depressing plays. Mari preferred Nasri's romances and comedies. Life could be dark enough without literature's gloomy cloud.

"We were happy together," he said wistfully. "Tell me honestly you never thought about marrying me."

Mari stared down into the murky dregs of her coffee. Right now she wished it was laced with something stronger than cream. The well-remembered sight of Nadir in the morning, carrying a basket of bread warm from the oven, a wheel of cheese, bacon, and an iron pot of tea swinging by its handle. The way he had made her laugh. Or cry. Or scream with so much anger she had to throw something. The long hours in the shallows of night, when dawn was a blush in their room and his face had been a landscape of light-brushed ridges and shadowed valleys. She had run her fingers lightly over his skin and wondered what their children would look like.

Now he worked for her father.

"No, Nadir. It wasn't anything I really thought about."

✳ ✳ ✳

After that, their conversation had stumbled into the realm of awkward inanities until Mari had decided she had enough. After a fumbling goodbye, she had fled into the city with her memories of the conversation—and of times longer ago—fresh in her mind.

They had been damaged, scared and feeling alone all those years ago. Mari doubted whether time had improved either of them much. Of all Nadir had said, it had been the questions about Belamandris that had upset her most. She had not seen him since Amnon. In fact, there had been no word of him at all since Amnon. She understood how Belam would be angry with her, but for him not to even try to speak with her? Each day she had debated whether to swallow her pride and go to him. Each day she thought better of it. To see Belam would mean risking seeing her father and that was something she was not prepared for.

Rahn-Erebus fa Corajidin: the man who would bring the witch covens back into Shrīan. In her most bitter moments she wondered whether it would have been cleaner for her father to have died. To have kept some semblance of the man she knew he could be. Moments later, time measured in heartbeats, or the angry tapping of her fingers on the hilt of her amenesqa, she would berate herself for her thoughts. Blood ties were hard to break.

Mari found herself back at the Carnat-Farhi Bridge at mid-afternoon. Crowds milled at the markets, faces from all across South-Eastern Īa: dusky eyed, bronze skinned Tanisians in a spectrum of vivid silks; olive-tanned Ygranians in their shirts, jerkins, breeches, and turned-down boots; Kaylish islanders, tall, muscular, and tanned, with their tribal tattoos and long dreadlocks. There were even a few of the lean, ponytailed, and leather-clad Darmatian horse speakers. She smiled at the sight of harlequinesque Seethe in their brightly coloured vests, close-fitting breeches, and high boots with their split toes. Children giggled and squealed by turns as the images on the Seethe trouper's glass masks changed from smiling faces of surpassing beauty, to leering monsters, to crying maids, to polished skulls. The Seethe troupers played their flutes, bells, sonesettes, and theorboes as they performed along the Gahn-Markesh. From time to time a Seethe Elder would spread their massive tinted wings, twirl and spin like they wore a galleon-sail cloak of white, pink, and grey feathers. At one point the Elder leaped high, wings cupping air, to soar above the crowd before landing light-footed amongst his troupe. An innocent part of her wanted to follow the Seethe to their lantern-like pavilions, bright with light and heat and colour, all care, all trouble, forgotten for a time.

Avānweh was so different from the dour emptiness that had fallen on Amnon. When the Seethe fled the Teshri's misguided persecution, it had been like they had taken the city's laughter with them.

She picked up her pace as she crossed the bridge. The Shoals were a combination of wharves, stilted guest houses and taverns, connected by a serpentine maze of cobbled lanes. There was nothing wide enough, or long enough, to be called a street.

At the far end of the Shoals, she saw the sun-bleached and weather-mottled canvas of Indris's pavilion. It was a simple construction that dropped in elegant folds from the forecastle and stern deck of the wind-galley. The phoenix-headed prow, broad wings with ornate metallic feathers and bird tail stern cast sharp-edged shadows on the pale sand. Without a thought for who saw the width of her grin, Mari lengthened her stride as she neared her destination. She felt butterflies in her stomach. Was light-headed and short of breath. She relished the warmth of anticipation that infused her.

Mari called out, but nobody answered. After a few moments she pulled aside one of the flaps and entered the pavilion. It was gloomy inside save where the light speared through the holes of eyelets and the slits in the canvas walls. Rugs had been spread across the sandy ground. Leather sprung camp chairs, cushions, and *ilhen* lanterns were set about a small, blackened oven. The curved landing gear had sunk into the sandy earth, leaving the bronze keel of the *Wanderer* a little less than a metre from the ground. The air was pungent with wood smoke and lavender oil. She climbed the boarding ramp to the deck. Called out again. Silence.

With a lazy smile she walked towards the stern of the vessel. Took the wide stairs down, past *ilhen* lamps like glowing crystal flowers growing from lacquered bulkheads. As she walked she unwound her sash from around her waist to let it fall to the deck. In sight of the double glass-panelled doors to the great cabin, she unlaced the front of her tunic before she fumbled with the buckles of her trousers.

Mari revelled in the wanton sway in her hips as she threw the doors open—

To find Roshana and five of her Lion Guard in Indris's cabin, along with another man Mari did not recognise.

They turned to stare at her. Rather than adjust her clothing Mari locked her gaze on Roshana. The Rahn-Nāsarat was her usual self: square-jawed, square-shouldered, and straight-backed. Something about her made everything she wore look military. Roshana's expression was somewhere short of friendly.

The Tau-se were known and dangerous, as were all their kind. It was the other man, the disarmingly casual one, who caught her attention. Slightly taller than average, he had an athlete's physique and the disturbingly placid, almost dreamy, eyes of a casual killer. He was handsome, blue-eyed, and fair-skinned beneath curled dark blond hair. When Mari looked at him she noted the way his expression changed to one of contrived blandness. *Assassin*, she thought. Her hackles rose.

"Where's Indris?" Mari asked from her place in the doorway.

"I'd ask you the same question, though obviously you don't know either." Roshana looked away, mouth downturned. "Are you going to cover up?"

"You're not the company I was expecting." Mari made no move to lace up her tunic or tighten the buckled trousers that hung precariously low on her hips. "Why are you here?"

"Business with my cousin," Roshana countered. "Nazarafine told me what she asked you to do. How many Feyassin are fit for duty?"

"Forty-seven are battle-worthy, with another eleven fit for light duties." She tried to banish the frustration from her voice. "There are eighteen too wounded to travel—they're still in Amnon for the foreseeable future. The others died defending the Tyr-Jahavān."

"Angry? I know it's little consolation, Mari, but it was their job."

"I know," Mari shrugged with equanimity. "I also know why they died there, in case you were tempted to remind me again of my father's actions."

"Wouldn't dream of it," Roshana said insincerely. "Shouldn't you be recruiting?"

"Haven't decided whether I'll take the job," she shrugged. Then smiled. "Maybe I'll just spend more time with Indris."

"Hmmm." Roshana frowned as she stood, the Tau-se looming over her, silken fur over iron muscle. The unnamed man seemed to glide to his feet rather than stand. Roshana took an unsealed letter from her jacket. She dropped it on Indris's desk. "See he gets that, will you?"

"Roshana?" Mari hated the tremor in her voice. "Has there been any word from the Arbiter's Tribunal about my father?"

"How can you care for that man after everything he's done?"

"None of our forebears are without sin, Roshana," Mari said with steel in her voice. Her hand curled reflexively around the hilt of an amenesqa that wasn't there. "What can you tell me from the Arbiter's Tribunal?"

Roshana gestured for her guards to leave, expression pensive. Mari felt a chill at the base of her spine. A small voice began to wail in panic in the shallow place where fear still dwelled in her. Once her guards were gone Roshana folded her arms and leaned back on Indris's desk.

"The Arbiter's Tribunal has yet to make its decision. That said we learned this morning that several of the key members of the Tribunal have changed their votes."

"Do you know why?" Mari asked.

"I have my suspicions your father or his followers are involved. The murders of the arbiters in the explosion yesterday were no doubt a strong motivator."

Start with a small gesture to let your enemies know they were vulnerable. Let them fear worse was to come. Nothing preyed on the mind quite like the imagination.

"We expect he'll be acquitted in a closed hearing today," Roshana said scornfully, "but nothing is confirmed as yet."

"What's going to happen?" The dread of her father's machinations rose in her chest, constricted her throat. "If he's acquitted will the Teshri let him run for Asrahn?"

Roshana shrugged. "The Teshri neither returned the governorship of Amnon to him nor restored his rank as Asrahn-Elect. But they're formalities. All the new sayfs he appointed from amongst the Exiles are an unwelcome complication. There's one consolation though."

"What?"

"My Jahirojin stands," Roshana smiled grimly, the tips of her fangs showing. "If we're lucky somebody will be inspired enough to kill your father and we'll not need to worry."

❉ ❉ ❉

When Indris returned almost an hour later Mari saw the tension in him. Reclined on one of the couches, her clothing in disarray, she did not feel desire so much as need.

Indris pulled up short when he saw her, a welcoming smile fighting through his overcast expression.

Their joining was a frantic thing of desperate hands, hungry mouths, and fever-hot skin. There was nothing of gentleness as they used each other. Mari exorcised thoughts and memories as she at once surrendered to, and mastered, Indris. He met her spiralling passion so much so she almost feared what troubles he was trying to banish in her.

Afterward, Indris frowned at her cuts and bruises. Muttered profanities in what Mari suspected were at least four different languages. Her skin tingled with warm pins and needles as he crooned a canto, his hands haloed with a pale corona as he drew away her sullen bruises. Sealed her skin and eased her pain.

They rested under the striped, coloured sunlight that streamed through the stained glass windows. Mari, her breasts pressed against his back and legs wrapped around his waist, traced the tattoos on his arms with her fingertips. She was hungry and thirsty, but too settled in her languorous afterglow to move. She explained what had happened to her at Nanjidasé and how Ziaire had taken her in.

Mari could not see Indris's face, though the way he hung his head told her their tryst had not improved his mood much. She told Indris of Roshana's visit as well as the letter that had been left for him. Indris stared at the letter from under lowered brows, eyes distant.

"Sending assassins to kill a Feyassin in Nanjidasé reeks of desperation," he murmured.

"There're only two reasons I can think of for somebody to want to act so rashly," she said into his neck. "Somebody doesn't want me to be Knight-Colonel of the Feyassin, or somebody doesn't want me around to interfere with plans to disrupt the Assembly."

"Who?"

"The most likely candidate for that is my father, but he wouldn't have me killed," she replied with certainty. The words felt right. Her father was many things, but a filicide was not among them. She hoped.

"Though his allies might not scruple. The Imperialists are big on setting examples."

Indris gently kissed the inside of her wrist. "What would you say if I asked you to come away with me?"

"Sorry?" she asked, surprised.

"Away." He turned in her embrace, his eyes gentle as his look caressed her. "To leave once the new government is in place. Rosha, Nazarafine, the others . . . I think Avānweh might get sick of us and I've a mind to be anywhere but here."

Mari felt a lump in her chest as her hearts skipped their beats. "Indris," she said too softly. She frowned as she cleared her throat. "It's not as simple as that."

"I'm sorry, Mari." Indris turned his face towards the window, where it became a mosaic of coloured panels across his high cheekbones and straight nose. The sun through the stained glass tinting his left eye yellow and orange. "I know it's a lot to ask and we've not been together long."

She looked up at him from under her shaggy fringe. Ran her fingers through his unkempt hair, amazed at how soft it was. Mari drew his head towards her own and kissed him as he turned in to her, relishing the taste of his lips.

"I can't control, and don't care, what people think," she murmured into his open mouth. She felt his arms tighten around her. "There's no crime in asking me something. Out of curiosity where would we go? What would we do?"

"Wherever we wanted and whatever we felt like," he breathed into her. "Away from other people's rules and expectations. Away from the past."

The past. Nadir. Her father. Amnon. Pillars of memory that she was sorely tempted to have sink beneath the waves like the cities beneath the Marble Sea. The chance for names to be words, without the burden of emotion. Or hurt. She remembered her conversation with Nadir. His revelations of joining her father's ranks. The inference of their experienced armies to be used to forward her father's ends.

Of witches.

From somewhere outside their window, the metallic tones of a sonesette could be heard. Shar's subtle way of telling them there were others aboard the *Wanderer.* The Seethe woman's breathy voice rose in a song in her own language. Mari did not understand the words, though the low, windy sounds were soothing.

"There's something I've been meaning to ask you," she said as she pulled back from him. The touch of his lips drew her attention away. The way his thumb grazed the outside of her breast, or his fingertips the soft skin on the inside of her thigh. Mari took his hands in hers as she bit her lip. "Later."

"What did you want to know?" he whispered into her ear.

"About witches." Indris pulled back, his question clear on his face. "Because I do," she said in response to his look. "I've seen what Wolfram can do. What would happen if they came back?" *Tell me they are not the nightmare history makes of them. If you say it's so*, she thought, *I might leave this behind and go with you anywhere.*

"It'd depend," he said cautiously, as if he could read her thoughts. "Not all witches are bad any more than all of most groups are bad. It was witches like Sedefke, Femensetri, Kemenchromis, Ahwe—and Yattoweh the Apostate—who helped found the various scholastic orders. It wasn't until the witches tried to wrest control of Shrīan, during the early years of the Federation, they became a threat."

"The Scholar Wars?"

"Hmmm," he nodded. "Thousands of innocents died and the centre of the country is still a wasteland with no natural disentropy. It's why they call it the Näq Yetesh—the Dead Flat."

"But how are they different from scholars?"

"There are more similarities than differences. We both subscribe to the various schools of thought that form the Esoteric Doctrines. Both scholars and witches channel disentropy to cause an effect in the world around them. We both use the disentropy found in the ahmtesh, like dipping into a big supernatural sea. Such talents and the senses we use are called the ahmsah. Within the ahmsah, scholars follow an Intrinsic Precept, which means our power is channelled, focussed, and exercised from within. It's based on the repeatable, predictable effects of the formulae we use.

"Much of the difference comes from the language used to express thought. The Sēq Arcanum is expressed in High Avān, which is a very complex, very subtle language similar to Seethe. However it has nuances that neither Seethe nor the common Avān languages have. Most witches these days would express their thoughts in Humanti, which is more about brute force and desire, than finesse."

"Are scholars more powerful than witches?"

Indris considered the question, his gaze focussed inward, before shaking his head slightly. "What we do is more *reliable*. Witches use an Extrinsic Precept, more like a conduit of force with their powers coming from outside themselves. They have less restraint. Less control over what they do. But their Arcanum, wild as it is, can be terrifying. Less disciplined though no less powerful. To be a scholar requires an awareness of self and our place in the world. To be a witch requires an awareness of desire, or basic wants. At our cores we tend to think differently, though some manage to bridge the gap. One of the coven's greatest universities, the Mahsojhin, was located here in Avānweh until the Sēq obliterated it. It wasn't one of their more honorable moments."

"Where did the covens go?"

"The Iron League, mostly. I know the pahavān in Tanis use them to help defend the Conflicted Cities. They're not unheard of in Darmatia, or Ygran. Ondea has the death penalty for witchcraft. The witches of the Golden Kingdom of Manté effectively rule the nation in the name of the Catechism— the collected leaders of the covens. The Angothic Witches are a powerful force also, ruling alongside the monarchy. And I don't doubt there are rogue witches in Shrīan and Pashrea. He leaned back to look at her thoughtfully, before grinning impudently. Indris asked her, "Why the sudden interest in all things arcane? I thought you were more about hitting things very hard, and often, until they didn't get up again?"Mari jabbed him in the chest with her stiffened fingers, which made him grunt in pain. "Oh, so now we're a funny bastard, are we? Indris, I . . . want to know more about what it is you can do." She leaned in to kiss him, then again more deeply, losing herself in her own distraction. She stopped herself when her own hands started to wander, smiling at his rueful laugh when she pushed him back. When she spoke it was in a mock little girl's voice, her eyes wide an innocent as she could make them. She knotted her fingers in his hair. "Maybe I can't defend myself! What happens when I have to fight a witch one day? What if some dirty old man like Wolfram tries to take advantage of me, or steal my virtue?"

"I think the virtue boat sailed a long time ago. Ouch!" He winced when she pulled his head to the side by the hair. They both laughed as they wrestled, she eventually sitting on him and holding her hands in the air in a gesture of her well-earned victory.

"I surrender!"

Mari moved her hips in small circles, grinding into him, her smile slow and lazy. "And who wouldn't? Ah! Hands to yourself. I may let you touch me later, but only if you're very good, and tell me all those secrets of the universe trapped in that handsome head of yours."

"What else can I tell you? The witches were, are, wild. Their art is extremely personal to them. I said witches are in touch with what they want. Part of this is reflected in the Disentropic Stain and the manifestation of their Aspect. Scholars call it the jhi, or Stigma, a visible sign of power. For me, it's my left eye. Witches take on illusory Aspects, which are often terrifying to others. It can drive people insane simply to see one. There are those who are animists, who summon and bind spirits to themselves, to use as they see fit. I'd heard they had also starting making devices, similar to a Sēq Master's mindstone, though I've yet to see one. It could all have been propaganda to justify the scholars trying to exterminate the covens."

Mari closed her eyes. Felt the warmth of her inhalation. The way her lungs expanded, the muscles in her abdomen flexing. The sense of hope sinking in her belly.

"Now all jokes and distractions aside." Indris's voice was soft. "Why do you ask?"

"What would happen if the covens came back to Shrīan?" she repeated her question. It was all the answer she could give him.

"*Are* they back?" his voice was so quiet, filled with a dread she had not heard in it before.

She went on to give Indris the highlights of her conversation with Nadir, as well as her recollections of what her father had revealed to her in Amnon. As she spoke, she realized she never revealed Nadir's name. For some reason discussing her ex-lover with Indris was something she could not do.

"This changes the Federationist's expectations," Indris said as he dressed rapidly. Mari followed suit. "Even if your father loses the vote to become Asrahn, he may still try to take control of the Teshri by force."

"Wouldn't the Sēq get involved if the witches made themselves known?"

"It would be a nightmare. In the name of all the blessed Ancestors, what's your father thinking?"

Indris took up Changeling and slung her across his back, buckled his storm-pistol on and hung his dragon-tooth knife from his weapon belt. He frowned when he saw Mari had no weapon. "You still haven't replaced your amenesqa?"

"The master smith hasn't returned to Nanjidasé and the smiths I've seen can't do the work I want." Mari nodded towards the weapon rack on his wall. "Do you mind?"

"Take your pick."

Mari quickly tried the weight of several long and short swords until she found a pair she liked. She thrust them through her sash, and made sure they were secure. She picked up the letter from Indris's desk. "What about Roshana's letter?"

Indris glanced at the envelope. "I'm pretty sure I know what's in it. I don't think it matters."

"What are we going to do now?" Mari asked.

"We're going to look for answers."

6

"Though we are educated by history, are guided by ethics, seek justice within the law, and are inspired by selflessness, we see these things subjectively. We need objectivity to understand how history will comment on who we have been. The best advisors are those who see us in context: they understand our past, have the courage to counsel us in the present, and will stand with us in the future."

—From *In Service to the People*, by High Palatine Navaar of Oragon, Second year of his reign (490th Year of the Shrīanese Federation)

DAY 349 OF THE 495TH YEAR OF

THE SHRĪANESE FEDERATION

The faintest scent of citrus hung in the air. Eyes closed, Corajidin lay on his bed and let the cool afternoon breeze flow across his skin. Close by came the sonorous tick of a clock and the susurrus of the wind through the apricot and mandarin trees. Further away, the sound of heeled shoes on marble-shod floors. Somewhere between, the hypnotic drone of voices from another room, other lives heard through an unwitting, disinterested voyeurism.

He sat up, robe wound about his legs. The sudden motion caused his head to ache. Eyes still closed, he focussed on the messages his body sent him. A slight cramp in his calf. Dull throbbing in his temples. Tightness in his lungs. Throat swollen. It was only the beginning. Eyes open, it took him a moment to focus on the deeper shadows that lurked among the lighter ones. Lacquered wooden couches. A few small tables on bowed legs, their hexagonal tops seamed with mosaics. A calligraphy chair and table, ornate scrollwork little more than a tracery of curled black lines, like ink in water. Beside him, glowing gently, the amber face of his beloved Yashamin. The Pearl Courtesan who wore it lay supine, planes of light and shadow gracing the curves and hollows of her warm body. He watched the rise and fall of her breasts. Wanted, for a moment, to run his hands over the length of her thigh. The flat plane of her abdomen, where it curved into the shadows of her ribs. Try as he had to lose himself in the illusion, she was not Yashamin. He had not heard Yashamin's voice and the afternoon light made a bitter fiction of his dreams.

Corajidin rose from his bed. Washed himself at the small golden basin nearby. Buckled himself into fresh clothes. He shrugged on his hooded over-robe as he limped the length of his long bedchamber. As he left the room, a squad of five Anlūki, banded armour and round shields sullen in the low light, fell into step beside him as he made his way to his office. Corajidin asked one of the Anlūki to ensure the courtesan in his chamber was compensated and escorted back to Venujoram, the Cloud Palace of the House of Pearl in Avānweh.

Nadir rose from his chair when Corajidin arrived, elegant with his lean lines and fine, if scarred, features. The light through the stained glass window shone bloody on his dark hair. Papers were scattered across the desk. Piles of gold coins and polished gems were stacked neatly on the desk near him, alongside several silk purses filled to bursting. The young warrior poured Corajidin fresh water from a silver urn, as well as aromatic coffee, which he flavoured with cinnamon and cardamom. Corajidin sipped gratefully, fingers heated by the porcelain cup, enjoying the hints of spice on his tongue.

Kimiya and Ravenet sat on a long couch in layered coats and trousers of Shrīanese damask, hair dressed with strands of precious gems. Kimiya, clothes in near wanton disarray, was reading from an old book. Ravenet, the older of the two and the one drawn to murder, listlessly tapped the hilt of the knife at her waist.

Moments later Jhem swept into the room with his swaying gait. The Blacksnake's hands and forearms were covered in fresh blood, as were his lips and chin. With the hint of a smile he went to a copper basin and fastidiously washed the blood away before wiping his hands dry. Corajidin was about to ask the Blacksnake who he had killed and eaten when Wolfram limped into the room, deep in conversation with Kasraman. The Emissary followed, her hooded over-robe of black and silver threads like a billowing thunderhead. Other than Wolfram, the others had not seen her before. Wolfram looked at the Emissary with a combination of fear and loathing.

"Your Majesty." Wolfram bowed his brindle head. "We've news from our allies in the Teshri."

"Good news, I trust?"

"The Teshri have agreed to convene an emergency session at the Tyr-Jahavān to vote on your eligibility to run for Asrahn," Wolfram said. "The vote will happen at sunset today, after the Arbiter's Tribunal delivers its ruling on the various charges against you."

"Nadir?" Corajidin looked at his adjutant.

"I'm confident the Tribunal's ruling will be in your favour, my rahn. Kimi, Ravy, and I have arranged some insurance against an unfavourable ruling, so doubt you'll need to worry."

"There are a number of Arbiters with more than a few skeletons in their closets," Ravenet said with disdain. "It gets boring hearing somebody say they have nothing to lose, though it's always interesting pointing out exactly what they *do* have to lose."

Kimiya looked up from her book to smile indulgently at her sister, before she turned a hungry glance at Wolfram.

"There was an Arbiter who had been questioning some of your sayfs," Jhem said, eyes unfocussed as if he were looking elsewhere. He smiled, a chill and brittle thing, before looking to Corajidin. "They have been taken care of."

"Not to mention Nix making them realize anybody could be killed," Kasraman said dourly. "Like father like son. Though murder isn't the way. We've enough attention as it is."

"Nothing will come back to us," Jhem said. He picked at his teeth, pulling a small gobbet of flesh. "There are advantages to the old ways, young prince."

Corajidin coughed, shaking his head for Kasraman to let it be. The others were looking at the Emissary with silent questions. Taking a deep breath, Corajidin introduced her.

"Friends, this is the Emissary." His hand shook as he gestured to her. He dropped it self-consciously.

"If I may?" The Drear Emissary asked. The hood of her over-robe plunged her face into deep shadow, save for her mouth with its pallid angular jaw and chin. The octopus pommel of her sword poked out, and Corajidin half expected the tentacles to writhe. "I have been working with Rahn-Corajidin and Wolfram, and will continue to offer what assistance I, and my allies, can."

"What allies would these be?" Kasraman asked. He narrowed his pale eyes at the Emissary, clearly troubled by what he saw. Corajidin shook his head when Kasraman looked at him. The Emissary smiled, a stretch of dead blue lips against slick, black teeth. "Powerful ones who've helped your father with his illness." She sat on the edge of a table, slender hands gripping its edge. "And now I have promised to help revive Belamandris from his sleep."

"And what will your help cost us?" Kasraman pressed.

"That's between your father, myself, and my Masters," she riposted. "But I will need your and Wolfram's help. It's not something easily done alone and there is no room for error."

"The Emissary has already spoken with me," Wolfram's tone was cool. "We'll do what needs to be done this afternoon, before the Assembly."

"And the matter of my wife's murderer?" Corajidin asked. Even as he heard the word, murderer, the Emissary's promise slid like oil into his mind. *Or, perhaps, have her restored—a much more difficult thing but not beyond my ability to deliver.*

"Your Majesty," Wolfram replied, "I've spoken with Sanojé regarding the matter of Yashamin's death. She's confident she can help."

Corajidin nodded, though his joy was momentarily soured by the knowing curl of the Emissary's lips. Then excitement waxed. He felt a thrill run through him at the thought of having his golden son with him once more. Almost against his will he looked at Kasraman with his high cheekbones, angular features, glacial blue eyes, and dark hair, and was reminded of the man's mother. Laleh of the Ars-Izrel was the daughter of a long line of powerful witches, their ancestral holdings near to the borders of the Immortal Empire. Kasraman was his mother's child; more like Wolfram, both students of the Esoterics. Both steeped in the moonlight and shadows of all they had learned, seen, and done. Belamandris and Mariam were children of the sun. Of summer days, warm oceans, and brightness. Of cleaner and more honorable methods.

"Corajidin," Jhem rumbled, "why do you need more witches? We've brought our own. I've seen what Sanojé and her allies can do. Believe me when I say it's impressive. Between those we brought with us, the Angothic witch, plus your own son—"

"You're dealing with the tidal pull of the Well of Souls, and energies best left undisturbed by the uninitiated." The Emissary's tone was scornful.

"Are you initiated?" Kimi asked, leaning forward, lips parted with avarice. Wolfram stepped closer to the young woman. Jhem watched the exchange, gaze frigid.

"Trust me when I say there are forces you're best left ignorant of," the Emissary's tone was introspective. "And they're best left ignorant of you. With care, Belamandris will rise again before the sun sets."

Jhem leaned over to whisper something to his son. Nadir smiled, bowed to Corajidin, then left the room on cat-quiet feet. Within a few moments he returned, leading four soldiers carrying a large brass urn engraved with tigers, serpents, and flowers. With careful hands they placed the urn—which came to their thighs—on the marble floor. Jhem waved the soldiers away then indicated for Nadir to lift the lid.

"In the spirit of rising again." Jhem bowed low, as did his son, "I present this to you as a sign of my allegiance, as well as my faith in your vision. I hope this marks the beginning of even closer ties between us."

Corajidin's breath caught in his throat. Gold ingots. Polished gems. Rings. A rahn's ransom in precious metals and stones glittered and shone. Though it was not as much as he had spent on the Amnon campaign, it was a staggering amount of wealth.

"And the other Exiles who've sworn themselves to you come equally burdened with their tithe, my rahn," Nadir smiled.

"How much is in there?" Kasraman whispered.

"Upwards of three million Shrīanese sovereigns," Nadir said.

"And a beautiful thing it is," Corajidin murmured, though his mind reeled at the idea of so much wealth in his hands once more. Transfixed, he let coins and gems trickle between his fingers in a shimmering, jangling rain. If all the exiles were so wealthy he would be able to settle his debts with Teymoud and the Mercantile Guild and have a fortune to spare. Let the grey-skinned leech choke on his coins. Corajidin looked forward to no longer hanging by the hooks of his debts. He turned to his allies. "We still have much to do, my friends. Let us hope you are as generous with your deeds, as you are with your money."

He looked at the Emissary.

"But first and foremost, I would have my son returned to me."

※ ※ ※

The walls of the rough cave deep within the Qadir Erebus were inscribed with lines of graceful, flowing glyphs. The irregular dome of the ceiling was covered with a mosaic of small, reflective silver tiles that shone from the afterglow of strong lights. The air was hot. It was redolent of sulphur, bitumen, and burned skin. Corajidin covered his mouth and nose, swallowing the urge to vomit.

A near naked Belamandris lay in a shallow horizontal cylinder of fluid, filled with bright motes that floated about him. He had been there for almost two hours. Metallic bands encircled the cylinder, making it the axle of a reflective wheel. The wheel was of a ring of long, rough-edged mirrors of polished gold. They spun around him like a broken wall, the wheel losing momentum with each second. Great gears spun slowly, their loud clunking sound dwindling as they came to a stop. At the head of the cylinder, tall metal coils and slivers of jagged crystal were thrust into a large bronze disk balanced on its edge. Faint sparks and traceries of lightning coiled in the charred air.

The Emissary stood by the device, hooded head bowed with fatigue. Kasraman and Wolfram were nearby, hair plastered to their skulls with sweat. Beside Wolfram kneeled a rapt Kimiya, eyes wide with adoration for the Angothic Witch, a broad metal collar around her slender neck. Corajidin scowled at the memory of Wolfram's last apprentice, Brede. Killed by Indris, he had wondered sometimes whether the Dragon Eye had done Brede a favour. To know Kimiya was now the object of Wolfram's attention made him worry for the young woman. He wondered what Jhem would say, or do, when he realized exactly what his daughter would be pursuing behind the closed doors of Wolfram's chambers.

Once the wheel of mirrors came to a complete stop, the Emissary stepped forward to examine Belamandris. Corajidin shuffled closer, eyes only for his son. In the image of the greatest of the Avān, Belamandris was a sculptor's dream of perfectly formed limbs, golden curls, and sun-brushed skin. His handsome face was refined in repose. His chest rose and fell in deep, even breaths. The only flaw was the ruby clot of blood that remained at the base of his throat, which no amount of cleansing could remove. A wound of hatred and vengeance, the Emissary had once called it. Thufan's final treachery, where he had shot Belamandris in the throat with a poisoned bolt.

The Emissary whispered softly to Belamandris as she worked. She ran her hands over corded muscle. Listened to Belamandris's chest. Peeled back the man's heavy lids to reveal the blue eyes beneath. Wolfram lurched across the room, supported by Kimiya on one side and his witch's staff on the other. The Emissary looked over her shoulder at Corajidin.

"My son?"

❊ ❊ ❊

"He'll not remember some of what happened," the Emissary said as she chewed a dried black lotus petal. She had regained some of her vigour after eating and drinking, as had Kasraman and Wolfram. They sat in a small reception room, a circular affair with half the walls given over to floor to ceiling windows of frosted glass. Late afternoon rain pattered, leaving long tear tracks on the glass. The room smelled of beeswax and leather.

"Why not?" Corajidin asked from the comforting depths of a couch. He asked his next question carefully, dreading the answer. "Will he be less than we was?"

"He'll be unchanged," Kasraman seemed almost boneless where he slouched amongst tapestry-fabric cushions.

"He will need to rest," Wolfram said. "But in a short time, the Widow-maker will once more show his quality."

"How much will he forget?" Corajidin asked.

"Only the events leading up to his, well, death." Wolfram stood, his hand on Kimiya's shoulder. Those old, long fingers kneaded the fabric of her coat like she was property. "We won't know until we've had the chance to speak with him to see what he remembers."

"My thanks to you." Corajidin breathed the words. He looked to his other son and smiled. "All of you. If it is in my power to give, ask and it shall be yours. But for now would you please leave me? I would speak with Belamandris and share with my son all we have achieved during his sleep. I will be telling him things that I will need you to support should he ask anything of you. Am I understood?"

The others bowed, then left. Corajidin was not waiting long before there was a knock at the keyhole door. He lifted himself to his feet, smoothing his over-robe, face split into an involuntary grin. He gave permission to enter.

Belamandris looked hale in his formal layers of red and black. His vermillion over-robe was set with hundreds of polished horse-heads carved from black onyx. The light lingered on his golden hair and made the blue of his eyes preternaturally bright. He smiled as Corajidin opened his arms, then came into his father's embrace. Looking into his son's eyes, he was taken aback by the cerulean depths of them, a blue so like Mariam's eyes, yet unfathomable and somehow . . . void.

For the next hour Corajidin told Belamandris all that had happened since Amnon, watching his son's expressions travel from horror to humour. Shock to pride. He deflected the questions about Mariam. Steered the conversation where it wanted to go. A clock in a nearby room rang out with the five chimes of the Hour of the Dragon. Corajidin looked up at the windows, noting the dying light as the sun dropped behind the towering snow-capped spear of Mar-Asrafah.

"Father?" Belamandris asked. He was looking at his hands, seemingly bewildered by them. He looked up and the light reflected from the backs of his eyes as if he were a cat, the effect vanishing almost immediately.

"What is it?"

"Can you tell me what happened to me? I remember being at the villa on the Huq am'a Zharsi in Amnon. We were leaving, I think. I'm not sure. There are fragments . . ."

Corajidin paused for a moment. He had been waiting for this question, wondering what he would say when it came up. There was no guile in his son's gaze. Nothing that indicated he was testing his father in any way. Now the question was out in the open Corajidin knew he had to use what gifts the fates lay at his feet. Feigning hesitation, he leaned forward in his chair to lay his hands on Belamandris knees. His son leaned back, apprehensive.

"Are you sure you want to know?"

"Do *you* think I want to know?"

Corajidin nodded, as if acknowledging the wisdom of his son's question. "We were escaping from the villa when Näsarat fa Amonindris attacked us. You went to our aid and showed him mercy. Your great soul was almost your undoing. He attacked me. Killed Thufan."

"I don't remember . . ."

"Because Indris attacked you, after you had released him on his word of honor. My son, he stabbed you in the throat and left you to die in front of me."

Belamandris's face stiffened with a barely constrained rage. He gripped the thick wooden arms of the chair. The warrior-poet breathed deeply, eyes closed. When he opened them they bored into Corajidin's.

"Where is he now, this oath-breaker and would-be murderer?"

"Here, in Avānweh, spreading his lies to keep your sister from us. Son, I need your help now more than ever."

※ ※ ※

"It's a dangerous road you follow." The Emissary had been waiting outside as a fuming Belamandris had stalked out of the room. "It won't take much for Belamandris to discover the truth."

"On the contrary," he said. "Almost every person who witnessed what happened is dead, or so far away as to make little difference. Belamandris has been returned to me. Now he will be unleashed as an instrument of retribution."

"As you will."

❋ ❋ ❋

Wolfram came to him with Sanojé in tow. The two talked quietly as they approached, the expression on Sanojé's doll face timid.

"Your Majesty," Wolfram said with a respectful nod of his head. "As to your request to find Yashamin's murder, Sanojé and I—"

"Can you do it, witch?" Corajidin towered over the small woman, who stood her ground. Corajidin resisted the urge to smile his approval for her courage.

"It can be done, my rahn, but don't you want to know—"

"I do not care how, little one. I only care it is done. Succeed and your future in Shrīan, or Tanis, or wherever you choose is assured."

Wolfram held up a gnarled hand. "Please, you should hear what Sanojé proposes before agreeing to her methods."

"Will they work?"

"Almost certainly," Wolfram said, "but—"

"Then there is nothing more to discuss."

"As you will, Your Majesty." Both witches bowed their heads before leaving Corajidin alone in the dark with his thoughts.

❋ ❋ ❋

The counsellors of the Teshri cried out across the floor or the Tyr-Jahavān. They reminded Corajidin of seagulls, squabbling over scraps. Counsellors, in their formal white cassocks and over-coats, flapped their arms as much as they flapped their jaws. In a rare moment of whimsy he wanted to throw food at them to see whether they would fight for it.

The great amphitheatre of the Tyr-Jahavān ascended in tiers beneath the massive dome above. The dome was rendered with a mosaic of the six seals of the original Great Houses who had authored the Declaration of Federation almost five hundred years before. There was the black and red horse rampant of the Erebus; the golden sunburst of the Sûn; the armoured silver and jade crab of the Kadarin; the white wyvern of the Dar-See At; the golden lion of the Selassin on its field of green; and the sapphire and golden flames and phoenix of the Näsarat. Looking upward he could almost feel the weight of all the stone and metal. In his mind he could hear the way the marble pillars groaned under the weight of the old ways, themselves born of rebellion against the Empress-in-Shadows. He wondered, if only for a moment, how much it might take for the whole thing to come crashing down.

On each tier sat pitted bronze spheres in lieu of chairs, each of them cast the day the Declaration of Federation had been inscribed into the pillars of the chamber. Corajidin knew from bitter experience he would never be comfortable sitting on the sphere. It was cold and hard. Had no support. Was easy to slide from if one did not balance well enough. The message in the spherical seats was clear: power is not meant to be comfortable. One could fall as easily as one could rise.

Historical essays, the dialectics of the great minds of Kayet Al Tham and Robaddin of the Hoje, the collected work of Sedefke—all spoke to the strength that came from challenging established thinking. The old ways had seen his people diminished in power and majesty. What was needed was a revival of the *oldest* ways, tempered with new sensibilities. A Mahj appointed by fate to sweep away the rubble and lead the Avān back to glory.

Padishin, the middle-aged Secretary-Marshall, rapped the metallic scabbard of his recurved dionesqa against the marble floor. With its scabbard tip on the floor, the pommel of the two-handed sword reached his shoulder. The senior official of both foreign and domestic affairs still looked more warrior than politician: tall, with a powerful physique and proud carriage. The way he gripped the hilt and scabbard of his weapon, as if ready to draw at any time, served as a reminder of the man's history as a hero of the nation.

Once the room quieted Padishin nodded to Kiraj. The chief justice of Shrīan and leader of the Arbiter's Tribunal was a slender, middle-aged man with a thick mop of red-brown hair. His tanned complexion and eyes, either blue or green, declared him an easterner from the Sûn Isles. He had in his hands a warrant with black, white, and grey ribbons affixed to the seal. Kiraj's expression was calm as he surveyed the assembled counsellors, though there was a flicker of rage when his gaze lingered on Corajidin and Jhem.

"The Arbiter's Tribunal met in a closed session." Kiraj's voice was stern and uncompromising, perfect for a man who epitomised the tenets of Avān law. Kiraj waited a few moments for silence in response to his opening statement. He lifted his chin and met Corajidin's gaze with equanimity. Corajidin felt his blood run cold.

"No doubt," Kiraj continued, "there are those among you who believe the justice system can be bought, or influenced. That we who safeguard the Avān way of life can be threatened. Let me assure you. You would be wrong."

Corajidin leaned closer to Jhem in the chaos of shouts and applause that ensued. "I thought your son had taken steps to assure a result in my favour?"

"It is done as it was said it would . . . be done." The Blacksnake's eyes were dead as ever, yet he refused to hold Corajidin's gaze.

He could almost feel the veins throbbing in his temples. "If I am formerly charged with any of these crimes, you will wish you had died in the filthy jungles of Tanis!"

Jhem shrugged indifferently as Corajidin turned his attention back to Kiraj.

"But today," The Arbiter-Marshall held up the warrant, ribbons fluttering, "the justice system proved itself. Arbiters on the Tribunal suspected of being compromised were removed from the judicial process, myself included.

"Rahn-Erebus fa Corajidin. Make your way to the floor."

Corajidin bristled at the tone of command in Kiraj's voice. Eyes darting left and right, he noted the positions of his allies and those of the Teshri guard, including the Feyassin. He planned his escape route with each step. From the corner of his eye he saw Nadir smiling. Part of him wanted to rush over and bite the handsome man's throat out. Schooling his expression to calm, Corajidin came to stand eye to eye with Kiraj. Corajidin wondered whether in his failing condition he could utter his jadyé—his blood curse—to plague all those who had failed him.

Kiraj's smile was bitter, one side of the man's mouth lower than the other. He wore a tiara of perspiration. Corajidin stared, fascinated by the gleam of saliva along the man's lower lip. The Arbiter-Marshall cracked the seal on the warrant with a hard jerking motion, as if he were snapping a neck. His expression was poised as he read the contents of the warrant to the gathered Teshri.

"We, the Arbiter's Tribunal of Shrīan, find insufficient evidence to prosecute Erebus fa Corajidin for the crimes of Treason, Conspiracy to Commit Treason and Regicide—"

Corajidin thought he would pass out as the uproar swamped him. He could make out the occasional word amidst the jeering, hissing, chanting, and cheering. His wide eyes took in the sour expression on Kiraj's face as he continued reading. Everything seemed to happen in slow motion. Noise echoed in his ears. He caught Nadir's slow nod, as if to say there was never any doubt.

"Did you hear what I just said, Rahn-Corajidin?" Kiraj sounded worn. "Though I would have had you incarcerated in the most foetid, dank hole in Maladûr gaol for the remainder of your pestilent life, my peers apparently are easier to influence than I."

"Thank you for a fair and unbiased decision," Corajidin said as the shock faded from him. "I have no doubt I will be in a position to repay your kindness soon enough."

Kiraj let the warrant fall to the floor, for all the good it had done him. Corajidin smiled at the defeated man.

Now to see whether his allies were worth their weight in gold.

❊ ❊ ❊

The old clock, with its exposed gears and cogs, chimed in the Tyr-Jahavān. An onyx cat bounded from the mechanism, as the golden and garnet hawk seemed to fly back into its clockwork den on the other side. Another hour marked. Another milestone achieved.

Corajidin sat on his cold spherical chair, his sense of relief so acute it left him feeling fatigued. Beside him Kasraman leaned forward, his expression bland even though Corajidin sensed his excitement.

Corajidin's nomination for Asrahn had been accepted and the Assembly would vote on the Accession and new government tomorrow. Nazarafine and her allies would work long into the night to prepare for what had become a contested election. Their outrage had been exquisite.

Let tomorrow come, he thought. *Fate has been patient long enough.*

7

"AT WHAT POINT DO WE SACRIFICE DOING WHAT WE KNOW IS ETHICAL, FOR THAT WHICH IS MORAL?"

—From *Ethical and Moral Conflict*, by Yalana Beq-Shef (396th Year of the Shrīanese Federation)

DAY 350 OF THE 495TH YEAR OF

THE SHRĪANESE FEDERATION

Across the city the bells tolled the Hour of the Serpent, the seventh hour of the day. The sun emerged from behind the shoulder of Star Crown Mountain, pried loose from the jagged rock so it could continue its arcing journey across the sky.

Indris, Mari, and Shar found Hayden, Ekko, and Omen at a tea house on the shore of the Shoals. The Copper Kettle was a busy place, a favourite of longshoremen, merchants, and mariners. Travellers were common, so a small group could come, go, or stay without attracting attention. It had the added benefit of providing a good vantage point overlooking the busy docks.

The incessant chatter of excited travellers, the clatter of plates, and the sizzle of cooking food drifted around them. Indris settled deeper into his seat, the old hessian cushions crackling as he made himself comfortable. The warmth of the sun felt good on his face, the wooden surface of the table coarse under his fingertips. He inhaled the mingled aromas of tea, bacon, strawberries, and freshly cut lemons.

"What news?" Indris asked as Hayden poured the new arrivals tea from a silver-chased copper pot. Indris cupped the rough tea glass in his hand, waving away Hayden's offer of honey.

"There were a lot of people found dead this morning." Hayden slathered butter on to a thick slice of bread still warm from the oven. He was pale, his skin almost grey, eyes red with fatigue, and his hands shook. "Seems there was a set-to between some Mantéan and Atrean Humans, against some Avān filled with the fire of their drink. It weren't pretty."

"Not long after Corajidin was acquitted, I take it?" Indris asked as he looked at Hayden with concern. The old drover looked almost at the end of his strength. *I forget how old he is,* Indris thought. *It'll be sad to see you go, but you're long overdue the peaceful years you deserve.*

"Omen saw some of what transpired," the Wraith Knight added, "the knives and swords and tempers fired. Many were the ones who fell, bloodied and broken, lost forever to the Well."

"Sassomon-Omen saw indeed. And then stood in the middle of it as the fighting passed by, talking to a statue on a fountain," Ekko said, shaking his head slowly with disapproval. "There was also fighting between the retinues of the Great Houses. The worst of it was between Näsarat and Erebus, and their colors. I witnessed your brother, Mariam, in the thick of battle." Ekko speared a sliver of raw salmon with a claw and popped it into his mouth. "He fought with a terrible fury. On more than one occasion he yelled out for Amonindris to come face him. I had not thought the man bore you such enmity, my friend."

"I think I should try and speak with him," Mari said. "Before it goes too far and somebody I really care for is hurt. Belam knows how I feel, and we've had this conversation before."

"His were not the words of a man defending his sister's honour, Mariam. He acted like a man intending to settle a debt, preferably in blood."

"I wonder what that's about?" Indris frowned his confusion. "When we spoke last, I'd told him to go and take care of his father. Better than one of us killing the other. There's no business between the two of us, as far as I know."

"Erebus. Näsarat." Mari's voice was sad as she covered one of Indris's hands with her own. "There's always business between us."

Silence, save for the rattle of cutlery on plates and the faint sound of chewing. Mari held up her hands, surrendering the idea.

"The people we were tasked to watch, errands a plenty and all in a rush." Omen's voice was a sepulchral echo from his ceramic chest "They have worked throughout the evening and night, yet have done naught wrong, look as we might."

"I figure there's been about twelve or so ships come and gone under darkness," Hayden added. "Those as come in last night are still here. We never followed them. There was too much fighting in the streets, and them at the docks seemed edgy as it is."

"Though the passengers were dressed as common travellers," Ekko rumbled in his velvet landslide voice, "the carriage of most was that of soldiers."

"I reckon they's here to cause a fuss. No way of knowing less we get a look-see at what they's up to." Hayden leaned back in his chair, pulling the brim of his hat down lower over his lined brow. "But maybe later? It's been a long night."

"We saw much the same at the Skydocks," Mari said. "It was a veritable who's who of Shrīan's entitled villains. All sayfs allied with my father, here no doubt for the vote tomorrow night on the Accession."

"Corajidin isn't taking any chances." Shar leaned forward to rest her elbows on the table, chin resting on her steepled fingers. Her pupils were black pinheads floating in orange irises. "From what I understand, Nazarafine was counting on being elected Asrahn uncontested. She would've had at least another five years to push the Federationist agenda and open Shrīan's borders."

"Under an Imperialist government, Shrīan would become as insular as the old Awakened Empire in the years right before the Insurrection," Indris muttered. "And *that* worked out so well for us. The Iron League kicked the Awakened Empire into near oblivion. I can't imagine them being any less aggressive a second time around. There are plenty of Humans who wish the Insurrection army had wiped the world clean of the Avān."

"Let's hope it don't come to that," Hayden said fervently. He coughed, his torso curling forward around the violence of it. His breath wheezed as he straightened. With a sad smile he looked at his friends. "But I think it's a fight I'll be sitting out, no matter what happens."

"And you'd be the luckier for it," Shar said, resting her hand on Hayden's. "But whatever is happening may start here, unless it can be prevented."

"True words. So what are they smuggling into the city?" Indris asked. "Maybe I should go and speak with the Sky Lord? Or Neva? They should be told what's happening."

Mari pointed to the ships. "The people with the answers are there." Her words almost tripped over each other they were said so rapidly. "I mean, we shouldn't bother the Sky Lord or his heir unless we have something of value to tell, neh?"

"Let's go have a look-see." Hayden's smile was weak beneath his long salt-and-pepper moustache. He yawned and stretched in his chair.

"I should be walking you to the Skydock and sending you home, my friend." Indris said gently. "You've done more than enough. Certainly more than anybody had the right to ask of you. Maybe you should sit this one out?"

"I've some fight in me left, lad." Hayden waved off Indris's concerns. "Let Ekko and I go do this thing. We'll be all subtle-like and back quick as a flash."

Indris shared a long look with Shar, who shrugged. Indris eyed Hayden. "Clearly you've forgotten how well your last side mission went. Remember the Rōmarq? When I asked you to not chase after Thufan, Belamandris and the Fenling? What happened?"

"We managed to—" Ekko began.

"You managed to get about half the Fenling in the Rōmarq chasing us through their *sherdé* swamp is what," Shar said, jabbing a finger in both men's direction. "I don't fancy being chased through Avānweh by *faruq* knows what, because you two see something shiny and get excited."

Hayden squirmed in his chair, face reddening in embarrassment. "That was different—"

"'That was different,'" Shar mimicked with an impudent grin. "I'm only going to save your leathery old hide a few dozen times more, Hayden. After that you're on your own."

The others laughed. Tea and coffee were poured. They set to the meal of raw salmon, warm flatbread, whipped butter, and bowls of tirhem, a slow-cooked wheatmeal paste with lentils, spiced pork, and lemon juice. They finished with slices of dried fruit, eating as they planned.

"Any questions?" Indris asked.

"Reckon I've got it covered," Hayden said, nodding. "I'll follow the next group porting cargo from the docks, and find out where they taking their goodies."

"I'll tag along with Hayden, all subtle and such," Shar said around a mouthful of lotus petals.

"I will maintain a watchful eye on the dock." Ekko added.

"And there it is I will lend my eye, with the giant one of golden fur, un-ravelling the thought and deed, of nighttime's dark and suspect curs."

Ekko moved his chair slightly away from Omen, his eyes fixed on the table. "Amonindris, I am more than capable of keeping watch—"

"None of us work alone, Ekko," Indris said. "I've not forgotten what we talked about, and I need your help to keep watch and make sure we limit the . . . unexpected. Please, remain here with Omen. Meanwhile, Mari and I will return to the Skydock and see what we can learn there. If we don't hap-pen across one another before hand, we meet back here at the Hour of the Phoenix."

"And if we happen across trouble?" Shar asked.

"You have to ask? Just do it quietly."

※ ※ ※

Indris and Mari were following a large wagon, creaking under the weight of its cargo, as it lumbered down the Fahz am'a Tayen. It was there they saw Shar and Hayden loitering outside the store of an antique dealer. Hayden leaned in to whisper something to Shar. She stepped into the crowd as it flowed down the Path of the Coins, towards the stair that joined the precinct of the merchant-caste, with the lakeside streets at the base of Sky Spear Mountain. Going for Omen and Ekko, no doubt.

When Shar returned with a silent Omen and a tense Ekko, Hayden led their small group into the antique store. It was mostly empty, yet afforded them a good view of the traffic on the street outside, as well as the frontages of the buildings opposite. Hayden pointed to one in particular.

"That's the old Maladhi-sûk," Hayden said quietly. "From what we seen, most of the cargo unloaded from the ships this morning came here. I figure the wagon you was following was one of many?"

"Yes," Mari said, "though that was the last."

"And there are no more from the ships at the docks below," Ekko added.

"The Maladhi-sûk was closed when Rayz and Nix were exiled. Nobody should be there." Mari leaned close to the glass, looking the building up and down. Indris joined her. Large wooden doors were detailed with sword-wielding spiders made of blackened iron, with iron webs crisscrossing the wood. The red stone walls to either side were carved with nightmare figures of giant spiders, armed and armoured, fanged and clawed, with facets of glass, or quartz, for eyes so they glittered with reflected light. "It's not a bad place to stay out of sight. If it's like the other sûks here in the city, it's a virtual fortress with its own barracks, kitchens, forges . . ."

"You could fit a lot of warriors in there," Shar whispered.

"And lots of cargo," Hayden said.

"The villains have nested, their camp in our sight. What for us now? To leave, or to fight?"

"Fight," Ekko growled, his tail swishing. He lanced Omen with a stare, his hackles rising. "Provided everybody is aware of their obligations."

"I agree with Ekko," Hayden whispered loudly.

"Of course you bloody do," Shar said.

"We came here to find out what was happening." Mari turned from the window to face Indris. "That's not going to happen if we stay here, flapping our jaws."

"We can use the main door of the sûk," Hayden said as he paid scant interest to some Kaylish scrimshaw, sea drake bones covered in intricate carving. "But it would be pretty obvious. There's another door out back. It's a ways off the main road. We'd need to follow a few rough paths and such to get there without being seen, but it ain't so hard going."

"Where's this other door?" Indris asked.

"At the end of an avenue in a narrow ravine," Shar said. "Most of the cargo from the docks was delivered that way."

"The vote for Accession is tomorrow night," Mari said quietly, "and we still don't know what they're up to. It's now, or we don't bother."

"Then it's now," Indris said. The others nodded.

❋ ❋ ❋

Hayden led them along the route he had chosen, taking the rough mountain paths to the back of the academy. The old adventurer was breathing heavily as he walked. Throughout the short trip Indris felt subtle ripples washing across the periphery of the ahmsah. It felt as if he and his friends were fish and a great silent shark swam the depths below them, unseen, though its wake was felt.

Several times Indris gestured for the others to wait while he cast his senses out. They were subtle nets of perception, fanned out to dust the world around them with little more impact than a fallen feather. Yet each time he drew the nets of the ahmsah in, they were empty. Whatever it was that watched them did so with amazing subtlety. The kind that only came with deep intellect.

After climbing down a narrow stair they came to a natural cul-de-sac. There were several large wagons there, all empty. The back door to the academy was nestled in a jagged crevice in the mountain. Hayden crept forward and tried the door, only to find it locked. It was the work of a few seconds for him to unlock it. Wary of detection, for he did not know who or what was inside the academy, Indris gestured for Hayden to wait while his arcane senses seeped through the door to trickle slowly into the empty spaces beyond. Whorls and eddies of disentropy washed against his mind, though nothing that raised an alarm. A sharp nod was all Hayden needed to open the door so they could make their way inside.

Walls, floor, and sharply arched ceiling were of dark red stone, veined with black and polished to a high sheen. Oil lanterns, scented with amber, gave the place a bloody glow. Noise drifted down long corridors. From up sweeping, shadowed stairways. Occasionally a laugh. A shout. A few times the bell of steel on steel reached their ears.

They crept from room to room. Some had surrendered to cobwebs and dust, empty weapon racks powdery with time. Rows of beds were lined against the walls of narrow cells, rope springing pallid as a sagging ribcage. Others showed signs of hasty cleaning and more recent use. Steam rooms were still warm and damp, the mortar between tiles spotted with mould. In another room heat from a recently used forge billowed over them when they opened the door, the floor rough underfoot from spilled carbon dust and metal shavings. Straight swords and shamshirs, long-knives and dagger, axes, arrowheads, and spear blades gleamed cold and new. In another room they found several ornate glass chests, lined with rotted silk. Most of them were empty, though in one were several baroque puzzle boxes. Each of the spheres, triangles, cubes, and hexagonal prisms had been opened. Indris saw the residue of ahm patterns on the puzzle boxes, old Wards for confinement and binding.

"What are they?" Mari asked.

"Dilemma Boxes," Indris murmured. Tempted as he was to take one, such things were valuable and no doubt whoever owned them would notice if one were missing. Better if the people who inhabited the sûk had no idea anybody had broken in. "The Seethe made Dilemma Boxes to trap powerful elemental daemons, too insane to be allowed their freedom. Once trapped the daemon faced the dilemma that it could either remain imprisoned for as close to eternity as it could imagine, or accept the opened door and be bound in servitude."

"Charming," Shar muttered.

On several occasions they were forced to hide when roving groups of women and men strode the corridors. They were dressed as members of different castes, freeholders, merchants, and artisans, but they clearly walked like fighters and were deeply tanned from time spent under a more northerly sun. One small group in particular was led by a sallow-faced man with long greasy hair. He spoke rapidly in a nasal voice. He had a Dilemma Box in his hand, the pieces of which he moved with erratic, sharp gestures. His ostentatious over-robe was stitched with overlapping spider webs in silver thread, with silver spiders for buckles. Also amongst the group was a haughty-looking woman who rolled her eyes at the man whenever his back was turned.

"The woman is Ravenet of the Delfineh," Mari whispered. "The daughter of the Blacksnake. The other is Nix of the Malahdi."

"An inbred little psychopath by all accounts," Indris said, his voice equally soft. "Your father would love him."

"Not if memory serves, no," Mari replied. "Father had little affection for the Family Maladhi at all. I doubt time has changed his attitude much, from some of the things I've heard him say in the past."

As they trod further into the academy, Indris felt the presence of whatever watched them growing perceptively stronger, though it was still unfocussed. It felt at times as if he was being watched by somebody's dreams.

Each room they searched showed similar signs of use, either as refurbished barracks, smithies, or storerooms for supplies of food, water, weapons, and armour. One dark stairway led down, though the stench of rot and mould caused them to move on. Indris lingered for a few seconds longer, however, certain he was being watched by something, deep in the darkness. He was about to head down when Mari returned and took him by the wrist, to join the others.

At an intersection Indris heard a commotion from a branching corridor and up a flight of stairs. He recognised the patois of dayeshi, the low-language common to merchants, people of the middle and low castes, and to professional soldiers and nahdi. The speakers were complaining about how hard it had been to store their cargo. Indris would have been happy to have moved on, were it not for the mention of how valuable it was . . . and the comment, *"Pah-Sanojé will have us flayed alive if we damage these things."*

The conversation continued for some minutes before Hayden stiffened.

"Balls. We got company behind us," Hayden whispered from the rear. Indris turned to see the old skirmisher raising his rifle. Omen drew his long, ornate shamshir. Indris heard the sound of booted feet approaching. The creak and jangle of leather and metal hauberks.

Indris looked to Mari who jerked her chin up the stairs to where the argument continued. Ekko grinned widely, as did Shar.

"I was hoping it wouldn't come to a fight," Indris murmured.

"But it has," Mari said.

"It usually does," Shar added blithely. She patted Indris's cheek. "No sense in wondering could've, would've, should've. We'll be quiet. Promise."

At Indris's nod, Mari led Ekko and Shar up the stairs in a silent lope-run. With a muffled curse Indris gestured for Omen and Hayden to follow.

Not far along the corridor at the top of the stairs was a row of ornate wooden doors. The soldiers were positioned before one of the doors on the right. The ceilings here were high, with glass panels letting in solid columns of harsh light. *Ilhen* lanterns on the wall shone a pale red behind tinted glass panels. Marble pillars, each capped with a brutish rusted spider, lined the walls. Rusted iron arches delicate as webs held aloft the mosaic ceiling.

Mari and the others struck in near silence.

Of the six antagonists, two fell rapidly. Mari, Shar, and Ekko engaged the remainder. Omen stepped in, blade swinging, then stopped abruptly. Shar danced back, blundering into the Wraith Knight, who rocked on his feet but otherwise did nothing. The Seethe war chanter swore at Omen to move as she rejoined the combat. Indris barely had the time to take three steps in their direction before a series of well-placed kicks and blows with elbows, knees, and fists had felled the others. Wasting no time, Indris's companions dragged the supine bodies through the door. Once inside, Indris closed the door behind them and turned the lock.

They waited several moments to see whether an alarm had been raised. Thankfully it had not.

"That went quite well," Ekko rumbled. His pupils were dilated, tail sweeping the carpeted floor.

"Omen?" Shar stepped up and waved her hands in front of his leering, sharp-featured face. When there was no response she looked at Indris, before turning back to the Wraith Knight and hissing "Omen! What in the name of the winds was that?"

Rather than answer, Omen straightened himself, emerald eyes sparking in the light, and started to walk around the room with his bird-like gait. Shar watched him go, jaw set.

Inside the suite were several small crates that, when opened, revealed various powders, ointments, and potions. Others revealed weathered books, scroll cases, ink bottles, and ornate bone-handled writing brushes. A larger trunk was filled with carefully folded clothing: cloth of gold, bold silks, and heavy red gold jewellery set with polished rubies, emeralds, and sapphires.

Indris's main interest was the largest box. Shards of light lanced down from quartz panels in the ceiling, illuminating the stray maiden's hair of floating web threads. The bright light made the shadows even deeper. He felt a chill as he neared the box. It was Tanisian, measuring two-and-a-half metres from end to end, almost a metre-and-a-half wide, and a metre tall. Its teak surface was polished with age, carvings worn away to almost nothing. Indris could barely make out the vague shapes of mammoths, tigers, horned horses, and fantastical birds set amongst vines and flowers. At one point there had been characters carved around the edges of the lid, but now they were worn down to mere dents. Reliefs of rag-wrapped skeletons peered from between other carvings. Massive bronze hinges were placed down one side with a set of yellowed ivory handles on the other. He saw deep scores in the box, where it appeared chains had once been laid tight about it to keep it closed.

There was the faint sluggishness in the ahm, which spoke to old traces of salt-forged steel.

Towards the far end of the box was a crest: a circle of grinning skulls around an inlaid crown of gold and bone, held aloft by two kneeling skeletons each bearing a sickle in their free hand.

Indris's breath caught in his throat as he stepped backward. He felt again the lick of a mind against his own, cold, dark, and dreaming.

"What's wrong?" Mari asked as she and Shar joined him. Indris caught her by the wrist as Mari was about to touch the sarcophagus. Shar's eyes narrowed in concern as she scanned the box more closely.

"Nobody touch this," Indris said flatly. He started to walk around the sarcophagus, looking for something that would tell him who was inside. "I think this is the sarcophagus of one of the old rahn's of Tanis."

"Why would somebody bring a centuries-old dead Tanisian monarch to Avānweh?" Ekko rumbled. "And why is it so dangerous?"

"Because I suspect this rahn's not quite as dead as it should be," Indris muttered.

Mari cursed vehemently. Her expression held the revulsion most Avān had of Nomads.

Indris scanned the many neat rows of High Avān characters. The Tanisian dialect was not very different from Shrīanese, though there were some segments that confounded him. Finally he found what he was looking for: the centre of a knot of story and allegory about the rahn's life and achievements.

The histories inscribed there revealed she had been the eldest daughter and heir to the last Mahjirahn of Tanis before the Insurrection. A fallen Nilvedic Scholar, a witch and necromancer. According to legend she was one of those who had willingly become a Nomad to extend an already long, cruel and malignant life. A heretic among a people who worshipped their Ancestors, she achieved immortality by becoming a lich: locking her soul in a Wraithjar while she animated the mouldering flesh and bones of her own dead body. She had been succeeded down the centuries by the dissolute and corrupt living members of her line, including Chepherundi op Sanojé, a known ally of Jhem. Legend had it the heirs of the Great House of Chepherundi would marry, produce offspring to maintain the family line, then if they had the power would follow in the footstep of their forebears. A family whose entire legacy was to defy one of the Avān's most central beliefs in allowing the dead the peace of the Well of Souls.

The once casual scrutiny Indris sensed with the ahmsah became sharper. He moved cautiously away from the sarcophagus, eyeing it with trepidation.

Omen stalked to the side of the sarcophagus, head cocked to one side as if listening. "She lingers on the edge of slumber, teetering to mayhap tumble to the numbness of rest or the gleeful evil which is her wont."

"She? You can hear . . ." Mari's mouth curled downwards in distaste. She backed away from Omen, her eyes on Indris. "Indris, what in the name of the hallowed Ancestors is in this cursed box?"

"Her name is Mahjirahn Chepherundi op Kumeri," Omen hummed. "A lich. There is in her a great decay, a longing and hunger for greater days. She has bound herself in history, hoping for final victory against all the wrongs she perceives have been done against her and revenge long overdue."

"Easily sorted." Ekko strode forward, hands extended to open the sarcophagus.

"No!" Indris snapped as he swatted Ekko's hands away.

"It needs to be destroyed," Mari said, steel in her tone.

"If what I've read about the few known liches is right," Indris warned, "this thing is protected by layers of arcane traps. If I manage to get past those without getting either myself or any of you killed, there's still the lich to face. Do you have even the most remote idea of the mind and force of will it takes for a mystic to do this to themselves?"

"You can destroy this thing!" Mari's belief was as much about trusting Indris as it was about *needing* the lich destroyed, and her eyes were wide with dread.

"Possibly—"

"You lifted a cursed ship and all its passengers, then flew it for hours across the Rōmarq," Mari urged. "This should be nothing."

"Lots of things should be easier than they are," Indris held her gaze. "But wishing doesn't make them so."

"We remove monstrosities like Nomads from the world." Hayden's moustache bristled. "We don't walk away from them. No offence, Omen."

"None taken." Omen tapped his onyx-nailed fingers together in a rapid tattoo. He turned his head from side to side, as if looking for the best place to attack the sarcophagus.

Hayden ran his thumb over the stock of his storm-rifle. "I conjure if we just destroy the box—"

"Hayden," Shar said, "haven't you listened to a damned word Indris said?"

"Hayden's got the right idea." Mari's expression had become intent as she stared at the sarcophagus. Her long-fingered hand was curled around the hilt of her amenesqa. "We must end this thing."

"Would you all just shut up for a minute?" Indris opened the ahmsah a little wider, then wider still, to take in the complex system of arcane analogues and metaphors Kumeri had woven about her sarcophagus. It was complex and subtle work on her part. The entire surface was crisscrossed with an irregular hair-fine tracery of disentropic filaments. Elemental totems had been made at the junctures of the strands, intricate knots of primal disentropy. To his heightened senses the sarcophagus was blistered with rapidly blinking, bloodshot mystic eyes that rolled in weeping orbits. Many of those eyes scanned his friends, though more of them stared suspiciously at Indris. Slack-lipped mouths opened and closed, streamers of flesh like gaol bars between the rubbery lips stretching with each idiot gesture. An intricate web of disentropy fanned out from the sarcophagus, lines of barely visible energy so subtle Indris could not fathom their purpose from their lack of colour or texture.

All of it gave him the oiliness of the soul he had come to associate with the Drear.

He flexed his aura and formed a gentle disentropic probe, lighter and gentler than a baby's breath. It stretched out, its tether becoming thinner until it snapped, leaving a shimmering blue orb the size of a pea. He manipulated it closer to the sarcophagus. Ever so softly he urged his disentropic bead closer, then relinquished control. It spasmed, a diaphanous droplet trembling in midair, before it started to slowly fall. As it dropped, the disentropic orb lost its imprint of Indris's soul, becoming neutral energy, as harmless as disentropy could be.

It touched the arcane net, which bound the sarcophagus.

The room was lit by a brilliant flash of ball lightning where the tiny bead of disentropy had landed. Smoke coiled from the spot. The air reeked of electrical storms and scorched air. Indris heard his companions swear, weapons hissing from sheaths.

With his senses still finely tuned Indris saw the disentropic web begin to flex. Their colours brightened. Elemental totems flared with gem-like brilliance. After several heartbeats the arcane defences settled back to normal except for the web of strands that spread out into the wider world. These flared with diamond light, pulses shooting outward like they were driven by a beating heart. It looked a lot like a mystic alarm going off.

Indris swore under his breath.

"What happened?" Shar asked.

"Time's up," he said to his friends. "Run for it and don't stop. We'll meet back at the Iron Dog an hour from now."

"So, situation normal then," Shar said cheerfully. Indris went with them as far as the door.

"What are you doing?" Mari asked over her shoulder as the others dashed for the stairs, weapons drawn.

"You all wanted it destroyed," Indris said grimly, "so I'm going to do what I can. Liches are nothing to mess with."

"You said you couldn't," she accused.

"I said I possibly could." Indris shrugged. "But I don't need to destroy it. I need for its defences to make enough of a disturbance in the ahm so the Sēq will sense it. They'll waste no time getting here, trust me. Then *they* can destroy it."

"What about you?"

"I'll be safer if I'm the only person I need to worry about." He took her head in both his hands and kissed her deeply. They waited for a few heartbeats, gazes locked, foreheads pressed against each other. "Please, Mari. Go. I'll meet up with you later."

"Promise?" she whispered.

Indris smiled in response. She nodded quickly then turned on her heel and sprinted after the others.

Facing the room, Indris opened more of himself to the ahmsah. Changeling crooned in her sheath. She trembled against his back. The disentropic wards and protections woven about the sarcophagus were incandescent. The mystic eyes rolled in his direction and the hundreds of rubbery mouths started chanting in discordant, atonal voices. Kumeri's defences detected Indris as he revealed his power.

Numbers and symbols danced through Indris's mind as he crooned defensive wards. Arcs of lightning crashed against the fractals of energy that circled about him. Fire blossomed around his feet and rained from above, only to be quenched by tumbling diamonds of blue white power.

For good measure he manifested a coiled spring of pure disentropy between his hands, then hurled it against the sarcophagus. Sheets of light and power flared, almost blinding him. When the light subsided the lid of the sarcophagus had been blown to splinters. Indris caught a brief glimpse of the ragged skeleton as it rose from its bed.

Indris felt the pressure of a handful of inbound presences, their power like a bow wave. He wove subtle layers of refracted light—shadow and illusion—about himself to mask his presence, tapping them to the wild disentropy that filled the room. He then closed his mind to the ahmsah. A snapped comment to Changeling quieted her.

As Kumeri rose from her smouldering bed—a petite figure of tattooed yellow bones, socketed with gems and sheathed in bands of rose gold, wrapped in the shredded rags of what had once been sinew and skin—there came distortions in the air around the sarcophagus. Kumeri's skull, with its mangy fringe of coarse-looking hair, turned diamond-filled eye sockets in his direction. Skeletal hands began gesticulating.

Her emaciated form blurred. Ribbons of illusion clothed her in golden flesh, dotted with precious sapphires and tourmalines. Clothing spun about her like a whirlwind, fragments of light and dust mimicking layered coat of golden leather made from mewling faces, which shrieked and gibbered and begged in an awful discord. Her arms became spined, bloodied tips dripping venom. Finally her mop-haired head vanished behind the grim visage of a horned tiger, orange stripes burning bright, eyes like jagged pits of night.

As precursors to the Sēq's arrival, the distortions in the air swelled like massive air bubbles rising from the bottom of a pond. They burst, and five Sēq Knights strode the air, weapons drawn and blazing with disentropic fire. Their power turned their flesh to backlit canopies. Black Scholar's armour shimmered with pallid radiance along the edge of each scale, plate, and along the ornate lacing. Round shields with half-moons cut in the waist were on their off-arm. High-cheeked helms with long horsehair plumes obscured their faces.

One of the Sēq Knights flicked a glance in Indris's direction, as if he saw something, before he and his comrades stepped from the empty air to the smouldering ground.

Tempted as he was to join the fray, Indris remained motionless as Kumeri's Aspect raised its spined and venomed arms. She wove fluid combinations of Nilvedic formulae and witchcraft. The Sēq responded with the a capella of their canto.

The temperature rose rapidly as near-incomprehensible volumes of energy were channelled, focussed, unleashed, countered, released then rechanneled. The lich used analogy after analogy against the Sēq: slavering wolves of splintered earth; rearing dragon heads spewing fire that burned stone, wood, cloth, and flesh alike; writhing serpents of poisonous water; and rip-faced tornadoes, which careened against the Sēq again and again.

In response, the Sēq used their shields to focus their spinning geometric wards while they unleashed the targeted, diamond precision of their cantos. The air trembled with the noise, beautiful and terrible as deadly symphonies.

Locked in stalemate, the irresistible force and the immovable objects battled while the room disintegrated around them. Another witch and a squad of soldiers appeared to help Kumeri. They were mowed down by coruscating parabolas of Sēq energy. One of the Sēq barely had time to shriek before she burned to ash. Another followed soon after and all the while the lich Kumeri wove her terrible blood-witchery.

The ceiling cracked in the corridor where Indris stood. Large sections fell in to smash on the tiled floor. Torn between escape and lending his aid to the Sēq—which would most certainly lead to them escorting him back to the Chapterhouse and from there to the custody of the Suret—Indris was still there to feel the massive wave of energy as two more presences approached.

Two Sēq Masters, their witchfire crooks burning an incandescent jade, appeared amidst booms of thunder. Indris knew neither one. They rapped their crooks on the ground, which caused the room to tremble. Concussive waves rushed outward and cracks appeared on the lich's Aspect. Together they sang a paean: one to bind the lich in serpentine coils of precise energy; the other to shut Kumeri off from the disentropy she needed to weave her witchcraft.

Seeing the way of things, Indris staggered up the makeshift stair caused by the collapsed ceiling. Though he would have been able to overcome the concerted efforts of three Sēq Knights, he doubted he would have prevailed against they *and* the two Masters.

Reeling from the amount of disentropy that whirled and crashed about him, almost drunk with its assault, he shambled away along a dusty goat track in an effort to distance himself from the strife behind him.

8

"WE ARE NOT FREE BECAUSE WE HAVE THE RIGHT TO CHOOSE. WE ARE FREE WHEN WE DO NOT HAVE TO."

— From *Principles of Thought,* fourth volume of the Zienni Doctrines

DAY 350 OF THE 495TH YEAR OF

THE SHRĪANESE FEDERATION

Mari had fought a running battle with the warriors who had spilled out of the Maladhi sword school in pursuit of her friends. It had been a case of run, stand, fight, and run. Bodies were left littering the ground in Mari's, Shar's, Ekko's, and Omen's wake. Between waves of pursuit they had decided to split up, making sure to lead nobody back to the Iron Dog.

Having evaded pursuit, Mari admitted to herself there was too much at stake to remain silent. Rather than head to the Iron Dog she raced to the Qadir Sûn. It had not taken overly long to relay her story to Nazarafine and the other Federationists there, though each word felt like throwing stones into a seemingly bottomless pit.

Nazarafine drew in a deep breath before releasing it slowly as she stared at Femensetri, Roshana, Ziaire, and Siamak. Through a set of partially open filigree doors, Mari watched Vahineh where she rocked and twisted on a low couch. Vahineh's dissolute cousin Martûm sat by her, turning his face slyly from time to time to see what was happening in the other room. The man had every appearance of caring for his sickly cousin, though knowing his reputation, Mari doubted the truth of his motivations. Becoming the Rahn-Selassin would solve many of his problems, while financing his mistakes. There were rumours the man's debts had been paid off, and certainly the glimmer of precious metals on his fingers and around his wrists and neck spoke to recent and newfound wealth. But who was his benefactor?

There were two others in the room. One was a solid, aquiline man whose hair was swept back like two glossy white wings. His skin was tanned, his eyes a piercing hazel flecked with light brown. He sat leaning on a gryphon-headed walking stick, youthful hands and face belying his almost two centuries of life. Sayf-Ajomandyan of the Näsiré—Ajo, as Indris called him—was the one they called the Sky Lord, ancestral governor of Avänweh. His granddaughter and heir, Neva, was with him. A statuesque woman with cropped mahogany hair, she shared her grandfather's fine features, though was less hawk-like, more beautiful in her intensity. The woman, of an age with Mari, was the commander of Avänweh's Sky Knights. She stood at her ease in a short armoured coat of leather and metal bands, her breeches covered by worn leather leggings affixed to a thick weapon belt. Neva and Mari shared a long, appraising look at each other.

It had taken the combined arguments of the others to stop Femensetri from returning to the Sēq Chapterhouse to mount an attack on Corajidin and the Imperialists. The Stormbringer's mindstone had blazed with a black corona, the witchfire crescent of her Scholar's Crook burning so hot it caused the air to steam around it. Cooler heads had prevailed though for how much longer was anybody's guess.

"And you left Indris there?" Roshana's voice was sharp as a sword edge. "You should've stayed with him!"

"He wanted me to—"

"Curse what he wanted you to do!" Roshana thundered. She glanced sideways at Ajo and Neva, who blushed as she looked down. "I've plans for my cousin that are useless if he's dead."

"Roshana, enough." Ziaire held up a slender hand for silence. "You wanted Mari to stay with Indris and fight a lich? What could she have done?"

"What could anybody have done?" Siamak asked reasonably. He smiled gently at Mari, gesturing for her to take a seat. "We had a lich once in the Rōmarq, when I was but a boy. My parents sent almost a full company of our warriors to root it out and destroy it. One hundred brave warriors and not one of them came back."

"I remember," Femensetri muttered. "It killed a Sēq Knight and badly wounded the Sēq Master we sent after it."

"Then Indris . . ." Mari felt a void opening in her chest. She remembered the taste of his lips. The quirk of the smile she had taken as his promise to return to her.

"Is a different coloured dragon altogether," Femensetri said quietly. Mari felt her spirits rise somewhat. If anybody knew what Indris was capable of, it was the one who had trained him.

The scholar continued. "Thank you for bringing us this intelligence, Mari. We learned of the lich when our sentinels went to contain it. But now we know that on top of witches and Nomads, they're smuggling and arming a fighting force. What numbers do you think the Imperialists have at their disposal?"

"And how many witches?" Roshana added, scowling. "That Corajidin allowed them into—"

"There's no proof my father knew his allies would bring witches with them into Shrīan!"

Roshana snorted with derision. "Your father knew well enough what he was doing."

"Your father has opened doors that were best left closed." Ajo's voice was sad but firm. "He wouldn't have done so if he didn't think the other Imperialists would support him. His son Pah-Kasraman and Nadir of the Maladhi were seen breaking into the Rahnbathra last night, amongst the other chaos. The Antiquities-Marshall is still trying to compile a list of what has been stolen."

"More troubling are the witches," Neva said. *Even her voice is lovely*, Mari thought. Low and throaty. The gryphon-rider asked the question Mari also wanted an answer to. "Scholar-Marshall, do the witches pose a threat to us and your Order?"

Femensetri leaned back in her chair, legs akimbo. She scratched at her chin for a moment in thought, eyes distant. Mari wondered at the cavalcade of wonders and horrors, victories, defeats, and disappointments Femensetri had seen in her millennia of life. How often had she seen the same mistakes played out to the same result?

"The Crown, the State, and the Sēq are at risk," she said flatly. "We always have been. Understand that when you talk about the scholars, there are three different Orders, each with their own internal sects and secret societies. We rarely, if ever, work together. Even during the Scholar Wars it was only the Sēq who fought the covens. I doubt the covens will forget that. The Zienni and the Nilvedic use Reductionist Canon, specialists in certain fields of the Esoteric Doctrines, none of which are particularly militant. Their presence is small in Shrīan. We Sēq practice a Holistic Canon fusing disciplines of body, mind, and soul. That said even the Sēq don't study all the Esoterics. Put simply, there's too much to know.

"But this is a difficult time, which some see as being filled with opportunity. There are many in my Order who believe we should be exerting more influence over the government. Others, like myself, believe we should be working more closely with the Crown and the State. Faction fighting has neutered us for decades. Our numbers are few and I doubt we'd act as a cohesive Order unless we all saw we were under threat. Even then, it may be too late."

"What about the Guilds of the fringe sciences," Ajo asked, "such as the Alchemists, Artificers, and such?"

"They've their own concerns." Femensetri spat derisively into her empty tea cup. At least Mari hoped it was empty. "They care more for money and the vulgar trappings of their possessions, than they do about the society that has mostly ignored them for centuries."

"But if the Imperialists—not the Humans—are bringing witches and Nomads into Shrīan," Ziaire said, "then surely that would be enough for you to join ranks? I've received reports from the Primes of the House of Pearl in Ygran, Tanis, and Kaylish all saying the witches seem to be preoccupied with some new agenda."

"You'd think so, wouldn't you?" Femensetri muttered. "There's only one way to know. I'll return to the Sēq Chapterhouse and confer with my fellow Masters."

So saying Femensetri rose from her chair and stalked from the room.

"I, too, find I'm needed elsewhere," Roshana said stiffly as she headed for the door. Her gaze raked Mari, who bristled. The warrior clenched her fists, knuckles turning white, willing the woman's head to explode for her interference in her and Indris's relationship. Roshana didn't seem to take notice. "It seems Corajidin won't scruple to fly in the face of our traditions. The man is virtually a heretic. It's time I used the means at my disposal to respond in kind before his reach grows overlong."

"You have your Jahirojin." Ziaire's tone was barely civil. "What else do you want?"

"You need to ask?" Roshana paused, one hand on the door with its many panels of frosted glass. She cocked an eyebrow at Ziaire. "And here I thought the Primes of the House of Pearl knew all the secrets of the world." She opened the door and started through.

Mari drew in a deep breath rather than say something she would regret. For she and Indris to continue seeing each other, she would need to have something less than Roshana's contempt. She flicked a glance across to Neva, then looked away when the woman met her gaze. Damn Roshana! Mari would excuse herself soon and head to the Iron Dog. She needed to know Indris had returned safely.

After Roshana had left the room, Mari took a seat next to Ziaire.

"What have I done to offend Roshana so much?" Mari asked softly.

"Her concerns are different now." Ziaire draped her arm across Mari's shoulder. Mari could smell the amber on Ziaire's skin. Henna and jojoba in her hair. "I think she sees you and thinks only of the hatred she bears for your Great House. The Näsarat and the Erebus have been at odds for millennia. You're also in the way of her plans. A renewed alliance between the Näsarat and the Näsaré is important to her. Sorry love, but don't think one battle—or you sharing Indris's bed—is going to change any of that. Ever."

Mari winced at the flatness in Ziaire's voice. Though her friend's expression was kind, her eyes were calculating. She wondered how much Ziaire knew about Roshana's plans. How much and for how long? It was said every secret in the world eventually crossed a pillow at some point. The Primes of the House of Pearl were perfectly situated to hear them all. Mari planned to speak less and listen more when around the painfully desirable woman at her side.

That said, she was piqued at the courtesan, so Mari shrugged Ziaire's arm from her shoulder. She poured herself a glass of tea. What she wanted was coffee: strong and black, with a hint of whiskey. Or honey mead. She raised the silver tea pot in Nazarafine's direction, though the other woman shook her head. The others likewise declined. Mari cradled her glass, hot against her fingertips and palm, the aromatic tea bitter against her tongue.

Ajo and Neva were discussing with Siamak and Nazarafine how they could best use the Sky Knights and the kherife in Avānweh to maintain the peace. Neva also suggested to Nazarafine the use of some of the Näsaré wind-skiffs and wind-galleys, a more subtle exit from Avānweh in the event of dire circumstances. She would personally command the Sky Knights to escort them away should the need arise. Mari admitted sourly to herself she actually liked Neva, as much as she did not want to.

They continued planning until Nazarafine asked whether she could have a few moments alone with Mari. Mari looked up, surprised and cautious as the others quietly left the room.

"Mari," Nazarafine began, "how has your father managed to survive this long? Surely he must be near the end of his strength. The Communion Ritual tonight will likely kill him. It is hard enough on a rahn in full command of their faculties. Your father risks his life by continuing his pursuit of the Asrahn's crown. Why does he not just—"

"Die?" Mari prompted coldly. People confused her estrangement from her father for hatred of him. "I told my father to escape, you know. Back in Amnon. I had to give him the chance for redemption."

"And now we all have to live with it," the other woman replied with barely disguised bitterness. "Your and Indris's mercy to your father may be our undoing. But I was going to say why doesn't he abdicate in favour of Kasraman."

"Everybody deserves the chance to redeem themselves." Mari was surprised at the conviction in her tone. "We're all, in one way or another, the architects of the folly we now find ourselves in."

An uncomfortable silence settled over the room like a pall. Nazarafine polished the amber buttons of her coat with her thumb, a frown creasing her brow. Mari maintained the distance between them, allowing the wordless gulf the time it needed to fill. The room darkened as clouds passed in front of the sun. The temperature dropped. The breeze through the window brought with it the smell of rain. When the metallic brightness of the sun returned, Nazarafine blinked owlishly. Her frown disappeared, no doubt in resolution to whatever conflict she had wrestled with. She reached for a small golden bell on the table beside her and rang it, the sound as bright as it was brittle.

Several minutes passed, during which the two women exchanged mindless and uncommitted pleasantries. Mari's eyes lingered on the door. Sende demanded she stay in the presence of her social and political superior. Too often Mari had acted on whim and known her reputation would save her. She was no stranger to scandal. Her eccentricities had made her popular. *Oh, did you hear about Mari?* people would say. Or, *Is it true that she . . .?* Unfortunately, the woman she shared the room with was not only the rahn of a Great House, come tomorrow she could be Asrahn of the nation. If there was ever a time to demonstrate restraint it was now.

So she was still there when a tall, solid man entered the room. His blond hair was so short it resembled more a scattering of sand atop his scalp, pale against tanned skin. His green eyes were angular, set in deep orbits. He wore a knee-length coat, fastened with buckles from throat to knee. His hands were massive, burn-scarred, knotted with muscle and corded with ropey blue veins. He carried a long wooden box with brass fittings and the sun crest of the Great House of Sûn emblazoned on the lid. The man dropped to his knees in obeisance before his mistress.

Nazarafine touched the man on the shoulder, who rose to his feet. His eyes never strayed from the box in his hands.

Nazarafine looked at Mari. "I understand you lost something at the battle for the Tyr-Jahavān," she said, smiling, cheeks once more ruddy with her usual good humour.

Many things, Mari was tempted to reply, yet overcame the petty impulse. "Yes, I did. My armour was destroyed beyond any ability to repair. As were my weapons."

"You had an amenesqa from the Petal Empire? Your personal weapon, rather than your Feyassin's blade?"

"It once belonged to Sayf-Mariamejeh of the Tyran-Amir," Mari nodded. "It was lost when Ekko rescued me on the stairs. No doubt somebody saw it for what it was and decided, given my chances of survival were slim, to keep a memento."

Nazarafine stood. With a gesture she invited Mari closer, then rested her hand on the box. Mari felt lightheaded. Had they found her weapon? There were few Petal or Awakened Empire weapons left unclaimed. Of the original thousand Awakened Empire amenesqa given the Feyassin, Mari knew there were less than six hundred accounted for. Each death had sometimes been a loss of history, as well as life.

"Though we couldn't find your old weapon, it was within my power to arrange a replacement for you. Though it is not the same, I sincerely hope you'll use it with pride and honour." Nazarafine took Mari's hands and gently placed her fingers on the clasps. When she spoke again her voice was a whisper. "This is the weapon of a hero of her people. One to be used in the defence of her Asrahn."

With cautious hands Mari thumbed open the cold metal clasps. In the moment between heartbeats—the moment the Poet Masters of The Lament had told her to release herself to the certainty of death and purity of action—she opened the box.

And almost forgot to breath.

Nuances struck her in the moment. The way the light wavered. The length of Nazarafine's eyelashes, a sooty brushstroke across the moist umber of her irises. The distant thrum of traffic on the street below as it merged with the roaring of her blood. The weight of her sword belt across her hips. The slight breeze that ran through the hair at the nape of her neck. The scent of sandalwood and the gathering storm.

Then came twin thuds in her chest, so heavy she thought her body had rocked with them. Heartbeats of exquisite strength. A singular moment. At rest on a bed of crushed silk was an amenesqa, styled after the longer blades of the Petal Empire. It was almost a hand span longer than the blades of the Awakened Empire, which were in turn longer than the single curved modern shamshir—what those with no romance in their hearts simply called swords. As if such a word could ever give meaning to something so elegant, so fit for its purpose. Her fingertips traced the delicate arabesqued designs on the *kirion* scabbard. Light coaxed near-invisible moire patterns of red and blue from the depths of the black metal. A golden sun was etched into the scabbard, as well as into the sharkskin binding the hilt and in the amber of the pommel. A seahorse was etched there as well, ruby red on silver blue. The colours of her mother's Family Dahrain. As Mari drew a mere hand span of the weapon she marvelled at the flare of brilliant golden jade light that burned there. Mari looked up at Nazarafine in wonder.

"A Sûnblade!" she gasped in awe.

"We make few of these now," Nazarafine said gently, "and they're only ever given as gifts to those who've risked all for the greater good. Was a time during the Awakened Empire when hundreds of warrior-poets, each an Exalted Name sworn to the Mahj, carried these. Yet sadly, those days of honour and glory are behind us. This sword will never dull, never tarnish, and never break. It will serve you for so long as you need, then go back to the ash when you do. A Sûnblade is literally a weapon for life."

"I don't know what to say." Mari felt the heat of unshed tears. "How can I repay your faith in me?"

"Say yes, Mari. Stay in Avānweh to help us rebuild. Help me. Keep me alive. Become the Knight-Colonel of my Feyassin."

❋ ❋ ❋

Mari sat in silence, her Sûnblade cradled in the curve of her arm like a child. The box felt warm, as if the blade were indeed made from a sliver of sunlight.

From time to time Mari looked across at Nazarafine as she spoke with Siamak and Ziaire, Ajo, and Neva, who had returned. They made no secret of their plan to replace Vahineh with Martūm, though Ziaire questioned the man as an appropriate choice. They talked of other options on the Ascension Role, ways of ensuring it was a Federationist who replaced Vahineh and ways to save Vahineh from the Awakening, which was killing her. These last heavily depended on Femensetri and Indris, though it sounded like Indris was unaware.

The portly older woman was no fool. By making Mari aware of such plans she was including her by implication. Though Mari had not accepted the offered post, Nazarafine knew the obligation she had placed on Mari in giving her the gift and sharing such knowledge.

Under sende nothing was for nothing. Every gift or favour was a move of obligation, one to another. For the first time in her life Mari had the chance to be free of another's demands on her. True, she could accept the blade at face value and walk away even though she knew the intent behind it. Ziaire had said as much. Nazarafine had plans for Mari that had nothing to do with Indris. It was as if the Federationists were conspiring to create lives for them in completely different circles.

What to do? To swap one saddle and bridle for another because they chafed less, or to dispense with harness and run free to face the unknown? What was it Indris had said about destroying the lich? *Lots of things should be easier than they are. But wishing doesn't make them so.* There was simplicity in service. In doing what she had been trained to do. Modesty aside, Mari thought there were probably no more than a score of people in the world who were her match in combat. Yet her encounter with the assassins had caused her to re-evaluate her position. There were probably no more than a score of people in the world she *knew about* who were her match. This then left a problem. What about all the warriors she knew nothing about? The ones who had trained their whole lives, who had left not a single living witness to their prowess. If such people existed, then was it not her obligation to protect the Families and the Great Houses who served the public trust—sayfs, pahs, rahns, and the Asrahn—from knives in the dark? By extension, it was also her responsibility to understand the techniques of such people. To adopt them. Adapt them. Evolve them into newer, deadlier, techniques. To draw a line across which the enemies of the State and Crown would do well not to cross.

To do such things required her to commit once more to something larger than herself. And once done there was no easy road back.

A clock chimed elsewhere in the qadir. Mari swore to herself when she realised she was two hours past when she was meant to meet the others at the Iron Dog. With a mumbled apology she took the swordcase by the handle and exited as gracefully as she could.

It was as she turned towards the Iron Dog that she saw Indris. She called out to him, then again. He stopped, eyes narrowed against the glare of the overcast. He looked like any other wanderer in his threadbare blacks and browns, the wind tugging at his unruly hair. Indris watched her as she approached, relief in his eyes.

And then, from the corner of her eye she saw Nadir, his sister Ravi, and the man Nix striding beside them. Their faces were painted with amiable veneers. She lost sight of them when a crowd passed between. Once the throng passed they where nowhere to be seen.

She looked about nervously. How long had they followed her? Tempted as she was to search for them, Indris was soon at her side. His left eye was slightly discoloured with orange and yellow flecks like sparks from a brazier, while his other had the gleam of dark amber. Mari reached out to touch him. Changeling purred softly.

"Shar said she lost you as they escaped," he said as he took her hand. Kissed her fingers. "Where've you been?"

"We separated and they lost me," Mari murmured into his mouth as she kissed him. He smelled of sea salt and coconut. "But now I'm found. Let's get away from here."

"Where to?" His eyes dropped to the swordcase in her hand. When they rose again, they were wide with wonder.

"Congratulations!" He grinned as he drew her into his arms. She felt the hard planes of muscle in his chest as she pressed against him. "A Sûnblade is a weapon to be proud of. Have you named her?"

"Not yet."

"I take it Nazarafine's given it to you as an incentive to—"

"I've not accepted," she blurted out, though the words denied the lie that had taken root in her heart. "Walk me to Nanjidasé?"

Indris pulled her by the hand along a quiet street, away from the clamour of wagon wheels and pedestrians. The street was narrow, its paving stones forming hexagonal lines of shadow underfoot, bordered with lush ferns and golden wattles. Eucalyptus trees waved in the strengthening breeze, their scent strong.

Mari leaned in to him as they walked. His hand was warm, muscles hard as bands of steel under the skin. The line at the gondola station was long, so Mari tugged on Indris's arm until he followed her towards the weathered bronze of the stairway arch with its clinging ivy. There were fewer people there and none seemed terribly interested in them. She looked southward over the rolling patchwork of the Lake of the Sky. The mountains on the other side were a dull smudge, wreathed in tendrils of grey like ropes of cloud joining the earth with the sky. Rain. Summer was coming to a close.

Together they exited the stairs on the Caleph-Sayf. Mari led them through the streets and lanes, past the high walls of the Habron-sûk, until they came to the polished red marble and alabaster of Nanjidasé. The Feyassin's headquarters was quiet, the long white banners with their white lotus blossoms snapping in the wind. Mari looked askance at Indris as he pulled to a stop.

"There are other things than service, Mari." His voice was low, almost a buzz, which tickled her ear. His breath was warm against her neck. His arm around her waist strong. "You've never left Shrīan. There are so many things you could see and do once the new Federationist government is in place. Amazing, wonderful things."

"There are amazing, wonderful things I can do here, too." She looked him in the eye as their brows met. "You could help me make the Feyassin something new. I know our techniques were first taught us by the Sēq, but I've watched you fight. It's like nothing I've ever seen." *Not even the assassins who tried to end me.* "Indris, I want to be remembered as something other than what history expects an Erebus to be."

"You will be!" he said, expression sincere. "I think you already are. But there's a world beyond Shrīan I'd dearly love to show you. Places I've never seen we could explore together for the first time."

"What would we do?" she demanded. "For the first time in my life I'm starting to do things for myself. Knight Colonel of the Feyassin is something I've dreamed of, yet never thought I'd achieve. You say there's more to life than service, yet service to others is the life I wanted. Convince me that whatever we do out there will be as important as what we do here."

"There're no certainties. I can say there's more evil in the world than we see in Shrīan. What lurks in the Rōmarq isn't unique. There're other places where worlds collide and where a few good people need to take a stand against those who'd dominate those weaker than themselves. People need help everywhere, Mari."

"What happened to you that you're always looking outward for what's inside—" The words were out of her mouth before she thought about what she was saying. There was no way of taking them back. Indris's face went still. His eyes narrowed. He looked away.

Mari took Indris in her arms. Rested her head on his chest. When he spoke, his voice was a deep hum in her ear.

"There's a place, a little tower near Memnon, overlooking the Marble Sea. As the sun goes down, the light shudders, as if the sea doesn't want to let it go. Bet then as the darkness pools out from between the waves, thousands of *ilhen* lamps shine beneath the water, still working, still lighting the old ruins after all this time. It's like watching a second sky, dusted with clouds and sparks and secrets in a darkness we may never know. And then, when the Nomads take shape in the moonlight and start to sing . . . And that's just one place, Mari. I'd like to see more, find more, and share more with you.

"If I'm going to lose myself anywhere, I want you with me. Will you think about it, Mari? Promise me you'll consider coming away when this is over?"

She felt the tears at the corners of her eyes. What he offered sounded so beautiful. "Only if you promise to consider staying."

"And if your father is elected Asrahn, Mari? What then?"

"It won't bode well for anybody, least of all the two of us." She rested her palm on his chest, and looked him in the eye. "The clock is ticking for us, one way or another. But I have to believe that while I'm here, I can make a difference. Otherwise, what point is there to any of it?"

9

"THOUGH WE SHOULD BE DIRECTED BY REASON, OFTEN AS NOT WE ARE THE SLAVES OF APPETITE. AND THERE IS NO APPETITE SO HARD TO APPEASE AS THAT FOR DESTRUCTION."

—Miandharmin, Nilvedic Scholar to the Ivory Court of Tanis, Fourth Siandarthan Dynasty. (171st Year of the Shrīanese Federation)

DAY 350 OF THE 495TH YEAR OF

THE SHRĪANESE FEDERATION

The arthritic fingers of the ruined dome of the Hearthall were crooked above Corajidin's head. Wind hummed through cracks in the crumbling walls. A smattering of tall trees grew amidst long coarse grasses where the stony ground had not been fused to a breeze-rippled pond in glass. A broken fountain, its round bronze basin dented and stained by verdigris and moss, was canted from true amongst tumbled red stones. The air was thick with the scent of geraniums and monkshood, which grew tenaciously in the upper mountains.

From time to time, Corajidin was startled by the appearance of shadows where they should not be, to find they were blurred echoes of dead people burned into the rock itself. To north and east the once proud remnants of the Mahsojhin—the great witch's university of the Awakened Empire—could be seen as broken towers, collapsed libraries, and rubble filled streets where the stone had been melted smooth. Almost all of the students and teachers had perished in what had been the final stroke of the Scholar Wars.

The Sēq were nothing if not thorough.

The Emissary stood at a tripod that held the Emphis Mechanism, stolen from the Rahnbathra by Kasraman and Nadir during the rioting last night. It was made of several round lenses of amber and adamant in a horizontal step pyramid. Around the lenses was a large wheel with many smaller wheels and gears, attached to a pendulum at the bottom and a clock face to the side. The old bronze device was pitted with the years. Gold and silver tarnished. Amber scratched. The Emissary looked through the lens at the dark vault of the Hearthall of the Mahsojhin.

Kasraman, Wolfram, and Sanojé stood in a loose perimeter.

"Will this work?" Corajidin asked.

"If it doesn't we'll never know," Kasraman said with false cheer. "We'll all be stuck in the damned Temporal Labyrinth."

"Do you mind?" the Emissary croaked irritably. She adjusted the amber lenses, then wound the largest of the gears forward. "Playing with mazes in time and space isn't the easiest thing I've ever done."

Corajidin peered at where the Emissary was making fine adjustments to the lenses and clockwork mechanism. "What in Erebus's name is she doing?" he said quietly, so as not to disturb her.

Wolfram explained how the amber and adamant lenses allowed the Emissary to see through the layers of the temporal maze. The clockwork mechanism was used to align the time and space within the Hearthall with the present. If the Emissary made a mistake, it was possible for the energies to spread outward, trapping a greater portion of the world in it.

"But time would still appear normal to us," Wolfram finished. He shrugged. "For all I know it may already have failed and we're trapped in the maze even as we speak."

"Wonderful." Corajidin said dryly.

"We're not trapped," the Emissary said as, with a final adjustment of the clockwork mechanism, the lenses began to show an image of red-robed witches and their brown-robed apprentices in defiant poses. Corajidin looked into the Hearthall with his own eyes, yet could see nothing. He turned his attention back to the lens, which showed him the image of the witches rooted to the spot.

"Is this what you want to do, Father?" Kasraman asked. "If we pop this cork, there's no telling what will spill out."

"The witches in there are still fighting the Scholar Wars," Wolfram added. The Angothic Witch leaned on his ruined staff. "For them, no time has passed. Their rage, their hatred, is undiminished."

Corajidin looked to an expectant, triumphant Emissary. There was something in her expression that should have given him pause. Voices in his head cried out a broken and scratched warning.

"Do it," he said grimly. "Bring one or two of them out so we can test the waters. If I like what I see, we will discuss liberation for the rest. And the price for doing so."

He pointed at Wolfram and Sanojé. "But first, I would have the answers you promised me."

※ ※ ※

"It would've been much easier," the Emissary said, "if you'd let me do this. I know you question my motives, but all we've done is give you what you want, and asked a fair and equitable price in return. Do you think you're being treated unfairly, Corajidin?"

"And how does Indris fit into your plans?" Corajidin said through clenched teeth, choosing bravado against the rustled steel in her tone "I mean for him to die."

"My husband is none of your concern," came the stern reply.

"Husband?" Corajidin could not help himself. "Surely you gave up—"

Corajidin felt coldness on his hearts as if icy fingers had curled around them. Chills pulsed through his body as if winter runoff, rather than warm blood, filled his veins. He tried to breath in. It felt like he was drowning.

The Emissary, taller than Corajidin, stared down from the depths of her hood. Her skin flickered as it were lit from within by an oil lamp. The putrescent mindstone in her brow flickered momentarily with a sickly green corona.

"My Masters would not punish me were I to end you here," she said blandly. Corajidin felt the beginnings of vertigo. He tried to move, to make some form of gesture for help, yet was rooted to the spot. "There are others like you. You happen to be the most useful and the one who is in the place we need them to be. That can change. Should I remind you of what it was like before I lent you the aid of the Drear?"

Agony scored his every nerve. Herds of steel-shod hooves tramped the insides of his skull. His abdomen clenched, his bowels writhed as if hungry rats gnawed on them. Every muscle in his body cramped, acid scouring them. His teeth felt loose in his gums. The old taste of bile on his tongue and the pain of reflux. His eyes unfocussed. Sounds were hollow echoes as if heard from underwater. All he could smell was his own sweat, urine, and faeces as he soiled himself. Tears welled unbidden in his eyes as all he wanted to do was curl up and let the darkness take him to its final—

"I can give all that back to you," the Emissary whispered. "If you don't need my help, just say the word. Yes you want my help, or no, you don't."

Wracked by shredding pain he did not need to think. As consciousness faded and the fever sweats rolled down his brow, he forced the word out with the last breath in his body.

"Yes!"

Instantly his affliction was gone. Replaced with a warm sense of wellbeing that bordered on a carnal bliss, for which he hated himself a little. He sucked in an enormous breath of cool, sweet air. Could almost taste the magnolia on his tongue. He checked himself to find what the Emissary had done to him was pure suggestion. Thankfully she had not made him soil himself in public.

"Then where Indris is concerned you'll neither question, nor comment, nor oppose a single whim of mine no matter how trivial it may seem. Am I understood?"

Corajidin nodded, face flushing with angry shame.

"Excellent. Now, you'd best take advantage of what the little Tanisian witch has prepared for you." The Emissary smiled coolly. "Given how many of your principles you've already sacrificed, another shouldn't bother you overly much."

With a terse gesture he bade Jhem follow him to the sealed palanquin where Wolfram and Sanojé waited. The Tanisian witch had been in a foul temper all day, a barely contained rage simmering beneath the surface.

Corajidin had heard of the disaster at Rayz's sword master academy where somebody—the Sēq no doubt, Indris if Corajidin made an unsubstantiated guess—had broken in and destroyed much of what Sanojé had smuggled into Avānweh.

Up close the palanquin reminded Corajidin of some of the family reliquaries he had seen kept by the Great Houses. Each ornate container would hold either part of an Ancestor, held after their death as a means by which their descendants could communicate with them, or one of their prized possessions. The Great House of Erebus had something similar, though Corajidin had always preferred to commune with his Ancestors in the more pure manner afforded him by his Awakening. Such methods were almost lost to him now.

"What is this?" Corajidin asked Jhem.

"Not the foggiest," the Blacksnake replied in his near-lisp. "Apparently Sanojé's family have access to ancient oracles and diviners who are privy to all manner of secrets. They will give you the answers you are after concerning Yashamin's murder."

Corajidin gestured to the box, his question self-evident. "Wolfram?"

"Your Majesty," the lanky witch nodded his head by way of a bow. "This is one of the Chepherundi Boxes, famous in Tanis and the Conflicted Cities as oracular devices."

"Rahn-Corajidin." Sanojé's bow hid her bitter expression. "The Chepherundi Box is always correct. Those who attacked us earlier destroyed something similar, though not as powerful. Thankfully others of its kind were kept hidden elsewhere. Please understand the answers can take time. The more obscure the question, the longer—"

"So it may not know who killed my beloved?" Corajidin heard the steel in his voice. Though he could not make the Emissary pay for her earlier affront, his vassals were another matter. "If you have wasted—"

"The question has been asked already, Your Majesty," Wolfram's eyes were bright behind the long spears of his brindle hair.

"Mahsojhin is where history will say your Renascence began," Sanojé's voice held a hint of awe. "A rebirth of classic Avān learning, new teachings, and discoveries, rather than the limits the scholars impose on us."

Corajidin felt a tremor of excitement. To be free of the scholar's yoke over the government. To finally sever all ties with the Empress-in-Shadows and rekindle the fire in the Avān spirit. This was what he was fated to do. The oracles had said so. Everything he had done, all he had endured, echoed the truth of their foretelling.

A chill shadow stretched across him. The wind increased in speed. Corajidin looked to the west to see the sun almost balanced on the horizon. Fear coiled in him. The Communion Ritual was less than an hour away. The Emissary had promised if he dosed himself on her potion he would survive, yet doubt was ever his companion when it came to her.

"I am ready," Corajidin said with as much certainty as he could muster.

Sanojé opened the Chepherundi Box.

Corajidin took an involuntary step backward. Surrounded by ancient gilt- and gem-encrusted weapons, fetishes, scrolls, candles, and embroidered banners in bright primary colours, was a skeleton seated on a gilt throne. Its eye sockets were set with amethysts and it had polished milkstones for teeth. A baroque crown was set amidst ropy, dreadlocked hair. Where not draped in vivid scarlet silk, the exposed bones were graven with rows of High Avān characters, encrusted with gems and set with bands of precious metals. Rings were on every finger and toe. A trick of the afternoon light caused the eyes to glow purple as if fires shone in their depths.

"What in Erebus's name—" Corajidin choked out. This was a profanity! To keep a small part of an Ancestor in a reliquary was customary. Better were it a prized possession. To keep an entire skeleton, to ornament it so, was an invitation for Nomads to flock! The dead were burned, their ashes interred. This was the Avān way.

"These are the remains of my father, Chepherundi ap Navaskar," Sanojé said reverently. "In Tanis, where the oldest ways of witchery have not been forgotten, this is how we venerate our Ancestors—"

"This is a—"

"Necessary thing, my rahn," Wolfram interjected smoothly. The decrepit witch looked on the skeletal remains with interest. "This is the oracle who will tell you what you need to know."

"It is a Nomad!" Corajidin's voice teetered on the edge of a shriek. He turned to where Jhem stood by, though the man seemed neither surprised nor perturbed. "Jhem? You knew?"

"I have served in the Conflicted Cities, my friend," the Blacksnake said quietly. There was the echo of terror in his serpent's eyes. "It is a different world outside of Shrīan. There were certain beliefs I needed to overcome in order to survive. To face one ally's Ancestor is nothing compared to what horrors and madness the Golden Kingdom of Manté can conjure."

"The lich is here, Your Majesty," Wolfram urged. "It has the answers you need. Make use of it while you may, and if you choose to never speak of, or to, it again, then none of us will argue. Regardless, no others will know of what transpired today. If you don't take this chance, I can't think of any other sure way we can find what you're searching for."

The air cooled again. Corajidin noticed his breath had started to steam. His skin prickled. There was the sensation of being appraised. He slowly turned his head to look at the remains of Chepherundi ap Navaskar.

"A question has been asked of me." The voice sounded like the humming wind across a deep well. Though the jaws of the Nomad moved, no sound came from them. Rather it echoed about, a multipitched voice from everywhere and nowhere. "Who is it who would hear my answer?"

"My thanks, Revered Ancestor," Sanojé dropped to one knee. "I have requested this boon on behalf of Rahn-Erebus fa Corajidin, who has taken your daughter into his patronage."

Corajidin took another step back. Then another. Jhem placed his hand on Corajidin's shoulder to steady him. Then he walked forward with him until he stood directly in front of the glittering Nomad.

"Then it is I who owe *you* a debt in return," the voice in the wind was as empty as it was emotionless. "Gift for gift. Blood for Blood. Life for life. This is the way of things."

"I do not . . ." Corajidin looked at the Emissary, who smiled at him grimly. Where had his obsessions led him? "I do not think I can—"

"You wanted to know who murdered your beloved Yashamin," the Emissary sneered. "This is how you find out. The dead know things the living don't."

"Nobody told me we would be using Nomads!" Corajidin spat as rage fired up in him. "My Ancestors turned their backs on our Mahj because she became a Nomad! The dead go to the Well of Souls—"

"Scholar's teachings," Wolfram said flatly. "Before the scholars rose to power, it was Sedefke himself who perfected his communion with the dead. He, a man you admire, was a witch before he was a scholar."

"And he never stopped perfecting his communion with the dead," the Emissary pressed on. "What exactly do you think Awakening is, Corajidin? You speak with your Ancestors at will. You traffic with them. You're even linked with the great mind of Ía, upon which things die every second of every day! Death is a constant. What difference between a spirit in the Well of Souls and one that clings to existence and experience—much like you! You need to open your eyes if you're serious about your cultural rebirth and using the witches as allies to get what you want."

Corajidin felt her words like blows on his conscience. He stared at her, common sense at war with instinct and years of conditioning.

"Think it through, Corajidin," the Emissary said. She came closer, a woman who had been presumed dead yet had instead undergone a profound transformation. Wolfram gazed at Corajidin, wolf-eyes bright as he nodded. Corajidin reached into the folds of his coat to touch the smooth amber of Yashamin's funerary mask. He needed, in these of all places and times, her wisdom. Yet the mask was simply a mask and her voice was not there to bring him wisdom.

In desperation he reached out with his Awakened spirit to see whether there was any lingering connection with his Ancestors. The veils between the waking here and the living parted to monochromatic flashes like moonlight on rushing water. Try as he might there was no conclave of those who had come before. His ears were deaf to anything they may have had to say.

He lurched towards the Nomad in the palanquin. Shadows clung there in the dying light of the afternoon. What little there was, shone coldly on gems, precious metal and inscribed bone. With little care for the consequences he grasped the open door to the palanquin and thrust his head inside.

"Very well, dead thing," he snarled. "To begin something new I need to end something old. Tell me. Tell me who it was who cut Yashamin's throat and let us begin my new age with vengeance!"

The answer was given as easily as the question was asked.

"It was Rahn-Selassin fe Vahineh who murdered your wife."

✳ ✳ ✳

Principles that had once meant so much, the foundations upon which he had built the house of his life, seemed like stones in his boots now. Solid footing broken over the years with every compromise and betrayal. Today had been the day for it. Releasing the imprisoned witches—enemies of his nation, no less!—trafficking with Nomads and now, by no means least, he would use the tools of the Drear to falsify his own success at the Communion Ritual.

No doubt there would come an accounting, yet if he managed to unify the Avān and bring them back to their place in the world, he would face whatever history and his Ancestors, would say of him.

It all came to this. Natural stone columns curved upward to the distant, jagged top of the cavern called the *Elhas Shion*, the Ancestor's Heart. Crystals in the living rock reflected the light of *ilhen* pillars like stars in the deep. The air was close and damp. Cascades poured from dozens of crevices in the cavern walls like sheets of lit, wavering crystal. Some fell into pools higher up, where they fed myriad streams in their journey to the red-tinted pool that filled the Heart basin. Others were launched into the air where they became heavy mist. Each pool and fall swirled into a natural basin at the central point of the cavern floor. The sound was phenomenal. Corajidin felt the roar of the world crash against him. It drummed against his skin, pounded through his boots to cause his whole body to vibrate.

He ducked his head involuntarily with the sense of the colossal weight of the mountain above. Beside him Kasraman stood mute in wonder, though it was not the first time he had walked the Heart with his father.

Before them the path led into the ruddy water. Halfway between this shore and the next was an *ilhen* pillar, upon which sat a stone bowl the size of a man's head. The Communion Font. A rough frosted geode, which legend had it Sedefke himself broke in two. One half remained here while the other half was locked in the great treasury of Mediin, used as part of the coronation ritual for the Mahj. One day soon Corajidin hoped to drink from that half, too.

On ledges above him, partially wreathed in mist and fractals of light caused by the moisture on his eyelashes, were the Witnesses. Corajidin could see the black, white, and grey coat of Kiraj, the Arbiter-Marshall. The heavy purple folds of Padashin's over-robe as the Secretary-Marshall. Rahn-Narseh, his only friend from amongst the Witnesses, in her grey-green armoured plates and over-robe of the Knight-Marshall. Lastly the haughty Femensetri, a shadow amongst shadows, mindstone flickering with a black corona and the witchfire of her Scholar's Crook shining like a hook of moonlight.

"Drink now, father!" Kasraman urged. His son took Corajidin's head in his hand and brought it close to his own. Even with their heads together Kasraman had to raise his voice to be heard. "Pretend a moment of pious contrition and I'll stand between the Witnesses and you so they can't see."

Corajidin smiled his thanks to his son as he dropped to his knees. Kasraman stood before his father, coat and over-robe partially soaked from the spume.

With hands that trembled as much from nerves as from agony and fatigue, Corajidin popped the stopper on the potion. This close to the source of the Water of Life, the tiny motes of light held in blue suspension flared to incandescence. He looked up at Kasraman in surprise, who stepped closer to his father's to hide the brightening glow.

"For the love of Erebus, drink before the others see!" Kasraman almost shouted into the tumult.

Corajidin downed the vial in one draught.

There was no warning. No delay. It was like an explosion that started on his tongue then trailed down his gullet. Fire scourged his veins, so much so Corajidin thought he saw his veins burn through his layered clothes and skin. From the base of his spine up to his skull he vibrated. He could feel every drop of moisture burst on his skin. Each breath thundered in his lungs. The movement of the air caressed him. Played him like a sonesette. Strummed his manhood. He could see the flickering of this world and all the worlds that crashed upon it in an endless symphony of light and sound and motion and there was so much to see his eyes began to flicker in time with the millions upon millions of pinprick detonations of pleasure in his head that flared like blossoming flowers in his eyes—

Filled with light he sprang to his feet. Kasraman's expression was shocked, though Corajidin had neither thought nor care for what his son bore witness to. He felt like he could punch the mountain away with a thought. Could drink the great basin of the Ancestor's Heart dry. The voices of his Ancestors sang in his head. He could feel the grasses in the breeze of Erebus Prefecture, see through the eyes of the hawk as it banked, run with the horses as they thundered across the fields. And more. And more. So much more. This is what it was to be Awakened!

Corajidin strode forward. The red-hued Water of Life swirled around his ankles. Unlike other years, where there had been a shimmering opalescence where he touched the water, this time the water shone as if the moon rose from within it. Blue-green light burned about him, igniting the water for metres in every direction.

Waist deep in the pure waters the Avān called the blood of the world, Corajidin took up the Communion Font. The geode was warm in his hand. The crystal shone in response to his touch. Without hesitation he dipped the geode into the water. Filled it to the brim.

The Communion Font was hot to touch, something he had never experienced before. Water droplets landed on his hand, raising the skin in small blisters, which healed almost immediately. He felt the nettle-sting as mist kissed the exposed skin of his face, neck, and hands. He paused, uncertain. This was the greatest test his people knew: to face the power of Ïa itself and be judged worthy or to be destroyed utterly, consigned to agony and writhing madness before somebody brought a swift and merciful end. It had happened before. He had seen it.

Yet to not drink was to admit he had been found wanting. He had come too far to slink away and give up everything in favour of his successor. No! Come what may, Corajidin would be Asrahn like his father and other Ancestors before him. They would see him and know he had their measure. He needed to trust the Emissary had done all she could to help him survive.

He raised the broken geode to his lips and drank his fill, desperate to end the ritual as quickly as he could.

Despite the Emissary's potion the ponderous awareness of Ía was not entirely fooled. His stomach knotted. Bile burned his throat as some of what he drank dribbled through his clenched teeth. No! He must not spit the Water of Life out, lest he fail. The veins stood out like blackened cords on the backs of his hands, rising centimetre by centimetre as the Water of Life infused the weakened vessel of his soul.

Corajidin slammed the Communion Font back into the pillar, where it rocked for several heartbeats, almost toppling. Once more the muscles of his stomach knotted. His thighs trembled. He wanted to—needed to—void his bladder and bowels to get the Water of Life out of his system. Vomit filled his mouth. The others could never see, never know.

Despite the pain he refused to surrender. He had sacrificed too much honour and integrity in the name of power to stop now.

Forcing himself upright, Corajidin concentrated on taking one step after the other to the other shore of the basin. There, out of sight of the witnesses, he frantically stripped off his clothes before he covered himself in his own soil. He vomited the Water of Life in an explosive heave, the clear waters tinted red with his blood.

Kasraman helped clean the mess, his face expressionless. Corajidin looked down at the blackened crescents of his finger and toe nails. At the additional seams that had appeared on his hands. When asked, Kasraman dutifully reported there was more white in Corajidin's hair and that his face was now more gaunt, the eyes sunken. It was the face of a mad man, or a prophet. Yet it was the face of a living man.

"Was it worth it?" Kasraman asked.

"I am alive and have another five years before I need do this again," Corajidin rasped through a burned throat. *Unless I get everything I want and change the laws that keep us beholden to the Sēq and their traditions!* The Emissary's potion was already doing what it could to heal him, though the pain was almost debilitating. "I would do it again tomorrow if it meant success, though hope to never do it again."

It took some time to push his aching body back into the complex folds and layers of his clothes. His eyesight was poor, though with each minute gained focus.

Together Corajidin and his heir made their way through the short corridor that led to the Tyr-Jahavān, the Assembly, and the pending vote for Accession. The Witnesses had seen him pass Ïa's hardest test. Now came the time to pass the test of his peers, another outcome he hoped he had skewed in his favour.

❊ ❊ ❊

It was a weakened Corajidin who arrived last at the Tyr-Jahavān, though he was feeling somewhat stronger than when he had left the Ancestor's Heart. He was shocked to see how many chairs were empty. Too many counsellors absent from this, the most important vote in five years.

A restrained Siamak accepted the congratulations of his friends as he was declared Rahn-Bey fa Siamak, and Bey Prefecture was returned to his custodianship. The Beys had not governed their prefecture for nearly five centuries, and the giant man stood proud amongst his peers. There was a . . . wonder . . . in him now. His eyes seemed brighter, as he saw wider vistas than ever before. On leaving Avāweh, Siamak would return to his prefecture, there to achieve Unity with the consciousness of Ïa, and to bind his body, mind, and soul with the lands he and his descendants would rule for generations to come. Quite the homecoming for the man, and one his Ancestors will no doubt rejoice in. Corajidin still remembered the wonder of his first Unity, walking under stars and the Ancestor's Shroud, barefoot through snow, field and sand alike, all the while feeling the consciousness of Ïa and the presence of his Ancestors blossom in him. Everything had seemed sharper: his vision and hearing, the scent of pine needles and the grass that broke under his feet. There had been nothing to compare to the way he had made flowers grow and blossom at his touch, or to *feel* the life in the wheat fields as he had walked them alone under moonlit skies. He had known, even from the beginning, how he could summon storms, cause floods, lower waters, heal livestock . . . with the uttermost effort even raise the dead, should he so want—*Yashamin!*—but he never had. In those days there were some abuses of which he was still respectful. But times, like needs, change.

He envied Siamak the experience he would have, all the while fearful of his reach for Unity with his own prefecture. No doubt the others would undergo their own private rituals. It came as no surprise Roshana and Nazarafine were confirmed in their positions. Corajidin could barely contain himself when Vahineh, who sat drooling on herself and unaware of her surroundings, was also confirmed. It was a travesty she was even allowed to be tested, let alone the insult she had succeeded.

He glared across the polished marble floor at Vahineh. The Rahn-Selassin rocked back and forth in her chair, chewing on the bloodied crescents of her fingernails. Corajidin doubted the imbecile woman would have the presence of mind to vote today, yet Nazarafine and Roshana would have her here just in case. *Keeping a watchful eye, eh? You, who've known all along what Vahineh did, but kept it secret! There is vengeance aimed at you, too.* The Communion Ritual had neither repaired Vahineh's shattered mind, nor seen fit to end her. Corajidin expected that her search for Unity—were she capable of it—might kill her. Or, in a case of cosmic irony, the soul of the world might actually heal the broken little doll of its ills. The last things he needed to contend with were the shadows of Ariskander and Vashne, both men he had murdered, conscious in, and whispering their malcontent to, their heirs.

Corajidin's throat constricted with fresh grief. Had he any proof he could share he would call down a Jahirojin on the Great House of Selassin and wipe them from the face of Ïa. Yet the secrets told by a Nomad in the windy ruins of Mahsojhin were nothing he would take to the Arbiters, or the Teshri.

Vahineh would die for her crime. It would be no more sanctioned than it would be merciful.

Corajidin leaned forward as Jhem crossed the floor. The former-exile's expression was contemplative as he perched on a cold bronze sphere beside Corajidin. The two men leaned closer so they could speak.

"There's no sign of our missing allies anywhere," Jhem murmured. It was impossible to tell what he felt.

"And the Federationists who are likewise absent?"

"Some easily explained. It was myself, Nadir, Ravi, Nix, and a few others. The kherifes found Iraj's corpse under the Naje-dar Viaduct this morning, not far from his mansion on the Huq am'a Jarhen." Jhem's lips stretched across his teeth in a satisfied smile. The tips of his fangs, decay mottling them the colour of old coffee, showed for a moment. There was a feral gleam in the other man's eye, which gave Corajidin pause. "They'll no doubt find others as the night wears on. It would appear the Federationists unsheathed their knives, too. There are others, though. Stories of corpses torn to shreds, their throats ripped and their hearts torn out. Somebody was up to some red work."

"If I had to guess I would say it was Roshana who showed the resolve to tip the odds in their favour," Corajidin said. He looked across at the square-jawed, square-shouldered woman. Awakened only weeks ago, she already displayed much of her father's strength. Even so—despite what he had just said to Jhem—he doubted Roshana would stoop to such savagery in killing as Jhem described.

Mind turned to the dark paths of shedding blood, Corajidin looked to where the strongest of the returned Exiles sat. Tahj-Shaheh and Feyd sat beside Nix and Sanojé, who looked on the inbred man with a smouldering gaze. *Nix was so much like his father, spinning his webs and watching as people were stuck fast.*

"It would be best if you kept an eye on Nix," Corajidin said. His lips curled as if he had a bad taste in his mouth he could not get rid of.

"Stick a knife in Nix, was that?" Jhem's eyes remained dead, belying his words were even remotely said in jest.

"One day. I don't trust Nix, and I trust his father even less. But Jhem, what have you and the others done? I was confident the Accession vote would go my way, with the players I knew already on the board. Now I'll need to deal with a different kind of game . . ."

"'Never ask a question you can't afford the answer to,'" Jhem said. His expression was bland, his eyes hooded and deep as all Corajidin's sins remembered. "You said yourself we should do whatever is necessary to put you in power, and it's best you know nothing of what we've done, in case the Kaylish Face Readers try their ways on you. Or worse, the Sēq Inquisitors."

"Is there anything else you need to tell me?" Corajidin asked curtly, not wanting to prolong his interaction with Jhem any longer than he had to. The thought of the Sēq Inquisitors made him shift in his chair.

"Nothing you'll want to hear. But remember there are those of us who can, would, and will do anything to bring about a new Shrīan with you at its head. We'll make you Asrahn, Erebus fa Corajidin. In return you will thank us by binding us more closely to your Great House and the throne. We will all ascend to greatness, or all fall trying."

Memory crashed through Corajidin. Of lurid rites. The foretelling in Wolfram's chambers in Amnon. Was Jhem an agent of his fate? Was the man, remorseless and single-minded as he was, here to pave the way for Corajidin's destiny?

Corajidin's ruminations were interrupted by motion on the chamber floor. Padishin, the middle-aged Secretary-Marshall, rapped the metallic scabbard of his recurved dionesqa against the marble floor. He nodded to his functionaries who made rapid time to gather the votes from the counsellors. Each functionary carried a locked wooden chest with a hole in the lid.

The rules to the Accession vote were both simple and deeply ingrained. With two main factions there were few complications with casting votes. You were either an Imperialist or a Federationist, or had promised your vote to one faction or the other for a return of some kind. Only a rahn of a Great House could be considered for Asrahn. Any vote going to Vahineh would be a complete waste, as the fidgeting halfwit lacked the capacity to even direct her preferences to another rahn. The Imperialists had himself and Narseh, and it was no secret that Narseh would forward all votes for herself to Corajidin. Narseh had made it clear that she was happy with being the Knight-Marshall, and had no aspirations for higher office. If Corajidin took the day, Narseh would be Asrahn-Elect whether she liked it or not. There was no other choice.

❋ ❋ ❋

The selection for the Federationists was more complex. Nazarafine was an experienced rahn and had been the Speaker for the People for almost fifteen years. A gifted diplomat, she had shied away from the Asrahn's throne at every opportunity. Roshana was new to her Awakening, yet she was the daughter of Ariskander who—and this made Corajidin's gums ache—would have been his most dangerous opponent, and the most likely candidate for Asrahn. Corajidin had heard the others talking, saying how much of Ariskander they saw in Roshana, though Roshana was harder and more prone to rash action than her father had ever been. Siamak was new, of a fine and honourable line, and had served Far-ad-din well. Yet it had been centuries since a Bey had been a rahn.

Corajidin hoped Roshana was not voted as the leader of the Federationists, let alone Asrahn. The woman would be dangerous, and difficult to deal with, more so when she finally grasped the insight and wisdom for which her father had been almost revered. It would only be a matter of time before she became truly formidable.

There came the dry rustling of reed paper as the forms were slipped inside the boxes. Some counsellors, more pretentious than others, caused delays as they waited until the last minute to seal their votes. Corajidin suppressed a snort as some counsellors thrust their scrolled votes into the ballot chests like spears. It was as if they could not wait to be rid of the things.

Once the chests with their votes had been returned to the Secretary-Marshall, he left to begin the count.

❋ ❋ ❋

Two hours later, Corajidin sat up as the Secretary-Marshall's voice filled all the empty spaces of the Tyr-Jahavān. It must have been close for it to have taken so long.

Not a very comforting thought.

Of the Exiles who had returned, most had been given lands and titles in Kadarin and Erebus Prefectures. Corajidin had taken comfort in the swelling of Imperialist ranks in the Lower House of the Teshri. Even should the Upper House be run by the Federationists, Corajidin would still control much of the will of the government. He revelled in the knowledge of the tithes his own client sayfs would pay for his patronage, though wondered how many had failed him to make the vote take as long as it had.

The seats on the Magistratum were announced with no changes, which came as no surprise. Narseh was still Knight-Marshall and an ally, while Femensetri as Scholar-Marshall was a known quantity he could deal with. The others were of little consequence, tending to be bureaucrats who adhered to policy rather than trying to shape it.

As each result was read, Corajidin felt the tension coil alongside the pain in his chest. His mouth was dry. His palms perspired. His eyes felt hot in their sockets. Jhem's presence was scant comfort. Narseh, the old Knight-Marshall and rahn of Kadarin Prefecture, locked her gaze with his in a sign of support. With each passing moment, he felt his closest allies draw nearer, an illusion woven by the stress of waiting for the final vote of who would be Asrahn.

A surprise came when the Speaker for the People was announced. Nazarafine's jaw opened in disbelief. She looked to her friends in shock, then across to Corajidin with apprehension. The wild card candidate Sayf-Cesare of Ashion—an Ygranian expatriate and one some would call a Dusk Avān behind their hands—had been appointed. Corajidin knew him by reputation. Unfortunately, he was a moral, honest man with blood relations to the Sky Lord of Avānweh. The ex-mercenary commander was also a cursed Federationist. He was inexperienced though, so time would tell how well he represented the voice of the State.

Corajidin felt like he had been punched in the stomach when Rahn-Näsarat fe Roshana was declared the leader of the Federationist Party, and Siamak her deputy. The pain was eased a bit when he glanced at Nazarafine—who seemed to crumple with the blow—who in turn was looking askance at an entirely self-satisfied Roshana. Siamak looked guilty, refusing to meet Nazarafine's gaze. The portly woman's face reddened in what Corajidin took to be either embarrassment, or rage at an unexpected betrayal. He clapped his palm against his chest in honour of Roshana's determination. As much as he hated her for her blood, he had to respect her ambition.

He clasped his hands so tightly they hurt when the final result was announced.

The Tyr-Jahavān vibrated with the force of applause. Stamping feet. Relieved laughter. Outrage. Jeers. Corajidin let the noise wash over him. Felt it crash in waves so loud he could feel it on his face.

He was Asrahn! Or would be, when he was crowned in ten days' time. But with the support of his Imperialist peers, and those wanting to curry more favour, the great work could start now.

He stood on weak legs. His face felt like a wooden mask as he was carried along by his supporters. They made their way from the bright Tyr-Jahavān and into charcoal blue mountain shadows.

Finally he would walk in the footsteps of his father. He would look him in the eye in the Well of Souls when the time came and know they had both governed a nation.

Outside, Kasraman and Belamandris waited, expressions proud. He threw his arms wide and embraced his sons, wishing in the moment Mariam was there with them. He felt lightheaded. Noise came as from a distance. The fingers of his left hand began to tingle as a profound pain settled in his left arm and chest and—

10

"DARKNESS IS THE NATURAL STATE OF THE UNIVERSE. LIGHT, FLEETING, COMFORTING AS IT MAY BE, MAY STRETCH TO THE VERY EDGES OF ALL WE KNOW. YET ONCE IT IS GONE, THE DARKNESS ALWAYS REMAINS."

—From *The Darkness Without*, by Sedefke, inventor, explorer, and philosopher (751st Year of the Awakened Empire)

DAY 350 OF THE 495TH YEAR OF

THE SHRĪANESE FEDERATION

Looking down from the beak-like balcony of the Sky Room, Avānweh was a bowl of varicoloured stars cupped in shadowy fingers. Indris leaned against the wind, listening to the tattered sounds of singing from below. There would be dark days to come with Corajidin as Asrahn. As if hearing his thoughts, lightning flickered on the other side of the Lakes of the Sky. The air smelled of storm and brine.

"I was wondering whether it'd be worth jumping," came Femensetri's hard, angular voice from behind him.

"Let me know how that works out for you," Indris murmured. "Might be less painful than what's to come."

"This is on you, boy."

"Really?" Indris feigned disinterest, masking his irritation. Ten days until the New Year when Corajidin started his five-year reign. What happened between now and then was anybody's guess, though Indris expected tensions to be high. No doubt there would be more blood in the waters come morning. "How's Nazarafine holding up? This must have come as quite the disappointment."

"You should've—"

"Killed Corajidin?" Indris snapped. He cast a withering glance over his shoulder at his former teacher. She was a wind-swept silhouette against the lamps of the Sky Room. "I hear that a lot. Funny, when last I checked I wasn't the only *faruqen* person in the country! You, or any of these others, could've slipped a blade between Corajidin's ribs!"

"It's what you were trained for."

"It's what I stopped doing."

"We remember how well you stopped doing it at Amnon," she said with a sarcastic smile. She came to stand beside him. Looked over the edge, leaning on her Scholar's Crook flickering with blue-green sparks. "You're happy to shed blood, provided it's for your own causes."

"And *only* when there was no other choice. My causes were your causes for a very long time, sahai. They got me little more than grief."

"You may not believe it, but I always had your best interest at heart. Your mother and I were friends, Indris. I swore to her I'd do whatever I could—"

"Including keeping secrets from me? Like the fact I don't actually know who either of my parents are?"

She scratched at the wind-blown mess of her hair. "Anything I can tell you, you've been told. There's a lot about your mother's life I don't know. Those answers most likely lie in Pashrea, with the Sussain."

Indris snorted. He had visited Mediin, though never spoken with anybody from the Parliament of Immortals. He had kept his presence quiet, he and Shar focussed on the search for Anj-el-din at the time. "Can you tell me anything about my father?"

"Of course there was plenty of rumour and innuendo." Indris thought it sounded strangely like trepidation in Femensetri's voice. He opened his mouth to ask another question, but was forestalled by her open hand in his face. "Pashrea has some of the most ancient surviving members of the Avān race, including a few First Bloods like myself and my twin, Kemenchromis. But no. Truth is I honestly don't know who your father is."

"But you've guessed, haven't you?"

The wind gusted more strongly, bringing with it the first sting of rain. Femensetri gestured for him to come inside as she left the exposed balcony.

It was a large natural chamber in the mountainside, with several irregular corridors leading away from it. One led to a long stair along the side of the mountain. Another outside to a path sheltered behind verdigris-stained screens to the gondola station. Others led to what had once been a barracks of Avānweh's fabled gryphon-riders, now turned to sitting and guest rooms.

Scores of *ilhen* lamps had been set into the stone, giving the room a cold radiance. Marble chairs and couches were forged into the likenesses of gryphons, worn smooth by time. Old uniforms and weapons of the Daiharim—the order of gryphon-riding knights and airship pilots—were sealed in glass cabinets. The antique swords and knives were long and curved with ornate hilts and scabbard furnishings. The uniforms were wool-lined leather with plates of bronze-chased steel, winged helms with beaked visors, bronze-rimmed goggles, elbow-length gauntlets, and thick scarves.

Guests mingled quietly, drinking, talking, nibbling on food intended for Nazarafine's victory celebration. There were few smiles and fewer laughs. No celebration. Not tonight for the Federationists, probably not for a long time to come. Even Roshana was noticeably absent, not joining her fellows to celebrate her appointment as leader of the Federationists. Indris heard the talk. The fear of antagonism between the young, headstrong Roshana and the wily old Corajidin. Such fears would not have been given voice had Ariskander been alive.

Hayden and Ekko sat together, speaking quietly while Shar strummed her sonesette nearby. Omen stood beside them, seemingly frozen, facing one of the uniforms in its glass cabinet. Hayden looked up at him sadly.

Mari stood with Ziaire, the two of them consoling a despondent Nazarafine. Indris smiled at Mari, who gave him a terse head shake in response. Neva and her brother were there, tall and lean in their flying leathers. The statuesque beauty gave Indris a warm smile from across the room, Indris responding with a casual wave. Mari's brow creased in an annoyed frown, at which Indris dropped his hand with a wan smile. Siamak, his petite Tanisian wife Vasanya and solid daughter, Umna, stood together, watching the storm gather. Vasanya looked like a tree between the powerful hill of her daughter, and the mountain of her husband. Siamak saw what passed for the exchange between Indris and Mari, and nodded his support.

Needing a cup of tea, Indris passed by where Martūm sat next to Vahineh in a small alcove. The long-faced gambler had maintained his role as the solicitous cousin, more so now Vahineh's condition had not improved. Poor Vahineh had not been healed by drinking from the Communion Font, despite people wishing otherwise. Her skin looked as if parts of it had been burned smooth as dark porcelain while chalky patches marred her like rot. Her eyes were dull beneath heavy lids. The right side of her mouth drooped.

Vahineh would never be the Rahn-Selassin. His heart went out to her. A young woman, her life one of promise that had barely even started, cut short by Corajidin's schemes. Of course Corajidin would never be brought to task over what he had done to Vahineh, her father, mother, and brothers. To Ariskander. To Far-ad-din and his family. To a long and nameless list of others who had suffered.

"She's not long for the world," Femensetri observed Vahineh over a goblet of yellow lotus wine.

"And Martūm?"

"Bloody disaster," she said without a glimmer of humour. "He'll use the Selassin fortunes to pay his gambling debts and litter his bed with courtesans. Ziaire's reports of him weren't encouraging. He's politically indifferent, just as likely to sell his votes to either faction, depending on where he benefits most. Unfortunately, he's the closest living relative. There are some other, distant cousins we're looking in to, but he's probably the only real candidate." She sneered. "I hope I'm wrong, though; Martūm is a polished turd at best."

"Charming. What are you going to do?"

"Sever her from her Awakening." Femensetri's tone was resigned. "We've ten days before Corajidin assumes office. We need another ally in the Teshri and I don't trust Martūm to butter my bread. If we can't find one of Vahineh's distant relatives, we'll have to elevate another Family to the royal-caste. If that comes to pass it would mean the end of the Great House of Selassin, and a chance for Corajidin to get another Imperialist in the Upper House of the Teshri."

Politically it was a difficult decision to make. There was a list of candidates from the Hundred Families who had been waiting centuries for their opportunity. The Sēq would examine each candidate, approving those who passed the tests . . . while striking candidates who failed from the lists forever, since failure at the Communion Font meant a painful death after protracted madness. It was not an end to be wished on anybody.

"You know how Corajidin will react if you try and appoint a rahn without his approval," Indris said.

"Badly," Femensetri shrugged. "I'm more concerned about how the Sēq will react. Our noninterference is still informal, but that won't last. There's not a great deal of time in which to help Vahineh before any such action is expressly forbidden. Even I have to take orders sometimes. There are a growing number of my peers who would relish a return to the days of Empire."

"Corajidin hates the Sēq. It will be the end of the Order's autonomy in Shrīan."

"Except for those who'd appease the cunning old bastard."

"Except for those," Indris echoed.

Lightning flooded the Sky Room with a moment's harsh glare. Seconds later came the snarl of thunder. Rain hammered down, a steady hiss that caused a small layer of wet haze to dance on the jagged balcony. The wind whipped some of the rain inside. Femensetri stared at it, lips curved into an appreciative smile. Was a time when she, the Stormbringer, and her twin Kemenchromis, the Skybreaker, had been known to call cyclones and tornadoes to destroy armies. As two of the First Bloods, they had been at Näsarat fa Dionwē's side when he sank the Seethe High Court and their entire country beneath the Marble Sea. Those were the ancient times, when every Great House had a Sēq Master as rajir. Indris wondered, not for the first time, what it would be like to have the benefit of a colossal, immortal mind and perspective at one's command. He frowned. Commanding a Sēq Master was about as likely as politely asking the moon not to set. The Sēq did not serve an Asrahn, nor did they deign to do anything not in their own best interests, or the interests of their long game.

As if sensing his thoughts, she levelled her opal-gaze on him.

"I'll need your help to do this Severance," she said.

"What?"

"I'll need your—"

"I heard you the first time." Indris shook his head, stunned. "You've Sēq Masters who can help you with this. People who've done a Severance before. I doubt there's anything I could do other than get in your way."

"You I trust," Femensetri said flatly. "The others? Not so much. Besides, the presence of a lich in the city has my colleagues on edge even more than usual. The Sēq who took Chepherundi op Kumeri into custody never reported seeing you there. Do tell me how you managed to hide yourself from Sēq Knight Majors and two Masters."

"Where was I again?"

"*Sherde!*" Femensetri gave him a withering stare. "I'm so glad you managed not to get yourself killed."

"Always happy to oblige with not dying."

Femensetri stalked off, muttering to herself. Indris allowed himself a small, if short lived smile, but then thought more on his old teacher's words. A lich was not something he had expected to find when they had gone to discover what the Exiles were doing. Only those who had lost touch with some of the Avān's oldest beliefs would traffic with the walking dead, or those who served them. Such were the type to deal with criminals like the Soul Traders, unscrupulous merchants—sometimes Nomads themselves— who traded immortal souls and sometimes even living flesh for the transient satisfaction of fortune and to appease their own desires.

But the presence of a lich spoke to a dark intent. Nobody dealt with such beings unless they had a powerful message to send. From what they had seen, the Maladhi-sûk could have housed hundreds of people; warriors, assassins, witches, or rogue scholars. Even Exiled sayfs, returned to Avānweh in secret. For all the Ancestors knew, liches and other foul things could have been lurking, like horrors under the bed, in the corridors of the sûk for weeks, if not months or years.

How much damage could the people who would deal with liches do, if they could act in total secrecy?

"Deep thoughts?" Mari's voice broke through the fog of his self-recrimination as she came to stand by him.

"Me?" Indris forced a smile. "Not likely. How's Nazarafine? You've been hovering over her just a lot."

"How do you think she is?" Mari murmured. But even as she said that, she smiled at him, slow and lazy. "Are you feeling abandoned, my poor man?"

"Is there anything to feel abandoned about?"

Mari leaned against the wall next to him. Her hand reached out amongst the shadows between them to grasp his. She felt warm. He rested his head against hers, relishing the strength of her. Thoughts of walking along the wide galleried streets of Masripur, or viewing the alabaster facades of Carcisa where they overlooked the clouded waters of the Marble Sea, seemed aged on the vine.

"Indris," her voice was as urgent as the way she gripped his hand. "I've not accepted the offer. I've been thinking about what you asked me and am more tempted than you know, but—"

"Mari." He had witnessed on many occasions how the world conspired. "You need to do what you need to do. Believe me, if anybody understands the call of duty, it's me."

"You're not angry?" Her wide eyes, such a vivid and beautiful blue between long blonde lashes and the faint shadows of their orbits, held his.

"I'm not happy," he admitted. "But I'm not angry."

"I understand." He loved the way she rubbed the back of his hand with her thumbs. Her fingers entwined with his, strong and supple. "Can we talk about it later? Tonight? Just the two of us?"

He leaned in to kiss her, her lips parting beneath his. Indris raised his hands to run his fingers through her hair as their mouths lingered just moments from each other. It was all the answer he was able to give before the sound of shattering glass echoed across the Sky Room.

"Mari!" a drunken male voice shouted. There came laughter from several people on the other side of the room. People's heads turned towards the ruckus. Then towards Mari. "Mari! I know you're here. It's time you came home."

"Erebus's withered balls!" Mari swore. "What's *he* doing here?"

"Friend of yours?" Indris asked. He placed his bowl of wine on a nearby shelf, next to an ancient scratched helmet and pair of goggles, light splintering from a crack in one of the lenses like a rainbow trapped in glass. The

Feyassin closed ranks around Nazarafine. Other guests backed away. Peripherally Indris saw Ekko rise to his feet, a mountain of fur and muscle. Shar glided forward, seemingly lighter than air. Hayden smoothed his moustache as he stood, hand on the hilt of his broad-bladed hunting knife. Only Omen remained motionless, although in the silence Indris could hear the basso tones of Omen's voice, talking to what appeared to be the empty air.

Mari moved towards the new arrivals, Indris in her wake. He gestured subtly for his friends to stay where they were.

A wide space surrounded the newcomers. All were in expensive silks, standing amid shattered glass and a growing pool of spilled sunberry wine. A man and two women, siblings by their look, wore the floor-length, hooded over-coat of the elite-caste. The others wore the knee-length coat of the warrior-caste. All of them armed with sheathed long-knives. Their clothing was all in shades of black and red, sleeves marked with the black stallion of the Erebus.

Mari addressed the silk-clad newcomer, "Nadir, you're not welcome here."

Nadir looked Indris up and down. "Is this the man you've dishonoured yourself with?" His speech was slurred.

Mari grabbed Nadir by the wrist and dragged him onto the balcony. The rain had paused, though the clouds still blossomed with lightning. Thunder rumbled close by, vibrating on the skin and rattling glass.

"You're pretty," said the younger of the two women to Indris. Her pupils were huge, her large eyes blackened by kohl, lashes long and dark. There was a hunger in her gaze that made Indris uncomfortable. He felt a faint stirring of disentropy as if somebody had dipped a finger in the ahm.

"He's a Näsarat and a Sēq, little sister," the older of the two spat. "Father won't forgive you if you bring it home."

The younger woman pouted then turned her heavy-lidded gaze to the other people in the room. The older woman gripped the sheaths of the long-knives in her sash, revealing an intricate floral tattoo on the back of her hands with skulls for flowers.

Indris heard Mari shout. Nadir responded in kind. Indris interposed himself when the sisters and their companions sought to move further into the room. Within heartbeats Shar and Ekko were in his shadow. He spared a glance for Mari and saw her gesturing angrily at Nadir.

Their argument rose in volume, the embarrassing residue of what was clearly a past romance. People in the Sky Room looked askance at Indris, who fervently wished himself elsewhere. Mari's swearing reached fever pitch. Neva's expression was one of surprised approval. With people's attention diverted, Ziaire ushered Nazarafine, drooling Vahineh, and nervous Martūm out via a different door. The Feyassin followed.

Then Nadir, clearly frustrated and close to tears, tried to grab Mari. Mari shrugged his hands off and backed away.

Omen pounded across the marble floor, his ceramic feet almost chiming in his speed. Hayden was not far behind, his hands outstretched. With one arm Omen drew Mari to the side, away from the balcony ledge. With the other, he struck Nadir a vicious blow to the side of the head. The man reeled. Took a dazed step towards the edge. Then another. He teetered.

The two sisters screamed. The elder of the two drew one of her knives and threw in one fluid motion. Indris felt the ahm stir as the younger sister began weaving disentropy.

Omen grabbed Nadir by the coat and held the man over the yawning emptiness. Looking down, Nadir shrieked in terror.

The thrown knife struck Hayden high in the chest. The old man reeled and fell to his knees. Blood welled through his clothes as he clutched the weapon that pierced him.

Indris slapped the younger sister's Disentropic Stain with his own, forcing her to stop what she was doing. The pretty young thing gasped in shock.

"Sassomon-Omen, remember where you are!" Ekko roared. He had one massive furred hand curled around the hilt of his khopesh and he strode forward, bristling with violence. "If you cause so much as—"

"Not now Ekko," Shar snapped. She glided forward on light feet, her hands loose at her sides. "Now, Omen, there's no need to go making a mess of this nice young man. He's a friend of Mari's isn't that right?"

Hayden scrabbled back, gasping, a dark stain spreading on his hunting shirt. Ekko pounced to his side and picked the old drover up in a sweeping motion, as if he weighed no more than a child.

Indris could feel the tension crackle in the room. It squealed in his head, a scraping, shrieking wall of noise interspersed with feelings of anger, of desperation, of incredible pain, and . . . murder! A bubble expanded in his brain, swelling against his skull. Bypassing his Disentropic Stain, it expanded until all he sensed was the single-minded intent to kill from somebody in the Sky Room.

"Stop!" Indris's voice boomed across the room, a wall of sound that brought stillness in its wake, compelling all who heard it to freeze in place. Indris looked about, to see Femensetri staring at him in surprise.

And on the balcony, Omen stood as everybody watched, holding the writhing Nadir over the precipice with a hand incapable of feeling Nadir's blows, once more still and silent as a statue.

11

"THE TRUTH OF POWER IS THAT IT EXISTS WHERE YOU BELIEVE IT EXISTS"

—Miandharmin, Nilvedic Scholar to the Ivory Court of Tanis, Fourth Siandarthan Dynasty (169th Year of the Shrīanese Federation)

DAY 351 OF THE 495TH YEAR OF

THE SHRĪANESE FEDERATION

"Your father knows who killed his wife, Mari," Nadir had slurred. *"He has people hunting her even now. It's only a matter of time before he finds her and kills her and those who helped her."*

Only a matter of time. The knowledge of Yashamin's murderer would be a thorn in Corajidin's hoof. Her father would neither rest, nor hesitate in claiming blood for blood.

Mari had stayed behind to argue with Nadir on the wind-battered ledge of the Sky Room. He insistent, she obstinate. It had always been like this between them. But this time they had not reconciled their differences in passion's heady embrace like they would in old times, as much as she could see Nadir wanted it. And try as she might, Nadir had refused to reveal the source of his information, though there was a hollowness in his gaze that spoke to something that frightened him deeply.

"Your father is sick, Mari. He needs you—he needs his family with him."

Now her boots splashed water as she sprinted across the High Weir, a series of weirs and parks that formed a long pedestrian walkway across Skyspear, World Blood, and Star Crown mountains. The watery path was rarely used in the cooler months and almost never in the rain, yet it was the fastest route to the Qadir Sûn. Flash floods had been known to sweep people from the High Weir, sending them careening into rivers or over ledges into pools and small cataracts. While most of the time it was not a fatal slip, there were exceptions. She was thankful for the lanterns on their stone plinths to light her way. From time to time she cast her glance skyward to see lightning backlight the clouds. Thunder boomed at the impassive snow-capped heads of the mountains, like angry children shouting at three somnolent elders at peace in their chairs.

She spared a glance down the mountainside, to the terrace below her and the bright ponds cast by the lanterns along the road. Buildings were soft-edged from this height, tiled and domed rooves slick with rain. There they were! Indris and his friends were sprinting along the lower road in an effort to find Nazarafine and her escort. Nadir and his sisters were being held by Neva and Yago on behalf of the Arbiter of the Change. They would be released, though not in time to cause any more trouble tonight. Mari doubted her father would be so rash as to assault Nazarafine directly. The Exiles on the other hand might do anything to curry favour with their new master.

Something glittered coldly up ahead. Mari leaped a balustrade. Sprang from rock to rock. Jumped over a small watercourse. She drew her Sûnblade as her booted feet pounded the road.

She sprinted to where a number of bodies lay in puddles by the roadside. Their mortal wounds were deep and precise. Blood swirled in shallow water, dark as ink. None of the dead were known to her. The air was filled with the hissing of rain. It sheeted the road ahead, forming a blurred grey-white curtain between the stencil shadows of buildings and the empty blackness of the terrace edge. Mari took a shield from one of the dead, its circular rim badly dented, then continued on her course.

The world became small. A thing of details, rather than broad strokes. Her eyes were focussed on the play of shadows in the rain. Looking for the telltale sign of reflections from the metal of sword, knife, and shield. She listened for the clash and clamour of steel on steel. The screams of the wounded through the driving rain. Cries for help. She spared a glance behind her and saw Ekko's mighty frame powering closer, beside the unlikely teetering gait of Omen. The others followed closely behind, even the shorter figure of Hayden, who had come despite his wounds.

With friends such as these, Mari doubted there was little she could not do. She had fought beside skilled people, brave people, and lucky people. Yet Indris and his friends were all of this and more. They believed in what they did, their fights were for causes with real consequences they could see and understand. If Roshana and the others were smart, they would give Indris anything he wanted to convince him to stay. She wondered whether his cousin or the others understood him at all. Her stomach sank at the thought of him being anywhere without her. Or him being with anybody else.

Mari continued along the road towards the Qadir Sûn. The world about her had been reduced to wet monochrome streaks in the night, the red stone of Star Crown turned grey in the uncertain light. She sped under the intricate bronze and marble arch of the Water Garden; a series of reflecting pools with white lotus blossoms scattered on their surface, fine gravel paths, pagodas, carved wooden benches, willow trees, and manicured stands of bamboo and flowering bushes. There was the sweet perfume of lotus blossoms, as well as mountain rose and teak oil. Ahead of her she made out the frenetic dance she knew to be combat: the elegant art of a few warrior-poets; the brutal workmanship of many more bravos; one lithe figure and another more rotund in Ziaire and Nazarafine.

On silent feet she changed her sprint to a loping run, springing from one foot to the next. Her Sûnblade was held low, almost dragging behind her; the shield rim curving just beneath her eyes, made bright and sharp in the lamplight.

As she drew close she synchronised her steps and breathing with the beating of her hearts.

Mind, body, and spirit as one, Mari ignited the Sûnblade as she fell upon her enemies.

❋ ❋ ❋

Mari stood poised in *White Wave Crashes,* one of the stances of the Water Dance. Calf-deep in a reflective pond, blood dripped into the water from the recurved edge of her sword, itself an extension of her arm. The blade shone white gold, reflected in blood-stained ripples on the water. The lush white petals of lotus flowers glowed in its light. Steam coiled from the blade as raindrops stuttered and bounced on the hot metal. Her shield was held above her head, rain drumming on it, trickling off its ruined edge. Water trembled on her eyelashes, bright with refracted rainbows. Her sodden clothing stuck to her skin.

The flare of solar brightness from her sword had panicked the bravos. The Feyassin had cut down a few more before Mari snapped at them to get Nazarafine to safety. Ziaire had nodded, folding her metal fan edged with blood, her pale grey-white coat was gore-spattered. Nazarafine stood, a short dagger held in a hand that shook less than Mari would have given her credit for.

The fight with those who remained had been brutal and relentless. Mari's shield had reverberated with the blows of sword and axe. She had felt skin part and bone break as she struck. Whatever she touched, died.

Indris and his friends had fallen on the remainder of the bravos like a breaker. She did not spare them a glance. Within minutes bodies bobbed in the reflective pool or lay, limbs akimbo in the blood trampled grass.

Save for one, who stood facing Mari with an expression close to terror on his hollow-cheeked face.

"Who hired you?" she asked, voice raised against the barrage of the rain.

The man remained silent, his eyes flicking left and right. Omen picked his way closer, steps crane-like, body slick with rain and lamplight. He reminded Mari for a moment of an insect, cold and predatory. The Wraith Knight muttered to itself, its voice at one with the moaning of the wind through the willows.

"This only ends one of two ways," Indris said. Changeling crooned in his hand. A radiant blue-green sliver. "You're a nahdi. Why defend a person who may as well have paid you to commit suicide?"

The bravo crab-walked to the edge of the terrace. Shar and Ekko pinned him in. Rain sodden, he spared a glance for the long drop behind him.

"You don't understand," he said in a voice rough from smoking and drinking moonshine, the potent spirit made by the Jihari tribes. "Once you're in the spider's web you ain't 'scapin.' You do for him, or you die. He gets you. He gets yours. Ain't no other way to it. You're wrong, lad. This ends one of one way . . ."

So saying, the man threw his short curved sword at Shar, closest of them all. As she dodged, the bravo flung himself backward into the emptiness. Mari, Indris, and the others trudged to where he had stood. Though Mari knew there was only one end for such a leap, it was a sense of morbid curiosity that made her look anyway.

✳ ✳ ✳

"Corajidin will kill Vahineh when he finds her!" Nazarafine snarled. "We need to get her out of Avānweh until he can be reasoned with."

Her face, usually florid as a fruit farmer's, was livid with rage. She trembled with a combination of shock and exhaustion, from time to time glancing at the almost artful spray of blood along the hem of her white over-robe and long kilt.

"We must face facts and understand Rahn-Corajidin's motivation if we're to form a strategy. Truth is, Vahineh murdered Yashamin without provocation," Qamran said into the silence. The Feyassin officer refused to meet Nazarafine's glare. "If you think a man who assassinated the Asrahn, Rahn-Ariskander, and Rahn-Daniush—among others—can be brought to reason, you're more optimistic than I, Rahn-Nazarafine."

"She was driven mad by her Awakening!" Ziaire said as she wrung water from her long dark hair. "Vahi can't be held responsible for her actions."

Mari shivered in her own damp coat and trousers, boots squelching when she shifted her weight. She looked at Nazarafine squarely when she spoke. "The others may not want to say it, but my father won't be reasoned with. I know him better than any of you. If he knows who killed Yashamin, he'll not stop until a debt of blood has been repaid."

Mari's body thrummed with the excitement that only came with threat to life and limb. She stood with Indris and his friends. Hayden's shirt was caked with dried blood. Indris helped the old man take his shirt off so he could see to the wound. She watched with held breath as Indris's hands shone like lanterns, bones and veins incandescent. The pain left Hayden's expression within moments as the wound closed. Shar helped the old rifle-man wash the dried blood away.

"At the least she'd be imprisoned, or Exiled." Indris shook his head, spraying water, then ran his fingers through rain-damp curls. "The law is quite clear. There was no Declaration of Intent, she wasn't acting under the auspices of Jahirojin, and there wasn't an Ajamensût declared between House Erebus and House Selassin. Had this been a War of the Long Knives—"

"You!" Nazarafine spat at Indris. "Were it not for you, we would not be having this conversation. Corajidin should be ashes. You were asked to do a simple—"

"It was never my place to murder Corajidin, so don't lay your mistakes at my feet." Indris's tone was so casual it took Mari a moment to realize what he had said. The Sûnguard looked at him angrily. The Feyassin tensely. Indris tilted his head to one side, eyebrow cocked, daring any of them to start. "You knew Corajidin could, *would*, buy the outcome he wanted. But you expected you'd win the election, so you didn't do enough to guarantee it. Now you've learned what somebody who really wants something is capable of doing to get it."

"Indris," Ziaire said, "you have to accept your part in this."

"So I keep hearing. Yes, I could've murdered Corajidin and made a criminal of myself." He shrugged. "I didn't. None of us did. That water has been spilled and we can't pour it back. It's time to move on and agree what needs to be done to save Vahineh."

"Why did you not kill him?" Nazarafine looked up from where she sat, voice hard, apparently unable to accept Indris's philosophy. "You were there at the villa. It would have been so easy for you to end the life of that evil bastard!"

Indris looked at Mari, his eyes haunted. *He didn't kill my father for me,* she thought. She felt tears welling at the corner of her eyes. *How was it fair for mercy to come back to haunt us?* He looked back to the Speaker for the People and the Prime of the House of Pearl. "Awakening gives the rahns immense knowledge. Hopefully access to some wisdom. Yet they can never forget. Nor does it seem they can forgive. The revenge and hatred and violence has to stop somewhere."

"That was not for you to decide!" Nazarafine rose from her chair. She stepped towards Indris, fingers curled into claws. Changeling rumbled threateningly while Indris waited, expression dangerously bland. Nazarafine looked at Indris with loathing. "Shrīan will have a monster as Asrahn for the next five years! The Imperialists control the Lesser House of the Teshri! The Iron League needs no better excuse to plan war on us."

"Because of your apathy, yes," Indris said with sorrow. The others looked stunned. "You didn't take action in Amnon, assuming I would mysteriously know you wanted Corajidin murdered and solve your problems for you, so you could have a clean conscience. Then you lost the election because you failed to act. And yet you seemed surprised at what's come to pass."

"Get out," Nazarafine snapped. She glared at Indris, finger trembling as she pointed to the door. Her voice rose to a scream. "Get out! GET OUT!"

"Nazarafine—" Ziaire said with a panicked smile on her face.

"Out! I want him gone from my sight, he and his useless comrades," Nazarafine turned her back on Indris, walking stiff backed to her chair.

"Indris . . ." Mari whispered. His face was stern, eyes like steel.

"I hope your mistress manages to find some sense," Indris said to Mari, avoiding her attempt at an embrace. He rested his hand on her hip. "You asked what happened that I search outside for what's inside. Ask the same of yourself, Mari. Don't live a lie. You've a duty to yourself, also. Nazarafine or these others will see you wasted and too soon planted in ashes."

He and his friends left without a backward glance, passing a stern-looking Femensetri as she walked into the room, Siamak and Ajo at her side. The Stormbringer turned to watch Indris walk away, then turned back to the others, hands wide open in question.

"Nazarafine told Indris to leave." Ziaire sounded as shocked as she looked.

"You *what?*" Femensetri said with disbelief. "Have you taken leave of your senses, woman? What possessed you to do such a thing?"

"Do not take that tone with me, Femensetri," Nazarafine said from beneath lowered brows. When she spoke it was with a quivering, righteous indignation. "You should have heard what he said! He blamed the loss of the election on me!"

"And he's wrong how?"

"*What?*" The Speaker's voice rose several octaves.

"You heard me." Femensetri shouldered past two of the Sûnguard so she could better loom over Nazarafine. "You know there was a lot more you could've done to win. Ancestors' sake, Indris even warned Roshana what to look for to prevent Corajidin from having the power base he wanted and you did nothing. Sûn love you, Nazarafine, there are times when you frustrate the life from me."

"We don't need him," the Speaker insisted with less certainty in her voice. "We survived for years without him and we'll manage to survive for years more."

"You've really no idea what that man sacrificed to keep the monsters from creeping out from under your bed, do you?" Femensetri said scathingly. "*Sherde!* If Corajidin could see us now, he'd be laughing himself silly. We're practically handing him what he wants if we fall on each other like this."

"The Federationists control the Upper House of the Teshri," Siamak offered in a calm tone. "Corajidin can not make any sweeping changes without our approval."

Ajo rested his chin on the polished silver gryphon on his walking stick, a troubled look in his eyes. "So long as Vahineh is not replaced and the balance of power changed."

"My father knows it was Vahineh who murdered Yashamin." Mari blurted. Femensetri seemed to stop breathing for a moment. She glowered at Mari, who held her hands up. "I didn't tell him! No idea who did. When Nadir was talking to me at the Sky Room, he mentioned father was going to kill Vahineh and any who helped her."

"Ahh," Femensetri said. "That explains all the dead bodies on the way and all the tightly puckered sphincters here. I'm glad you're all safe."

Mari felt the need to defend Indris, to try and remind Nazarafine he had always put himself at risk for others. "Indris had a lot to—"

"Stop speaking his name!" Nazarafine yelled. She held a trembling hand to her forehead. A few moments later a bound-caste servant arrived with a tray of sweets and glasses of hot chocolate. Nazarafine pounced on them with a vengeance, jaws working rapidly as she ate, stopping only to drink. Mari wondered whether she might lose a hand to Nazarafine if she reached for a pastry. The smell of chocolate, honey, nougat, and caramel made Mari's mouth water.

The others remained quiet as Nazarafine's expression changed with her altering mood. Lightning flared through the windows as rain tapped against the glass. The matronly Speaker lost some of her angry colouring. Her brown eyes warmed over time. Once or twice she smiled, a faltering, fledgling thing. More substantial food was brought in. The aroma of minced chicken, coriander, and mint filled the room. They sat down to a quiet meal over watered-down wine and polite, if somewhat tense conversation. Once Nazarafine had resumed her typical good humour, Ziaire turned to the topics at hand.

"Femensetri?" the courtesan asked as she lined the folds of her over-robe along her crossed legs. "Were you successful with the Sēq? Will they help us with Vahineh?"

"As to that," the scholar stretched her legs out, joints popping, "my Order is about as fractious as the Great Houses. A Severance is a dire thing. Some of them see the benefits in saving Vahineh. Other's care less about her than who would be Awakened in her place."

"And that is the rub, is it not?" Ajo observed.

"Pretty much. There are those amongst the Order who want to see where the openness of the Federationists can take us. They realise the monarchs of the other nations fear what they don't know and want to ease the pressure with our neighbours."

"But?" Siamak leaned back, the sweeping breadth of shoulders barely contained by the chair.

"There are others, more, who want a return to the heady days of power." Femensetri's voice was hard as steel, and dagger-sharp. "There are some of us who remember what it was like to serve a Mahj. They have the taste for real power. Many of us know such power comes with a terrible price. Sadly our Mahj, the one power we've all sworn to serve, remains silent in Mediin. We who left to help guide the Avān in Shrīan will find no wisdom from the one person who, by rights, can order us to come to a resolution."

"So where does that leave us?" Nazarafine sounded defeated. "Vahineh can not survive as she is. If Corajidin gets his hands on her, Sûn herself only knows what he will do."

"Can he influence who she Awakens?" Ajo's gaze was sharp.

"It's possible," she nodded. "He'd need a properly trained Sēq to help guide him . . . or a witch from before the Scholar Wars who may remember how it's done."

"Can *you* help Vahineh, without alerting your Order?"

"Nazarafine just told the one person I needed to get out." Femensetri grimaced around the words.

"He only ever helps himself," Nazarafine muttered bitterly.

"With respect, Speaker, you seem to have a bit of selective memory." Mari felt her face flush as she spoke. Nazarafine drew in a breath to speak, but Femensetri held her hand up for silence. The black-robed scholar nodded to Mari to continue.

"You know as well as I do Indris acts from his duty of conscience. He cares what happens. He just won't be lied—or dictated—to." Mari spared a glance for Femensetri, who glared back. Nazarafine's expression was haughty. Ziaire, Ajo, and Siamak nodded their approval. Mari continued. "For all his service to Shrīan, when the time came for the Crown, the State or the Sēq to help, he was abandoned in the slave pits of Sorochel for two years to then escape by himself. Yet he risked his life again for all of us. The dust hasn't even settled after the Amnon fiasco, and you seem to have forgotten everything he and his—how did you put it, *useless comrades*—did."

"You speak from infatuation, child," Nazarafine said with the barest hint of compassion. "Indris will end up on a pyre before too long. He has chosen a dangerous path and made too many enemies. Besides, you know there is no future with him. Roshana and Ajomandyan have already entered into discussions regarding a proposed marriage between Indris and Neva."

"Be that as it may," Mari said with rising anger, "his path has helped people and he continues to do so. He'll help Vahineh, regardless of how poorly you've treated him."

"How can you be so sure?" Ajo asked.

"Because it's the decent thing to do."

12

"OUR LIVES ARE MADE OF RISKS AND REWARDS. OUR ENDEAVOURS, LOVES,
AND HOPES ARE ALL PRONE TO THE GREAT RISK OF FAILURE. YET TO RISK
NOTHING FOR FEAR OF FAILURE IS TO LIVE IN A SHUTTERED BOX IN A
WORLD WHOSE WONDERS YOU WILL NEVER KNOW."

—Madesashti, the Prime of Amajoram, the Cloud Palace of the House of
Pearl in Avānweh (276th Year of the Shrīanese Federation)

DAY 352 OF THE 495TH YEAR OF

THE SHRĪANESE FEDERATION

Finally there had come an end to the nightmares—but only in that he
was now awake.

What felt like days ago—though it had only been a few hours—
Corajidin had woken screaming, tangled in soiled sheets, his limbs palsied
and aching. In what voice he had to his name he had yelled. In his ears it had
sounded loud enough to bring the three mountains of Avānweh down
around his ears. It had taken what felt like a very long time for Nadir to
come to his aid. Neither one of them spoke as the young man washed
Corajidin's body. Helped him change into new, clean clothes. He thought he
was going to pass out from the pain in the time it took for Nadir to give him

a generous dose of the Water of Life. He found he needed more of the potion as the days wore on, the doses large enough to relieve most of the pain, most of the time.

But even with the Water in his veins, Corajidin felt drained as he slouched on an ornate couch in a sunroom at the Qadir Erebus. Through a metal lace ceiling fitted with glass panels, he could see the towering heights of Asrafah, Īajen and Silamari—Sky Spear, World Blood, and Star Crown mountains—stretching upward and back into forever. The sun hung in a cerulean sky, beating down on the three great mountains, whose tops were perpetually mantled with snow. The image reminded him of some of the watercolors Mari had painted: long dark thumb strokes of forest; the diamond-dust rubbing of mist from the waterfalls; and the fine chill blue strokes of rivers that eventually fed the aqueducts, canals, streams, and ponds of Avānweh before they emptied into the Lakes of the Sky.

Weighted by his residual pain he tried to summon resentment at the memory of his wayward daughter. But alone, surrounded by the vault of the sky and mountains that pierced the sky, he allowed himself to miss her like he had missed his son. Like he missed his wife, too. He allowed himself to cry. While those who counselled that revenge against Vahineh would accomplish nothing, he disagreed. Some argued that after Corajidin had ordered the murders of Vahineh's father, mother, and brothers, Yashamin's death had been an almost inevitable consequence.

Those people were mistaken.

He sat on the sluggish edge of wakefulness. Sunlight felt thick and heavy on his skin. A large marble fountain, surrounded by potted fig trees, burbled merrily. Small red and black birds warbled. A Seer's Window, a mist-flecked crystal pane of glass in a silver frame, was propped in a baroque golden horseshoe set with cogs and flywheels. A high-backed chair faced it with a small wooden table beside. The room smelled of smouldering rosemary and peppermint.

It seemed like a world at peace, though was there truly such a thing? Weariness pulled at his limbs. He caught himself nodding as his body jerked back to wakefulness. Yawned wide enough to cause his jaw to pop. Tired as he was, he did not want to return to sleep and the horrors that waited to reveal themselves behind his closed eyelids.

For two nights and a day he had lain in torpor, his body struggling with the strain put on it at the Communion Ritual. When he had awoken it had felt like acid scalded his veins. His chest was still tight, though. It felt as if it had been hit by a hammer, and he had been reminded of the savage blow of Thufan's hook not so long ago. The pungent smell of his own faeces and urine in his soiled bed had been thick in his nostrils. Part of him imagined he could still smell it.

The perfume of success.

Every time he blinked there came flashes of the turbulent visions that had plagued him.

Blue-green clouds had swirled above, shot with wavering pillars of light. He had panicked, for fear of drowning, holding his breath until his eyes burned and his chest ached and his hearts thundered in his ears and he had to take a breath and when he did there was—air. Shapes flitted about him: people, yet not. Heads, torsos, arms, and legs, yet proportions were wrong, as if their limbs had been fused with great diaphanous fins. Or backlit wings, dyed with rainbows. He heard his name called by familiar voices. Memories caressed the surface of his mind. Conversations held in different times in different rooms by different people resounded in the confines of his head.

He was sinking. The voices told him to swim. Some of the shapes came close, to show faces half-remembered from other lives. Their voices collected in him, like sediment, so much clamour he could not make out words. Only noise. It made him heavy. He kept sinking.

Below was turbulent darkness as if light was held captive there. Things moved. Heaved. Gave out great bellowing groans. Screams. Giggles and shrieks and laughs and cries. Sobbing. It was cold. Much colder as the darkness swaddled him in a great heavy blanket. Down he spiralled.

Tentacles coiled about each other, like snakes the size of fortress towers. Great clusters of orbs for eyes, unblinking as they stared upward, so large Corajidin would walk on any of them. He saw other beings down here, wheeling like birds flying underwater. Tiny compared to the leviathans below. Sound boomed upward, buffeting, causing his body to thrum. Words dark, phlegmatic, and stentorian rolled across him. One of the flying shapes came close. Her pallid, corpse-still face was set with a polished tourmaline in her brow, which flickered, radiant.

"What can we do for you?" she asked.

He was sinking—

Corajidin rose feebly now. He shuffled to the Seer's Window, wincing with each step. The Emissary's potion had most certainly saved Corajidin from dying during the Communion Ritual. He held tight to the all too brief joy of Communion with the soul of Īa and his Ancestors, something long past for him. Days after the ritual, the world blood that remained in him was taking its toll. As he reached out to adjust the Seer's Window, he saw the raised, ugly blisters on the insides of his arms, mottled red brown and yellow green. The skin around them was tender and hot to touch.

Out of curiosity he scratched at one. Foul-smelling pus burst out, to dribble slowly down his arm. Sickened, Corajidin wiped the filth on the hem of his over-robe. He would have the cursed thing burned, rather than washed. He would have everything he was wearing burned. His bedding, too. Better there was no reminder of how his body had betrayed him.

Turning his eye to the Seer's Window, Corajidin used the flywheel to adjust its angle and direction. He was overwhelmed by a sense of vertigo as his eye tried to track objects near then far then near. Eventually he found the landmark on Īajen-mar he was looking for: two enormous diorite statues of a hooded woman and a hooded man, Scholar's Crooks held angled so they formed a high arch. There was a heavy gate beneath the arch, the metalwork a thing of intertwined, thorned vines with lotus flowers scattered amongst them. Changing the angle of the Window he followed the sheltered passage along the mountain face where it climbed steeply to a natural turret. From there, a long stair had been carved into the rock. Boulders and sharp pieces of stone rose from it, the original builders leaving as much of the natural stone formation as they could. Diorite columns lined the way, each topped with an *ilhen* sphere.

At the top of the stairs, two hundred metres above where the Caleph-rahn sprawled on neighbouring Star Crown, a great archway had been carved. Almost five metres in height, the stone within had been arabesqued around a recessed door that stood three metres tall. The door was *kirion* black, shot through with clouds of red, blue, and green like an oil stain.

The doors to the near-fabled Amer-Mahjin, the Deep of the Wise Ones, were without lock or handle. The Sēq Chapterhouse of Avānweh had once drawn the greatest minds of many generations. No longer. After the Scholar Wars people had started calling it Amenankher: the Long Shadow. The Scholar Wars and the terrors that had come with the century of scholar-witch conflict had left some deep scars on the society who had survived it.

Corajidin would stand there the day the witches blasted those doors from their hinges. He would watch light flood in and banish the shadows of long-kept secrets. Stride the timeless corridors, filled with knowledge the Sēq had kept from the Avān in their long-held arrogance. The world deserved answers to the questions that plagued it . . . like the cure for his illness and the weapons of ages past when the Avān had ruled all they had laid their eyes upon.

Whispers filled his head. His vision swam with the illusions of other-memory. The same place, a different time. A different person. In a quantum of insight he knew he was Asrahn-Erebus fe Amerata, the Red Queen who had ruled Shrīan during the Scholar Wars. She had died in them, fighting against the Covens.

Superimposed above the sheltering sky he watched as the firmament burned. Clouds seethed red. Flame sprouted on the mountain heights. There came the echo of shrieks from the city below. The Stormbringer stood in the turret near the gates, mindstone blazing with dark energy, her Scholar's Crook glittering with fractals of light. She raised her pale beautiful face to the sky and sung down blades of wind, hailstones, and scourging rain, amongst lightning bolts that struck to kill. Others near her cut the air with planes of incandescent light, orbs, arcs, and prisms of energy that detonated like murderous fireworks. Witches wheeled in the sky, and fell from it. Wrapped in the frightening illusions of screaming tornadoes, dragon-headed monsters, flying insects with glowing entrails, and worse, they cast down bolts of fire, or commanded daemons of the water, earth, and air to tear Avānweh from its foundations. He felt the phantom tears stream down his face as he remembered the anguish of so much loss of life—

"Finally you see what it is you've forgotten," came the creaking groan of the voice from behind him. Corajidin turned to face the Emissary. Her hood plunged the ravaged beauty of her face into shadow, though there was a faint hint of what she had been. The squid on the pommel of her sword seemed to flex its tentacles where they rested on the end of the hilt. There came a faint rasping, little more than a distant whisper, with each movement. "You are once again Awakened, Corajidin. At least for a little while, until the Water of Life leaves your body."

"Will I ever be able to be what I was?"

The Emissary shrugged. "We've given you the means to be more, yet you hesitate to do what needs to be done. You want to conquer Pashrea. You want to become Asrahn—or to rise even higher and unify your people. Yet you still resist our gift, and the dawn of your returned power stays forever beyond the horizon."

"Are you here to plague me, Emissary?" he asked peevishly, idly rubbed at the lesions covered by his coat. "I left orders I was not to be disturbed."

"The witches of the Mahsojhin have been waiting to meet you."

"Ahh," he said, nodding. His smile was as false as any he had ever given. "And so it is I can start paying off my debt to you, Emissary."

❋ ❋ ❋

Trepidation and excitement filled Corajidin in equal measure. He had sent for Kasraman, Belamandris and Wolfram, waiting for them to arrive before giving the Emissary leave to admit the witches freed from Mahsojhin.

The Emissary went to the door and gestured to people outside. She stepped aside as a woman and a man in ornate, layered vermillion coats strode past her. Both had rings of silver, gold, and bronze on their fingers and thumbs. They wore thick torcs of twisted gold and silver strands like metallic rope. The ends were sealed: hers with a jet goat's head; his with a blackened silver octopus that reminded Corajidin of the Emissary's sword pommel. Both carried tall staves of stained oak, set with polished metal ingots and smooth gemstones.

The woman was a petite thing, her features disturbingly symmetrical and cold. She called herself Elonie, a creature of milk skin and spun-sugar hair with eyes the colour of cornflowers. The other, Ikedion, was a confectionary-coloured obese man of middling height, with shiny round cheeks, rubbery lips, and eyes sunken in flabby pouches. His chubby fingers twitched as he looked around the room, gigging to himself.

Neither witch made obeisance, nor showed Corajidin the slightest honour for his rank or station. He looked them up and down with some disappointment. A tiny, frigid-looking woman and a tittering fat man. He turned his gaze on the Emissary, one eyebrow raised as if to say *Is this all?*

"Rahn-Erebus fa Basyrandin fa Corajidin," the Emissary said, "Elonie is formerly of Nienna and a Magnate of the Stone Witches. Ikedion of Corene, in Atrea, is a Master of the Sea Witches. They would negotiate with you on freeing of the remainder of their brethren. They are amongst the most senior of the professors at the Mahsojhin."

"No doubt." Corajidin leaned back in his chair. Elonie of Nienna? Ivoré and its capital city of Nienna had been wiped from Ïa almost two hundred years ago by the Angoths. Elonie's family and friends, husband and children if they existed, were long gone to ashes. The glittering towers of candy marble and limestone reduced to rubble. Her glorious knights a memory. He wondered whether anybody had told Elonie the fate of her famously beautiful homeland, gone to ruin in her oblivious incarceration.

"The question is, are they worth the trouble?" Kasraman asked pointedly. "The Sēq taught them the limits of their power once—"

Where Elonie stood there was now a tall, gaunt phantom crone. Her long hair streamed like a dirty mop in a gale, her shredded coat translucent and wrinkled, rotten skin translucent so the putrid blue grey of her organs shone through the skin. Her eyes were two gelid blue stars and her teeth blackened fangs in grey gums. Her oaken staff became crooked, a bleeding goat's head with weeping eyes at its top. A whirlwind formed about the edges of the room, turning even the most harmless of debris into a lethal projectile that ground against stone and splintered wood.

Ikedion had likewise changed, the obese man replaced by an even more obese octopus whose tentacles flayed in a mire of ink-like cloud. A cluster of eyes like blazing golden coins against flesh that burned the colour of hot coals. One of the tentacles lashed out and smashed a table to kindling. The octopus continued to grow, taking up more and more space in the room. The heat was incredible.

Corajidin felt his bowels loosen at the sight of the lashing tentacles. So much like his vision! He tried to crawl back through his chair and away. His mind was bombarded with the need to run. Run! RUN! He almost wet himself with fear and his hearts faltered in his chest. His left arm was virtually paralysed by a blinding pain.

Belamandris had drawn his amenesqa and stood, pale-faced yet reso-
lute, between the terrors and his father. Wolfram likewise took station to
defend his master. Corajidin looked on as Kasraman stood, his back to his
father, facing the two horrors. There was a brilliant flash as if lightning had
sheeted across the room. Corajidin thought he heard a thunderous voice
boom with authority in a language he could not understand.

One moment the room was filled with the visions of nightmare. The
next Elonie and Ikedion were standing, pale-faced and almost fearful, eyes
downcast before Kasraman, who loomed over the both of them. The two
witches gave trembling obeisance.

Corajidin did his best to stop his own limbs from trembling. His chest
ached, mirrored by a stabbing agony behind his eyes. He smoothed his coat
and sat himself more authoritatively on his chair. The room was none the
worse for wear: furnishings in place, walls unscathed. Only the Emissary
seemed unperturbed, though she looked at Kasraman with a newfound respect.

Kasraman turned to his father and bowed. "I believe our guests are
more than ready to discuss terms with you, father."

"We apologise for our outburst, great rahn," Elonie said in a subdued
tone. Ikedion nodded his agreement. "Please understand we've come to understand the world has changed much in what has been centuries for you,
but moments for us. Much of what we knew, what we loved . . ."

"The betrayal by the Sēq," Ikedion kept his face down, "as well as by
Asrahn-Amerata, is something that only occurred hours ago. Our passions
are high."

Corajidin stared them down, taking the time to control his still-shaky
extremities. He cast a glance at Kasraman, who looked no different than
before. Yet he was sure it was his heir who had dominated these two. The
question was how? He wondered what else his son was capable of.

"It would please me to take you into service," Corajidin said graciously,
"provided you take Kasraman's orders as if they were my own."

Elonie and Ikedion nodded quickly. Kasraman looked at the two of
them thoughtfully, no doubt wondering the true strength of the weapons
given into his hands. Wolfram came to stand by Kasraman, to whisper in his

ear words Corajidin could not make out. Kasraman nodded once, lips twitching in a smile.

"Now to business." Corajidin clapped his hands together briskly. He gestured for Elonie and Ikedion to be seated. "There are things we need from each other. I understand there are more of you locked in Mahsojhin and I am eager to help you set your friends free. However, let us start our newfound relationship by what you can do for me, shall we?"

✲ ✲ ✲

Corajidin poured himself a tall glass of coffee, spicing it with cinnamon. He closed his eyes with pleasure as he sipped. It was moments like these, devoid of pain, when life was almost as good as he remembered it being.

"Will you really make use of the witches, Your Majesty?" Wolfram asked from where he leaned on his crooked staff. The old witch reached down to massage one leg beneath the worn straps of his callipers.

"I would think so," Corajidin said. Memory of their demonstration of power still lurked like childhood fears. "They carry with them such . . ."

"Hatred?" Belamandris offered. "Danger?" He pushed himself away from the wall, expression troubled. "This is a reckless course you pursue, father!"

"They're what we need, little brother," Kasraman countered. Corajidin's heir pulled at his lip as he pondered. "They bring a terrible power, but it's a power we need to control. The Sēq are unlikely to ever do anybody's bidding save their own. We can forge the witches of Mahsojhin into something that will serve the Great House of Erebus."

"Speaking of which." Corajidin withdrew from an inside pocket of his over-robe a scroll case. He tossed it to Kasraman, who caught it deftly. At his cocked eyebrow he gestured for his son to open it. Kasraman read far more quickly than Corajidin would have thought possible. It was as if he had taken in the entire contents in a single long glance. His oldest child looked up wonderingly. The scroll was passed to Belamandris, then Wolfram, before the Emissary had the chance to read it.

"You know the Stormbringer," Corajidin said to her. "Your thoughts?"

"She'll not be happy to read this," the Emissary said, one side of her mouth twitched into a smile. "Do you really expect the Scholar-Marshall to come to you, to discuss the future of the Sēq in Shrīan? She doesn't bend."

"Then she and the Sēq will break," Corajidin snapped. He glanced quickly at Belamandris, then back to the Emissary. "This is what was agreed, neh? Part of your price? The scholars will bend a knee to me as Asrahn, or they will find they have no place in Shrīan. Now that I have an alternative, their days of unquestioned authority are over."

13

"So a garden can not thrive without sunshine and water, the garden of the soul can not thrive without love or compassion."

—From *The Nilvedic Maxims*

DAY 352 OF THE 495TH YEAR OF

THE SHRĪANESE FEDERATION

The Seethe troupe sang unaccompanied, using their breathy voices for layered vocals and instruments both. Gathered in the comforting darkness of a deep, oval arena in the mountain, hundreds of people from myriad backgrounds watched the troupe in wonder. The night sky was littered with stars. The coloured cloud that was the Ancestor's Shroud stretched part of its cowl over the night-sharpened edge of the arena. Some thirty Seethe, including Shar, sang their beautiful choral work where each voice caused tall radiant crystals to shine a different colour and brightness in time with their voices. Indris spared a glance for Mari's face, her profile lit with innocent wonder, tears forming at the corner of her eye. He smiled. Let his own tears flow at the beauty that caused his spine to tingle and chest to tighten.

As the music swelled to a breathtaking crescendo, a number of the troupers took to the air, pirouetting in open space, skin shimmering from within and gem-like eyes bright as candles. Those who remained on the ground mirrored them in a complex, swaying, heart-breaking perfection of movement.

As the piece came to a close, the crowd surged to their feet. The roar of their applause, hands clapping against chests, feet stamping, all of it filled the arena to overflowing. Hayden's eyes were bright, wrinkles deep etched at their corners with his smile. Ekko's tail beat the seat, his enormous velvet paws clenched together and eyes half-closed with joy. Neva and her brother, Yago, shouted their appreciation. Only Omen remained sitting, his head cocked upward and to the side as if listening and watching things only he could see and hear. Shar searched them out from the round, face lighting with pleasure. She clapped her hands and bounced on her feet, smile wide.

These were the moment Indris loved best.

"Thank you," Mari leaned in to him, threading her arm through his. "That was incredible!"

"I can't believe you were stationed in Avānweh and never saw a Seethe troupe perform before. Have you seen the Näsaré Flying Cirq?"

"The one your cousin, Neva, performs in?" Mari shook her head, smile faltering at the mention of Neva's name.

"We'll see it tomorrow, if you've the time."

"Let's play it by ear," Mari said without conviction as she looked away pensively.

Indris followed her gaze to where Nazarafine, Roshana, Siamak and their retinues were seated in a cordoned-off area of the arena. Ajo was there, as were Kembe of the Tau-se, his partner Ife and their tawny-maned children. Bensaharēn and Maselane sat together, nursing polished drinking horns and laughing quietly. Guards formed a shield wall around the royal-caste guests and their friends. A sullen-looking Martūm sat beside Ziaire who, in turn, was seated her with her hand in the lap of Esid of the Mandarhan. Esid was the sayf of a very wealthy Federationist Family, his parents recently killed when their wind-skiff crashed during a heavy storm. The young man had been trained by the Zienni Scholars in Kaylish and was reputed to have a prodigious mind and a sublime generosity of spirit. He was also a distant cousin of Vashne's. From Martūm's expression it appeared he knew he was no longer the only choice of the Federationist cabal.

"So what happens with the Feyassin, now that your father will be Asrahn?" Indris asked.

"Do you mean what happens with the Feyassin," Mari leaned closer and smiled, squeezing his hand, "or my place with them?"

"Either. Both."

"I can't serve my father," Mari said. She gazed at Indris shrewdly. "But there's something shady going on between Nazarafine and Roshana. I've been told we'll both be pariahs if we continue seeing each other. Do you know what they're planning?"

"They want us both for their own purposes," Indris shrugged. Let Rosha plan all she likes. As much as Neva was a potentially good match for the Näsarats, Indris was interested only in Mari. He looked at her, though her expression gave naught away in the vague shallows of night. Part of him wished his strange new gift would choose the moment to manifest itself, unfolding her thoughts for him to hear. A greater part chided himself, hating the thought of invading her privacy. "Do you care?"

"My head and my hearts are colliding. It's all a bit of a mess, and there are moments when I think I'm falling apart." She smiled at him the way he loved. "Are you here to save me, Indris?"

"I can't imagine anybody who needs it less."

"Good answer."

※ ※ ※

The two of them sat comfortably together, hands entwined. Down in the round the troupers were taking up their instruments. Conversations faltered, then stopped as the painfully beautiful voices of the Seethe troupers once again filled the night sky with wonder.

For the next hour the troupe continued with singing, dancing, and feats of acrobatics and martial skill. The Seethe war-troupers in glowing *serill* armour with their long, curved swords were a particular favourite. The face masks of their helms flickered from shape to shape: beautiful maidens, leering insane faces, crying skulls, to flaming eagle heads. Their armour shone all the colours of the spectrum, sounding like wind chimes as they moved.

When the performance was over, Indris and his friends waited for Shar. Mari was joking with Hayden, their laugher bringing a smile to Indris's face. Ekko loomed above them all, eyes wide, whiskers twitching as he inhaled the world and the stories it told him.

"Omen sees the Stormbringer approaching," the Wraith Knight intoned. "Her soul is bright, it bends and burns, around many subtle twists and turns. There is seething anger in her—not at Indris, but at another."

"Is he always like that?" Neva whispered to Indris.

"Pretty much."

The Wraith Knight rested his glazed hand on the hilt of his sword then froze, motionless as a statue. Smiles withered on faces as a grim-looking Femensetri came to join them. The ancient scholar caused a wide circle to appear as people fled her presence, whispering and pointing.

"Go on, the lot of you," Femensetri muttered in her crow's voice. She eyed the patrons darkly as they moved away in the casually hurried way of nervous people. "Keep going. Don't come back."

"Good evening, Femensetri," Indris forced a smile. "Your arrival is subtle as always."

"That's for your jokes, boy," Femensetri said, snapping her fingers in Indris's face before spitting on the ground. She looked left and right, nervous enough to make Indris mouth dry with apprehension. "We've business that can't wait, you and I. My learned colleagues of the Sēq are about to enforce their non-intervention policy, until they can unpucker and come to some form of overdue agreement. We need to act now."

She went on to swear, long and comprehensively, in High Avān. Once she ran out of colourful phrases in one language, she switched to Seethe to round things out. Even Shar, who arrived in time for the tirade, blanched at the vitriol.

"I'll help," Indris said, "Has a proper replacement even been found?"

"Doesn't matter," Neva observed. Mari looked at the woman askance. "Though you can't prove it was him, Rahn-Corajidin or those who wear his colours have already made one attempt on Vahineh's life. It won't be long before there're more."

"Neva is right." Yago stood with his thumbs hooked behind his weapons belt. "The Imperialists have scented blood with Rahn-Corajidin's victory at the Election. There're plenty of people who'll want to be in his good graces who don't see the Federationists as much of a threat right about now."

Mari looked over to where the cabal of Federationists were leaving the arena. Nazarafine looked around, found Mari, saw who she was with then made an imperious gesture for Mari to join her. Indris saw the gesture and snorted.

"She can't be serious," he muttered.

"I'll see her back to her qadir, then meet you after," Mari said. "Where will you be?"

"Safer if we find you, girl," Femensetri's voice was barely above a whisper. "We'll send word when it's done. Better there be no Rahn-Selassin than Corajidin get his hands on Vahineh and force her to Awaken somebody of his choosing. Still, Nazarafine, Rosha, and Siamak had best agree on a bloody replacement quickly!"

"Yago and I will come with you," Neva offered, Yago nodding his agreement.

Indris saw the smile freeze on Mari's face, the lazy, seductive twist of her lips almost a grimace. Mari flicked a glance to Neva, who was talking quietly with Yago. There was something in Mari's look, neither loss, nor hurt . . . more a speculation. The far away blur of doubt, gone far more slowly than it had appeared.

"I'll not be long, Mari," Indris said. He kissed Mari farewell. Her open mouth clung to his, even as he drew away. He could taste cinnamon on her tongue. Her fingers were entwined in his and she pulled his arms around to the small of her back.

"See you soon?" she asked, when she drew back far enough to speak.

"As soon as I can." He kissed her again, then joined Femensetri as she stalked out of the arena, his friends at his side.

Once they emerged onto the wide streets of the Caleph-Mahn—the mercantile precinct on a terrace not too far above the great basin of the city proper—Femensetri led them along a circuitous route. Down stairs. Across parks. Over bridges and through tunnels, always checking to ensure they were not followed. After crossing a bridge over a river filled to the brim by the recent rains in the mountain, she led them to a gondola station.

The old building was made of timber and stone with massive bronze wheels, taller than a tall man, protruding from it. Cables thick as Indris's wrist stretched up and down the mountain. Within minutes they heard the whine and creak of gondola cables as the spherical carriage bobbed into the station. Made of polished timber, steel, and brass, it hung suspended from the thick cable that stretched up and down the mountain face. The top hemisphere was set with thick glass windows, the bottom on a pivot and four large wheels that kept it stable. They took the gondola up the terraces of Mar-Silamari, the cabin redolent of old leather, polished teak and oil. Wind hummed through cracks around the window frames. The cabin swayed up the steep incline to the Caleph-Sayf—the elite precinct and home to the hotels that housed many sayfs, as well as the villas of wealthy members of Avânweh society.

Another short walk brought them to an older villa, which had seen better days. The windows were shuttered with iron and the entrance was secured by a heavy, fretwork iron door and a couple of armoured Tau-se nahdi. They looked Ekko over as he walked past, who was seemingly oblivious to their curiosity. Inside, *ilhen* crystals shed a parchment-coloured glow on stone floors and wood-panelled walls.

"She's this way," Femensetri said. "I had her brought here the night of the failed attempt on her life. Some of the female members of the Feyassin have been taking turns impersonating Vahineh at the Qadir Selassin, in case there's another attack."

The room where Vahineh lay was gloomy and chill. Stale sweat permeated the claustrophobic darkness. Air seemed still, almost solid the way it pressed upon Indris's skin. Femensetri's profile was a pallid crescent in the black, marred by the thumbprint of her mindstone. She gave orders for Indris to follow her, the others to remain outside the room, but to stay alert.

Femensetri went to stand beside the bed where it rested against the far wall, her expression inscrutable. Indris came to her side. A whimpering cry came from the huddled sheets. Femensetri whispered softly, coaxing myriad fractals of gelid white light to tumble within the sickle-like curve if her crook. Fingers of radiance stretched outward, revealing the person on the bed.

Indris fought down a gasp. Vahineh's face was gaunt, a skull inside skin stretched too tight across her brows and cheeks. Her eyes were sunken in their sockets. Her hair, what shanks of it remained, clung in matted ropes against her brow and neck. Beneath her light tunic, Indris could see the high ridges of her collarbones and shoulders where they threatened to press through flesh. Her mouth opened and closed like a landed fish. Her hands clawed in the sheets, though could not move far for the straps that secured her wrists to the bed.

"Her Awakening did this?" Indris found his mouth suddenly dry.

"If you could call it that," Femensetri leaned on her crook. "It wasn't something she was ever supposed to have experienced."

"The restraints?"

"She was becoming a danger to herself." Femensetri pointed towards the livid lines of fresh scars that marked Vahineh's body. "We never know who she is from one moment to the next. She can't control the Ancestral Conjunction. At the moment her mind is about as stable as a house of cards and it's getting worse."

"What do you need from me?"

"You were Awakened, boy!" she said with a hint of wonder. "I was there! I sensed what you did. You managed to not only prevent it from happening, but to reverse it with no ill-effects."

No ill-effects? He wanted to laugh. Even so, perhaps there was a way he could find out what he needed. One service begat another.

"I'm not trained to perform a Severance," he frowned at Femensetri. "What I did with Ariskander was from desperation, not skill."

"Six of one, a half-dozen of the other," she said with equanimity. "If we don't act, she'll die."

"I know. But if we do this, she may still die."

"Or not," she shrugged. "Which is a better chance than she'd otherwise have. I can guide you through what needs to be done, but I can't do it myself."

"Because of the schism in the Order?" Indris sat on the edge of the bed and took one of Vahineh's hands in his own. The skin was hot and paper dry, the skin of an old woman, not a young adult. "What's happening, sahai?"

Her expression turned venomous. "They seem to have forgotten our mandate is to learn from the past, to advise and educate in the present, to preserve the future. There are few of us suited for thrones and crowns, boy."

"I'd say none of us are suited."

"Which is why we agreed one would fit you well enough."

"Not a chance."

Femensetri grunted. To return to the days of the Mahjirahn—the Scholar monarchs—or worse, to become the enforcers of the will of a flawed monarchy and government, was terrifying. It was why the Sēq loved and hated in the abstract. A Sēq owned nothing, needed nothing, for they were provided everything in life by the Order. It was meant to remove avarice for mundane possessions, jealousy over power or the accumulation of wealth. To unleash such powers as they had for earthly advantage was a path the Sēq had proven they were ill equipped to follow.

"If you'd allowed Ariskander to Awaken you, none of this would've mattered. In time you could've unified the Order and the Teshri both under a common vision."

"I'll not be the puppet of the Sēq—or the Teshri."

"So you keep saying, yet you come when trouble calls. I think you protest your disinterest too much. You're too governed by your adherence to truths, rather than the pursuit of facts."

"You'd never know *you're* the one who wants *my* help," Indris murmured. "And since it's apparently going to be my head in a vise when people ask who did this because you're—"

"Choose your words carefully, boy." Femensetri's mindstone flared into nacreous life. The fractals spinning around her crook flared as bright as miniature suns. Indris watched, a pit forming in his stomach, as her Disentropic Stain swelled to become a snarling corona. "Strong as you are, you've things to learn."

He bowed his head as she reined in the magnificence of her power. She needed him. It was time to bargain. There was no guarantee Chaiya would succeed. Femensetri could get him access to what he needed without him being in her debt. There was also the matter of his ancestry, something which had never bothered him until Ariskander's comments after his death and Rosha's scheming.

"I do have things to learn. Some of them are the price for helping you," he said.

Femensetri scowled for a moment, her gaze thoughtful. She shrugged. "If it's in my power, you'll have what you want."

"Good. Once we're done here you can start with my family, then we'll see where that takes us."

❄ ❄ ❄

Vahineh muttered to herself, sentences that changed in pitch and cadence every few words. It was as if she spoke with the voices of a dozen or more people. The accents, intonation and inflection changed constantly. Her eyes were partially open, glistening slivers of white against sooty lashes.

"This will be difficult," Femensetri said. "Severance is usually done in concert, by two or more Masters. You're going to have to do it yourself. I'll be tuned with your mind—"

"No, you won't!" Indris snapped. Once Femensetri was in his mind, there was no telling what she would unearth. He could not afford for her to see into the deep recesses of his psyche, casting her crow-like gaze into places he barely understood himself.

"Don't be ridiculous!" she scoffed. "If I don't show you the way, you could kill her. Or worse pass her Legacy to somebody at random. If it makes you feel more comfortable, screen your mind. I promise I won't peek."

"You can count on that," he muttered.

Femensetri began her own preparations while Indris chanted the Inner Fortress. He visualised adamant walls, diamond shields with thousands of sharp facets around the core of his psychic apparatus. History, memory, hopes, wants, and dreams all cordoned off behind mental mirrors.

Indris felt the warm caress of Femensetri's mind against the outer perimeter of his psyche. As he suspected she probed the Inner Fortress here and there. Her touch was light, and she stopped when Indris glared at her. The Sēq Master shrugged as if to say he knew she was going to try, despite what he said. He gave her one last, hard look to show her he didn't appreciate the attempt regardless, before focusing on the task at hand. Seconds later, he felt the warm water of the Tuning run across his mind. At first it was like two powerful streams coming together. A cataract that crashed against rocks, the foaming, boiling rapids of two minds. After a few minutes the current calmed. The two streams became interspersed. The flow strengthened as they entered pséja—the marriage of minds.

They loitered in a moment between moments where time expanded. In a realm of pure thought, almost infinitely faster than speech, Femensetri showed Indris the way.

Neither of them needed to represent themselves through any kind of construct or metaphor. Their communication was as intimate as the two halves of a shared mind could be, each with the intrinsic understanding of the other. Indris felt the mass of Femensetri's psyche. Its power. Its age. Its majesty. A primal part of him was in awe of her brilliance, wanting to lose itself in such solar radiance and never return. Yet he resisted the urge, and Femensetri led him, and together they flowed through the talus Vahineh's mind had become.

There were no cohesive thoughts. Her representation of herself was fractured. Worse than fractured—it was shattered. Her mind was a thing of canted mirrors, their surfaces cracked and jagged as if struck by hammers. Indris saw Vahineh as she saw herself. Childhood conflicted with adolescence at war with adulthood. Yet there were other faces. Other voices that yelled and pleaded and demanded. In her broken mirrors Vahineh saw herself as dozens of people: her Ancestors, all clamouring around the jagged rents of the past. Indris wanted to cup his hands to his ears to drown out the din. Femensetri held him close. Together they raced through the maze of rattling mirrors, under the eyes and mouths and ears and fragmented faces of Vahineh's Ancestors, until they found *her*.

She stood, a whirling dervish of light and shadow, at the centre of the storm. Vahineh was like a marionette stretched between scores of clanking chains at wrist and ankle. Bleached of colour, garbed in tattered rags, she span in a circle with arms thrown wide and head flung back. Eyes staring and mouth slack. Shards of memory span about her, a lethal cyclone of detritus. Indris felt his own mind assailed, nicked and cut as he moved through the maelstrom to fly beside her.

A sense of urgency washed over him. Femensetri's wordless commands resonated in his mind. He circled Vahineh, his speed growing. Eventually, battered and torn, he and she seemed to be motionless relative to the world spinning about them in a chaotic shadow play.

Indris focussed his mind into a chisel. With as much force as he could muster, he slammed the hard edge of his psyche against the chains that held her. The chains rang, rippling as if made more of fluid than metal. Above and below, space roiled like an ocean in a storm. Blue-white light lanced into them, cold and painful. Vahineh's mind was drowning in the turmoil of the Font and Ĩa was reluctant to let her go.

Shards of her mind, her soul and those echoes of her Ancestors pierced him. They sliced fragments from his Fortress. The casual weapons of her broken mind flayed him. Still, Indris stuck at her chains unrelentingly. Links broke away to strike him. He reeled from each impact, yet refused to abandon her. One by one, the chains that held her broke away with a clash of falling bells.

He tenderly took Vahineh in his arms as the last chain broke. Comforted her, his mind bathing her in warm softness, even as he flexed his will to slow them from their reckless whirl.

Holding her tight, Indris brought her to a gentle stop. He coaxed her to seal the cracks in the mirrors of her mind. To find and hold on to her sense of her living self, rather than the selves of the dead. Mirrors fell from the invisible walls. Puffed away into fragments so small they were little more than powder. Images, though bent from true, were once more whole: Vahineh herself, no older than a child on the cusp of adolescence, surrounded by the falling autumnal leaves of her experiences.

Indris opened a window in her mind. Light from the outside cleared the darkness that pooled at her core. Together they walked towards the mirror and the smiling young woman whose visage seemed so at peace.

Then he felt the sharp stab against his Inner Fortress.

He reeled. Try as he might to hold on to Vahineh, he could not. He was wrenched away, mind battered, hoping he had done enough.

❋ ❋ ❋

Through the pain that threatened to split his head, Indris saw Femensetri standing over him, mindstone burning. Flares leaped from it, to collapse against her forehead. The blue-green-black opals of her eyes shone like the panels of a lantern.

Yet it was *another* Sēq Master who plied Indris's mind with razors of thought, besieging his Inner Fortress in an attempt to claim the treasures of his mind. His head felt hot, lanced through with pain as he came to one knee, hand on Changeling's hilt.

"No!" Indris roared. On instinct he sent a thought lance to pierce the prying Master between the eyes. The woman reeled, mouth a lopsided tear in her face. He caught sight of Femensetri surrounded by five other Sēq Masters. Their crooks flared into an incandescence that almost blinded him. Disentropic Stains thrashed as they collided, casting long shadows on the ahm. The other Masters were tame compared to the Stormbringer; slick in their silks with mindstones polished, smooth and small as fingernails. One of the Masters faltered, then collapsed. Shortly after another one reeled. Femensetri's face was lit with a savage smile. Shadow spiralled around her mindstone.

The man who had fallen away from Femensetri came to stand over Indris, levelling his crook at Indris chest. Indris drew and struck. Changeling howled. The Master's crook belled, shards splintering away as it broke. With a muffled curse, shock etched onto his features, the man stumbled back. Before Indris could defend himself, another Master flung a glittering net of light around Indris, which engulfed his body, and squeezed.

Shar and Ekko stormed through the door, weapons drawn. They were blown back by a spinning ring of light that also brought down part of the wall. Rubble crashed from the ceiling, his friends buried under dust and debris.

"Stormbringer!" the oldest of the Masters thundered. He was a tall, powerfully built man with feline features, angular and proud under long white-blond hair. Tongues of honey coloured fire lashed around him, almost obscuring the man's features in heat haze. Through the pain, Indris remembered him as Zadjinn. An Erebus from the time of the Awakened Empire. "Relent or I kill the pup you so ably trained!"

Femensetri cast a glance at Indris, calculating. The web tightened, biting into Indris's skin. It sizzled with power, burning him. He bit down on a scream of pain with only limited success.

Expression apologetic, Femensetri dampened her power. She looked at the other Masters with disdain. "How weak the Order has become, if you are what passes for Masters."

"I saw such things . . ." the Master who had looked into Indris's mind murmured, hair in disarray. Her eyes were still unfocused. "The things you know. The things you have seen and done."

Zadjinn frowned at Indris before casting a curious glance at Vahineh.

"Bring the Stormbringer, the apostate, and the girl to Amer-Mahjin," Zadjinn commanded. "The others are of no consequence. Collapse this dung heap on their heads, and be done with it."

"No!" Indris yelled. He struggled against the binding net, felt the threads of energy burning through his clothes and searing his skin. The smell of burned flesh was in his nostrils. He glared at the Sēq Master who had cast his binding. The pressure in his mind swelled rapidly, seeming to expand beyond his skull, bypassing his Disentropic Stain. He spoke in a voice he barely recognised as his own. "Release us! Now!"

Indris's voice rolled around the room, filling the corners, then rumbling back across the people around him. The Master he had targeted began to relax her control over Indris's bindings when Zadjinn lashed Indris with a whip of fire. Indris yelled with the pain, losing the tenuous control he had with his new, and uncertain, powers.

The Master sneered at him and spitefully clenched the web around Indris. The air was forced out of his lungs. His bones creaked. Blood welled from deep cuts.

The world seemed to splinter. Cracks formed where they should not. Walls, floor, and ceiling cracked and fell away.

Vertigo.

Nausea.

Darkness.

He shrieked as he tried desperately to breathe then all his senses focussed into a single point of a nothing, which was everything, and he screamed as the world writhed and he saw—

14

"DECISIONS ARE LIKE STONES, YET YOUR APPROACH TO THEM SHOULD BE AS WATER."

—Nimjé, Gnostic Assassin of the Ishahayan and Master of Spies for the Great House of Näsarat (371st of the Shrīanese Federation)

DAY 353 OF THE 495TH YEAR OF

THE SHRĪANESE FEDERATION

Poet Master Bensaharēn had said to Mari that schooling her in patience had been one of the hardest tasks he had ever faced. She had suffered through hours of her teacher having her sit and do nothing, time she could have spent doing almost everything else she found more important. Fidgeting constantly on the inside, mind flitting across the lessons she enjoyed more, Mari had learned enough composure to, if not fool Bensaharēn, at least allow him to accept with good grace she was not going to master everything quite so easily.

Patience was something she had learned, but still struggled with. After hours of waiting for Indris, Mari made speed to the armoury of the Qadir Sûn in search of armour. The streets had become dangerous since the Accession vote, and she was not going to take the chance of being knifed in the dark by some zealot who masked himself in the fervor of a patriot. The best armour she could find was an uncomfortable and ill-fitting leather hauberk, studded with steel scales that showed the rust of disuse. Swearing at the laziness of the armourer, regretting not having something that fit, Mari left the qadir to find Indris and their friends.

He said he'd come, she thought. *Unless he was unable to.* The thought he may be unwilling flickered across her mind, followed shortly by an image of Neva's lovely face. She banished her doubts with a snarl. Indris should have been back by now, she was sure of it. Something must have gone wrong.

Spurred on by a growing dread—ears tuned to the distant sounds of fighting in the streets, and the shrill whistles of the huqdi, the street dogs who were more thugs and ruffians than warriors—Mari held her sheathed Sûnblade in her hand as she jogged to the Qadir Bey. The guards there had neither seen, nor heard, from Indris. Another, faster run took her to the Qadir Selassin where Martūm's indolent guards were uncivil and unhelpful. The man who made the improper suggestion as to how they could spend their time together was lucky to have kept his teeth in his head, saved only by Mari's constantly growing concern.

On her desperate way to the Qadir Näsarat, her dislike of Roshana at war with her doubt, Mari saw squads of kherife racing towards the sullen glow of a fire in the distance. Jaw set, Mari followed them to where a small crowd of people were gathered around a collapsed villa, along with a small hemisphere of the mountain that was broken around it. Flames licked at exposed beams of wood, but the rest of the stone looked as if it had been pounded by a hammer the size of a house.

The kherife were speaking with some Tau-se nahdi, all of whom were covered in cuts and rock dust. Blood glistened darkly on their fur. Mari edged closer to hear what was being said. She had to control herself when she heard that the villa had belonged to the Scholar-Marshall. When she heard there had been others inside, she shoved through the cordon to where the Tau-se and the kherife stood.

"Who do you think—" one of the kherife began, then recognised Mari for who she was. He and the other kherife gave her the Second Obeisance, fingertips to their hearts as they bowed. "How may we help you, Pah-Mariamejeh?"

Mari bowed her head, as much in respect for the kherife's manners, as to gather her thoughts. "What happened here?"

"We're not certain, pah," one of the Tau-se replied in his deep, plush voice. "We were guarding the exterior of the villa, with orders not to enter. We do—"

"Who was inside?" *Am I speaking too quickly?* She wondered. *Is this what panic feels like?*

"The Scholar Marshall and some of her guests, including ser-Neva and ser-Yago, the Sky Lord's grandchildren."

"Are they . . .?"

The Tau-se became stiff, eyes wide. Their tails dusted the street in agitation. "We were rendered unconscious, pah. When we regained our senses, the villa was as you see it. We have been clearing rubble with the help of the kherife, and some of the local residents, but have found no sign of the Scholar-Marshall, or her guests."

"How long ago?"

"Almost three hours, pah"

Mari looked at the massive weight of stone. Felt the heat of the flames even at a distance. She opened her mouth, and sniffed, trying to fight back the warmth of the tears without touching her eyes. *Could anybody have survived that, for so long?*

Heedless of the danger, Mari joined the front ranks of those who helped clear away the rubble. By the time they managed to enter what remained of the building, she hoped she would be too tired to cry at what she saw there.

✳ ✳ ✳

Two hours or so later, Mari had not been listening to the clocks and the smoke and the overcast obscured the stars, she dropped the last load of rubble she could carry. Every muscle ached. Her eyes were red raw from shallow tears and smoke. Her skin and hair reeked. Other than the Tau-se, who seemed incapable of fatigue, there were none who remained from the workers she had initially joined. She vaguely remembered being told to rest, as much as she remembered with shame her ungracious, and often hostile, responses. But they had been right then, and there was nobody left to tell her to rest now.

On unsteady feet, Mari shuffled back to the Qadir Sûn. The guards in their polished armour, with their mirror-bright shields and spears, looked at her bedraggled figure in consternation, but said nothing. Some looked at her with compassion, others kept their faces as cold as chiselled stone, eyes resolutely forward, avoiding any form of contact or recognition. Such was sende that a person could, upset, burned, and filthy, walk the halls of a qadir without being questioned, or offered the assistance she did not ask for.

Staggering into the antechamber she had started from, Mari stopped in shock.

Shar, Ekko, Omen, and Neva were battered and bruised. Hayden looked the worst. Pale beneath a deep cut on his brow, face dirty, two fingers on his left hand bound together.

"Where have you been?" she wanted to shout, but found herself grabbing faces and kissing them in relief. She even took a surprised Neva in a rib-creaking embrace, so glad was she to see them alive. But not all of them. She grabbed Shar's arm as she snapped, "What happened? Where is Indris?" Then, remembering the others, she said, "And what about Femensetri and Vahineh?"

"Taken." Shar said miserably.

"*What?* When? By who?" Mari asked, although she thought she knew the answer to the last question. She rose to her feet, attaching her Sûnblade to her weapons belt. How had her father or brothers known where to look? There would be no time to waste.

"Too long ago, and we've no idea." Neva was furious, her face streaked with dirt and blood. "We've been waiting here for hours!"

"Can you tell me why my friends were kept waiting?" Mari snapped at the Sergeant-Major of the Sûnguard, who stood nearby. "People could've been searching all this time!"

"Apologies, Pah-Mariam," he said. "Knight-Lieutenant Sûn fa Navid was under orders not to admit anybody to the qadir. Your friends told me their tale when I started my watch, so I brought them here. Unfortunately, you were absent and nobody knew where you had gone."

Mari winced at the subtle rebuke. Her absence did not excuse Navid, though. Nazarafine's nephew was a warrior-poet from the Sûn Isles who had done his training at the Saidani-sûk, the Four Blades School of the Great

House of Sûn. He was a proud and prickly man eager for recognition and glory, yet had done little worthy of either. Navid was in need of a few reminders that not all orders needed to be followed slavishly, no matter whether he was his aunt's favoured relative, or not. For now, there were more important things to be done.

"Tell me what you know," Mari said to her friends.

"Never saw 'em enter," Hayden muttered, "nor leave."

"We tried to help," Ekko rumbled. "Whoever was responsible collapsed part of the corridor leading to the room before we could get a look at them, though. Then the rest of the ceiling followed. We were trapped for almost an hour in the rubble." The Tau-se looked at Omen with respect. "Were it not for Sassomon-Omen being there to help, working in the flames as he did, we may not have been so fortunate."

"Such is the task in times of strife, to aid, to risk, to save a life," Omen hummed absently as he stared into the grass at the base of a potted plant.

"Whoever it was, clearly were after either Indris, Femensetri, or Vahineh," Neva said, looking askance at Omen. "Yago's gone to tell our grandfather what's happened. This is another of many attacks in the city over the past couple of days. Tensions are high all over after the election."

"We must get Indris back!" Shar said, cutting off Neva's train of thought. Her orange-gem eyes were bright with unshed tears.

"It is true that we must act,"—Omen said—"let us not wait when we can attack."

"I'm likin' the sound of that song," Hayden nodded. His eyes looked slightly unfocussed. Ekko growled, tail slicing air.

"Hayden," Mari said, "you're wounded. Maybe you should let us do this."

"I'm fixin' on gettin' me some payback, young miss." Hayden's jaw clenched. "Just try and keep me away."

"But where do we look?" Neva asked, exasperated. "We don't know who has them or why they were taken."

"I've an idea," Mari said. In her mind there were few people who would want to, or could, take Indris and Femensetri. She knew *she* could not defeat Indris in a fight. She was a better sword-fighter, yet his scholar training gave him an advantage she could not match without salt-forged steel. Belamandris, now he knew what he was dealing with, was probably also a fair match for Indris, sword-on-sword. However it would take a special combination of people to enter a guarded villa, defeat Indris and Femensetri, then steal away with a third hostage. Given the third hostage was Vahineh, the list of candidates dropped considerably.

Mari remembered her conversation with her father in Amnon. His obsession with the witches. He had confessed how he had turned to them for an answer to his illness. Nadir had spoken of nahdi armies and witches brought back from Tanis.

"Neva?" Mari turned to the tall gryphon-rider. "Do you think your grandfather would spare the time to see me?"

"Why?"

"Because he's the Arbiter of the Change and I don't want to go kicking over a wasps nest without him knowing why."

"He's a great admirer of yours," Neva admitted, "if not of your family. What do you think he could do for you?"

"Give me some advice on how far I can go before I walk the wrong line of the law in his city."

"When do you want to see him?"

By way of answer, Mari drew her over-robe on over her armour and gestured towards the door.

"I don't know how long I'll be gone," Mari said to the Sergeant-Major. "When you've the chance, please let Rahn-Nazarafine know I've gone with my friends to see the Arbiter of the Change. She can send people after me. Or not. I really don't care."

"The rahn won't be happy, Pah-Mariam," the soldier replied.

"It's going around."

Mari led her friends via the most direct route out of the qadir, which also took them far from the galleries housing the royal chambers. Bound-caste servants in pale yellow tunics bowed their heads as Mari and the others passed. Sûnguards stood at their stations, polished cuirasses and gold-washed scale hauberks shining. The guard's tall shields were polished so brightly it seemed to Mari she walked down a hall of mirrors. Nobody tried to stop them. Silently she thanked the Sergeant-Major for giving her the time to do what she needed, before anybody foolishly tried to impede her.

Even at this hour of the night the streets were well lit. To the south the brightly coloured cloud of the Ancestor's Shroud loomed over the horizon, surrounded by the sequined black velvet of the night sky. The Ancestor's Eye blazed a brilliant blue in the impenetrable depths of the empty cowl around it. Rough-edged ponds made from sheets of red stone surrounded layered pools, red-beaked swans drifting like obsidian shadows on the rippled water. There came the faint twang and hum of cables from a nearby gondola as it made its way down the terraces. The air was cool. Perfumed by wet grass and eucalyptus. Mari and her friends followed serpentine paths, where lantern posts and hollow-eyed statues of Avānweh's long-dead great were clad in the lush finery of orange trumpet vine.

Crossing a small bridge they came to the Caleph-Sayf. Armed members of the warrior-caste stood in doorways, or escorted their patrons with watchful gazes. Some were nahdi, while others wore the colours of a Great House or Family. Avān, Tau-se, Human or Seethe, there was work these days for those handy with steel. Those who could afford it paid well to ensure their blood stayed in their veins where it belonged.

Mari schooled herself to patience, though her natural instinct was to run as quickly as she could to Ajomandyan's door. She wanted to laugh at herself. Or cry. Indris, the child of her family's oldest enemies, and she had developed feelings for him. It went against everything she had been taught, which was perhaps why she allowed her feelings to grow. Her mother had always said Mari's contrary nature would be the end of her, though it had not been.

Yet.

There were times, curled in his arms, his breath sweet and warm against the back of her neck, when she had entertained the thought of a simple life. In the drowsy golden reverie of dawn she had wondered whether he was like her other lovers, the women and men who had come, lingered a while, then left her life. Then she thought of how it felt when she was not with him. The yawning ache that made her want to find him. To talk, to ask even the most banal of questions for the sole reason he would speak and the timbre of his voice would thrill her. In the past she had always managed to disguise her emotional apathy with bravado and the illusion of excitement for the life around her. It worked most of the time, until her own ennui infected her partner and they drifted listlessly apart.

Emotion had crept up on her, masked in all the usual safe feelings, yet hiding something dangerous. Even in her own head she could not bring herself to say the word, for fear saying it would either damn it, or make it real, either of which might cause it to die.

She had faced death many times, but now—confronted with the thought of a life . . . she had never been more unsure of herself. It had been so simple, when she had not cared deeply enough to be bothered overly much with the consequences of her actions. Had she died, it was only her life that would be lost. But now, the way she felt about Indris—thought of losing him almost choking her with panic—she wondered how so many people managed to feel so deeply, for so long, and not go mad. An admission of love, like the revelation of guilt, the confession of wrongdoing, and the taking of life, was something you could never undo.

"We're here," Neva's voice broke her reverie.

The Näsaré villa was a tiered home built into a wide defile in the mountain. A beautiful bronze awning shaped like a gryphon's beak shaded the tall keyhole door, itself banded in iron with a robust fretwork grille in front of it. Armoured soldiers in the Näsaré blue and grey—armed with spear, axe and heavy bow—guarded the door.

Neva led Mari and the others through long corridors and up sweeping flights of stairs until they reached a small circular sitting room. The walls were covered in blue and white tiles, the ceiling a dome of blue-stained glass. Mari rested her head against one of the windows where it looked out over the gardened interior of the villa. Ferns, figs, and gardenias grew amongst miniature pines, clinging to the cracks between sharp-edged rocks.

"My granddaughter says you want leave to cause havoc in my city," Ajo's voice came from the circular doorway nearby. The two-century old sayf looked somewhat dishevelled in his sweeping grey over-robe, the white wings of his hair swept back from tanned aquiline features. He leaned on his gryphon-headed cane. Yago was behind him, a younger version of his grandfather. Ajo looked Mari and her companions up and down, his expression rueful. "At least you're polite enough to ask first, despite obviously being in the wars already."

"I need to understand how far I'm allowed to go before I cross the line of the law." Mari said. "As the Arbiter of the Change it's your task to oversee the smooth transition of power, but—"

"That gryphon has fled the eyrie," Neva muttered.

"True," Ajo replied, looking at Neva with hard eyes. "But not to the point where it can not be brought back. Why do you ask, Pah-Mariam?"

"Because I fear my father has made some more poor choices."

Ajo gestured for them all to sit as Mari explained what had happened. "I'm sure you understand I want to find Indris, Femensetri, and Vahineh before something else terrible happens," she said when she had concluded, "But I also need to speak with my father about our problems. Ignoring them won't make them go away."

"How does your father know who murdered Yashamin?" the Sky Lord asked softly. "If what you say is true, there are none save your trusted circle who were privy to this."

"I've no idea. Nadir was the one who told me, though he didn't tell me where they learned what they did. True to his word, there were mercenaries who assaulted Nazarafine and her escort on their way to the Qadir Sûn."

"I had heard of this," Ajo said. He rested his hands on the head of his cane, his chin on his hands. "Most troubling. Is it in any way connected with the savage murders, or the abductions, happening in my city?"

"I doubt it."

"Grandfather," Yago urged, "we must help them find Indris! He's our blood."

And somebody Roshana is trying to marry your beautiful granddaughter to. Mari flicked a glance at Neva. The tall gryphon-rider was dashing in her flying leathers, long-limbed and hair tousled, beautiful no matter the grime and dried blood on her skin. She was the kind of woman Indris liked.

"What proof do you have?" Ajo asked.

"They've no proof!" Roshana said from behind Mari. Nazarafine, Siamak, Ziaire, and Martûm were with her, all looking as if they had dressed hastily and ridden hard to get there. Martûm, hunched into an expensive over-robe of indigo silk, stitched with amethysts, stared fitfully about. Bensaharēn blinked owlishly, his hair escaping his usual tight ponytail and braids. Yet there was nothing remotely tired about the way he gripped his sheathed sword. Roshana came to stand in front of Ajo, hands on her hips. "I apologise, Sayf-Näsaré. This is a private matter, which doesn't need your attention. For all we know, this was another attack on us by the Humans."

"Private matter?" Mari asked incredulously. "And the Humans? Seriously? You sound like my father."

"Mari!" Ziaire shook her head quickly. "Best leave this alone."

"I have been told much already," Ajo said. He glowered at Roshana, Nazarafine and Siamak. "Many disturbing things have come to my attention. Is it true you have decided to Sever Vahineh from her Awakening?"

"What business is it of yours?" Roshana asked, chin lifted beyond the point of belligerence.

"Everything that happens as part of the Change is my business, girl!" Ajo rapped his cane against the tiled floor with a sharp crack. "Look to you. A rahn for weeks, all puffed up and itching for carnage! Your father would never—"

"My father is dead and saw fit to Awaken me—"

"Because Indris refused!" Shar spat. "Never forget you have everything you do because of him! Your Great House still exists, because of him!"

"Watch your mouth," Roshana snapped. "Because Indris puts up with you, don't think I will."

"Regardless of how it was said, it's the truth," Mari countered.

"And what about the Stormbringer?" Hayden asked. "Or young Miss Vahineh, who you said you wanted to help?"

Nazarafine's eyes looked tired and sad amidst deep crow's-feet in her rounded apple face. The portly woman looked her age and then some. Mari noted more white in her hazelnut hair.

"We balance on a knife's edge." Nazarafine said wearily. Ziaire sat beside her, taking the woman's hands in her own. Nazarafine gestured to Ziaire, who produced a rolled parchment, which she handed to Ajo.

"What is it?" Mari asked. She stood. She could see the black and red ribbons and the rearing black stallion of the Erebus that were affixed to the document. Ajo broke the seal and read the message.

"It's Corajidin's demand for Nazarafine to observe the Third Dictate. He demands Vahineh be delivered for examination into her participation in the murder of Rahn-Erebus fe Yashamin."

"It's an excuse to escalate hostilities," Roshana said. "He hopes to gain the sympathies of the moderates. Vengeance for the murder of a loved one is something most of us understand."

"What's our next course of action?" Martūm looked to each of them. "Does anybody know whether Femensetri and Indris managed to—?"

"Keep your tongue behind your teeth!" Roshana cut the air with her hand. Her features danced from anger, to calm, to sorrow, and back. Mari looked at her with a kind of sick horror, wondering whether Roshana, too, would be overcome by the force of her recent Awakening. Mari further wondered what it would be like to have the memories of a murdered father in her head.

❀ ❀ ❀

"Martūm was about to say they don't know whether Indris and Femensetri were successful in Severing Vahineh from her Awakening." Shar's voice was hard.

Roshana glared at the Seethe woman, though said nothing to refute her. "It's to save her life."

"I do not doubt such is part of it." Ajo leaned forward in his chair. "So. You took it upon yourselves to appoint a new rahn, without conferring with anybody? This is why we have the Ascension Role."

"The rahns ultimately decide who Ascends," Ziaire said reasonably. "And if Roshana, Nazarafine, and Siamak all agree on a candidate, they'll carry the vote."

"The law states a Mahj, the Asrahn, or a few members of the Magistratum, such as the Secretary-Marshall, the Arbiter-Marshall, or the Scholar-Marshall, can appoint a rahn. You are none of those things. You would have robbed your fellow rahns of their chance to be heard. It is not so different from what you accuse Corajidin of doing.

"And while I do not challenge the legal right to suggest a candidate, I do challenge the right to withhold the knowledge of a murder against one of the royal-caste. By law you are all implicated—"

Roshana snorted. "For the love of the Ancestors you can't—"

"Be so kind as to keep your mouth shut," Ajo growled. He pointed his cane at Roshana. "You, who knew of Yashamin's murder. Who proclaimed a Jahirojin! Your abuse of power and manipulation of truths is equally as vile as Corajidin's."

"You forget yourself old man," Roshana snapped.

"I forget nothing, girl," Ajo said softly, eyes hard as chisels. "I'm Arbiter of the Change, and you had best remember your place."

"What can we do to Sever Vahineh's Awakening . . . and save her life?" Martūm asked impatiently, his closing words seemingly an after-thought.

"Your motives are far from altruistic," Ziaire said, hearing Martūm's hesitation and levelling a dark look at him. "Just who does settle your debts these days, Martūm? I'm reasonably certain it's not the Banker's House or the Mercantile Guild anymore. Is it the Malefacti you've turned to, or the League of Silence, perhaps? No, they're not forgiving of delinquency. A patron from the Hundred—"

"My situation is none of your concern!" The words tumbled out of Martūm's mouth.

"Peace!" Ajo said. "For the Ancestors' sake, would you all take a deep breath. Think this through. Your approach to helping Vahineh is laudable, the methods highly questionable. Hired swords attacked Nazarafine and her companions—one of whom happened to be Vahineh—on their way to the Qadir Sûn. But you've no proof of wrongdoing on the Erebus's behalf. Only conjecture they were involved, based on Nadir's drunken ramblings."

"A man who sells his sword for gold," Omen hummed, "reminded us of hearts turned cold, of spiders and webs held iron fast, of villains from the recent past."

There was silence in the room. Ajo looked at Omen as if he did not know what he was looking at.

"I figure Omen's talking about that Nix fellow," Hayden offered. "The last of them bravos mentioned something about being caught in a web and he ain't ever getting out. He reckoned whoever he worked for would do for his family, too. It ain't much, no doubt, but it's something."

"It is thin," Ajo shook his head, "and not something I could take to the Arbiter's Tribunal for them to act on."

Mari went to the Sky Lord and rested her hands over his, smiling her slow and lazy smile. "We saw him in the Maladhi-sûk talking with Ravenet of the Delfineh the day the Sēq captured the lich there. The Maladhi were ever the shadowy killers for the Erebus. The Delfineh were no better. Add a malign Nomad to that, and surely it's enough to raise questions! If they were involved, it was to execute my father's will. Is it enough I could start kicking over some rocks?"

"I forbid it, Mari," Nazarafine said. "You're the Knight-Colonel of the Feyassin—"

"But I'm *not*." Mari refused to look at Nazarafine, though heard the matronly woman's sharp intake of breath. "Seriously, how could I be, with my father as Asrahn? Even if we came to some common ground on what happened between us, I could never serve him."

"You could serve as my new Poet Master," Nazarafine said. "Or take on your mother's title. Her estates of Dahrain on the shores of the Sûn Isles are there for you, should you want them."

"There is always a place in my household, Pah-Mariam." Siamak smiled shyly. "We lost almost everybody of experience when Far-ad-din left, and the Teshri invaded Amnon. You would be of immense value to me in Bey Prefecture."

"But it would all be conditional on me doing whatever you wanted of me." Mari shook her head regretfully. "I think I need to be my own person for a while. That means going after Indris and the others on my own terms. Remember, Vahineh will be a point of contention for my father as well as a point of pride. He will want her brought to justice, no matter what."

"You'll be just another ashinahdi," Roshana said, "alone and friend-less—and that's how you'll die if you proceed with this. Worse, your father may take you into custody and then where would you be? You know every-thing we've planned and at some point, everybody reveals what they know. As Ajo said, think this through."

Before Mari could respond, Siamak said thoughtfully, "Hardly friend-less. You did a great service in saving my city and my Prefecture, Mariam. You gave your life willingly and I would be a poor rahn, unworthy of my station, if I were to let you do this alone."

"And I'll do what I can." Ziaire smiled at Mari. "I knew fixing you up when you came to my door would be a mistake. But I'd be a poor friend to desert you now, when you're becoming even more interesting."

"*Far* from friendless," Shar said, building on Siamak's words. Ekko and Hayden nodded their agreement. Both Neva and Yago stepped forward. Shar moved across the room to kiss a surprised Mari. The Seethe woman almost thrummed with excitement, her orange eyes blazing, skin flickering like a candle.

Roshana came to stand next to a downcast Nazarafine. The two spoke quietly for what seemed a long time, then nodded. Mari looked on apprehensively. Regardless of the cessation of hostilities they had shared in Amnon, the fact remained Roshana was a dyed-in-the-wool daughter of the Näsarat. She had been taught as a child the long list of crimes the Erebus had committed. Had no doubt learned by rote all the various blows and counterblows, the seemingly endless list of Jahirojins and Wars of the Long Knife the two houses had unleashed on each other. Now the memories of her Ancestors were in Roshana's mind, to be played out as if she had witnessed them herself: including the memory of her own father's assassination at Corajidin's hands. Roshana need merely open her consciousness to the long line of her Ancestors to be reminded why she hated the Erebus. The fact Mari had tried to help break the cycle was like damming a river with a pebble.

Mari watched as Roshana smoothed the folds of her suede over-robe. There were no rings on Roshana's calloused hands. No chains about her neck, nor jewels at her ears. Hers were the hands and the sensibilities of a soldier who ever saw the cloud of war looming. She was more like Corajidin than she knew, or would ever admit.

"I recognise the inevitable," Roshana said finally. "Understand me clearly, Mari: I'm not happy, but you'll go ahead and do this with or without my support. At least if I help you, I may have some control over the outcome."

"I'll not take your fury to my Father's door," Mari warned.

"If your father has abducted a Prince of the Blood of the Great House of Näsarat," Roshana said icily, "then it's for me to resolve the matter using whatever means are at my disposal."

"If you can prove he has done so," Ajo agreed. "Otherwise you will be breaking the law and will be subject to its penalties."

"I'll burn that bridge when I come to it. Pray we're all not in the middle when it happens."

15

"VENGEANCE IS THE CONFESSION OF A WOUNDED HEART."

—Marak-ban, Sēq Knight to the Sussain (345th Year of the Shrīanese Federation)

DAY 354 OF THE 495TH YEAR OF

THE SHRĪANESE FEDERATION

Stretching the kinks from his muscles, Corajidin observed his inner circle as they sat around a large octagonal table. The mother of pearl top had a slick, almost oily nacre under lamplight. Nearby several braziers were filled with firestones, the glowing red rocks washing the black walls, floor, and vaulted ceiling with a bloody glow. Scores of gold-plated skulls were arrayed on the walls, fanged mouths wide and silently screaming, eye sockets empty: trophies of those who had defied the Great House of Erebus and not lived to regret it.

Corajidin had staffed his house almost as it had been in the days of the Awakened Empire. Kasraman was his Master of House, perfect training for the day when he became rahn, or more. Golden Belamandris would be his Poet Master, the shining hero who drew the finest soldiers in the realm to Corajidin's colours. Feyd was his Master of Arms, the old tribesman more cunning than most of his so-called noble counterparts amongst the Shrīanese elite and royal castes. Tahj-Shaheh brought the tactics of subterfuge and piracy as Sky Master and Master of the Fleet. Jhem would serve admirably as Master of Assassins; something Nix would need to come to terms with, or find his path elsewhere. The man was like to become another Thufan and use what he knew more for his own purposes than his Master's, and that was something Corajidin could not abide. Wolfram would continue to serve as rajir, his most trusted Lore Master. And, in the future, Wolfram would do so openly, rather than from hiding. Everybody who counted knew Wolfram advised the Great House of Erebus, and it was only the banality of tradition for nobody to mention it.

Since the Accession vote, more followers had come into the light. Or, in some cases, had taken a step closer to the edge of shadow. The Malefacti and the League of Silence had sent their advocates to open negotiations, and both the Banker's House and the Mercantile Guild had made overtures now that it was clear Corajidin was a man of what appeared to be extraordinary means. The bankers and merchants knew too well that people with ambitions would always need money to grow them, no matter how much money they already had.

"What news of Vahineh?" Corajidin asked.

"She has not been released into our custody," Jhem said.

"I'll confront Roshana about it at the Assembly today." Corajidin's tone revealed his irritation. "I'm more concerned about retrieving what we can from Mahsojhin before too many of the witches are freed. There are weapons in there, I'm sure of it!"

"If memory serves," Wolfram mused, "the witches of Mahsojhin did have a powerful weapon they were developing. I was young at the time, a novice, so I only heard the rumours. Whatever it was never got unleashed against the Sēq."

"And there's no mention of it in history," Kasraman said. "If it existed, chances are it's still there. Certainly the Rahnbathra was a disappointment when it came to finding something we could use for our cause."

"Except this." Belamandris held up a curved knife in a verdigris sheath. "Salt-forged steel—something that will come in handy when I face Indris again."

Kasraman and Wolfram gave the weapon sidelong glances, subtly distancing themselves from it. The Emissary looked at it disinterestedly.

"You'll need more than that to defeat Indris," the Emissary smiled. "Besides, the Sēq have everything of any real value that was in the Mahsojhin. They're like crows, flying over the fields and picking up everything shiny to take back to their nest."

"Including the Destiny Engine we found in Fiandahariat." Kasraman's voice was rough with frustration.

"Then you, Wolfram, and Kimiya will go to the Mahsojhin," Corajidin said. "I'll not be robbed again. Protect whatever you find."

"I'll go with them," the Emissary said. "Even with the Emphis Mechanism we'll need to take extreme care in unfolding the Temporal Labyrinth."

"Without destroying the city in the process," Feyd muttered.

"Will you announce the disbanding of the Feyassin today?" Belamandris asked, his ruby scale armour and scarlet over-robe sullen in the ruddy glow of the braziers. "And what about Mari? Will she—"

"Your sister's fate is undecided," Corajidin said. The question gave him the beginning of a stress headache.

"I understand you resent her, but she did what she thought was right."

"Is it right she defiles herself with the man who tried to murder you?"

There was a commotion at the door. A dishevelled and bloody Martūm was thrust into the room, Nix almost capering behind him. The tatterdemalion killer bowed with a flourish, the long clumped locks of his hair sweeping the floor. Martūm cringed, holding his hand to his split lip. His left eye was bruised, swollen almost entirely shut. The battered man eyed the others in the room nervously.

"Is this any way to treat our friend?" Corajidin asked, though he did nothing to help the hurt man. Instead, he gestured for Martūm to pick himself up.

Nix rolled his eyes, face transitioning through half a dozen expressions in as many seconds. Corajidin took an unwilling step backward. *Is this what happened to all eaters of flesh? Or perhaps it was the inbreeding?*

"Hmmm." Nix scuttled to a chair, turned it round and crouched on it. His arms dangled over its back, fingertips poking through tattered leather gloves. "It wasn't me who gave him a thrashing. I saved him!" He reached out to ruffle Martūm's already mussed hair. His grip soon tightened, squeezing until Martūm darted away. Nix flicked a slender blade from a wrist sheath, gaze flat. His voice dropped when he spoke, losing its customary nasal whine. "I love this little man! He's so full of juicy facts I just want to cut him and gut him to see what squirms inside."

"There's no need to cut anything!" Martūm sounded panicked. "I went gambling last night in a less than salubrious establishment, and found my liquid assets were somewhat short of my debts. Even the courtesans turned me down! Bitches. They should be happy to have the new Rahn-Selassin in their beds."

"And *are* you the new Rahn-Selassin?" Tahj-Shaheh asked. "Or are you still an impoverished man-child, always crying to his benefactors to pay off the debts of his excess?"

"Watch your tone, woman!" Martūm warmed. "Has the salt air robbed you of your memories of sende? I may not be a rahn, but I am a son of the Great House of Selassin and you'll respect the bloodline." He stood up straight. "And of course I'll be rahn. Who else can take Vahineh's place?" He paused, before muttering, "Though Roshana and Nazarafine seem to be looking to anybody with a drop of Selassin blood in them."

"Are they now?" Corajidin asked darkly

"You bought me, Asrahn-Corajidin, and I know enough of your reputation to stay bought." Martūm straightened his clothing with what dignity he could muster. "But your investment in me will never give you rewards if Roshana and her lack witted cabal choose another to replace Vahineh."

"Ah," Feyd smiled a very small smile, a flash of white in his short iron beard. "But is the reward you offer something we'll find useful?"

"Or something we can get somewhere else"—Tahj-Shaheh added—"at half the price?"

Martūm turned to Corajidin, his expression desperately eager. "If you keep me locked in the warm lips of outrageously expensive courtesans, with enough gold for me to live as I want, you'll find me the most useful thing in the world, Asrahn. I don't want power. Never have. I just want the wealth, toys, and perversions power can buy."

Corajidin looked over steepled fingers at the man. Clearly the resemblance to Vashne was purely skin deep, the man a Selassin in name only. Yet he could still be the means to several ends.

"The question, Martūm, is can you deliver what you promised me?"

"Please, Asrahn, consider me an investment in the future," the man said as he rubbed his hands together briskly. "Last night, prior to my foray into the more dubious haunts of Avānweh's dark and delicious underbelly, I was with the Federationists. Maintaining the dutiful cousin story, you know. Anyway, I learned the Federationists were trying to Sever Vahineh from her Awakening."

"They *what*?" Wolfram snapped.

"I thought that would get your attention," Martūm smirked. "Oh, they also told Ajomandyan the Sky Lord all about how you have snatched up Indris and Vahineh. It was quite a tense topic of conversation, how they intended on dealing with that."

"You do not say." Corajidin held his hand up to forestall the others from talking. "Martūm, would you excuse us? Ask one of the Anlūki to point you in the direction of the baths, so you can make yourself more presentable before heading home."

"And about my minor financial hiccup?" The man smiled ingratiatingly.

"You will be well taken care of, trust me."

When Martūm was gone Corajidin rubbed his face with both his hands in an effort to mask the expression of pure rage and frustration he felt forming there. He ground his teeth, instantly regretting the shooting pain from his missing molar. He could feel a trembling in his elbows and knees. Taking his hands away he looked at the creases on his fingers. The deep-etched lines on his palm. So like squinted eyes, a flattened nose and curled lips. It was as if he had imprinted his fury into the skin.

"As pathetic a man as he is, Martūm could be useful if he Ascends, Your Majesty," Wolfram said.

"Were the Federationists going to Awaken him," the Emissary leaned forward in her chair, elbows on her knees and legs akimbo, "Martūm would've been there at the Severance to take on Vahineh's legacy. They'd need scholars of Indris and Femensetri's skills to help him order all the thoughts that would otherwise break him. I think they're seriously looking elsewhere for their new rahn."

"I agree. But why not have the Sēq do the Severance?" Kasraman asked.

"Maybe they wouldn't," the Emissary mused. "Maybe they couldn't. From all I hear, the Order is in turmoil."

"Where in all the depths of the Well of Souls are Indris and the others, then?" Nadir asked. "We don't have them."

"I'm sure Roshana and the others are manipulating Ajomandyan," Wolfram said. "If they can send enough doubt our way, they might be able to make others take another look at recent deaths and disappearances."

"They'll find nothing," Nix yawned, looking bored. He began to carve into the back of the chair with his knife.

"Let's take some more precautions. Jhem?" Corajidin said to his old friend. "I need you and Nix to arrange for the most likely candidates for a new Federationist rahn to leave the city." Seeing their eager faces, he quickly said, "No blood! There's been enough shed already. While you're at it, get the list of my preferred candidates from my desk. I want them all protected!"

"Does that include myself, my rahn?" the Blacksnake said emotionlessly.

Corajidin tried for patience. "There are those who have waited a long time for this, Jhem. Their Families have been on the list for Ascension for centuries. I will do for you what I can."

Jhem rose from his chair and took Nix with him, the shorter man almost hopping with excitement.

※ ※ ※

Corajidin sat in the windy chamber, his pristine white Teshri coat flapping about his legs. The large room was cold, the air crisp where it carried with it the hint of the high mountain snows. The pitted bronze sphere he sat on felt like ice, causing his lower back and thighs to ache. Even so it was refreshing to feel mundane pain for a change.

Nazarafine seemed to have shrunken in on herself, expression wan. Roshana's gaze was sharp as a sword blade, face hard as a shield. Siamak sat tall and still, a snowy mountain in his coat while Vahineh's absence was as predictable as it was vexing.

It was Mariam's appearance that had startled Corajidin at first. It was apparent she had recovered fully from her near-mortal wounds in Amnon, her movement feline and easy. Belamandris looked at his sister with affection, though his expression hardened at Corajidin's glare. Her smile faltered, an embarrassed hurt flushing her skin. Corajidin was surprised when Mariam did not assume her place with the Feyassin. Rather she took a seat at the back, in the ambivalent territory between the factions, populated by those lone voices in the political wilderness, or those seeking to attract patronage from those more influential than themselves.

It should have come as no surprise Mariam would distance herself from the Feyassin. Unlikely she would be comfortable serving her father, the man she had so recently betrayed, as the Knight-Colonel of his personal guard. Given he intended on disbanding the Feyassin—their treachery at Amnon was not forgotten—it hardly mattered, though it was a small, petty wound he could no longer inflict on his estranged daughter.

As expected, the Ambassadors from the Iron League wasted no time in accosting Nazarafine with their list of grievances. There was the usual litany of attacks by Avān nahdi on Iron League soil. The rebuttal of Manté's ongoing war against the Avān along the Tanisian border. Prattle about ancient territories, hereditary rights and claims to lands and the oft-won, oft-lost Conflicted Cities. Each time Nazarafine deflected a question, giving the Ambassadors the politically correct and comforting answers from the current administration, Corajidin was then asked the same question about his impending government. Yes, there would be a proposal to create the Royal Shrīanese Columns, a standing army loyal to the Crown and State. Yes, these would be similar to the Imperial Legions of the Awakened Empire. Yes, Shrīan would be reviewing its foreign policy, as well as the rights of non-Avān in Shrīan. No, it was not dissimilar from the attitudes adopted by the Iron League against the Avān for the past five centuries. Yes, more proactive support of the Tanisians would be considered.

The expressions on the faces of the Iron League Ambassadors were not encouraging. The Humans had made their antipathy well known when they had tried to exterminate the Avān during the Insurrection. After more than one hundred and fifty years of war, which had seen the end of the Awakened Empire, both sides were impoverished wrecks, spitting invective through what remained of their chipped and bloodied teeth. After almost five centuries of what people called peace, some called a détente and the informed called a stalemate, attitudes had not improved. Even the Ambassadors from the neutral nations of Ondea, Darmatia, Kaylish, Ygran, and Kaarsgard were suspicious. The Salt Islanders, little better than freebooters and mercenaries anyway, seemed to not care one way or the other. It was easier for them, since Corajidin could not imagine anybody wanting to occupy the Salt Isles who did not have to. Only the Tanisian Ambassador seemed pleased. No doubt he expected the Royal Shrīanese Columns to some sailing across the skies, in the armada of airships that did not exist, with weapons that had not been made, used by soldiers who had neither been recruited nor trained.

The Ambassadors left the open session of the Teshri unhappier than they had entered it. Corajidin rubbed the bridge of his nose between thumb and forefinger, trying to muster enough energy to care. He wanted to blame Vashne's government for the tensions, though there was unlikely to be a person in South-Eastern Īa who would believe such a claim. It was not a case of tensions mounting; it was a case of them never having eased, a full glass waiting to overflow.

"Is there any additional business?" Padishin, the middle-aged Secretary-Marshall, asked.

"I have a matter that needs to be clarified." Corajidin rose from his cold, uncomfortable sphere. He stretched his back, smiling at his fellow counsellors. "The architects of the Teshri certainly had the last laugh."

"What do you want, Rahn-Corajidin?" Roshana asked, glaring at those who chuckled at Corajidin's levity. She wavered on the fine line of civility demanded by sende. He bit back his instinct to school her on her manners. Though it was a young woman's face he saw, behind her eyes was the long line of those who had come before. Including Ariskander. Even dead, the echo of the man was not to be trifled with.

Instead, Corajidin bowed his head precisely as sende demanded, touching his fingertips to his chest, over his hearts. *I see you and hear you and show you I carry no weapon.*

"It is the outstanding matter of Rahn-Selassin fe Vahineh." Corajidin said. "We appreciate she was Awakened under tragic circumstances, yet know her ongoing position as rahn is untenable. It was a miracle she survived the Communion Ritual. Why prolong the inevitable? I propose we petition the Sēq to Sever Vahineh from her Awakening, in order to save her life."

"So you can take it?" Nazarafine had to raise her voice over the cacophony that rang about the chamber. The portly woman waved her arms around, try as Roshana and Siamak might to restrain her. "We know you want to bring her before the Arbiters, for—"

"For my suspicions that she was involved in the cold-blooded murder of my wife?" Corajidin asked quietly. He looked around the chamber, nodding at the shocked expressions there. "It is true. I do want Yashamin's murderer brought to justice. If it is Rahn-Vahineh, then let justice take its course.

"And while it is true I have lodged a petition with yourself, Rahn-Nazarafine—as well as the Arbiter of the Change—for this matter to be investigated, my primary concern is for the effective government of our country."

Ajomandyan leaned forward, balanced on his gryphon-headed walking stick. His eyes were eagle fierce either side of the beak of his nose. "It is true. Rahn-Corajidin has observed the forms with his petition. It is also true that, as Arbiter of the Change, it is my responsibility to advise the Teshri that we need to find Rahn-Vahineh's replacement quickly."

Roshana looked around the room, jaw muscles clenching. "We have been assessing appropriate candidates for her replacement."

"What of her cousin, Martūm?" old Narseh said in her parade ground voice. The Knight-Marshall glared at the world with one eye narrowed. Even in her formal coat of State, she may as well have been wearing armour. "Is he not the only full-blooded Selassin left alive?"

"He is," Siamak agreed, "though the man has—"

"If he is not suitable, say it so we can move on!" Narseh snapped. Civility had never been one of her strong points, the woman better suited to bellowing orders on battlefields.

"Is this true?" Padashin asked. "Is Martūm unsuitable?"

Nazarafine gritted her teeth. "We are deliberating—"

"And yet," Corajidin pressed, "I was informed you tried last night to have Vahineh Severed from her Awakening by the Scholar-Marshall and Pahmahjin-Näsarat fa Amonindris—"

The room burst into an uproar. Corajidin covered his smile by lowering his head, though not before Roshana, Nazarafine, and Siamak had seen it. *Let them rage!*

It was only the sharp crack of Padashin's dionesqa on the marble floor that brought order to the chamber. The one-time war hero looked as if he were ready to draw and use his weapon if such were necessary for silence. After a few moments the noise reduced to eddies, then swirled to a gentle murmur, before it became still as glass.

"This is a dangerous accusation to make, Rahn-Corajidin," Padashin growled. "Do you have proof?"

"It came to my attention from a reliable source, though the witness is not here."

"Convenient," Roshana sneered. "You bring this to us with no proof? Why waste our time?"

"It is my understanding the truth of the matter was revealed in a conversation with the Arbiter of the Change, at which the rahns Roshana, Nazarafine, and Siamak were in attendance."

"Ajo?" Padashin said quietly.

Corajidin knew that for the Sky Lord to obscure the facts, or deny them, would undermine everything the post of Arbiter of the Change stood for. If it were proven he had misled the Teshri, there would be dire consequences, not the least of which was the review of his role as a sayf and his governorship of Avānweh. And yet, Corajidin hoped the Sky Lord *took* the risk, so Avānweh could be governed by somebody more tractable.

All eyes were on Ajomandyan as he stood, bowing his head to the Secretary-Marshall. He looked at Roshana and the other Federationists with equanimity, for Corajidin knew for him to look apologetic would be a mistake.

"It is true," he said as the room erupted into chaos once more.

Corajidin nodded as he sat, revelling in the outrage of his peers, while privately disappointed the Sky Lord's honesty had robbed him of a chance to consolidate his power.

16

"LEFT TO ITS OWN DEVICES THE IMAGINATION CAN BECOME
YOUR WORST ENEMY. PAIN HURTS LESS THAN THE FEAR OF PAIN.
THE UNKNOWN OFTEN MORE TERRIFYING THAN THE KNOWN."

—Zamhon, Father on the Mountain for the Ishahayan Gnostic
Assassins, and Master of Assassins to the Great House of Näsarat
(259th Year of the Shrīanese Federation)

DAY ? OF THE 495TH YEAR OF

THE SHRĪANESE FEDERATION

Indris felt the ache in his shoulders and hips from where he was suspended, spread-eagled and naked in midair. The metal cuffs around his
wrists and ankles were hot: not quite painful, yet far from comfortable. There
was the faint snap and growl of energy tethers that connected the cuffs to the
frame around him. Sweat trickled down his arms, torso, and back. His thighs,
calves, and shins. A cold breeze whistled in from somewhere behind him,
chilling the sweat as it formed so he burned and was chilled at once.

There was barely enough light to see the rough, irregular facets of the
obsidian walls. He was held motionless in the centre of a large metallic wheel,
inlaid with formulae in gold wire, set at regular intervals with metallic disks
wound with copper wire and heavy-looking magnets. When he craned his

neck he could make out a circle of lightless *ilhen* crystals above, another below.

Sēq Inquisitors called the contraption he was in the Circumscription Well. Others called it the Potentiality Sink—a device that held its occupant tighter, the more energy they used to try and escape. While Indris remained quiet and did nothing, it let him be. The moment he exerted either physical or mental force, it was drained into the Well and stored for who knows how long. Knowing it would be futile—though needing to exclude it as a possibility—Indris tentatively used the ahmsah to see what could not otherwise be seen. He swore. Beyond the curve of the Well, the room was a cat's cradle of disentropy, shot through with hints of hot color: the hues of militant energy.

Can this thing be overloaded? He had never heard of it being done, but there was a first time for everything.

He extended his senses. Slowly at first, gradually gathering more of the world's latent energy until he felt pins and needles begin in his spine. Awareness became discomfort. Discomfort became pain. Pins and needles turned to vicious shocks that caused—

❀ ❀ ❀

When he opened his eyes the room was exactly the same, save for the smell of singed skin and hair.

And the squat form of the man in the wheeled chair before him.

"Do you know who I am?" came the rasping whisper, as if either the man or woman struggled for breath.

"Do you know who *I* am?" Indris asked.

Pain lanced through his body, causing him to thrash. His teeth snapped together while his muscles convulsed and his back arched like a bow. There was fire burning his—

❀ ❀ ❀

"Do you know who I am?" came the question again, a rasping whisper from the darkness.

"A strangely off-putting person in a wheeled chair?"

There was more pain this time. Unfortunately the darkness took longer to claim him.

❈ ❈ ❈

"Do you know who I am?" came the rasping whisper from the darkness once more.

"*Faruq yaha, yaha mehel felyati!*"

"That was not polite."

As Indris's body spasmed in agony and his eyes rolled back into his head, he felt his bladder and bowels empty. He went beyond pain. His last sense was of the reek of sweat and his own filth.

❈ ❈ ❈

"Do you know who I am?" came the rasping whisper from the darkness.

Indris's protracted silence brought more pain.

Then welcome darkness.

He cracked rheumy eyes open to see the blurred outlines of people. They began to beat him about the chest, back, stomach, and thighs with truncheons. Each blow hammered his already sensitised body. Every lash of their dauls was like being branded. As much as he did not want to admit the screams that echoed in the small cell were his, he knew better.

Consciousness remained as Indris was pummelled. Furious—and careless for the harm it would cause him—he tapped into the ahm. Numbers raced across his narrowing mindscape as his senses were overloaded. His Disentropic Stain flared. His left eye burned and the room was filled with a conflagration. In a brief moment he saw their faces, frightened and shocked, before they puffed away into dust.

Only the man in the wheelchair remained, expression surprised as the flames writhed about the spinning fractals of the man's protective wards. Indris knew him.

A face from childhood. Taqrit. One of the Eight . . . and, before Indris was given his Writ of Release from service, one of his best friends.

When darkness stole Indris, he had the time to imagine it was Mari's arms into which he fell.

❄ ❄ ❄

"You killed four Sēq Scholars in that little demonstration of yours," Taqrit wheezed from his wheeled chair. The man was much changed and looked older than his thirty-five years. His face was deep etched with the roads he had travelled beneath patchy white hair. His eyes were strangely colourless, the pupils twinned dots floating in milk. His hands were little better than emaciated claws. A daul hung from his belt: a whip of plaited leather and witchfire studs, with a curved handle bound in gold and silver wire. A heavy strand of jade meditation beads hung about his neck, set with the shepherd's crook and eye sigil of the Inquisitors. "I'm curious as to how you managed that little trick."

"Four? I was hoping for five." Indris tried for a conversational tone, yet his voice was hoarse, his mouth dry. He coughed and tasted blood. The circle of *ilhen* crystals above and below him shone with a clean white light, reflecting from the harsh angles of the irregularly faceted black walls.

He struggled against his bindings in vain. The room smelled of urine, faeces, sweat, and burned flesh. It made him gag.

"I know you're thinking about how you'll escape," Taqrit said. "Let me assure you it's highly improbable you'll do so. Usually I use the word impossible, but it's you we're talking about so we've taken some additional precautions."

"Why are you—?"

"Nobody outside these walls knows you're here," Taqrit continued as if Indris had not spoken. "Nobody is coming."

Indris stared down at Taqrit. "What happened to you?"

The Inquisitor smiled a very small smile. "*You* happened to me, Indris. After you left they were much harder on the rest of us. Didn't want more of their special generation slipping through their fingers. Ironic, given most of us Fell to the Drear anyway. They were demanding and dangerous years after you left. Ones I shan't forget. But in the here and now *I* have the questions and you'll give me answers."

"And you needed to drag me in here to ask them?"

"We dragged you in here because the opportunity presented itself. Though the Order may not be united in its approach, there are those of us who'll put the interests of the Order before the life of any individual." He rested his hand on the handle of his daul. "It's always been thus."

"I don't have any secrets the Order would be interested in, Taqrit," Indris said, eyeing the daul apprehensively. Every member of the Sēq Order was familiar with the signature pain-giver of the Inquisitors. When combined with some of their other tools, such as the Memory Trawl, the Spiritrack, or a Mind Lens, the pain of the daul usually delivered quick results. Even for those trained to compartmentalise their minds it was usually only a matter of time before it was too much to bear. The most basic level of proficiency required for a person to be a Sēq operative was to be a nayu-adept— one who had mastered their body and could isolate pain and the fear of pain. Yet as the Ishahayan—the sect of Gnostic Assassins—said, *Everybody breaks and everybody talks because everybody, everywhere, has a point beyond which they can not endure.*

"Allow me to be the judge of what the Order is, or is not, interested in." Taqrit lips stretched in a wan excuse for a smile. "What can you tell me of the Soul Traders?"

"The what?" Indris was not certain whether he had heard correctly. Taqrit gestured with his hand and a surge of heat scalded Indris's nerves. He glared at the man in his wheeled chair, choking back a curse. "What? The Soul Traders are a myth."

"You've met them. Tell me about them."

"What do you mean I met them?" Indris frowned. "I'm pretty sure I'd remember something like that."

"You think you'd remember your three years on the Spines," Taqrit wheezed. "But apparently not. Now, tell me what you know of the Soul Traders."

The Soul Traders had been one of the nightmares of Avān legend for millennia. Reputed to steal the souls of the hallowed dead, and then sell them to collectors or those who would use them for their own ends, the Soul Traders were an abomination. "I heard rumours, years ago, that the Soul Traders were Nomads fishing the Well of Souls. But I've not dealt with them. I help Nomads with their transition or, if it's their choice, help them keep a foothold in a world they're not ready to leave. I don't trade their souls."

"How wonderful for you. A soft-hearted heretic, and traitor to his Order. You do us proud."

"The soul is eternal, you cretin," Indris said scathingly. "The Well of Souls can wait until a soul is ready to be at peace. If a Nomad harms none, why should we harm it?"

"Tell me about your dealings with the Soul Traders."

"I've never dealt with them." *At least I don't remember dealing with them.*

"So you say. What is their connection with the Dream Key?"

"The what? Taqrit, I've no idea what—" Indris's screams felt like they were going to tear his throat apart. When the pain stopped he was left panting, limbs twitching, glaring at the crippled Inquisitor. "When I escape from here, I'll kill you."

"No doubt you'll try and no doubt you could succeed," Taqrit said, unperturbed. "It's why at the end of this we'll fix you with a Docilator Crown and put you out to stud. What days you have left will be spent as a pacified imbecile, fathering children for the Order so we can at least realise some use from you."

"I've done nothing wrong!" Indris shouted. He thrashed in his bonds. May as well have tried to move the mountain.

"You were ever our better," Taqrit mocked. "You took everything you had for granted while we struggled under every trial and lesson Femensetri, Ahwe and Madiset tasked us with. You were so oblivious in your superiority."

"You're torturing me out of spite?" Indris asked, aghast.

"No." Taqrit shook his head, a small smile of genuine pleasure on his face. "Well, not entirely. Now—what is the connection between the Soul Traders and the Dream Key, why did Sedefke name you to find it, and what was the date and year you should start your search?"

✳ ✳ ✳

Indris lost track of time.

The frequent bouts of pain. The wax and wane of awareness. The same senseless questions. Who are the Soul Traders? Are they Nomads? What is their relationship with the Dream Key? What do you know of Sedefke? Is

Sedefke still alive? Why did Sedefke name you as the one to be sent to the Spines? Is the Dream Key on The Spines? Who are the Soul Traders? Are they Nomads? What involvement do the Soul Traders have with the witches? Why is the Drear now more active? Is there a link between the witches, the Soul Traders and the Drear?

On and on it went, a never-ending circle of questions Indris had no answers to.

Sometimes moments of clarity came where he pinned the questions to the Possibility Tree, following root to trunk to branch to twig to leaf. Yet there was no common source from which to extrapolate effect from cause. His mind raced with variables, too many possibilities and too few probabilities—like fruits that grew, withered, and died on the vine more often than not. There were too many pieces missing.

His body felt distant when he woke, smothered in a rough and uncomfortable blanket. His breathing was laboured as if he breathed through a leather bag. Hot air swirled around his face. His head felt heavy. There were voices, though whether inside or outside his head he could not tell.

"Have you found what we are looking for?" came an older male voice, lion-proud and booming. Zadjinn? *"Did he find the Dream Key?"*

"No," came the wheezer. Taqrit? *"I've searched the outer layers of his mind to no avail. Our questions, intended to provoke his memories, have caused him to extrapolate causality."*

"And?" the lion asked.

"It's the symptom of somebody trying to discover answers, not of a person who has them. Or knows he has them."

"What do you mean?"

"There is a block in his mind," the wheezer said. *"An Anamnesis Maze set up around part of his memory. It's complex beyond my ability to navigate. If I dig too far, I may never find my way out."*

"So, he does have something to hide," came a sultry contralto.

"I can dig deeper," the wheezer said. *"There're no assurances as to what state he'll be in when I finish. The Mind Lens can be more invasive than we predict."*

"Time is against us," came the booming lion. *"Our brethren know something is amiss. We can not hide him here forever."*

"Do what needs be done." This masculine voice was gentler than the oth-ers, though cold. *"I can keep the Suret diverted adequately enough. Our spies tell us the witches are on the move, and we are unprepared for what is to come."*

"If this is the harbinger of the return of the Inoqua," the sultry contralto said, *"we must act soon. Neither the Sēq nor the rahns are as powerful as once they were."*

"The Empress-in-Shadows has abandoned us to our own devices," the cold voice muttered. *"And Shrīan is not Pashrea. Break Indris if you must, but find out everything he knows. He is the only one to have gone to the Spines and returned."*

"There's another," Taqrit said hesitantly.

"No!" the lion snapped. *"The Order believes she is gone, and that is the way it must stay. At least for now. Besides, she has revealed what she knows, and will-ingly. I am certain of it."*

"Will you gamble all our futures on your infatuation with another man's wife?" the contralto taunted. *"If Indris were to—"*

"Enough!" the cold voice snapped. *"Our answers may be in Indris's mind, and we need to find them first if we are to control the direction of the Order! Dig deep, Inquisitor. But dig quickly."*

"As you command," the wheezer said.

❋ ❋ ❋

Hours passed. Perhaps days. Indris could not tell.

Time was marked by the passage of indignities. The scourging of his skin. The flaying of his mind. They force fed him and poured water down his throat through a funnel, all to keep him alive so they could question him a little longer. They injected him with serums to make him more pliant, all the while breaking down his physical and mental control.

Everybody has a point beyond which they can not endure.

Indris hung his head and stared at Taqrit from under sodden hair gone lank. Breathing through his nose almost choked him, the filth of his un-washed and abused body too ripe in the enclosed space. Breathing through his mouth was little better, though, as he could taste the smell, a foul residue that caught at the back of his throat.

The Inquisitor sat in his wheeled chair beside a long table. Devices lay upon it in neat rows, some of which Indris recognised. The bronze and leather helmet of the Mind Lens, with its many external lenses, nodes, spines, and vanes. The carved and polished wooden circlet, fitted with hundreds of crystals around its inner circumference, was a Memory Trawl used to fish memories from a mind, whether they were consciously known or not. Beside them were crystal lances, long jewel-topped needles and vials of fluid in dozens of different colours. There was a strange, mesmerising beauty to their form. An artistry set loose by a mind fixed on a singular purpose, hiding said purpose within intricate carvings, faceted gems, polished metal, and tooled leather. An elegance where style met function, regardless of how grotesque the function was.

Changeling lay lengthwise by the implements of torture. Beside her was Indris's dragon-tooth knife and holstered storm-pistol. His clothing lay neatly folded beneath his satchel. His journals, ink, and brushes nearby.

Taqrit noticed Indris's glance. He gestured towards Changeling. "This is another question that needs answering. Where did you come by this weapon?"

"I made it."

"Where did you make it and how?" Taqrit leaned forward, pupils little more than pinheads of coal set in snow. "One would think it quite beyond you, talented though you may be, to make a psédari. You did not have this when you left, and no Sēq Master would have taught you the skills since you returned. So how, then?"

Indris opened his mouth to speak, the answer on the tip of his tongue, though the words would not come. He knew he had made Changeling. Had felt the blast of volcanic fire against his face and the cold metal haft of the hammer in his hand. Yet he could not say where, when or how. He closed his mouth again.

"And there we have it. If you didn't make it, you must've stolen it."

"You know that's impossible!" A mind blade could only be wielded by the one who made it, the weapon crumbling to nothing within hours of its maker's death.

"Is it?"

"Try unsheathing her and find out." Indris bared his teeth in a wild smile. Changeling seemed to chuckle where she lay, causing the glass vials and metal objects to rattle together in imitation. Taqrit looked at the table with alarm, wheeling himself back. "You know what happens to somebody who tries to use another's mind blade, don't you?"

Taqrit nodded reluctantly.

"Then how could I wield her and live?"

The placid Inquisitor went back to preparing his instruments. Indris subtly tested his bonds. As expected they were still firm. He flexed his Disentropic Stain the barest fraction, little more than a lick of the ahmsah, to find the pins and needles of feedback still there. With Changeling so close it was almost worth unleashing the fullness of his power, though Indris doubted he would remain conscious long enough to take advantage.

He was reasonably certain he was somewhere in Amer-Mahjin, hidden amongst the currents of disentropy. He imagined the scholars all around him. Studying in the Amber Library. Transcribing older manuscripts from handwritten pages to print on huge presses. Drafting new inventions, experimenting with formulae, examining artefacts brought back from across the length and breadth of Ïa. Meditating. Undergoing the rigorous physical training required of all the Sēq: for of all those who studied the Esoteric Doctrines, it was the Sēq who sought the unity of body, mind, and spirit. It was one of the first things one learned: one plus one plus one equals one.

Awareness of his body dwindled to the distant sound of his own breathing, deep and even as the surf. He allowed his consciousness to climb away from the flesh, inhabiting the ephemeral bastions of the psé: the place of the pure mind that cohabited with the kaj, or soul. Indris drifted through the lapis sea of his mind. It was a place of analogies and metaphors. Thoughts became clouds of crystal filaments, coloured slivers that rotated as they grew, merged, or repulsed each other to form new shapes. New ideas, carrying postulates, assumptions, and calculations. Axioms, ambiguities, and paradoxes. All forming, changing, colliding, branching out in something larger and more profound than any Possibility Tree.

The psé was immortal. The Nomads were proof of this, their bodies dead yet retaining memories and able to learn new things throughout the stretched span of their years.

As a psé-adept, Indris had been taught his psyche was like the interior of an almost limitless bubble of possibilities. Nothing was ever forgotten, though a person could misplace memories, hide them, or have them hidden.

Indris opened himself further, stretching the cord that bound nayu and psé together.

Freed from his body for the moment, he changed his perspective. Rather than look inward at the downwardly curved vault of his mind, he pierced the mental walls to see himself standing on the outside of the globe of his soul. His kaj was only one drop in a boundless ocean filled with an infinity of bubbles drifting along currents as old as the beginning of the universe.

Indris had experienced firsthand the realm the Nilvedic Scholar Vedartha referred to as the ahmtesh: the fluid infinity of disentropic energy surrounding the qua. It was here the ternary nature of existence shed the need for the physical, or the temporary. This was the place of the psyche and the soul. The former carried the will, intellect, and memories; the latter the context of a person's existence, their emotions, and drives for enlightenment in a complex and overwhelming universe.

He drifted in a place of no time and no space. His dhyna, the inner eye, flicking across the vista before him in this place where all things were connected. He caught the glimpse of distant formations obscured by brilliant, undulating streamers of pale blue. There were schools of formless light, swooping and wheeling. Coming together and parting. He wondered how many of his friends were there, long dead and living in eternal peace? Did his Ancestors remain here, or had they drifted to the surface to be reborn and experience the world anew?

The thought of his Ancestors reminded him of Ariskander's cryptic words. *My sister was a vessel, one who willingly accepted her great burden. Your mother risked all when she sent you forward. Sedefke saw that one day the Scholar Kings would be needed.*

Indris felt his metaphoric footing slip. His psé reverberated. No doubt Taqrit was going back to work, trying to rouse him. Fluid space grew more turbulent, the warm lapis sea becoming cloudy.

But this venture had not been without profit. Here in the Amer-Mahjin he was surrounded by both psé- and kaj-adepts. So while he could not physically use disentropy, there was nothing stopping him using its essence to send a cry for help. It was much the same way a man who could not swim could still throw stones in the river. In Indris's case, he intended on throwing some very large stones.

Kneeling, he used the metaphors of his fists to beat on the surface of his soul. He had no time to be choosey of whom he alerted. Things could hardly get worse than what was planned for him already. Ripples spread. A repetitive boom in the great currents of the ahm. He only hoped somebody would hear and find him, before it was too late.

17

"WE ENJOY THE TRIUMPHS AND TOLERATE THE FAILURES OF FAMILY
BECAUSE BLOOD IS BLOOD. WHEN ALL IS SAID AND DONE, IT IS THE BONDS
OF FAMILY THAT DRIVE US TO THE EXTREMES OF ACTION AND EMOTION."

—From *Immortality of the Bloodlines,* by Tamari fa Saroush, philosopher
of the Awakened Empire

DAY 357 OF THE 495TH YEAR OF

THE SHRĪANESE FEDERATION

For three days and nights Mari searched Avānweh for any sign of Indris. She only slept when exhaustion took her. It was more sleep than Shar or Omen enjoyed. The Seethe war player ran on the ragged edge of exhaustion, while the tireless Wraith Knight spent the shallow watches of the night, to the blue-grey haze of predawn, hunting down the sources of even the slightest rumour.

Mari sat in bed, her back resting against the cool mosaic wall in her room at the Eyrie, an elite hotel on the cliffs of the Caleph-Mahn. What little sleep she had was not restful. The dream was so vivid, of Indris laying beside her, speaking, though no sound came save the metronomic beating of his hearts as if from underwater. If she closed her eyes she could still hear the faint, metronomic beating. Every day he was missing made her heart ache all the more at the thought he would never return.

But now there was a lead that might bear fruit.

The sun had not yet risen. With the balcony doors closed the gentle hum of the wind was barely audible, the sky beyond a flat, featureless grey expanse. Mari unfolded the parchment in her hand, its crackling preternaturally loud. She did not need the decrepit light of the guttering lanterns to read it. The contents were well known to her.

It had taken Corajidin two days to respond to Mari's request for an audience. His timing sent her a mixed message that was no doubt deliberate. When the Seethe had made the Avān in their Torque Spindles, they had taken Humans and blended with them the traits of big cats, wolves, and other animals, as well as the Seethe themselves. The result had been something that, while looking almost Human, felt and thought profoundly differently.

In their early generations the Avān had been wild and uncontrolled. After a few generations of war, the first rules of sende had been penned. They provided to the aggressive, territorial Avān a structure of etiquette and social interactions that prevented them from exterminating themselves. Over generations it had become more intricate: a subtle and profound way for a passionate people to express themselves and declare the intent of their behaviour. Like the beasts of the wild, the Avān remembered what it was to protect their territorial interests, to mate so the fittest bloodlines endured and to defend the weak. Hence the caste system, which defined strict rules of conduct. The board game of tanj, complex and convoluted as it was, was the embodiment of sende, often used to teach children how to behave.

Corajidin's response told Mari many things. The timing said he still thought of her as a member of the family, though not as closely as once he had. The quality of the parchment was expensive, meaning he still valued her, yet the ink was not laced with precious metal, so she was not elevated in his regard. It had been written in his own hand, rather than by his adjutant, which showed he had taken time to compose his message. The black and silk ribbons, with their bars of black and red gold, as well as the wax seal with its polished rubies and black lodestones, told her she was still precious to the Great House of Erebus and should find her way home. The written words were precise and spoke of neither commitment to a resolution, nor her jeopardy. The fact he had invited her to a public dining house said he had nothing to hide and she would leave the meeting alive. Under the rules of sende. Nobody murdered a guest where food and drink had been shared. Even the choice of messenger—Nima, a respected cousin and Knight-Lieutenant of the Anlūki—told her Corajidin took her seriously and recognised her military prowess. It all said, *I see you, Mariam, for what you are and know you are to be respected, possibly feared. Yet blood is blood.*

He had sent a gift that placed a further obligation on Mari to respect the codes of conduct: it was her old amenesqa, thought lost at Amnon. Mari had been dumbfounded to see it, restored to pristine condition. It was sharp, reminding Mari of the nature of truth. Reminding her where she had come from. She laid it beside her Sûnblade, one weapon the dark reflection of its sister.

Roshana had been pleased with Corajidin's response. She insisted Mari take a retinue. Originally, Roshana had wanted to send Bensaharēn and a squad of the Tau-se, yet one did not send Shrīan's foremost warrior-poet and the lion folk anywhere, without it sending a message. Besides, her father had never been comfortable with any non-Avān, which also meant taking Shar, Hayden or Ekko was out of the question, let alone Omen. Siamak had offered some of his marshland warriors. In the end Mari had agreed to take two soldiers each from Roshana, Nazarafine, and Siamak. The message implicit in such a gathering could not be lost on her father.

Mari bathed hastily and dressed. Her tunic, tall supple boots and trousers were of black suede, her light hauberk of red quilted silk with mirror-bright silver scales. These were colours of both the Erebus and her mother's Family, the Dahrain. She wore her antique amenesqa across her back, while the Sûnblade was attached to her weapons belt opposite a recurved long-knife. Over this she wore the white hooded over-robe of the ashinahdi, declaring she acted outside the purview of her Great House. The consequences were hers and hers alone.

The sun was a bright fingernail pairing over the eastern range by the time Mari arrived at the Näsaré villa. As Arbiter of the Change, Ajo had agreed to attend as a neutral party. Neva and Yago were his witnesses, the latter carrying an Audio-scroll Apparatus in a carved mahogany box. Shar, Hayden, Ekko, and Omen waited there also. As the other six attendees arrived, Ajo reminded Indris's friends they were not to interfere. Ajo extended to them the hospitality of his home until the meeting was done. Neither Shar nor Hayden appeared happy, Ekko was as opaque as expected of a Tau-se, and Omen simply stood there like a giant porcelain doll.

Ajo led them to the nearest gondola station where they boarded one of the ornate spheres. As the gondola descended, rocking slightly in the wind, Mari was thankful people seemed calm. She appraised those the rahns had sent in their names. She trusted the rahns to have exercised good judgement, given the lives of many hung in the balance of today's discussions.

The marsh-warriors were nut brown, their hair tied up in high ponytails, feet clad in frayed reed sandals. A man and a woman, they were lean and lithe, worn clothing hanging from their spare frames. Their hands were wedge shaped, narrow with ropey muscle. The hilts of their weapons looked well used. Nazarafine had sent two of her nephews, sun-kissed youths who looked as if they had known little save the salt tang of the ocean and the summer on their skin. Yet their movements were quick and sure, their twinned swords and dual knives slung according to the style of the Saidani-sûk, the Four Blades School of the Sûn Isles. Roshana had sent a woman and a man, both of whom were so innocuous as to raise Mari's hackles. Their expressions were bland to the point of being non-existent, clothing and weapons of little note. Neither man nor woman met her gaze.

The public dining house Corajidin had chosen for their meeting was The Twelveway, a prestigious establishment on the Caleph-Sayf situated in a dodecagonal building of lacquered wood and viridian glazed tiles. It was set on carved stilts over one of the streams that fed into the Ascendent's Court, a broad, deep defile between Star Crown and World Blood mountains. At the bottom, amongst lichen- and moss-covered stones and natural pools, was the Ascendent's Memorial: twelve painstakingly crafted bronze statues, each thirty metres tall, of the twelve Ascendents of the Great Houses of the Avān. Green with age, the mists adorned the statues with liquid diamonds that glittered white. The court was webbed at various levels with delicate covered bridges and stairs of polished alabaster and red marble. There was a constant rumble as small cascades spilled into the court, to swirl around ferns and lotus flowers, then to pour away down the mountainside to the terraces below.

Mari inhaled the lush perfume of the ferns and lotus flowers. The air was cool and damp. There were no other people about. The Hour of the Serpent, seventh hour of the day, had only moments ago sounded from clocks across the city.

"It seems fitting we talk in the hearing of the Ascendents, neh?" Corajidin's voice echoed around the court. He made no secret of his entrance, escorted by a squad of Anlūki including Belamandris and her cousin, Nima. Corajidin made a striking figure in his red velvet over-robe, the black damask sleeves embroidered with rearing horses. His red-blond hair and beard were streaked with white, but his complexion had lost the jaundice it had at Amnon. His carriage was erect and proud. The long-knife he had used to assassinate Vashne was thrust through the sash at his waist. Golden Belamandris looked healthy, his bright blue eyes rimmed in kohl like any fashionable Avān of means. His expression when he looked at Mari was wistful, his smile a fledgling thing that died too soon.

"Thank you for coming, father," Mari said. She bowed lower than was necessary of a daughter to her father. It was the bow of a subject to her Asrahn.

"Shall we?" Ajo gestured to the double doors of The Twelveway. Belamandris and Nima went first, then Ajo, Neva, and Yago, followed by Nazarafine's people. There were no shouts of treachery. Mari was aware of her father's stare. The way he read in the messages in her clothing and choice of weapons. She saw him smile from the corner of her eye before he lifted his over-robe away from the wet ground and entered The Twelveway himself. Mari followed, the others behind her.

The food was a simple affair, something to be found in any Avānese home. Porridge, with cinnamon and honey. Slices of mandarin, orange, and apple. Blueberries and raspberries. Unleavened bread hot from the oven, goat butter melting into its pores. Silver urns of tea and coffee with porcelain jugs for the cream. An alabaster vase was filled with floating yellow lotus flowers and baby's breath, the scent remarkably like orchids and vanilla.

Corajidin and Belamandris sat opposite Mari at the twelve-sided table. Ajo and his children took station between. The guards remained alert and on their feet.

"How have you been, Belam?" Mari asked as the key people arranged food for themselves. "You look well."

"Well enough, considering." Belam's expression was one of sweet melancholy. He reached out a hand towards her, stared at it for a moment, then drew it back slowly across the table under the sharp scrutiny of their father. Belamandris dropped his gaze to stare at the patterns in his coffee. "I hear you won't be taking the role with the Feyassin. What are your plans?"

"Not sure. I may do some travelling. I've missed you."

"And I . . . suffice to say life is different without you around." He cast a quick glance to their father who seemed absorbed in surveying the dining house, though Mari was not fooled. Belamandris opened his mouth to speak again, then closed it with a frown.

Yago opened the Audio-scroll Apparatus. Within the waxed wooden box were bright metal gears and wires. He unfolded a broad-lipped tube, much like a great flower with delicate silver petals. It was the work of moments to inset a scroll into the recorder. Once ready he indicated they should begin.

"Thank you for arranging these talks, Mariam," Corajidin said. He bowed his head politely, touching the fingers of both hands to his chest, over his hearts. "I must say I was surprised when it was you who made the overture of peace."

"Something had to be done." Mari stirred cocoa and cream into her coffee. Inhaled the pleasant aroma and sipped, giving her time to think. Every word could either bless or curse what she was trying to achieve. She set the cup down with an audible click. "Shrīan stands at a precipice. Unfortunately, we passed the crossroads some time ago and now all eyes are fixed on what happens here. Amnon weakened us. We don't need more fighting between the Great Houses or the Hundred Families."

"Well said," Ajo nodded. The Sky Lord rested his fingertips lightly on the table. His fingers were long, encircled by bands of white gold, silver, and sapphire, the long nails painted white. The skin was remarkably unlined for his age. "I mean for the change in authority to go without further incident."

"Surely there is much about the present level of unrest that is beyond our ability to control?" Corajidin riposted. "The Iron League have already stated they intend on continuing their war against the Avān on all fronts. Even High-Palatine Navaar of Oragon says he fears Ygran will become the object of the Iron League's ire."

"Not to mention Tanis," Belam said. "Was a time when the Avān thought of themselves as a nation. Now? Truth be told, I've no idea what we are anymore."

"Well here is a good a place to start if we're of a mind to mend fences." Mari leaned forward, hands palm upward on the table. "The issues of a new rahn to replace Vahineh and the abduction of Indris, Femensetri, and—"

"I know nothing of any abduction," Corajidin shook his head. "It is entirely too convenient a story. As much as I have neither love for Indris, nor the Stormbringer, you know as well as I the kind of power it would take to overcome the both of them."

"Convenient? How is it even remotely . . .?" Mari heard the chill in her voice. She saw Ajo shake his head. Inhaled slowly to centre herself.

"Perhaps we can talk of the issue of Vahineh's replacement, then work from there?" Ajo suggested. "Let us take hope an early agreement will make us amenable to others as the morning progresses."

"I would have been content to follow the names on the Ascension Role," Corajidin said, "had the Federationist cabal not tried to subvert the accepted process. Reparations need to be made for their flagrant disregard of their peers."

"And these reparations would be?" Mari asked, dreading the answer.

Belamandris produced a document, which he passed around the table to Mari. Mari cracked the wax seal with her thumb, then unfolded the parchment. It was an edited copy of the Ascension Role. The names Kashir, Aram, and Nouri were penned there, known quantities who had been promoted up the list. Jhem was entirely new, a person who had not even undergone the Sēq testing to see whether he could be Awakened.

"Those names," Corajidin pointed at the list, "are the ones who will be given first chance at being Awakened. The three who already existed on the role have been approved by the Sēq; they are unlikely to die in the process of Awakening. Jhem is to be assessed by the Sēq for his suitability within the day."

The names on the list were all Imperialists. Should one of them become a rahn, it would even the balance of power in the Upper House of the Teshri. Of the three approved by the Sēq, Kashir was the most reasonable. Aram was one of Corajidin's longtime supporters and Nouri would cheerfully wage war on the rising sun, if it meant the Avān would rise to eminence on Ïa once more.

"I can take this to Nazarafine, Roshana, and Siamak this morning," Mari agreed. She passed the list to Ajo, who eyed it with trepidation as if it might bite him. "They will no doubt have a preference for the order."

"That is acceptable," Corajidin said. "Provided there is a third Imperialist rahn in the Upper House of the Teshri, I am willing to be flexible as to whom it is."

"If none of your candidates pass their Awakening, we will return to the order on the Ascension Role," Ajo said. The next five names were all Federationists, some Families having waited for centuries for the chance to be elevated to the royal-caste. It would be up to Roshana and the others to explain why they would need to wait longer still.

"Agreed," Corajidin nodded. He popped a piece of strawberry into his mouth, chewing contentedly.

"Father!" Mari and Belam both yelled. The soldiers around the room reached for their weapons. Eyes darted accusingly. Belam went to take the strawberry, something poisonous to their father, out of his mouth.

"I am well!" Corajidin slapped his son's hand away. Her father chewed contentedly, pausing only to dab at his lips with a napkin. He reached for another. "Such an amazing fruit! It is a shame I was unable to eat them for so long!"

Mari sat slowly, mind racing. Her father's renewed vigour. His seeming lack of pain. How he had managed to survive the Communion Ritual. The fact he could eat a fruit that would have been toxic to him even a month ago. It was clear her father had found something potent indeed to restore his vitality and stave off what had seemed like an inevitable death.

It was also clear that this was something beyond Wolfram's abilities; otherwise the Angothic Witch would have helped her father sooner. No, Corajidin had some new allies that he had yet to share with the rest of the world. Perhaps, with these new allies, his protestations of innocence when it came to Indris's disappearance were nothing more than empty air.

"Now, to the topic of Indris and Femensetri," Mari said. She eyed her father with newfound suspicion. The man seemed oblivious to Mari's scrutiny, deftly dropping strawberries into his porridge and pouring honey atop the lot. "We will want them released by sunset today. If you want to—"

"I told you I do not have them," Corajidin's voice was hard as an anvil. He pointed at Mari with his food-crusted spoon. "And having Vahineh handed over to the authorities is something upon which I will not waver."

"On what crimes?" Ajo asked. "You have made an accusation, though have provided no proof of any kind Vahineh was involved in Yashamin's murder."

"The same way you accused me of murdering Vashne and Ariskander? If memory serves I was robbed of my position as Asrahn-Elect and Governor of Amnon because of those accusations!"

"Is that really the card you're going to play, father?" Mari thrusted. Corajidin glared back.

Ajo cleared his throat then said, "If you can prove Vahineh—"

"No, Ajomandyan!" Corajidin rose to his feet. His voice cracked with unshed tears, of rage or grief Mari was unsure. "My. Wife. Was. Murdered! Under my own roof. A place, Mariam, that should have been safe had you only been there. I will have vengeance!"

"You may have justice," Ajo countered, "when you bring proof to the Arbiter's Tribunal. Even an Asrahn is not above the law, Rahn-Corajidin."

"You would enjoy that, would you not, Sky Lord?" Corajidin wiped tears away with shaking hands. He winced, as if beset by an unexpected pain. "Would you test my resolve? Do I need to issue a Jahirojin? Though Vahineh be a witless girl driven mad by her Awakening, she will pay for what she has done!"

Corajidin slumped back to his seat, breathing deeply.

"And Indris?" Mari asked, anger rising. "Femensetri? What are your plans for them, Father? Your idea of negotiation seems about as self-serving as I remember it."

"Mari!" Ajo snapped. "This does not help anybody."

"No," Corajidin waved his hand to silence the Sky Lord. "Lance the wound, Mari. Let your poison out!"

"You've betrayed your peers in the Teshri." Mari stood, struck the table with a stiffened fingertip. "You've perverted the course of our government with your bribes and malcontent. You even assassinated an Asrahn and a rahn, thinking all the while there'd be no consequences. Now you'd dare slap the Sēq in the face?"

"The Sēq are done in Shrīan, Mari." Surprisingly, it was her brother who spoke. Belam rose to his feet, his fingers curled lovingly around the hilt of Tragedy. His face was stern, eyes hard as chips of blue marble. "You turn your back on your family, to defend a man who tried to destroy it."

"Indris defended himself and the nation after our family tried to bend it to their will!"

"Your lover tried to kill me, Mari!" Belam shouted, colour rising. "He left me for dead in Amnon—"

"That's not what happened!" Mari saw the self-satisfied look on her father's face. She turned, pointed a trembling finger at the man. "You can't even tell Belam the—"

From the corner of her eye Mari saw the first flicker of movement. A knife flashed through the air. Belam diverted it with his hand. Rather than piercing her father's eye, it sliced across his temple.

Roshana's people! One of them flowed forward, movement so fluid it seemed he hardly moved at all. He glided from foot to foot, part run part lope. Her own hand froze on the hilt of her Sûnblade. She recognised the movement.

It was the assassin from the rooftop of Nanjidasé!

The assassin leaped high, long-knife an extension of his arm as he shot towards Corajidin. Belam drew Tragedy faster than Mari thought possible. The red-hued blade cleared the scabbard as Belam slid sidewise. Became a living shield for their father. He knocked Corajidin from his chair and diverted the assassin who turned his fall into a roll.

Roshana's other assassin moved forward. Nazarafine's and Siamak's warriors drew steel. The Anlūki did likewise.

Corajidin turned to Ajo, furious. "You see? This is what comes of my trust in a faithless, heartless, bitch who lives only to torment me! You hear me, Mariam? Do—"

"I had nothing to do with this!" she cried.

Roshana's assassins moved to attack. Belam smiled his small smile, so like Mari's yet so cold.

"Stop this now!" Ajo yelled. "As Arbiter of the—"

"Kill them all!" Corajidin screamed, spittle flecked, veins almost bursting from his temples and throat. Blood tracked down his cheek and jaw.

Mari did not draw steel. The same could not be said of the others. Nima and one of the Sûn warrior-poets faced off, blades shrieking. The Anlūki left Belam to defend Corajidin, their faith in the Widowmaker well placed. Mari swayed under a sword, pirouetted away from another. She lashed out with a boot, caught one of the Anlūki under the chin. Spinning, she smashed the base of her palm, then her elbow, into the temple of the other. Both warriors fell to the floor like so much meat.

Belam faced the two assassins alone. Mari wanted to go to his aid, yet it was Ajo, Neva and Yago she needed to see safe first. The Sky Lord had withdrawn towards the door with his heirs, though none seemed interested in attacking the Arbiter of the Change. Corajidin had scrambled away and stood, knife drawn, at the door to The Twelveway.

"Neva. Yago." Mari said. "Get Ajo and my father safely away. Please."

The Sky Knights nodded. They huddled Ajo towards the door, who spoke briefly to Corajidin. Her father glared at her as he left.

The battle was a frenetic blur. Nima had killed his assailant and moved on to the other Sûn warrior-poet. The marshlanders from the Rōmarq fought like dervishes, their shamshirs and hand axes throwing up a net of steel that seemed to draw blood at every turn.

Yet it was Belam who Mari concentrated on. Both assassins assailed him. Alternating. Then together. It did not matter. Tragedy seemed to be everywhere at once. Belam moved faster than Mari had ever seen before. Footwork precise. Parries perfect. Strikes flawless. She rejoiced to watch such an artist at work, though quailed when she saw the stony expression on his face. It was new to him. There was none of his savage joy. None of his humour, or personality. It was as if he were an automaton. Some golem made to rive flesh and bone.

He ducked. Swept his amenesqa in a low cut. Grey coils of intestines spilled to the floor amidst a flow of blood. An assassin crumpled to the floor, looking shocked. The Widowmaker grabbed the other assassin's wrist. There came the snapping of bones like dry twigs. The man who had attempted to kill Mari on the rooftop of Nanjidasé tried stabbing the Widowmaker with his other hand. The blow skittered off the Widowmaker's armour. With his other hand the Widowmaker grabbed the assassin's throat. Mari watched in horror as her brother, without even a hint of remorse, crushed the man's windpipe. He threw the body to the ground like it was so much waste.

Her brother turned his passionless eyes on Mari. He economically beheaded the assassins, taking the heads by the hair.

"Belamandris!" Corajidin yelled from outside. "Anlūki! To me! The faithless Näsarat's may have other assassins in wait."

Those who remained standing were covered in myriad wounds. None looked to be fatal, though some bled profusely through the fingers that covered them. Belam cast a disinterested glance around the room, then flicked the blood from Tragedy's blade.

Without a sound he left The Twelveway, Nima and the one conscious Anlūki behind him. Mari watched him walk away in silence.

All she could think about was the iron in her brother's gaze, like he was a different man entirely from the brother she loved, and the knowledge it was Roshana who had tried to have her killed.

Friends, like trust, seemed to be growing scarce.

18

"BETRAYAL IS THE MOST BITTER INSTRUMENT ONE CAN USE TO MURDER TRUST."

—Embarenten, Swordmaster of High Arden, 369th Year of the Shrīanese Federation

DAY 357 OF THE 495TH YEAR OF

THE SHRĪANESE FEDERATION

Corajidin sped through the dimly lit streets as rapidly as his legs would take him. The cut on his temple stung, the blood already turning tacky on his skin. The sweat of panic prickled his scalp. Left a long cool trail down his spine and across his chest. His hearts hammered against the prison of his ribs. Everything was in monochrome. The edges of the world were inked in black; parchment shapes pasted one atop the other to give the illusion of distance and depth.

Nima took point, feet flying across the road; hand on the hilt of his shamshir. The wide legs of his trousers made a snapping sound in the wind of his passage. Belamandris loped along beside, scowling. He held the two severed heads by their long hair, blood dripping from the stumps. The last Anlūki on his feet trailed behind, listing badly, leaving a trail of red in his wake. Corajidin spared a glance for the man, who dropped further behind with each passing moment. If the man made it back to the Qadir Erebus, then the fates had decided he would survive this morning's disaster. If not, there were others who could take his place.

Ahead, his nephew flagged down the driver of a Spool-Carriage, lightning flickering from the spinning layered cogs of the Tempest Wheel set behind its front axle. It was an opulent affair. Wooden panels arabesqued with brass. Teardrop door handles burnished. Iron fretwork screens over glass windows. Sun Globes in iron settings flickered in the shadows, fluid swirling bright in thick crystal. Nima held the door open until Corajidin and Belamandris were safely inside. He tossed a golden crown to the driver, more money than he would earn in a month, with orders to take the passengers as quickly as possible to the Qadir Erebus.

"What of you?" Belamandris asked.

"I'll wait on Yotep," Nima muttered. He took a bandanna from a pocket of his over-robe, used it to wiped his face and hands clean of blood. "We don't leave our own behind."

He rapped on the side of the carriage. The driver pulled away.

Corajidin huddled on the plush seat, hands folded into the sleeves of his over-robe. The cabin was redolent with leather and beeswax. The gentle rocking motion, as well as the faint hum and crackle of the Tempest Wheels, helped ease his fractured nerves. He stared at his son from beneath lowered brows, taking in the disinterest there. An ennui that had never been a stamp of the old Belamandris. The son who had gone under the Preservation Shroud was the not the son who had come out from it. It was as if part of him still lingered on the lip of the Well of Souls, gazing in.

"It seems your sister has shown her true colours," Corajidin grumbled.

"So it would appear, neh?" His son continued to gaze out the window to where the world scrolled by.

"Defiling herself with a Näsarat was one thing. Siding with them to assassinate me is something else! It shows she—they—can not be trusted."

"No more than we," Belamandris said distantly. He turned to face his father. "It was you who escalated this, remember? You murdered Vashne in the streets. Abducted Ariskander to wring from him what you needed to save yourself."

"I needed to live and the Iron League forced us to need a warrior, not a man of peace!" Corajidin snapped. He petulantly kicked at the seat Belamandris reclined on. "You're beginning to sound like your sister."

"She tried to save you, Father." Belamandris's voice was a monotone. "Perhaps you invent too many monsters in the dark places your mind is want to wander? Her recollection of events in Amnon seems to differ from yours."

"Perhaps it would be best if we continued in silence, if you are going to be morose."

Belamandris gave an elegant shrug. They rode the rest of the way in silence, Corajidin glad when the Spool-Carriage rattled beneath the yawning arch of the qadir. The gate was flanked by two massive horses that seemed to be rearing from the mountainside. There was a moment of shadow as they passed beneath the weight of Star Crown Mountain, then sunlight again as they came to the palm and olive tree garden that led to the qadir proper.

Anlūki in their blood-red and black armour snapped to attention as Corajidin and Belamandris stepped from the carriage. Corajidin looked up the irregular defile into which the qadir was built, taking in the polished stone of balustrades, prow-like balconies supported by horse-head reliefs and the all-seeing eyes of keyhole windows.

"Bar the outer gates," Corajidin ordered. "Double the guard. Nobody enters without my permission."

Corajidin stalked through the corridors, his long over-robe sighing across polished stone floors. *Ilhen* crystals in blackened iron sconces swamped the shadows. Potted plants softened the obdurate rock into which the qadir had been carved. The air seemed still and stifling as he stomped past stairwells, arabesqued doors, paintings, and statues collected over centuries not for their intrinsic value, more for their value to others.

When he came to the Hearthall, he paused. Every Avān residence had one, no matter how humble. It was the centre of a dwelling, the place where people came to take comfort in family and a sense of belonging. The Erebus Hearthall was a yawning cave formation, its walls mirror smooth. Stalactite and stalagmite teeth had been carved into lace trees, beasts and statues of ancient heroes of the Erebus. A wide stair spiralled upward and downward, *ilhen* light reflecting from quartz crystals and veins of silver, turning the blackness into a star-filled sky under the mountain. Several braziers of firestones burned. Lounges with cushions and thick woollen blankets surrounded hexagonal tables with brightly coloured mosaic tops.

It had not occurred to him before how much a cold and empty place it was, littered with things rather than filled with life.

"Your Majesty. You've returned early." Wolfram's voice was sepulchral as he ascended the sweeping stair. His eyes burned lupine and hungry through the tattered length of his fringe, his teeth a yellowed rip in the mat of his beard. The old witch limped in his callipers, ruined staff seeming to bend under his weight. Kimiya, ever in his orbit, stared at Corajidin with dark and troubled eyes as if the young woman were privy to sights she could not forget as much as she may wish to. Wolfram frowned at Corajidin. "You're wounded."

Corajidin growled at his witch, crossing the Hearthall to climb the wide staircase that led to the suites, which held his offices, audience chambers, and a small, though opulent, dressing room, bedroom, and bathroom. He gave himself a perfunctory wash in an alabaster basin. Steam coiled across the surface of a large tub that had been cut into the rock nearby, fed by the natural heated springs of Star Crown. It was tempting to soak there, having his body servants scrub him with mineral salts and massage scented oils into his skin as Yashamin had so often done for him. Time, however, was pressing.

Changed into fresh clothes, Corajidin headed for his office where his sons and some of his advisors waited. The Emissary entered not long after, followed by the frigid-faced Elonie, and Ikedion, the buck-toothed and obese Sea Witch with his long sideburns who reminded Corajidin of a walrus. He barely suppressed a tremor of fear at the memory of their illusory Aspects.

The others waited while Corajidin settled himself, glancing briefly at the small pyramid of scrolls and the stack of reports on his desk. Yashamin's Funerary Mask seemed to glow under *ilhen* light, the eyeholes dark and mysterious as her eyes had been in life.

"*I told you Mari would betray you, my love.*" Her voice was soft as smoke in his ears. He closed his eyes for a moment, imagining her hands on his shoulders. At the nape of his neck. Her lips pressed to his ears. "*You extend your hand to that treacherous slut, when you should have demanded my killer be thrown to your feet!*"

"I'm sorry." He reached out to touch the mask, the amber warm. "I promise it will be done."

"Avenge me my love." Her voice buzzed against his earlobe. *"Become the man of war your people need and take what is destined to be yours!"*

"Destined, not fated, to be mine."

"What will be yours, Your Majesty?" Wolfram asked. Corajidin looked up, unaware he had spoken aloud. The Emissary stared at Corajidin, eyes boring into his as if she were trying to read his mind. Corajidin jerked his head aside, suddenly afraid.

"What we set out to achieve," Corajidin said. He was brief in his recitation of Mariam's betrayal. Curt in stopping Belamandris short when he tried to defend his sister and cast a more positive light on her actions. Kasraman chewed his lip as he listened; glance flicking between his brother and Corajidin.

"So where is Vahineh if the Federationists don't have her?" Kasraman asked.

"It's a ploy to buy them time, nothing more," Nix said, rotating tinted glass balls on the palm of his hand, long fingers supple. He spun them so rapidly they almost blurred into a rainbow. Nix bobbed his head from side to side, hair swaying like a sagging reed thicket. "With every passing day they undermine Rahn-Corajidin's authority. Too long have their barbs gone unanswered. The response needs to be simple, yet instructional."

Nix allowed the globes to spin out of his hands, smashing into brilliant fragments when they hit the floor.

"I agree," Corajidin said, showing no sign of displeasure at Nix's liberties, his eyes transfixed on the rainbow-hued destruction on his floor. "I am going to be crowned Asrahn in three days' time. I will make what I do now, legal later. There was a time the Avān paid for what they wanted in blood. Let us remind them."

"Father," Belamandris said, "we're not at war. Please be wary. Remember Amnon? It nearly undid us."

"Your near demise unman you, Widowmaker?" Nadir asked.

Belamandris levelled a hard look at Nadir, his fingers curling loosely around Tragedy's hilt in a smooth and oft-practiced gesture.

"Nadir," Corajidin growled, "I remind you, you are my adjutant. Keep a civil tongue in your head if you wish to keep either."

"My rahn, I apologise for any offence." Nadir bowed low, face flushed. The man did not understand how close he had come to his own swift demise.

"I hear your warning, Belamandris," Corajidin said. "But this is a different matter. We risked much in Amnon for great reward. We are about to reap that reward and more."

He sat at his desk and took a piece of parchment. The words were not long in coming, as this was something he had given more than passing thought to over past days. He signed it, then dusted it with sand from a golden shaker in the likeness of a stallion's head. Kasraman whispered a word and a tiny fire spirit danced on the head of a candle. Corajidin pooled wax, then set black and red ribbons and a seal of red and black gold to his missive.

Corajidin handed the writ to Belamandris. "Take this writ and ten squads of your best Anlūki—"

"You want fifty of my Anlūki?" Belamandris asked, shocked.

"No. I want your fifty *best* Anlūki. The rest can guard the qadir. Take the writ and go to Ajomandyan of the Näsiré. Kindly inform the Arbiter of the Change I am invoking ayo-kherife. Given there were enough witnesses at this morning's debacle, including himself and his heirs, he is unlikely to question my rights."

"Then?" Belamandris asked quietly.

"Then you will go to the Qadir Näsarat and make a caste-arrest of Rahn-Roshana fe Näsarat! They were Roshana's assassins in Mari's retinue and she will be held accountable. No Arbiter would ever deny me justice, when the perpetrator is so obvious."

"And when they resist?" Nix tapped the fingers of his hands together in a rapid tattoo.

"Which they will," Jhem added.

"It is something I am rather counting on," Corajidin said. He turned to Belamandris. "Kill whom you will to send a message, but I can not stress this enough: under no circumstances is Roshana to be counted amongst the dead! Do I make myself clear? I can not afford for her to Awaken another."

"Especially not Indris," the Emissary said.

"He declined it once,"—Kasraman countered—"why would he take it if offered again?"

"Because he can see what's happening in his country," Wolfram said grimly. "The growing unrest, the strife brewing with the Iron League. He may already know about what has been happening at the Mahsojhin. This is a man the Sēq trained to either topple, or save, governments. And that's only what we know of his overt work. Who knows what he did while covert?" He idly stroked Kimiya's hair, the woman only barely flinching, before she leaned in to the contact.

"Were Indris to weigh the threat of the witches' return, or a war with the Iron League, against what he could do to prevent it as a rahn," the Emissary nodded, "he'd allow himself to be Awakened. I know Indris better than any of you. Know what he's capable of and why the Sēq have kept their eye on him. Indris being Awakened isn't something you'll ever want to deal with if he's your enemy."

"Very well," Belamandris bowed to his father. "But I'll kill Indris if I see him and bring Mari home, should I find her. I'm sure I can talk sense into her. But I will not abandon sende. There'll be no killing of civilians, or any other innocent."

The Emissary laughed and clapped her hands, then her laughter stopped, her smile turned cold and she pointed the fingers of her joined hands at Belamandris. "Aren't you the sweetest thing? A killer with a conscience. And manners! But I've been through this with your father. *Nothing* is to happen to Indris. But if you do decide to cause a fuss, take a lot of people with you. Preferably ones you don't mind losing."

"For the love of . . ." Corajidin said, voice dark with frustration. He gave Belamandris a look that clearly said: *Kill Indris if you have the chance, my son, and bring my daughter home where she belongs, away from the corrupting influences that steered her wrong.* Corajidin then took Nix and Jhem in with a glance—their eyes were hard at the thought of causing mayhem. Their savagery would be a boon. "Jhem and Nix, you go with Belamandris. Once you have finished with the Näsarat, move on to the qadirs of the Sûn and the Bey. Kick over as many stones as you need to. Stamp on whatever scuttles out. Do whatever it takes to bring Roshana and my wife's murderer to me."

Nadir and Ravenet stood together, talking quietly amongst themselves. Kimiya looked on, her body leaning towards them, expression longing, though the collar about her tanned throat and Wolfram's broad palm on her shoulder kept her where she was. Corajidin was again reminded of Brede, Wolfram's last apprentice. He wondered whether she too had been this way, before becoming Wolfram's creature, heart and soul.

Corajidin gestured for Nadir and Ravenet to come closer. He walked them to the door, leaning close as Ravenet opened it.

"I need you both to find Mariam," he whispered. "Bring her back. Do whatever you need to do, but bring her back alive and unharmed."

Brother and sister bowed, then slipped quietly from the room.

"What of the rest of us?" Kasraman asked. He watched the warriors leave the room, his expression troubled.

"We are going to remind the Sēq there is a new world on the way."

❄ ❄ ❄

Corajidin led his small retinue from the qadir aboard a wind-skiff. With Kasraman, Wolfram, Elonie and Ikedion in train, Corajidin had little to fear. Or so he hoped. Though he may dislike the Sēq for their arrogant superiority, there was no denying they had gained their reputation for a reason. The streets were no doubt being watched and air travel was by far the most direct route to the heights of Ïajen-mar and the long-abandoned Eliom Dei, also known as the Qadir am Amaranjin, named for the Mahj who had made it. Amaranjin. Son of Dionwē, the Näsarat who had sunk the Seethe beneath the Marble Sea, and first Mahj of the Awakened Empire.

Kasraman sat comfortably at the helm, guiding the wind-skiff with sure hands out over the Caleph-Rahn on Star Crown, across wooded ravines and cool, damp gullies to the harsh cliffs and jagged rocks of World Blood Mountain. From the deck of the wind-skiff, Corajidin could see the tall smile of white marble pillars that was the Tyr-Jahavān, set into the mountainside. Stairs, bridges, paths, and streams crisscrossed the mountain. Giant waterwheels were silent at this distance. Aqueducts bright lines of white stone filled with rippling diamond streams.

The Eliom Dei was built over almost one hundred vertical metres of the mountain, between Amenankher below and the Shalef-mar Ayet—the Temple Mount Shrine—above. Arabesqued reliefs were carved into the mountain face, smoothed and hardened by extreme heat so they shone like veined mirrors. Hundreds of windows and balconies faced outward, glass winking. Gardens hung. Water streamed from fountains to sculpted streams before turning to spume as it poured from the mouths of phoenixes: wings spread wide in intricate friezes now partially obscured by vines and small persistent trees.

A long beak of stone, deceptively fragile-looking, jutted outward. It was topped by a ring wall; arches filled with crystal panels. Kasraman turned the wind-skiff into the stiff breeze, landing amidst the spark and sizzle of Tempest Wheels and Disentropy Spools. The skiff bobbed as it settled on its crab-leg landing gear.

Wind howled through cracks in the ring wall. Clouds were brushstrokes of grey white, stretched thin and long. Grasses and flowering weeds grew between cracks in the stone. A long pathway, straight as a spear, led from the landing platform through a lush garden long gone to seed, all the way to the high keyhole doors of the Eliom Dei.

Corajidin led the way as they walked silently towards the great doors, closed for centuries. Statues dedicated to long dead grandeur loomed larger than life amidst oak, pine, and cedar trees, their faces lost in silhouette against the bright vault of the sky. Apples lay rotting in the long grass. Wasps droned. Wolfram's callipers creaked with every limping step, his staff striking the ground sharply. Flurries of thistledown tumbled in the wind. A giant mountain hart, several hind, and their fawns stopped to watch. The hart raised its red furred face; ebony antlers sweeping as far as Corajidin could stretch his arms.

Marble phoenixes flanked the path; time-dulled *ilhen* crystals grimy slivers in their eyes and mouths. Sandstone slabs were set between each phoenix. Corajidin counted hundreds of them as he passed, where loyal Feyassin would have stood night and day to protect their Mahj. It made his eyes burn with unshed tears to think how far his people had declined since the Insurrection. Once, an Avān rahn had ruled every nation in South-Eastern Ia. Corajidin's ancestors had once governed the Atrean islands, blessed by the sun and kissed by sea salt and the cerulean depths of The Westron Divide. Now the power of the Awakened Empire was little more than legend.

Tall pillars surmounted with the twelve-petalled lotus of the old empire flanked the round door. The door was carved to resemble the imperial lotus, with one petal for each of the original Great Houses of antiquity. Corajidin rested his hand against the doors and they opened, smoothly and silently. Inside, crystals ignited sending gelid fingers stretching across dust-covered walls, floor, and a ceiling so high as to beggar belief. Cobwebs fluttered in the sudden breeze like gossamer curtains.

"I remember reading a story of this place," Corajidin murmured. Somehow it seemed wrong to break the age-old silence. The visages of ancient people stared down from long glass panels, expressions obscured by grime. Rugs were brittle underfoot. There was a marked chill in their air.

"Before the Empire, Avānweh had not even been a city. There was nothing save Amenankher, which had been built by Sedefke, Kemenchromis, Femensetri, and a few others as a place of study. After Dionwē created the Marble Sea with the help of the first Sēq Masters, he built Avānweh and made it his capital. It is why, even though we do not have an empire anymore, we still come to this city as our seat of government."

"It's beautiful," Kasraman said. He craned his neck to look up at what could be seen of the intricately carved ceiling, set with ornate fretwork in what had once been rich enamels and precious metals.

"Yes." Corajidin wished he could summon the memories of those Ancestors who had walked these halls in their glory. He tried, yet received nothing more than shooting pains behind his eyes for his efforts. The Water of Life had left his system, taking its puissance with it.

Corajidin led them up a long corridor, the ceiling set with panels of frosted quartz. Long veils of web were draped between pillars and statues. Crystal orb spiders; bodies translucent as glass and wider than a man's hand, reared in warning. Wolfram gestured with his ruined staff and the entire web went up in flames. Elonie and Ikedion both whispered under their breath, hands making complex signs in the air. Within moments there came the plopping sound as hundreds of orb spiders fell from the ceiling above. Rats squealed and died. Cockroaches struggled on their backs, legs flailing.

Elonie took in Corajidin's surprised expression. "Crystal orb spiders are drawn to disentropy—though mostly they're drawn to rifts between here and both the under and overworlds."

"The lady speaks true, Rahn-Corajidin," Ikedion tittered, lips rubbery amidst his round cheeks and many chins. His opulent blue silk robe was pattered with sweat under the arms. Left crescents beneath his flabby breasts. "We should be cautious. This is a place of power across many worlds."

"Why are we here, Your Majesty?" Wolfram asked. The old witch leaned on his staff, breathing heavily. What little of his face could be seen behind his tangled fringe and wild beard was flushed. Corajidin rested his hand on the man's shoulder, sympathetic to the physical ordeal the long walk had been for the witch's ruined body. Yet he did not answer.

Instead, he quietly led them along corridors and up stairs. Across bridges that arched over deep, dark chasms filled with nothing save the roar of water far below. Through natural caves that stretched upward to razor cuts of light in the distance, or downward to spiralling trails of coloured radiance, where paths led to unknown and abandoned vaults.

After crossing a long bridge of what appeared to be spun *serill*—faceted black drake-fired glass—Corajidin led them to a tall door of mirror fragments. He looked at himself, broken and split, the doors revealing him in pieces yet never as a whole. There were two large porcelain handles, each shaped after the imperial lotus.

Above the door was an inscription in the fluid High Avān script: *Ishii qiel yaha rem. Dijar bah yaha vahin. Beware who you are. Respect what you want.*

His hand wavered for a moment. There was the faintest trembling. The merger of fear, desire, and anxiety. He looked at his shattered reflection in the broken-mirror door, slivers of his face, or eye, or chest showing him to be the broken man he was. There was a deep crack running down one eye. Another across his lips and a long split that severed his image above his hearts. Each time he blinked it seemed as if the mirror pieces had moved, showing him different images of himself. He spared a glance for the others, saw the looks of distress on their faces.

Closing his eyes, Corajidin turned the handles and pushed the doors open.

The throne room was a bell-shaped chamber of crudely faceted obsidian, with a dome made of thousands of tinted crystal panels in all the colours of the seasons. In its day it had been called the Obsidian Heart, a place where decisions were made that could be sharp and dark, rending the hearts and soul of the Mahj who made them. Like the spherical seats of the Tyr-Jahavān, it was a reminder that power was nothing to be envied. Keyhole alcoves lined the round wall, where Feyassin and Sēq Knights would once have guarded their Mahj. Tall, black-lacquered chairs were spaced in a semicircle around the wall, facing inward. In the centre, in a broad beam of honeyed light, squatted a giant tourmaline throne, like somebody had carved a huge faceted chair from a piece of the sea. The Canon Stone.

Beside it was a small, ornate wooden chair, lacquered black. It was so old it was seamed as an old man's skin. Its high back was surmounted by two fist-sized orbs of flickering witchfire.

And on that chair sat a man in a black cassock, so dark it seemed to drink the light from around it. The man was short and stocky. Ruddy, with eyes the hue of fresh cut grass set in deep orbits lined with kohl, his mind-stone an oval without facet or imperfection. His long hair and beard were the colour of clay, shot through with terracotta. A ploughman's hand, nails rough, was wrapped around the iron stave of his Scholar's Crook, its scythe-like top a narrow razor of witchfire. Power crackled in traceries of lightning about his head and hands. His eyes shone as if they burned from within. He stood.

"I am Sēq Master Zahiz." The words were quiet, though the pride in his voice almost filled the room to the exclusion of all other sound. Fractals of energy began to spiral within the curve of his crook, sending patterns of bright colour across his brow. "Why do you come to the seat of the Mahj?"

Corajidin fought the impulse to bow. Flicking his eyes right and left he saw the loathing on both Elonie's and Ikedion's faces. The abject fear in Kasraman. The animal in Wolfram's yellow-toothed snarl. Nima had dropped to his knees.

"I am Asrahn Erebus fa Basyrandin fa Corajidin," he managed to grind out. The urge to bow and scrape grew stronger. He felt his knees trembling. "I come here to discuss the terms of the Sēq's surrender to my authority, or their exile from my country. Where is Femensetri, the Scholar-Marshall? It is she I would speak with."

To either side of him the witches glared at Zahiz. Corajidin wondered whether the Sēq Master had been one of those who had sealed them inside Mahsojhin? Zahiz looked back at them with equanimity, though his skin began to flicker like a paper lantern. The whites of his eyes shone bright.

"Femensetri no longer speaks on behalf of the Sēq," Zahiz said. "Another has not been appointed to replace her."

Corajidin was stunned. The Stormbringer had been the Scholar-Marshall for centuries, advising generations of Asrahn. Before then she was part of the Mahj's inner circle. What had happened? Was this the result of the schism the Emissary had mentioned, or something else?

"Days ago I informed the Scholar-Marshall there would be changes in Shrīan. Namely, the status of the Sēq and my requirement for them to rest their brows at my feet in homage."

"And why would we do this thing?" came the condescending response. "We bow to none save the Mahj. It has always been so."

"It was always so when the Mahj was a scholar, the Awakened Empire existed and you were in Pashrea." Corajidin stood tall. "Shrīan is not Pashrea. We have no Mahj here. From this point forward you and yours will bow . . . or you will leave."

Zahiz's eyes went slightly out of focus for a moment, as if he were seeing sights and hearing conversations in a different room. It lasted a few seconds only, before his eyes sharpened on Corajidin with needle sharpness.

"I can not agree to what you ask," Zahiz said.

"Then find somebody with the authority to talk about the future," Corajidin gestured to the witches, "or you may die before you see it."

19

> "FRIENDS AND ALLIES ARE VERY DIFFERENT THINGS. A FRIEND
> WILL DELIVER ALL AND EXPECT NOTHING. AN ALLY MAY
> DELIVER NOTHING, UNTIL YOU'VE GIVEN ALL."

—High Palatine Navaar of Oragon (495th Year of
the Shrīanese Federation)

DAY ? OF THE 495TH YEAR OF

THE SHRĪANESE FEDERATION

"Finally!" Taqrit's voice pierced the swaddling around Indris's mind. "I thought I'd lost you! And that, old friend, simply wouldn't do."

He lay on something cold and hard. Metallic. The sour reek of his own body had been replaced by the scent of crushed mint and tea tree oil. The fine woollen cassock with its high collar felt cool against his skin. His wrists and ankles were cuffed in what felt like a combination of metal and leather. Despite these material comforts, the muscles of this shoulders, back, and chest were afire with agony. He cracked an eye open, blinking against the glare.

"You're quite the prize." The leonine voice came from a blurred silhouette hovering over Indris. Wisps of white-blond hair were an aureole around the planes of the man's face. Zadjinn, the centuries-old Erebus Master who had led the attack on he and Femensetri.

"Lucky me." Indris's tongue felt thick in his parched mouth. "Where are Femensetri and Vahineh?"

"Femensetri is undergoing Censure. The Stormbringer has tested the patience of the Order one time too many. She is no longer the Scholar-Marshall and another will be appointed in due time. Vahineh, that useless woman-child, is no concern of yours anymore." His face slowly came into focus, handsome and lion-proud. His cassock was impeccable, black damask with diamond-studded buttons and heavy turned-back cuffs in the modern style. His crook was tall, the curve at its top extended to almost make a circle of it. "Rumour is you were the one who performed her Severance, making her useless to Crown and State. Yet another thing you shouldn't be able to do—unless somebody has made you a Master and not told anybody."

"I dare say there's plenty about me you've no idea about."

Taqrit flailed Indris across his upper thighs with his daul. It felt like his legs had been struck with a branding iron. Though he knew it to be fiction, part of his mind could smell the burning flesh. Could imagine the welts turning to blisters that would become infected and septic over time. He contained the thought before it took hold, enforcing his will over the subtle psychic barbs of the daul.

Indris felt the fire burning behind his eye, infusing his brain. It ran down his spine using nerves as kindling. The Inquisitor frantically wheeled his chair back. Nervous sweat beaded his brow. A drop trickled down to tremble on the tip of his nose.

"You're a dead man," Indris nodded, gaze boring into Taqrit's milky eyes. "I'll be free of this and there's no place on Ia where I won't find you and end you."

"I think some salt-forged steel shackles will keep you pliant enough." Zadjinn said. Indris wanted to beat the smug expression from his face. "I hear you're already acquainted with salt-forged steel, so I don't need to tell you what you'll experience. Until then the Marionette Tether will have to suffice."

Indris thrashed in his bonds, memories of his years in the slave pits of Sorochel not distant enough. *Hard stone floors, the dust of undisturbed ages in his throat. Muscles aching from day after day after wretched day of swinging pick and hammer. Runny gruel to eat and dirty water to drink. The reek of both the living and the dead in claustrophobic tunnels, like too many rats. And the con-*

stant nausea/burn/ache/vertigo/fatigue of the salt-forged steel cuffs worn by he and the other mystics imprisoned there, digging up the treasures of a civilization gone and better left forgotten. Tears of frustration came unbidden. He inhaled deeply to master himself.

Zadjinn picked up an ornate cylinder, crystal rods and metallic coils poking from it like a crown. It had several small wheels, which he began to turn. Indris sat up straight. Try as he might, Indris was unable to stop the strange, exaggerated motions of his body as Zadjinn pulled his strings. More moving of the wheels. He swung his legs over the edge of the table.

Standing, Indris had a better view of the room. This was not the gloomy cell dominated by its torture device. This room was airy, slit windows showing a cloud-scudded grey sky. It was neither large, nor ornate, made by hand unlike most of the Amer-Mahjin whose warren riddled Ïajen-mar. On a table lay Indris's satchel, his weapons belt with storm-pistol and dragon-tooth knife, and a long recurved shape wrapped in black damask, studded with silver. Changeling.

"Where are you taking me?" Indris asked.

Taqrit went to strike Indris with his daul. Zadjinn waved him off. The Sēq Inquisitor shot Indris a sullen look from his wheeled chair. Rather than sheath his daul, he kept it in his lap, one clawed hand curled possessively around its hilt.

"Firstly we will gather the Selassin woman as a gift for our esteemed Asrahn. Word is he has placed quite some value on apprehending her. Then my peers in the Dhar Gsenni are excited about speaking with you."

Dhar Gsenni. A bastardisation of the High Avān phrase, *for the good of all*, it was a name out of history. A sect of the Ilhennim who had existed before the scholastic orders were formed, then navigated the halls of power for centuries after. The myth had them as being powerful mystics who defied the mandates of the Covens, then of the Orders, pursuing their own agendas in search of knowledge. To them, so the myths went, knowledge could not of itself be evil: there was only ever evil done in the application of knowledge. Or the power that came with it. Legend had it was they who had sponsored the open syllabus taught at Khenempûr, the ancient city in Tanis with its curved walls, doors, and streets, which passed from dying culture to dying culture over the millennia.

Indris knew there were many secret societies within the Sēq, each fighting their quiet wars with each other, as well as with orthodoxy. But of them all, the Dhar Gsenni were the most insidious, with tales of them tugging at the reins of the Sēq for millennia. Clearly, Zadjinn and his fellow cultists were desperate enough to abduct Indris and try to hide him in the Amer-Mahjin. *But there's more to this tale that needs telling.*

"Why?" Indris often found the simplest questions were generally the best.

"Will you walk," Zadjinn said, ignoring the question and holding up the box with its crystals and coils and wheels, "or will you be tiresome? I have studied you a great deal, Indris. It would be beneath you to be marched in like some witless golem."

"If you've studied me, you know I'll escape and probably kill a good number of you on my way out."

Zadjinn shrugged, manipulating the wheels to make Indris march towards the door. Taqrit rang a small bell, at which the door opened and another four Sēq entered the room. They wore over-coats with the hoods drawn up. Plain cassocks of black wool. Unadorned. No insignia of rank like Zadjinn, with his Master's insignia embroidered in silver thread on the hems of his turned-back sleeves. Or Taqrit with his crook-and-eye sigil stitched in white. These others were not Sēq of rank. Novices, most likely. Librarians, perhaps, or even inexperienced Scholars. Students swayed by whatever promise of grandeur Zadjinn and his ilk had spun from opiates, seductions, and dreams. They carried long-knives thrust through their sashes, the leather-bound hilts not yet stained with use. The new arrivals took up Indris's possessions, following as Zadjinn led the small group through the door. Taqrit trundled after, wheeled chair squeaking.

It had been more than seven years since Indris had stepped inside Amer-Mahjin, yet his recollection was still strong. Long irregular corridors lined with volcanic glass. Polished marble columns in black, white, and grey. Stained glass windows, taller than trees in some cases, sending coloured beams across mirror-bright floors, carved wooden desks and long rows of shelves and cabinets, and doors leading to one wonder after another.

On occasion they would see other black-cassocked Sēq: Novices, Librarians, Scholars, Knights, and the rare Master. Each time Zadjinn would lead them in a different direction to avoid contact. Clearly the factions were ill at ease with each other if he went to such lengths to avoid contact.

Indris barely controlled his surprise when Zadjinn spoke again, the man's tone wistful, as if they were old friends sharing confidences on park benches, with little more to their days than playing tanj, drinking tea, or feeding pigeons.

"The Sēq are so few now," Zadjinn said. "Since the Scholar Wars, the perception of our value has diminished. We remain aloof, for the most part, from the affairs of the people. It is a tragedy, given we know so much that could benefit the world."

"Before we became part of the political apparatus," Indris mused, "the Sēq used to discover things. Build things. Advise and suggest, using everything we knew for the common good. Now the Order hides in long shadows, nesting in the detritus of yesterday while ignoring the present, let alone the future."

"Dhar Gsenni," Zadjinn agreed. "The good of all. There are those of us who have walked Ia, recovering the most exquisite, beautiful treasures from around the world. Knowledge thought long forgotten. Wandered moonlit paths lost even to myth and legend. Been witness to sights that beggar the imagination. It is enough to make one weep. Yet nothing is as heart-breaking as those who could make a difference, but do not."

"What do you and yours propose, then? Has the Mahj given you leave to interfere in Shrīanese politics?" Indris looked over his shoulder at his captor. "Shrīan is not Pashrea. Though you cling to the fantasy of your elitism, there's nothing stopping an informed Asrahn from cutting the Sēq off at the knees."

"And Corajidin will do this, unless we can offer him a reason not to." Zadjinn turned Indris. "Giving him Vahineh should be a good start in build-ing a relationship with the man who would change a nation."

I'll do my best to make sure Vahineh does not become your bargaining chip. Surely you realise the moment Vahineh is Corajidin's care, her life is over? The balance of Shrīanese politics possibly altered for decades to come.

But Indris said, "What do you want with me? I've no interest in your agendas."

"But you're exactly the kind of person we need," Zadjinn nodded briskly, feline features creased in a smile. "You and those few like you. You knew when to disobey! You knew when to stand up and tell the Order they had done wrong! So many of the Sēq these days are sheep, taught by rote all they think they need to know. The gift of intellect is *not* knowing what questions to ask, rather questioning what you are taught. Every axiom must be challenged in order to grow.

"Besides, there are far too many secrets locked away in your head for us to let you go on as you have done. Your time on the Spines. Your knowledge of the Soul Traders. The memories of Sorochel and the wonders you must have seen, digging amongst Inoqua ruins. Actually touching relics made before the Time Masters had risen to the height of their power!

"Then, of course, is the information everybody wants: why Sedefke himself, centuries before your birth, sent you to find the Dream Key."

Indris looked on the man with horror. His years in Sorochel had been one nightmare after another. Had he and Shar not escaped, he wondered how much longer he could have survived the punishing conditions. Yet this man saw nothing save the abstract of knowledge, without consideration for the price or consequences such learning demanded. He was like a child playing with fire in another person's home, seemingly careless of what may burn down around him. Zadjinn was an idealist, without the altruism to temper his moral or ethical compass.

They came to a set of embossed silver doors. The leonine scholar-master nodded to one of his followers. She went to a nearby door and knocked. Within moments the door opened. Shortly after, a hollow-eyed Vahineh was escorted out to join the small group.

From all outward appearances she had been treated well. She had been bathed and fed. Some of the hollowness beneath her cheeks had filled out. Her hair was clean and brushed; clumps of it missing yet dressed to hide the worst of it. Her face was still piebald and drool collected at the corners of her lips in tiny bubbles that expanded and contracted as she breathed. Her fingernails were lacquered, jagged edges filed smooth. Somebody had dressed her in a simple hooded robe of fine wool, the laces along the sleeves and bodice drawn tight, the deep hood pooled around her shoulders. Indris smiled at her. She looked at him with the vague comprehension of somebody who hears a song, though is sure neither of what it is nor where she heard it.

Loud voices came from ahead. When they turned the corner there were a number of the Sēq talking amongst themselves. There were no doors along the corridor. *Ilhen* crystals hung from the wall in curlicued sconces, coaxing veins of russet, orange, and brown from the faceted obsidian walls. One of the Sēq was a Master, a tall man who looked like he hailed from a land of towering pines, snow-covered mountains and long, star-shot winter nights. His mindstone was a rough thing, all edges against his tanned brow. His crook was tall, the sickle top a bright jade-hued talon. Beside him was an armoured Sēq Knight and what Indris took to be more Librarians, faces fresh and eyes still bright from the horrors they had not yet seen.

Indris was tempted to shout out, though was unaware what kind of reception he would receive from the strangers. Zadjinn's and Taqrit's response was less doubtful: it would be something swift, violent, and unpleasant.

"Wait here, all of you." Zadjinn then handed the control box to Taqrit, who took it with an evil glint in his flawed pearl eyes. Zadjinn stared at Indris. "Do I need to warn you to remain silent? Yours is not the only life in the balance here. Remember the woman."

"Vahineh is about the only reason you have for me not ending you here in the corridor." Indris smiled, though his gaze was hard. "Can't make any promises for the immediate future, though. I do intend on misbehaving, if the warning is any help."

"My patience goes only so far, boy," the leonine man growled under his breath. He stamped away, Scholar's Crook held primly above the ground as if he did not want to sully it. He met the other Master. Heads were inclined as politely as sende required, though expressions were tense. After a few moments, Zadjinn walked into a distant room with the others. The door closed behind them.

Once Zadjinn was out of earshot, Taqrit squealed forward on his rickety chair. The man's face was pensive, the mottled skin and snow-blasted eyes stark against the sombre tones of his cassock and the faceted glass walls.

"You could have a place with the Dhar Gsenni," he said. Indris cast a glance down at the daul clutched in the crippled hand of the broken man's lap. He suppressed a shudder at the thought of how many people had been given a similar offer, under similar duress. "All you need do is tell Zadjinn and the others what they need to know."

"And then they'll use what I tell them for the good of all," Indris mused, "or for the good of the few? Such has always been the way of secrets, Taqrit."

"Says the man with the secrets. Zadjinn and the others are great schol-ars. They could make a difference for our people."

"The man with the secrets thinks Zadjinn may be a great scholar, which does not make him a great man." Indris gazed down the corridor to where the man in question had disappeared with the other Sēq. "I think in his case it makes him a great liar."

"You'll learn your place!" Taqrit's voice was savage. He spun the wheels on the control box, forcing Indris to his knees and freezing him in place.

Taqrit struck Indris's shoulders with his daul, the Marionette Tether making it impossible for Indris to move. Again and again he struck. The torturer growled imprecations from between spittle-flecked lips.

Indris bore the punishment silently, afraid what would happen to Vahineh should he sound any kind of alarm. Time and time again came the crack of the daul, in time with Taqrit's grunting and the hissing of his sour breath.

Vahineh began to whimper and wring her hands. A tear leaked from her wide, dark eye. Something lurked in there. Something caged and wanting to be free, if only it knew the way.

"Will one of you shut her up? Taqrit snarled at those around him. One of the others stepped close and raised a fist over Vahineh. The girl cried out, her voice echoing down the corridor.

Out of control, Taqrit whipped his daul across Vahineh's abdomen. The woman buckled, shrieking. Indris smelled urine. Saw the widening pool of moisture on her robe, then the small puddle on the floor. Eyes bulging, Taqrit backhanded Vahineh in the face, the daul in his clenched fist. There was a small detonation as the woman was knocked back against the wall, lips split. Blood sprayed across her cheek, mixing with drool as it trickled down her chin. She slumped to the floor, eyes rolled upward, breathing ragged.

Around them the walls began to blossom with frost, tendrils like vines spreading across the polished obsidian. Indris felt a familiar chill across his skin.

"*Chaiya,*" Indris thought. The warm tingling along his spine told him better than words who had heeded his desperate call.

"Corajidin can do without you, girl," the crippled torturer spat, arm raised for a final blow. His expression grew perplexed, though, as he noted the frost. The temperature dropped suddenly, his breath a white plume. The daul cracked against Vahineh's shoulder, rather than her brow.

"Mistake," Indris grated through clenched teeth.

"What have you done?" Taqrit gasped.

The lights went out.

Chaiya stood there, a glorious sculpture of jade light and deep shadow, her outline flickering. Taqrit shrieked, his wheeled chair colliding with one of his co-conspirators as he tried to back away.

"I need you!" Indris thought desperately. *"Please, help me! I can't do this alone."*

The lights flared. Chaiya disappeared. There was a silence that felt like an eternity. The other Sēq looked about nervously, hands on their weapons. Taqrit began to murmur under his breath, causing ripples in the ahm.

Indris worked to marshal his strength, aware his efforts may be fruitless yet unwilling to let Vahineh suffer any more.

Then Chaiya was with him. Or rather, more than with him.

She *was* him.

There was no sense of the individual. Her memories and ambitions. Her patience and constant wonder at a world she will see spin for centuries to come, until she forgets why she lingered. They shared everything they had ever been. Every memory. Experience. Love, loss, triumph, failure, and joy. One plus one plus one equals one. Plus another and the whole became much greater than the sum of the parts.

Two souls in concert, willing and equal in the name of a greater good. Chaiya understood what Indris wanted to do as if she had thought of the idea herself. To her, she had. Indris understood Chaiya's connection with all the other kaj, orbs of light floating, talking, communing in an endless ocean of the energy that fuelled all life. A great net of information. Every voice that had lived. Everything that had ever been known, drifting free on currents of pure disentropy.

Chaiya embraced his mind. Sheltered those parts that still knew fear, doubt, or pain. She was the cool balm around his nerves, allowing him to act while she buried the backlash of agony under layers of soothing thought.

Indris felt the fury burn. He felt his power rise, entwined with hers. It pooled in all the deep places in him. Ran tingling across his soul. The

Dragon Eye opened, tinting his vision with furious hues. The Marionette Tether puffed away into ash as Indris stood.

He reached out with his mind. Cloth-wrapped Changeling flew into his hands. The black fabric around her burned away at his touch. Changeling snarled, low and menacing. The inexperienced Sēq around him froze in panic. Some fumbled for weapons. Others stepped back. Only Taqrit acted, his skin brightening like a lamp being turned up as he sang his first canto.

But too slowly, the Inquisitor stammering with fear.

Indris's eyes blazed as the power of his jhi was unleashed. Taqrit was swept down the corridor on a tongue of fire, a mess of raggedy limbs in his kindling chair. Indris's Disentropic Stain expanded, whirled like a dervish as it scattered his captors like so much chaff.

Training and experience took over. He did not think of six enemies, for there was only ever one at a time. He did not think at all. He kept the murmuring Changeling sheathed as he twirled it like a baton, spinning from foot to foot in the steps of the sword-dances he had learned from a dozen Masters across South-Eastern Ïa and beyond. Perfected on what had felt like an endless number of battlefields. Every step was designed to cause harm, else what was the point? *Leaf on the Wind* led to *Dragon Sweeps Down*. *The Wyrm's Tongue* became the *Headsman's Caress*. Changeling hummed as it tore the air, the black kirion sheath a blur as it struck and struck and struck. And where it struck, a person who should have been a protected brother or sister of the Order was laid low.

Perhaps they will have learned a lesson, when they wake, for some reputations were made, while others were earned.

❇ ❇ ❇

Chaiya slowly unfolded from his soul, her presence the lingering memory of a kiss. She gave him time to order his thoughts and lock the pain away in scores of tiny boxes, to be dealt with later. He felt her soul caress his in the kind of understanding lifelong lovers sometimes feel. She appeared next to him, a juddering image in the uncertain light.

Indris stood over a panting Taqrit, who was curled in a foetal position. His fingers were bent, the hands now useless clubs of charred flesh. The remainder of his hair had been burned away, eyes seared from his head leaving scorched sockets. With a word, Indris quenched the smouldering of the man's cassock, though it would do Taqrit no good. The odour of cooked meat and burned hair was overwhelming.

"Kill . . . me . . ." Taqrit wheezed.

"I already have." Indris looked down on the man, trying to summon some emotion, such as hatred or satisfaction. Even remorse or regret. But he couldn't find it in him. There was a place in him, not a void, merely a place like all people had such places, waiting to be filled by better things, for better people. He had no room for Taqrit.

"They'll . . . never . . . stop . . . looking . . ."

"I don't imagine they will." Indris knelt by the man. *There but for the sake of the Ancestors lay I.* Was this the fate he had missed, by leaving the Order before they could wring him dry, leaving little more than a bitter husk who fed on secrets and suffering? He thought of Femensetri. Her brusque manner and idiosyncrasies developed over a count of years Indris could not begin to imagine. Was this her fate, too?

"You . . . could have helped . . . us."

"No, I couldn't. I wouldn't, even if I knew what the Dhar Gsenni wanted. I made a choice a long time ago to care about people. Not power, nor politics or riches. Your struggles are none of my concern."

"You don't . . ." Wheeze. Pant. Gasp. "Believe that. Amnon. You came back . . ."

Indris looked down at the man and was surprised to feel a faint stirring of loss for what the man had once been. "Of eight there are now two. How our teachers must weep at the thought of how far we fell short of their dreams."

Taqrit's breath was dry as it whined through his scorched throat. His daul was burned into his hand, the fingers sticks of burned meat and blackened bone. The other flexed spasmodically.

"Kill . . ."

"You'll die the death you deserve," Indris murmured. He looked away to where Vahineh lay, unconscious and bleeding on the ground. Heavy hearted, he turned back to the dying man at his feet. "We were taught many things. Many terrible, Ancestors' awful things. Things I wish I could forget. One of the things we were taught was to make decisions, many of which would return to haunt us.

"I try hard to be a moral, ethical man. It's why I love the Tau-se so much. They live their lives with quiet integrity and honour. They believe in *nemembe*—that they get back from the world threefold what they give it, both in kindness as well as suffering. May your Ancestors forgive you, Taqrit.

"But I can't. I won't."

So saying he turned away from the dying, mewling Taqrit to take Vahineh in his arms.

Zadjinn would return soon. As, no doubt, would others. He needed to get Vahineh to safety while he still could, before the Sēq bartered the woman's life away to a vengeful Corajidin.

"I can't fight for you," Chaiya's sad voice was like satin draped across his soul. *"Helping you as I did went against everything I believe in . . . but with the life of a friend in the balance it seemed a fair price. I will not blend my soul with yours again, Indris . . . but I can show you the secret ways out of Amer-Mahjin."*

"Thank you, Chaiya. I could not have escaped alone, and I'm terrified of what they want to know, that I can't remember."

"Well, I hope you don't forget this," she replied, and Indris could feel the timbre of her smile without seeing it. *"The hallowed dead have answered your question, my friend. There is one living who can tell you of the Mah-Psésahen."*

"And I owe you my thanks a second time."

"Perhaps . . . not." Chaiya's imagined smile faded. *"When you've the chance, look for a man named Danger-Is-Calling—he wanders with the Nomadic orjini who travel the Dead Flat. He is old, Indris. Frighteningly old. But he has the answers you are looking for."*

"Why wouldn't I thank you for this? You've been a great help."

"Because Danger-Is-Calling is but one of his names, and though the dead know him by many, it's his place of origin you'll find most troubling. I'm sorry, Indris, but I wish it were otherwise."

Indris closed his eyes, feeling the lightness of hope turn dark and swollen as a rain cloud in his chest. There were places Indris was wary of, but few of which he was frightened.

"Isenandar." The Pillars of Sand.

20

"THE EASIER PATH TAKEN HAS THE SINGLE REWARD IN THAT IT IS EASY."

—Zienni proverb

DAY 356 OF THE 495TH YEAR OF

THE SHRĪANESE FEDERATION

"You reckless, selfish, careless woman!" Mari did not care how harsh her words sounded. Roshana deserved them all and more besides. The sunroom at the Eyrie echoed with Mari's indignation. She flung the list of preferred new rahns at Roshana, who opened it as if Mari were not standing in front of her.

Mari had raced along narrow mountain streets until she caught up with what remained of her envoy after the bloodletting in the Ascendant's Court. Neva and Yago escorted Ajo to the Eyrie, while she sprinted to the Qadir Bey with the two marshlanders in tow. There, Mari had asked Siamak to send messengers to Roshana and Nazarafine, asking them to meet in secret at the Eyrie. Neva had gone to get Shar, Ekko, and the others herself. The Eyrie was the only place Mari could think of that was in a remote location, was neutral territory, and was nowhere her father or brother would think to look. It was also close enough to the Royal Skydock, High Skydock and the commercial Skydock known as The Southface for an escape, if it came to such.

It had taken almost two hours before Roshana had arrived with a nondescript man in warrior-caste clothing whom Mari took to be another assassin, a pensive Bensaharēn at her side. Nazarafine had been accompanied by her nephew, Navid. The man had prowled into the hotel, soft-footed, head low, shoulders inclined. Ready to fight the world at the slightest provocation. From what she had seen of the warrior-poets of the Saidani-sûk today, unfounded arrogance was one of the four blades they were taught to use. The arrival of Ajo and Yago, as well as Kembe of the Tau-se and his lithe bodyguard, Ibamu, had been a welcome relief. Neva had arrived sometime later, windswept from her gryphon-back reconnoitre of Avānweh's skies.

Mari had told those assembled what had transpired in as unemotional language as she could. It was Roshana's casual indifference that had given rise to Mari's temper. Now everybody sat in the uncomfortable aftermath of truth.

"Are you quite done?" Roshana asked, sounding bored, eyes flicking over the list of names Corajidin had penned. The soldier-turned-rahn waved the parchment in the air. "And you agreed to bring me this? Fah! I'll not have the appointment of a new rahn held to ransom.

"There was a chance to end your father's tyranny before it plunged us into war. The Iron League nations will take the time to build their forces, unless we do something to allay their fears. It was a calculated risk and I took it. It failed. Now we need to decide how to proceed."

"You're wrong," Shar's breathy voice carried in the stillness. "So terribly wrong. If Corajidin has Indris, you may as well have wielded the blade that killed him yourself."

"Are none of you listening?" Roshana sounded incredulous. She pointed out the window to a salt-and-pepper clouded sky. "The Iron League will come. Their Ambassadors have said as much. We already suspect the Humans of attacking us. The murders in the streets, the abductions. This is all in response to Corajidin being confirmed as our new Asrahn. If we don't do something we'll be at war within two years, three at most. Shrīan can't stand against the combined might of Manté, Angoth, Atrea, Imre, and Jiom. The Neutral Nations are unlikely to help or hinder, and Pashrea will doubtless remain silent as it has done for centuries."

"What about Kaasgard?" Ajo asked. Neva looked at her father in surprise. "It has been centuries since we have dealt with them, yet they were Avān before their exodus after the Insurrection."

"Kaasgard?" Benshaharēn shook his head. "Most of those who fled there were of the orjini. The ice and frigid seas have turned their blood cold. They took giants and other, less wholesome things to their beds to breed a race we would hardly recognise anymore. Better to negotiate with the winter, for both would do as they would regardless of our needs."

"Nobody is coming to help us," Roshana said. "We need to get our own house in order."

"So you thought possibly starting a civil war, so close on the heels of Amnon, was the best way of doing it?" Ajo asked, aghast. "You tried to assassinate Corajidin! He was under a peace pact, agreed by all parties. Did you care about the lives in the balance, or the outcomes of what you've done?"

"It was a foolish act, Rahn-Roshana," Bensaharēn added disapprovingly. "And one that dishonoured you and the Great House of Nāsarat."

"I question whether your motives are as selfless as you say, Roshana." Ziaire paced the room, slapping her steel-vaned fan against the palm of her hand. She came to stand with her back to the window, haloed by the afternoon. "Your Jahirojin, signed and sealed by the power in your own blood, sets your feet in motion where common sense might otherwise say be still."

"He's an Erebus," Roshana said flatly. "I'm a Nāsarat."

There it was. Six words that had seen tears and bloodshed in frightful measure over the generations. Mari held back a groan of frustration. The Iron League monarchs, without the living memory granted them by Awakening, let feuds rest where they would. What happened two generations ago was history. Two centuries ago was a curiosity. Five generations ago things became legend, and after a thousand years legends turned to myths. The Human hatred of the Avān was less a thing of legend than it was an ongoing friction between two peoples who refused to relent.

For the rahns it was not so easy. What happened a millennium ago was as fresh as if it had happened yesterday. Festering wounds stayed open, bleeding down the long count of years. An Awakened rahn in control of their power could influence the weather in their lands. Assure a good crop. Set an example of peace, of love, humility, morality, and ethics that trickled through to everybody who dwelled there. On the reverse side, such power could be used to inspire hate, prejudice, paranoia, and aggression when a rahn was weak of character, or bent on destruction.

Whereas some simply drifted, unwilling to be the agents of much-needed change. The reluctant Nazarafine, so loath to hold the Shrīan's tiller, was quiet. The woman wrung her wrinkled, fleshy hands together as if she were cold. A tray of sweets lay untouched beside her. The steam from her tea had stopped coiling. She looked her age; skin loose, hair thin and lustreless.

"This is my fault, is it not?" Nazarafine asked of nobody in particular. She looked up, a haunted look in her eyes. "We provoked Corajidin and made bad moves in a game he plays better than we. I assumed a victory in the election and have doomed us all with my complacency."

"Including Indris," Shar muttered. The Seethe woman's eyes burned a bright orange in her sharp face, the silken quills of what passed for her dawn-toned hair hanging loose about her shoulders. She switched her gaze between the rahns. "He is missing because he was trying to help you."

"Peace, little one." Kembe rumbled. The Tau-se patriarch lay deceptively still upon his couch, tail swishing on the floor. Passing clouds dimmed the sheen from the fortune coins braided into his white-gold mane. "It seems to me there have been many hands on the shovel that dug this well, hoping to find water when all we have found is dust and the bones of those who have dug here before."

"Reckon Shar has a point," Hayden said from where he leaned against the wall by the window. He hugged his long-barrelled storm-rifle to his chest. "I ain't one for the schemes of lordly folk and such, but I figure Indris is a brother in blood, and he ain't been done right by."

"There is nothing but sorrow and waste in all this death and feckless haste," Omen fluted. "To set a crown on a hard man's brow, when peace is needed here and now."

"Well there's more sorrow and waste to come before any brow is crowned," Ziaire said. "Belamandris and his Anlūki have been scouring the streets looking for Vahineh."

"And Indris," Bensaharēn added. "There is a story there of which I'm unaware. Belamandris rides on the back of a reckless hatred that will not end well for him, or anybody involved."

And how much of that is because of me? Mari thought.

"After this morning's little escapade," Ajo said, "Corajidin has invoked ayo-kherife. He's going to make a royal-caste arrest of Roshana, another barb to tarnish the Federationists in front of anybody with eyes to see, or ears to hear."

"There were too many witnesses to this event for her to come away unscathed from this." Neva leaned against the wall, arms folded under her breasts. She had not changed out of her flying leathers and seemed ready to go into action at a moment's notice. She looked at Mari. "I'll do whatever you need."

"If Rahn-Roshana is convicted of attempted regicide and treason," Ajo added grimly, "she'll be stripped of her rank and her place in the Teshri. More than likely she'll be given the choice of Exile for the duration of Corajidin's life, or sent to Maladûr gaol."

Roshana sat quietly on the edge of her chair. With the personal consequences of her actions heard out loud, they seemed to finally hit her. Her lips were a hard line across her angular face.

"Corajidin escaped a dire fate," Omen said, "his plots and schemes founded in hate. Is there no way this rahn can escape the web that may yet seal her fate?"

"What's done is done and I was right to do it," Roshana said. "The alleged assassins are dead. It's pure supposition I ordered them to do anything. Corajidin has gotten away with much worse."

"Hollow words, if we lose you." Siamak rose from his chair, his lean and deadly marshlanders behind him. "If the Arbiter's Tribunal brings you before Kaylish Face Readers, the truth will be known. Thank the hallowed dead Corajidin doesn't use the Sēq. Their Inquisitors would strip every secret from you, whether it was relevant or not. We need to plan what comes next carefully."

"Then lay it at the feet of Mariam and be done with it." Roshana shrugged indifferently. "You need to ask yourself whether I add more value as the Rahn-Näsarat and a member of the Teshri, or as a renegade. Mariam is the darling of the Avān! People would see it as little more than a wilful daughter acting out against her father—which she has done before—and then forget about it. Corajidin survived, after all."

Both Siamak and Bensaharēn looked appalled at Roshana's rationalisation. Nazarafine's eyes narrowed shrewdly. Mari schooled her features to stillness, refusing to look at Roshana lest she launch herself across the room and beat the life from her. *My father survived, just as* I *survived your assassins, Roshana.* Mari felt anger infuse her at the memory. *Don't think it's something I've forgotten, you cold, hard bitch.*

There was a pregnant silence, before the birth of commotion when voices were raised all at once.

Mari stepped back from the conversation, taking solace in the tangible presences of Shar and Neva. Hayden and Ekko, too—and to a lesser degree Omen, whom she did not understand. The leaders of the Federationists fenced with words. Roshana sat with her typical military bearing; square jawed, square shouldered and aloof, her eyes watchful. Her guard, a man neither named nor introduced, was tall yet stooped to hide it. Dark-haired and dark-bearded, he was sword slender with sharp eyes on either side of a blade for a nose. Bensaharēn sat neatly, like a well-groomed cat, his sword across his knees. Beside Roshana, Nazarafine slouched as if both her physical and emotional weight bore her down. Navid, her prickly proud nephew, hovered over her. The way his hand hovered near the hilt of his sword, it was as if he waited for an excuse to draw it and prove himself the fool Mari suspected he was. Ziaire stood amongst it, watching, listening, offering sage advice when necessary. Yet mostly she took it all in, inhaling the events around her.

Siamak and Kembe seemed almost at ease. Siamak and his marshlanders remained standing, poised yet nonthreatening. Even at rest a Tau-se was menacing: there was no help for it when one was two metres of steely muscle sheathed in silky fur. Yet Kembe and Ibamu remained still. They avoided direct eye contact and the only indication of agitation was the occasional widening of their eyes, or a swish of their tail.

Time passed, measured in the inexorable march of a translucent beam that shone pallid through the window. It marked all of them in its passage, leaving cutouts in the spaces behind people as it passed over them. Hayden leaned on his rifle, head nodding as he drowsed, then jerking sharply as he came awake. Shar absently juggled her *serill* knives, the black faceted glass glittering. Ekko and Omen stood silent—the former may as well have been a statue in fur.

Tired of the foreplay in the conversation, Mari was about to suggest she and the others leave the rahns to it when she caught sight of something blue flapping by the window. Taking it to be a bird she was going to ignore it, yet it kept butting against the glass, sounding more like a moth than a bird. Distracted, she turned to look.

And let out a sharp bark of near-hysterical laughter, followed by a relieved sob. A surprised silence stole over the room.

Mari flung open the window and the small blue bird flapped into her hand, then lay still. Tears in her eyes, Mari carefully unfolded the paper phoenix to read the message Indris had sent her.

❋ ❋ ❋

Without a care for who saw, Mari threw herself into Indris's arms when she met him in the narrow ravine above the Qadir Selassin. She hugged him so hard he grunted. His arms encircled her and she felt as much as heard the gentle resonance of his voice.

She took a step back to look at him. He seemed none the worse for wear, though there was a tension at the corners of his eyes and mouth she did not like. Dressed in a formal cassock of fine black wool he looked severe, silver buttons in cold contrast against the soft black. His longish hair was unruly, tangles snatched by the exhalation of the wind. Changeling's scaled dragon hilt rose over his shoulder, one sapphire eye seeming to stare at Mari where she stood. Seeing him this way, rather than the relaxed vagabond he worked so hard to pretend to be, Mari could understand how people might fear him. There was an implacable strength in his stance and a fierceness in his gaze that would have given anybody pause.

Watching the man in his sleep, lids slightly bruised and lined with long dark lashes . . .

Hearing him breathe . . .

The way he hugged his knee when he read, one long finger holding the page still . . .

Listening to him laugh at himself for something poorly said, or clumsy . . .

That was not the man who stood in front her now. What she witnessed here, for the first time, was the killer of men and destroyer of nations and it caused her breath to catch in her throat.

Shar wiped a bright tear from her cheek, before turning to bury her face in Ekko's chest. When she turned back, she was beaming. Hayden's grin split his weathered face, causing his long moustache to bristle like a living thing. Omen stood poised and silent, enamelled simulacrum gleaming. Indris beamed at them, the look of the killer replaced by genuine affection.

"What happened to you?" Mari asked.

"We need to get Vahineh out of Avānweh before she's retaken," he said gently. "Corajidin's made a deal with a faction in the Sēq: his continued tolerance in return for Vahineh."

"Don't avoid the question," Shar prodded. "Where have you been?"

"Amer-Mahjin. The Sēq extended their—"

"What?" Shar yelped as if bitten. "The *Sēq* had you?"

"Yes, though it's a tale for another time. There are Erebus soldiers throughout the city, as well as more than a few stray dogs they've picked up for whatever coppers were lying around. I've had to deal with a few of them, but they'll regain consciousness soon and report they've seen me. Where are the others? They need to be warned."

Indris walked further back up the ravine. She heard him speak quietly. A bloodied and bruised Vahineh walked out where the others could see her. Mari wondered at the improvement in the woman, though Vahineh seemed overwhelmed at the attention. Vahineh hid shyly behind Indris, clutching his hand like a child, her eyes wide when she looked at Ekko.

"Is she . . .?" Mari asked, not wanting to use the word *sane*. Indris shrugged with his eyebrows.

Mari led them along pedestrian walkways, across gardens and narrow bridges and down secluded flights of stairs. Though Avānweh was a cosmopolitan city—its citizens used to seeing Seethe, Tau-se, and Humans—Mari doubted they were used to seeing such a mixed group. People bobbed their heads in respect when they saw Indris. Some, mostly of the older generation who had been raised with sende as an integral part of their upbringing, went so far as to drop to both knees in the Third Obeisance. Others, younger and raised in a more casual manner, gave him the barest courtesy, or looked at him with barely contained fear. Indris said nothing, hardly recognising their presence at all, as a Sēq would do. Once they passed he muttered under his breath about this being the reason why he never wore the formal cassock of the Order.

They paused at the base of the long Kiridin Stairs, screened on either side by tall bamboo and a wall of weathered stone. There was a modest butkada to the Family Masadhe there, though age had made use of it. Pigeons nested amongst the split timbers of the domed roof, while spiders made their webs amongst the legs and fangs of their graven kindred. The broken fretwork screens of the butkada and its thick wooden pillars, varnish peeled away like dead skin, gave Mari and the others a place to observe. The Caleph-Mahn was a major mercantile district, its main road lined with merchant factors, jewellers, weapon and armour smiths, tailors, scribes, general stores, dining halls, and narrow tea houses with iron pots hanging from chains by the door, clanking in the wind.

Hayden gave his storm-rifle to Indris to hold, then casually walked into the flow of the crowd. The moustached man smiled pleasantly, tipping his hat at a sour dowager and what Mari took to be her equally unattractive ward. Then he was off, walking bandy-legged in his old buckskins, sun bright on the ends of his bobbed salt-and-brass hair.

"He's a great scout." Indris leaned against a wooden pillar as far from the road as he could get. "He can pass for an Avān or a Human and being older, few people suspect him of being up to any trouble."

"Will he be safe?" Mari asked.

"Safe as the rest of us."

"So no, then."

"Not so much. Excuse me a minute." Indris asked Shar and Ekko for some money. He left Changeling and unbuckled his weapons belt, leaving it folded neatly on the narrow seat that ran the length of the butkada. For a moment he looked at his weapons, then thrust the dragon-tooth knife through the sash at his waist. Joining the crowd—who gave the Sēq in his fine woollen cassock a wide birth—he walked down the street a way before turning into a clothier.

"You get used to him," Shar said from where she came to stand at Mari's shoulder.

"Pardon?"

Shar nodded down the street to where Indris had gone. "I saw the look on your face. You get used to him. Who and what he is. The walls he sometimes puts up, and forgets to bring down until something reminds him he's among friends again. Most of the time he's the man you've come to know. Caring, passionate, gentle . . ." Mari frowned a little at the wistful nature of Shar's voice. Clearly there had been more than friendship between her and Indris. Shar shrugged it off, then said, "But then there are the times he just needs to be what he was trained to be, and you see how cold, hard, and intractable a man he is. I feel sorry for his enemies. I'd never want to have Indris mean me harm, I can tell you that for free."

Mari nodded, relieved but not overjoyed. With all that had happened, she was beginning to wonder whether he had decided to keep his distance from her. He certainly had not been as . . . demonstrative, or warm, on seeing her as she would have hoped. But then she did not know what he had experienced at the hands of his former teachers and comrades.

It was something else they would need to deal with, the secrets that lurked in their pasts, which might come out to bite them. Mari settled herself in the shade, stretching her legs, and resting her back against a warm wooden column. She breathed deeply, picturing her anxieties trickling down her arms and legs, then out her fingers and toes, draining away to leave her clean and thinking clearly.

Hayden had not returned in the thirty minutes it took for Indris to emerge from the clothier wearing an outfit of the warrior-caste: black trousers bound with brass buckles in the style of the southern mountain clans; a dark brown coat to his knees, sleeves studded with bronze and buckled across the chest; soft-looking black boots and a hooded over-robe in the same dark brown. Now people scarcely looked at him, save for a few women who gave him admiring glances once he had passed them by. He stopped at a nearby dining hall, bringing back ekfi—soft flour flatbread wrapped around spiced rice, beans, parsley, mint, and shredded lamb. These were passed around with a flourish and the small group set to eating, looking little more than visitors taking their rest in the shade of a busy market street.

"I'm going to miss those old boots of mine," he mused as he looked down at the square toes of his new boots. Mari could see the leather shift as he wriggled his toes. "Took me years to break the damned things in."

"You should go ask the Sēq to have them back," Shar said with a wicked grin.

Indris gave her an exaggerated fake smile, before turning back to the street. Hayden appeared not long after, taking his time as he meandered back. The rifleman stopped to look in the window of a sword maker, thumbs hooked in his belt.

"That's the signal," Indris said. He helped Vahineh raise her hood, then walked into the street accompanied by Shar and Omen. Ekko followed, Mari trailing behind. They met up with Hayden a score of shops down the road, who reported there was nobody he could see watching the Eyrie. Indris handed the old man back his storm-rifle.

Mari took the lead, somewhat more relaxed. Nearing the Eyrie they passed under one of the many zaihin gates; tall arched gates set as waypoints along the road, their supporting columns thick as polished tree trunks. This one was carved to look like the columns were two thick snakes, scales lacquered black, grey, and white. Looking up she saw a coiled black serpent carved on the lintel, amongst renderings of jagged leaves and thorned roses.

The snakes reminded Mari of Nadir, his father, and sisters. The ones whose Ancestors, as legend had it, learned their wisdom, subtlety and fighting techniques from the great wyrms of the Mar Ejir. The man she had once been infatuated with—as was her wont to fall quickly and hard for certain women and men—had changed much since their time together. He was more like the snake of his Family these days. Warmed by the sun, or by contact with others, rather than having any warmth of spirit. His blithe mention of war, of bringing carnage back to Shrīan, had been warning enough to show children often grew into the shoes of their parents. It was a reminder Mari hardly needed, yet was instructional all the same. Mari had no interest in the feel of her father's stride.

The more time she spent with people who had tasted true freedom, the less she wanted to walk anybody's path save her own.

Exiting the far side of the gate, Mari was blinded a moment by the afternoon sun. She turned back to see her friends. Indris laughing at some jape of

Shar's, holding Vahineh's hand as they walked. Omen walking with his stork-like gait, Shroud flowing around his mechanical limbs, emerald eyes gleaming. Ekko and Hayden following, the enormous Tau-se walking with slow strides so the shorter rifleman could keep pace. Hayden was gesticulating wildly with one hand, his storm-rifle in the other. Ekko's eyes were half closed in happiness.

In this moment it became clear to her what she must do. She smiled for the joy of it, at the same time fearing what such a change in her life may mean.

The arrow took her in the back, driving the wind from her lungs and dropping her to her knees.

✸ ✸ ✸

"Erebus's shrivelled balls!" Mari grunted. The pain was incredible. It felt like being hit by a hammer between the shoulder blades.

As she rose the arrow fell to the ground with a thud. It rolled past her. A roundhead, tipped with a ball of resin, and used to incapacitate rather than kill.

There was a sound like a swarm of angry wasps. Arrows shredded the air. Mari dashed towards the cover of the zaihin gate. The next arrow hit her high between the shoulders. The force of the blow sent her careening face first into a stand of tall, green bamboo. She gasped for air as she tried to rise, the muscles across her back and shoulders protesting the abuse.

Indris raced forward to her side, using a sheathed Changeling to swat arrows out of the air. Behind him Omen stood in front of Vahineh, a quasi-living shield, a long antique shamshir with an ornate filigreed hilt held in his mechanical hand. Ekko had drawn his powerful short bow and Hayden his storm-rifle, both men firing at targets as they presented themselves.

All around them civilians screamed as they sprinted for cover. Wrapped parcels, baskets of food, bolts of cloth, and other goods were dropped in their haste. Wagons were abandoned, or used as cover as artisans hid themselves beneath them.

"Can you move?" Indris asked, hand extended to help her to her feet.

"I can bloody well move out of here!" Mari snarled. She took his hand and was pulled to her feet. More arrows fell around them, the closest parried by Indris until Mari drew her Sûnblade and joined him in their defence. Together they threw up a web of whirling steel, slicing and swatting arrows from the air.

There came a scream as a body fell from a balcony, pierced by an arrow through the throat. Then another as a person collapsed in a doorway, blood fountaining from a rifle-bolt to the eye. Mari scanned the street, seeing only enemies now the civilians had fled. There were some twenty of them, clad in mismatched light armour, knee-length coats, and loose-legged trousers. They carried wooden swords, nicked and dented from use. From the look of them the bravos were huqdi—street dogs—impoverished soldiers who were little more than ruffians. Deserters, traitors, and thugs without the honour needed to survive as a nahdi, or to serve in the retinue of a Family or Great House.

The hail of arrows stopped as the huqdi dashed into the street. Hayden remained where he was, the crack-hiss of his rifle the metronome of battle. Where he aimed, a huqdi died. Ekko left his bow and, drawing his sickle-bladed khopesh, sped into battle. Omen stood motionless in front of a silent, wide-eyed Vahineh. Arrows bounced from his glazed frame. The girl's fingers gripped the Wraith Knight's shoulders with white-knuckled intensity as she hid behind him.

When the huqdi met them, Mari, Indris, and Ekko were more than ready. The Sûnblade flared into life, blade sizzling as it took the sword hand from the wrist of her first target. Ekko slipped sidewise and spinning, back-handed his khopesh deep into the waist of a man, just above the hips. Reversing, the Tau-se swept his blade out, up and over to take the man's head. Indris had not unsheathed Changeling, using the moaning blade as a club where it whirled about him, breaking bones and knocking teeth from mouths in a bloody spray.

Mari kept a peripheral awareness of her friends, focussed on her enemies. In all her years at The Lament in Narsis, then the years of combat experience that followed, Mari had learned to trust to the rhythm of her aipsé—the place of the no-mind. Her eyes and ears saw and heard, her body sensed movements in the air and changes in the ground. Her training interpreted. Muscles responded. She became what she was trained to be: a living weapon, where hands, feet, and her Sûnblade were melded into one instrument of havoc.

Lightly armoured in soft leather and quilted silk, Mari felt the stings and pains of cuts. Such were unavoidable when the few fought the many in such chaotic confinement. Still, she, Indris and Ekko moved in a lethal dance, weaving about each other as they advanced, the three of them striking, parrying, and riposting as they glided amongst their enemies.

Then she saw faces she recognised. Nadir and Ravenet, hovering at the back of battle, watching, desperately wanting.

Distracted, a blow to the face split her lip. She disembowelled the man. Another opened the skin above her eye, impairing her vision. Then another across her ribs. She probed with her tongue at where it felt like a tooth was loose after she had leaned away from the worst of a blow along her jaw.

She lost sight of Nadir. Then saw him again as he appeared in front of her. Mari smashed him in the face with the hilt of her weapon and the man went spinning into Indris's path.

Ravenet pounced into the combat line. Rather than a wooden sword, which could kill as well as a metal one, she used twinned daggers with lightning speed. Mari needed blade, elbows, forearms, and the suppleness of her body to avoid the serpent-strikes of the fangs in Ravi's hands.

Mari stumbled over one of the corpses that littered the road. Slipped sideways. She saw Ravenet's eyes and knew the woman intended to kill, not wound. Her face was lit with a sick, glorious wonder.

Turning her fall into a roll, Mari twisted under Ravenet's blades. Came to one knee. Cut with a powerful horizontal stroke that severed air, skin, muscle, then air again. Ravenet stumbled backwards, blood pouring from the wound in her abdomen. She spiralled to the ground, knives clattering, trying to keep her entrails from slithering between her fingers.

Rising to her feet, Mari looked down on the woman as the life left her eyes, fodder for the crows. Near her lay Nadir, his face smeared in blood. She checked his pulse. He lived yet.

She felt no remorse for Ravenet, who had never been a friend to Mari. She only felt sorrow for the storm that would no doubt follow.

21

> ## "EVERY DECISION IS A DOOR THAT CAN OPENED BUT ONCE AND NEVER CLOSED AGAIN."
>
> —Penoquin of Kaylish, Zienni Scholar and philosopher
> (325th year of the Awakened Empire)

DAY 356 OF THE 495TH YEAR OF

THE SHRĪANESE FEDERATION

"They should have been here by now," Wolfram muttered. The Angothic Witch wrapped his large-knuckled hands around his staff, protruding bones like knots of wood in his age-whorled skin. "The Sēq can't be trusted, Your Majesty."

"I expect not." Corajidin had taken one of the black-lacquered chairs facing the Canon Stone. The play of colour that flowed through the tourmaline was mesmerising, streams and clouds that constantly changed like the colours of waves in the sun. "Yet this is a conversation that must be had, one way or the other."

Zahiz had left them some hours ago. Wolfram, Elonie, and Ikedion had padded about like cats on a hot metal roof. Kasraman seated himself as comfortably as one could on one of the uncomfortable chairs, reading a small book taken from within the folds of his over-robe. Nima had patrolled the room several times before coming to stand beside Corajidin. The Anlūki prowled away again, muttering to himself nervously.

Corajidin had started to nod off when there came the sound of yelling from outside. The witches fanned out around the Obsidian Heart, eyes intent. He stretched and yawned, keeping an eye on Nima as he went light-footed to the door. Cracking it open, the soldier peered outside then opened the door wide enough to admit Belamandris, Jhem, and Nix. All of them were bloody, Nix most of all. Corajidin heard the creak of armour and scuff of many boots outside. The Anlūki, no doubt.

Belamandris's expression was tormented, his eyes red. Jhem's fingers clenched as if he wanted to throttle somebody. Nix, covered in the grime of war, had a grin painted across his narrow face.

"What happened?" Corajidin asked cautiously.

"We did as you asked," Belamandris said, voice hoarse. He looked down at the dried blood on his hands. There were rents in his crimson over-robe and one sleeve hung half ripped from his shoulder. "There was opposition, which we met with force. There were losses—"

"It answered the question as to whether Pah-Mariam was lying," Nix said, walking around the Canon Stone. He extended a hand to touch it, then draw it back sharply. Legend had it only a Mahj could sit the Canon Stone—all others being struck dead. Nix looked up with a wry grin. "She was."

"You can't prove that!" Belamandris protested angrily.

"Your sister was with the Dragon Eye and the Selassin girl when Ravenet asked for them to surrender themselves!" Jhem said in his near lisp. The man's gaze was cold and hard as an iron ingot. "How can she not have lied about knowing where they were? My daughter is dead because of her!"

"What happened?" Corajidin asked again. He could feel the tension of secrets as yet untold in Belamandris and Jhem.

"Nadir, Ravenet, and some stray dogs went hunting." Nix crouched near the Canon Stone, blood-soaked arms wrapped around his knees. There was even blood in his hair and at the corners of his mouth. "Their eyes were bigger than their teeth and claws, I'm afraid. They'll be planted in ash before the sun sets, for such are the wages of folly."

Jhem seemed to glide across the floor. Knives appeared from the sleeves of his battle-torn coat. Nix uncoiled from where he crouched, grinning madly, eyes bright and wild. He bounced on his toes as he stretched his neck first left, then right, arms held loosely at his side. The lean, inbred man started to giggle.

"Enough!" Corajidin snapped before the men came within killing distance of each other. Jhem stopped dead, brought to heel. Nix almost vibrated with energy where he stood, eyes rolling, dirty locks of hair waving with his every movement. "I will not have this, do you understand? I will not! Belamandris?"

"Nadir found us after we had a running fight with some of Nazarafine's Sûnguard." Belamandris's tone was sour. "Why Ravi used such bottom feeders as the huqdi I'll never understand. But if we're being told the truth—and I say if, as there're no guarantees—then it was Indris who opened Ravi's belly. Mari was with him and his carnival show friends from Amnon."

"Was Vahineh with them?"

"Apparently."

"Where is Nadir?" Corajidin asked. "I would have words with him about what happened."

"Resting from his wounds. He and Kimiya are back at the qadir."

"Indris is fodder when I get my teeth into him," Jhem turned his serpent's eyes on Corajidin. "His span is numbered only in the heartbeats it takes me to find and finish him."

"Good luck with that," Belamandris said dismissively. "As the saying goes, better men and such."

"And you are—"

"Better, yes." Belamandris rubbed his palm along Tragedy's long hilt. "Come the day, come the man—but every man his day, for good or ill. Indris will plant you in ashes, Blacksnake, and not even sweat doing it."

"Whoever is going to do it, can do what they will to Indris," Corajidin said, even as the Emissary's words regarding her one-time husband echoed quietly in Corajidin's head; he did not much care. If Belamandris, Jhem, or anybody else slaughtered Indris, it was something long overdue. He eyed Jhem darkly. "But my daughter comes to no harm. Do not test me on this, Jhem. If Mariam suffers, so will you and yours."

Jhem bowed sinuously, knives vanishing into his sleeves as he backed away. Nix still trembled from the excitement of near mayhem. The two men eyed each other wearily. Corajidin knew one would end the other at some point, though who would murder whom was uncertain.

Belamandris was talking quietly with Kasraman, grief clearly etched on his face. How would Belamandris reconcile his feelings for Mariam? Would her involvement in Ravenet's death be enough for Belamandris to harden his hearts and give himself fully to Corajidin's agenda? Ravenet's death was unexpected, yet casualties were inevitable if Corajidin was going to shape a nation. By the looks of Belamandris and the others there had been some hard fighting. There would no doubt be more when the Sēq rejected Corajidin's proposal. Something he was counting on.

Kasraman and the other witches looked up.

"Father," Kasraman said, "they're coming."

The air blistered, then ripped, as black-robed and black-armoured figures appeared from the torn air. There were a half-dozen of them, brooding and sombre, intricate scaled and banded armour dyed and laced in black. There were recurved swords thrust through the black sashes at their waists. Each carried a Scholar's Crook subtly different from the others and all had mindstones boring their foreheads like dark, twinkling stars. Zahiz loitered amongst the gathered women and men.

A leonine man with long pale hair stepped forward. Corajidin recognised him from family portraits. Zadjinn, who had joined the Sēq Order of Scholars shortly after the formation of the Shrīanese Federation and one of those who had fought in the Scholar Wars. The man crossed half the distance to where Corajidin waited, then stopped.

Corajidin remained where he was, silently watching, expression schooled to neutrality. After a long awkward minute, Zadjinn bowed his head in the First Obeisance: the honour of greeting amongst equals. The others followed suit. Corajidin did not.

"I see from your expression you recognise me, Rahn-Corajidin," Zadjinn said. Corajidin bristled at the use of the title, forcing himself to patience. He was still rahn until his coronation, an annoying fact though true. "And we hear you wish to negotiate with the Sēq as to our standing in Shrīan. My colleagues and I are happy to listen to whatever you may have to say."

"Can you speak for them?" Corajidin said with a raised eyebrow. "Can I take whatever you say with more than a grain of salt?"

"You can," Zadjinn responded coldly. "Though it is I who should ask what gives you the authority to makes demands of us?"

"The Sēq are in Shrīan because our forebears suffered you to be," Kasraman said. The other witches had gathered to his side, wild and on edge. Corajidin could see the apprehension in the scholar's eyes. "Now we do not. My father demands you bow at his feet like any other vassal, or you disband what remains of your Order in Shrīan."

"We will take the service of those individuals who wish to stay," Corajidin spread his hands in a gracious gesture, "though the Sēq would not be permitted to exist in the Federation."

"Much as the Asrahn-Erebus fe Amerata did with the witch covens after the Scholar Wars." Kasraman added with steel in his voice. "There is a precedent. Though *we* won't lock you in a Temporal Labyrinth."

"Probably not," Wolfram muttered, Elonie and Ikedion nodding.

"We would also expect full access to your stores of knowledge, weapons, and anything else that would be of benefit to our cause in strengthening Shrīan."

There was barely a flicker of his eyes as Zadjinn replied, "Of course. We exist for the good of all."

He then turned to his black-cassocked peers. Corajidin watched as their eyes went out of focus, the corona around their mindstones pulsing larger and darker. It was only a dozen or so heartbeats later when Zadjinn faced Corajidin.

"We six agree in principle," the scholar said. Corajidin doubted it, from the expressions on two of the six. "I will present your proposal to our peers."

"More waiting?" Wolfram snarled. "More time for your trickery?"

"Not at all, witch. We will ensure the others agree. Those who do not will be dealt with."

"I will know if you lie to me," Corajidin murmured. The Emissary had been correct in her other intelligence on the Sēq. He expected she could tell him whether the scholars intended to comply, or resist. "I am not convinced of your good intentions, Zadjinn."

"Allow me to offer you a gift, then, great rahn." Zadjinn looked over his shoulder at his peers. Four of them nodded while the other two watched, stone faced. "A token of our good faith."

"Indeed?" Corajidin's interest was piqued, though swaddled in caution.

"We understand you are looking for Selassin fe Vahineh?" the scholar smiled, a smug stretch of his lips in his tanned face. "The one whom you believe murdered your late wife?"

Corajidin froze, as did the others in his retinue. He looked at Zadjinn from under lowered brows, suspicion rising like flood waters.

"And how would you achieve this?" Corajidin asked with genuine interest, given the last time Vahineh had been seen was with Mariam, Indris, and his rag-tag entourage. "My sons and all our retainers have been unable to secure her."

"We took her into our custody some days ago, as part of another piece of business."

"And she is with you now?"

"Of course." Zadjinn's smiled never faltered. The same could not be said of those who stood with him. "We would need a modest amount of time to prepare her for you, but delivered she will be."

Corajidin turned to Kasraman and Wolfram, who both nodded. They whispered to Belamandris, Elonie, and Ikedion. Nima excused himself and left the Obsidian Heart. His voice could be heard faintly as he gave orders to the Anlūki outside. Corajidin turned back to the scholars, brows raised in enquiry.

"This is . . . good news," he said. "So you promise me you have Vahineh and you promise me you will speak with your peers in the Sēq? Your Order will rest their brows at my feet, to serve me and no other?"

"I swear it. All I have spoken is true," Zadjinn said, making the Second Obeisance: dropping to one knee, head bowed, hands held palm upward near the floor. Slowly, the other Sēq followed suit.

"Do what you need to do," Corajidin said quietly. "I expect to see you and the other leaders of the Sēq, along with Vahineh, tonight at the Hour of the Boar at the Tyr-Jahavān."

"It will be so."

Zadjinn and the others rose to their feet then vanished, one by one, into liquid rifts in the cool air.

Corajidin stood silent until they were gone. The air smelled of lightning storms with the barest taint of corruption for some seconds after they had left.

"What do you want to do, father?" Belamandris asked as he and Kasraman made their way to their father's side. Corajidin rested one hand on each of his son's shoulders.

"It is clear they can not be trusted, making promises they can not fulfil. Tonight you will kill the liars and be done with it."

❋ ❋ ❋

Corajidin was carried through the depths by the strong current. The world around him was cold. Sluggish. Blues and greens were muted to near black, the brightness above obscured by dark stars of sediment that had been pried loose by aeons of slow, inexorable movement from those below. Basso voices burbled in the deep, sending vibrations across his skin. A scaled mass, thick as a tree trunk, coiled nearby. The force of it sent him tumbling as when he was a child off the shores of Erebesq, when the waves were strong and the rip tried to carry him under. A faint singing reached his ears, echoed, wet, and atonal. He shrieked when something frigid and grey swept from below to caress his flailing legs.

Corajidin squeezed his eyes closed, yet the blindness made his imagination start at every slither, shriek, gibber, and burbled moan. He opened his eyes to a hazy world where fingers of sediment stretched improbably long, swirling slowly. As his eyes adjusted he saw through the gloom to the shapes that writhed against, with, and around each other. Bloated bodies. Fleshy tendrils dotted with a nauseating, pulsing radiance. Tentacles scraping across each other like thousands of giant, malformed octopi mating in a muddy ditch.

Then She opened her vast, hill-sized eye and fixed its putrescent yellow gaze on him. She called his name.

He screamed.

The Emissary was perched on the head of his bed, leaning forward so far he wondered how she did not fall. The thunderhead of her over-robe was draped about her, merging with the shadows of the room. Things slithered against each other under her robe, a dry hissing coming from the secret places amongst its folds.

"You've seen She Who Writhes in the Deep," the Emissary whispered reverently. "The sister-mother of the Black King of the Wood and the Storm Rider. Paramour of the Heart Which Burns in the Night. They're—"

"It was an obscenity!" he gasped, scuttling to the foot of his bed. He turned back to see the Emissary, an angular thing of contrasts looming like some shrine daemon. Her mottled skin shone. Her broken sapphire eyes glowed eerily in the dim room. "Are these what you serve?"

"They're what nature intended them to be and true to their nature, beyond the comprehension of that which is born, lives, and dies. Serve them or not, it makes little matter. They are. They do. They endure."

Corajidin's fists curled in the silk sheets, trembling. The Emissary's voice had been so gentle. It reminded him of when he had spoken to his children about their Ancestors and the boundless love of those who came before. His lip curled in disgust, then he pressed them together against what felt like snakes fighting in his belly. His bowels churned. Bile rose in his throat. Flinging himself from the bed he barely made it to the bath chamber where he vomited a rank mess, stained red brown, into an urn. He wiped his mouth with a shaking hand. It came away with streamers of blood-tinted spit.

"If you're quite done," the Emissary asked from the open door, "your people would speak with you in your office."

"You were of the Sēq once. Does it not bother you that I bring about their destruction?"

Her expression was glacial, neither confirming nor denying. "What does it matter what I think? You say you're serving destiny by clinging to your notion you're fated to do this thing. If it's meant to be, then it'll happen. Or it won't. My Masters would have me help you. Neither understanding, nor my agreement, are required for my obedience."

"To me?"

The Emissary gestured towards the door to his chambers, waiting for him to take the lead. She fell into step at his side, her high split-toed boots making the barest sound as she walked, tails of her over-robe sighing across the floor.

His sons stood by Corajidin's desk, speaking quietly to each other. Wolfram and Sanojé, Elonie, and Ikedion stood close by, having a heated, if quiet, debate. Kimiya stood in Wolfram's shadow, listening intently, only occasionally touching the thick collar around her neck or rubbing at the bruises on her wrists. Nix crouched with his back against the wall, nimble fingers turning the pieces of a puzzle sphere, a burned and blackened thing of scuffed precious metals. The man mumbled to himself, head waggling from side to side.

"You do know what you're toying with there?" Kasraman asked Nix.

"Do you mean whether I know this is a Dilemma Box? Yes. Is there an elemental daemon locked inside? No. The Soul Traders also had some that were empty—old relics from the Petal Empire—I could use for practice. The different shaped boxes open uniquely, and they're not the kind of thing you want to get caught on the hop with."

"Just as bloody well," Sanojé muttered anxiously.

"If you are quite done chatting," Corajidin asked tersely as he took his seat, "has anybody seen Jhem or Nadir?"

"We've not seen them since you took your rest, Your Majesty," Wolfram said. "The two of them left the qadir a couple of hours ago."

"Revenge is on the menu, I'd think." Nix bashed the sphere against the floor with a loud chime. Frustrated he shook it, then chewed on it, before he resumed trying to solve it. He looked up with a sly grin, fingers still working the puzzle. "Looks like one snake dying wasn't enough. They decided to empty the nest. Except for Wolfram's bed-warmer—sorry, apprentice."

"Your mouth will be the death of you," Belamandris murmured.

"Poison in his food will be the death of him." Kimiya glared at the little man. "Or a snake in his bed."

"You'd climb into my bed, dove? That's sweet. And flattering. And on any other day . . . but Wolfram wouldn't like that one little bit," Nix giggled. He sobered when Wolfram glared at him through the jagged fangs of his hair.

"How will we proceed, father?" Kasraman asked in an effort to divert attention.

Corajidin outlined his plan. Zadjinn had made it clear with his statement about Vahineh he could not be trusted. If one word out of the man's mouth was a lie, chances are the others were also. As much as it would have been of benefit to have the Sēq on his side, it was not to be. He would have preferred a foil to the witches, something to keep them in check, yet had to work with what fate was giving him.

Amenankher was too tough a diamond to break. The Sēq were burrowed into their place of strength like ticks. His plan was for the witches to cause such a distraction the Sēq would be forced out into the open, where the witches could face them on a more even footing. Then the witches could take their revenge, leaving the way clear for an esoteric order that would follow Corajidin's dictates.

"This will be the end of Shrīan as we know it, father." Belamandris stood with his fists clenched, golden brows drawn together. "Are we sure we want to do this? With respect to my brother and our witch allies, the Sēq got involved in the Scholar Wars because the witches tried to seize power. Is opening the door on a second scholar war really in our best interests?"

"He's right." Sanojé turned the golden bands on her thumb. "Once our blood is up, we will fight until this is over. It will be chaos."

"And Shrīan and its people will burn in the middle of it." Belamandris stood tall, catching his father's gaze and holding it. "This is a no-win situation for you, Father. For any of us. If the Sēq are victorious, you've lost the witches and will be executed, or exiled for life. The Great House of Erebus will be more infamous than the Empress-in-Shadows for what it's done. If the witches win, you lose the Sēq, who were the only force to counter them. You'll have unleashed an esoteric plague with nothing to stop it."

"The Empress-in-Shadows and the Sēq in Pashrea would take the field." The Emissary seemed to savour the taste of the words in her mouth. Wolfram and Sanojé looked at her with suspicion. "Can you imagine it? Truly immortal esoteric masters wielding all the power they'd gathered over the millennia?"

"Father," Belamandris said imploringly, "what then when the Catechism uses the covens to seize political power in Shrīan and we live, albeit briefly, on the funeral pyre of a nation you set out to save? I'm not sure even you're prepared for so much irony."

"We would see sights such as had not been seen in a very long time," the Emissary said wistfully.

Kasraman looked askance at the Emissary, then gave his brother a reassuring smile. "We'll control the witches. Breaking the Sēq only snaps the back of a monopoly, giving us options. Other groups will rise to fill the gaps, and we'll benefit from it."

"I'll follow you," Belamandris said, "though am filled with misgivings. But Father, what of conscience and consequence? How much can we tread on sende, before our boot prints mask it entirely? We abandoned the old ways for good reasons."

Corajidin shivered as a cold streak raced up his spine, to settle at the base of his skull. The vision of tentacles so large a dozen men with arms extended could not encircle them; the mad gibbering in the depths and the bitter cold that seemed to know nothing of sun-warmed grasses, the myriad scents of spring or the joy of . . . anything he could understand. Perhaps he had been right in not drinking too deeply of the gifts the Emissary had given him. Destiny had chosen him for this task, yet was it his fate to survive and prosper as the result of it? What purpose if Corajidin were to be the father of the empire, if only to sing the eulogy as the entire world died to make way for a new one he would never see?

Kasraman and Belamandris. Wolfram. These were men he could trust, who had bled for and almost died for him. Wolfram had served three generations of the Erebus and would, events conspiring, be there to lend his wisdom to Kasraman when he was Awakened. Yashamin should have been here to share this with him. He closed his eyes for a moment, hoping to hear her voice. Opening them again he stared into the corners where shadows pooled like the edges of doors into worlds unseen, for the smallest hope she was there.

Nothing. *I do this for you, my love,* he thought. *This was your dream as much as it was ever mine. And soon, the soul of your murderer will be flung to the deepest parts of the Well of Souls, there to face your wrath until you choose to be reborn again, or I come to join you and share the time stolen from us.*

His thoughts went to dark, proscribed places. So many of his beliefs had been brought into question. It was said the victor determined the right of what they had done, yet how far was too far? At what point did he forsake everything he believed in, to satisfy his own needs?

Or for love. Could Yashamin be returned to him? Her body remade to rule by his side as the perfect metaphor for the birth of a new world? The Emissary had said her Masters were powerful beyond the petty imaginings of mortals. For them, all things were possible—though for a price he had feared to ask, lest he willingly pay.

All decisions came with a price, each choice made, a door opened that could never be closed. The consequences of cause, hidden by the mists of effects yet to be seen. Witches. Scholars. The Empress-in-Shadows. The fate of his people. The war machine of the Iron League, who would invade Shrīan whether Corajidin was Asrahn or not. Sometimes there were only bad choices to be made where a current situation was untenable and doom waited, either way.

He looked to dark Kasraman and broken Wolfram. To golden Belamandris. Saw faith when they looked back at him. Corajidin smiled then.

"Conscience and consequence are words for those without the conviction that they do right." Corajidin stood and rested his knuckled fists on the hard surface of his desk. He looked to each of them in turn, resting last on Belamandris and Kasraman. *My instruments in this. The men who will rule the world after I am gone.* "Such words keep the timid cowed and the cautious still. Belamandris, gather your Anlūki and finish what you started. Leave no two stones together if you have to, but bring Vahineh back to me. Alive."

"Nix?" The little man stopped his playing to look at Corajidin. "Unleash your daemon elementals. I want the people of Avānweh to see the horrors that hide in the dark places of the world."

"Your wish is my welcome command," Nix said with a wicked grin.

"And Mari?" Belamandris asked quietly.

"She chose her new friends over her family." Corajidin looked at Kasraman, his lips a hard band against his teeth. "Gather the witches you trust, the ones we'll take on our grand journey. Rouse the rest, the fodder, from the Mahsojhin. We'll let them finish their war, though it be the last thing they ever do. Summon whatever spirits, shed whatever blood, make whatever bargains you deem necessary—but draw the Sēq from their halls so we can break them. Let us give our people the crisis they need—an unprovoked attack by the Humans of the Iron League—so we can save them."

22

"REGRET OVER THE PAST AND FEAR OF THE FUTURE ROB US OF TODAY."

—From *The Ternary*, by Sedefke, inventor, explorer, and philosopher
(586th Year of the Awakened Empire)

DAY 357 OF THE 495TH YEAR OF

THE SHRĪANESE FEDERATION

The gardens that hung from the narrow, sculpted terraces on the mountain had been flattened. Bodies crushed flowers, and bled onto long grasses whose blue flowers were spattered with red. Flurries of wind were not enough to remove the metallic hint of open wounds from the air. There was a brief shadow. The blur of motion. Indris parried the incoming Anlūki's blade, then backhanded him across the face with the sheathed Changeling. The weapon moaned as the *kirion* scabbard smashed into the Anlūki's temple, sending him to the ground.

Indris spared a glance for his friends. Ekko—surrounded by the dead and dying, his khopesh stained and dripping red, his armour and fur likewise slick with blood—breathed heavily. The great Tau-se favoured his right leg, which had a deep gash in the calf. Shar danced amongst the Anlūki and those other soldiers who flew the colours of Corajidin or his supporters. Her voice was raised in a song that raised Indris's spirits, while it seemed to lower those of her opponents. Her *serill* blade flickered like a blue-tinted net, chiming as it struck metal, though more subdued when it pierced flesh. There was a long bloody track down her cheek and jaw and her right arm was held close to her chest, her fingers curled into a claw. She winced with every blow. A grey-faced Hayden puffed like a bellows, lips flecked with spittle, wheezing with each swing of his sword. One eye was sealed closed, the skin swollen and bruised. One of his ears bled profusely. Blood flowed down his neck and onto his buckskins from a gash on the side of his head. The old man took a sword to the thigh—but Mari swooped in, blade a humming plane of light. She hacked through the Anlūki's arm at the elbow. Covered in blood—though Indris could not tell how much was hers and how much from those she had killed—she stood over Hayden while the man squeezed the wound in his leg closed, teeth gritted against the pain.

Since dawn, wave after wave of flesh and steel had hunted Indris and his cohort down, with no relief in sight. First they had fought Nadir, Ravenet, and their huqdi. As the sun rolled across a cloud-shredded sky, Indris and his friends had been driven from one battle to the next, each further away from the Eyrie. Though the huqdi had run, the street dogs had brought more of their mongrel pack back with them. Defeated, they would scatter, only to return with bigger dogs. And bigger. Until eventually it was wolves in steel they faced: Belamandris's Anlūki, the heavy Kadarin infantry, and the Exalted Names and bravos in Corajidin's colours out to make reputations for themselves.

Towering mountain shadows collapsed across Avānweh as the last score or so of enemies flung themselves out of a side street. Indris led his friends in a fighting retreat up a set of stairs carved into the mountain, a slack-featured Vahineh stumbling before them, Omen serving as her moving shield, the shafts of spent arrows rattling in his Shroud like quills. They made their stand in a flattened stone turret between bends in the stair.

With an exhausted grunt, Mari levelled a scything blow that cut the throat of the final warrior to come against them. Then she staggered to one knee and leaned on her Sûnblade, which smoked from the blood that burned off its blade. Mari rubbed a thumb against her split lip, her cheek swelling outward as she probed the inside of her mouth with her tongue. She leaned forward to spit out blood, as well as a small chip of tooth.

All day Indris had been expecting help to arrive, but nothing. At the very least the Avānweh kherife should have intervened. Indris had seen some of the green-coated kherife a few times during the day, though the constabulary had not interfered, and Indris did not know why. Even if nobody else came to help, Roshana certainly should have gotten involved if for no other reason than to save Vahineh. Besides, it was Roshana's foolish action that had started the violence at a time when the nation was meant to be at peace.

Indris held Changeling in both hands and let her trickle energy into him. Within moments the worst of the fatigue was gone. It was tempting to take all she could offer. The sense of overwhelming euphoria, the belief he could do anything and that he had no limits. Yet that euphoria, he had learned from bitter experience, was hard to let go. He loved and loathed the blade in near equal measure, though none of what she did for him was malign. She simply gave him what he wanted, so that he could do what was needed.

His friends were almost done, all wounded in some way and breathing hard. Even Omen's ceramic body had large divots missing from the once-smooth surface, two fingers were missing, and one emerald eye had been shattered. Shar's skin flickered with a combination of rage and pain. She cradled her arm like it was broken. Hayden's leg was leaking a lot of blood, which would have been much better off inside his body. Ekko took a hesitant seat with his back to a worn stone crenulation, carefully cleaning the blood from his nicked khopesh. They were silent, save for the Vahineh's loud and panicked breathing.

"We can't do this anymore," Mari said as she rose to her feet, stretching the soreness from her muscles. She shot a glance at the mountain, behind which the sun was hiding, invisible on its journey from evening and into night. The sky on the western horizon was as bruised as Indris felt. "They'll keep coming until we're dead, or taken."

"You're right," Indris made his way to Hayden's side. The old man's face was waxy beneath a layer of sweat and dried blood flecks. His moustache bristled with pain, and blood from his wounded leg seeped between his fingers. Moving Hayden's hands away, Indris pressed his own hand to the wound and channelled enough energy to seal the cut, then a little more to restore some of the colour to Hayden's chalky features.

"Is it a little late in the piece for me to go home now?" the old man wheezed.

"Soon." Indris patted Hayden's leg, then looked to Ekko, who nodded towards Shar, giving her precedence. Shar smiled her thanks, a brittle thing too easily gone from her lips. Indris inspected her forearm, his gentle touches eliciting a string of muttered invective. The forearm was broken in two places and cut in quite a few more. He could treat the cuts, but the broken bone was not something he could treat where they were, not in the limited time they had. Indris told her as much.

"*Faruq ayo, hir ajet*," she whispered in breathy, backward-sounding Seethe. "A lot. Do what you can."

"I know it hurts, Shar. I'll take care of the cuts and numb the pain. We'll find somewhere you can rest and I'll set that bone for you. Preferably on the way out of Avānweh."

It was a matter of minutes for him to heal her cuts and bruises. Hayden broke a small branch off a tree in one of the old flower beds. He snapped it in half, then used his knife to smooth it down. Cutting a length from the end of his shirt he handed the bundle to Indris so he could splint Shar's arm. She bit her lip between her teeth, staring into Indris's eyes the entire time while holding Hayden's hand in a white-knuckled grip. Shar gave a stuttering sob once it was over, then lay back on the stone.

"Your fighting day is over," Indris said. He picked up her *serill* blade and sheathed it for her. Seeing Hayden was out of ammunition, Indris gave him the dozen or so bolts he had left for his storm-pistol. The old marksman's face lit up as he reloaded his rifle.

"Indris?" Mari called out. She had walked to the edge of the turret to see the stairs below. Indris picked his way over the dead and unconscious bodies to join her. The stairs were spattered with gore and littered with bodies, limbs thrown wide to make haphazard shapes in leather, metal, and flesh. At the bottom of the stairs more *huqdi* waited, a greasy collection of thugs in mismatched armour, while more Imperialist soldiers arrived.

"Don't these people ever run out of soldiers?" Indris asked.

"Well, yes, they do." Mari smiled over her shoulder. It was a mildly grotesque thing with her swollen, bloodied lip, the scratches on her face and what looked like the beginning of a black eye of heroic proportions. "They just haven't yet. I don't think they've understood the invitation we've sent for them to go f—"

"Indris!" An echoing cry in a familiar voice from below.

"Sweet Erebus, no!" Mari whispered. Indris froze.

Belamandris came to stand at the head of a group of grim looking Anlūki. The other soldiers made a path for him. The man appeared fresh, lamplight slick across his golden hair and the ruby scales of his armour. He rested a booted foot on the bottom stair, hand curled around Tragedy's sheath.

"Indris, I know you're up there."

Indris could hear his friends muttering behind him. He gestured for them to remain calm, though it was about as far from how he felt as could be. He looked down the stairs and met Belamandris's gaze over the carcass-strewn distance between them. Belamandris smiled, a little tug at the corners of his lips. "Come down, Indris. Only one more person needs to die today."

"I appreciate the offer, but we're quite fine up here."

"Tell him to piss off," Mari muttered.

"You tell him to piss off," Indris said.

"I'll tell him to piss off," Shar offered as she joined them. The Seethe trouper leaned down the stairs and shouted, "Hey, Golden Boy. Piss off." She looked at Indris and Mari with a smile. "There. It's done."

Indris and Mari stared at Shar in stunned silence.

"What?" she said as they both stared at her as she walked away. "My arm hurts."

"That was . . . unexpected." Mari grimaced. "I doubt Belam would've liked that much at all."

"Really?" Indris said sarcastically.

"Is that your answer, Indris?" Belamandris asked. "Too many people have already died needlessly. Why prolong the inevitable? You'll never make it to safety and the longer you resist, the more likely it is your friends will die."

"You'd kill me, Belam?" Mari asked sadly.

"You? Never." He clenched his fist. "Once this is over you can come home and help me guide father away from the madness that consumes him. But the future has no place for Indris. Come down, Indris, and let's settle what we started in Amnon."

"What in the Ancestor's names is he talking about?" Mari asked.

"I've no idea," Indris muttered. "I resisted the Jahirojin and walked away, letting your father and brother go. It was Thufan who betrayed them both, not me."

"You're in no condition to face my brother, Indris."

Changeling murmured over his shoulder, a soothing balm on his nerves as she sluiced him with fresh energy. The aches and pains he had endured vanished, cuts and bruises on his hands fading away. Mari swore to herself as she watched days of healing happen in a matter of heartbeats. Indris clenched and unclenched his fists, turning his hands over, frowning where all the new wounds were almost gone.

"It seems I'm in a condition to meet your brother after all."

"Did you . . .?"

"Me? No! Changeling does things for her own reasons as often as not."

"You can't fight him, Indris." Mari jerked her head towards where their friends were gathered. Indris looked across and saw how ragged and worn they were. "And we need to get them somewhere safe."

"Is there such a place in Avānweh? My staying could buy the time you need to get our friends away."

"You staying will get you killed," she said flatly. "Your friends would never leave. And Belam is a better swordsman than you and has about, oh, a million friends down there to lend a hand."

"A million?" Indris looked down and pantomimed a count. Mari elbowed him in the ribs, expression stern. "There aren't a million people down there, Mari."

"No. But there're more than enough to put you down. And that I won't have."

"If we run, they'll follow." Indris shrugged. "Red work if we do, red work if we don't."

Belamandris had taken a few steps upward. Indris was about to respond by going to meet him when a large shadow swept overhead. The wind of its passage whipped his hair into his eyes. It was followed by another, then more. Gryphons! Then there was the crackle-and-snap of a wind-skiff as it turned towards the mountain. Indris peered into the growing evening gloom to see the blue and grey colours of the Family Näsiré flying from the stern.

The lead gryphon banked, as did the one immediately after, dropping to land near where Indris and Mari stood. The other gryphons circled above Belamandris's soldiers. Even in the limited light Indris could see the gryphon riders had their bows out, guiding the well-trained mounts with their knees and voices.

Neva unbuckled herself from her high saddle and slid to the ground, pulling her goggles up and unwinding the taloub from around her lower face. She slung her longspear across her armoured shoulders, the blade shaped to be a metre-long, razor-like feather. She looked irritated.

"Fine bloody mess you two have made," she said by way of hello to Indris and Mari. "Do you have any idea how many bodies are gathering flies in my city? I suppose I should be at least thankful you followed sende, and didn't kill civilians."

"We—" Indris began.

"Later," Neva cut him off. Yago remained in the saddle of his own gryphon, though he did give them a cheeky wave. Indris and the others raised their hands in wan response, grimacing. Only Vahineh waved with any enthusiasm, her face lit with wonder as she stared at the gryphon. Ekko hurriedly held her hands still and allowed her, his expression fixed, to stroke his mane. Neva glared at them all, then gestured towards the wind-skiff that made its careful way over the stairs, then stopped close to the turret. A side panel opened and a long boarding bridge, roped off at both sides, crossed the distance. Neva nodded to the skiff. "All aboard."

"Stop!" Belamandris yelled. He leaped up the stairs a few at a time until Neva held out her hand for him to stay. Belamandris slowed his progress to a walk. A second gesture from Neva and one of the gryphon riders fired a heavy-looking arrow that ricocheted from the stone a metre or so in front of Belamandris's feet. The warrior-poet looked at Neva angrily. "You've no right to interfere in the business of the Great Houses!"

"Erebus fa Corajidin fa Belamandris, by the order of the Arbiter of the Change and the Sayf-Avānweh, you and your soldiers are ordered to disband and return at once to your lodgings."

"That's not going to happen."

"Really?" Neva asked with raised eyebrows. "Just how many arrows can you and your friends dodge at one time? I'm betting . . . not nearly enough."

More archers appeared at the rail of the skiff, short but powerful bows in their hands, arrows held to the string. The two squads of gryphon riders maintained their lazy circling, bows likewise evident.

"Now go, Belamandris, while my grandfather is still inclined to mercy."

"You'll regret this! My fight is sanctioned by the law!"

"There's no doubt I'll regret many things," Neva replied. "But this won't be one of them. Widowmaker indeed. Tell the innocent families of those warriors you killed, or maimed, about the law—the grudge—that guides you. I doubt it was ever intended to harm them. Perhaps our regrets should start there?"

❈ ❈ ❈

It did not take long for the skiff to drop them in a secluded garden within a stone's throw of the Eyrie. Neva and Yago landed their gryphons nearby. Silent in her fury, Neva said nothing as she dropped from her saddle and marched, stiff backed and white knuckled, to where her father, the rahns, and the others waited.

Stories were being told, excuses made, reasons given, heard, and refuted, as Indris washed the blood from his hands in an aged stone basin. Shar's arm had been reset, the breaks fused with two slivers of gryphon bone he had taken from an old ornament. Even so, the injury still caused her pain. He had seen to Mari and Ekko's wounds too, and now a weight of lethargy sat across his shoulders. He looked down, eyes half closed. Clouds of red marbled the water, spreading outward, becoming darker each time he dipped his gore-soaked instruments. Though Changeling had healed Indris's wounds, the blood of others remained; soaked deep into the lines of his hands like the sins he tried to forget. He rubbed at old scars, pale roads on his tanned skin that tracked over the blue shadows of veined rivers and the corded muscles, which made hills and valleys on his skin.

There was a time when he had hoped his hands would build rather than destroy. He smiled to himself, inured to the clamour of voices around him, seeking peace in the memory of holding an ink brush. The feel of parchment under his hands while he designed new devices. Or the cool weight of a hammer, plane, chisel, wrench, or screwdriver that brought his designs from the page into reality. They were the tools he had loved best, yet his hands had been set to darker work for purposes he had once thought he understood.

He looked down at Changeling where she leaned against the moon- and lamp-streaked wall. She crooned, sensing his scrutiny and the darkness of his mood. It was not her fault. She, like him, had been built for a fell purpose. His hand, no other, had baptised her in the blood of carnage in much the same way the Sēq had done for him.

Regret was pointless. Everything he had done had led him to who and where he was now. What he did and the man he was now would set his feet on the path for what he was to become. All he could do was act with a thought to compassion, conscience, and consequences. To trust the living now would set his feet in the direction best for himself and the ones he loved.

Somewhere in the Eyrie, the leaden ticking of a clock was interrupted by a single basso chime. The Hour of the Phoenix. He glanced out the window at the deceptively still velvet darkness blanketing Avānweh, pinned by jewel-coloured chips in the patterns of streets and backlit waterfalls. Out there, obscured by the depths of night, warriors carried bitter weapons for purposes they, too, thought they understood.

A brooding, sullen weight grew over the city. He could feel it like oil on his skin. Somewhere out there, in the endless darkness of laneways and door-ways and mountain passes, disentropy was being pooled like clouds before a hurricane. From the streets drifted the stench he had detected on the ahmsah, like the smell of pus after a scab has been ripped off an infected wound. And voices filled his head; the tinny whisper of conversations he did not want to hear yet could not escape from. His head pounded.

He glanced up at the mirror to see the reflection of those in the room. Hands gestured wildly. Faces were strained, ruddy in the subdued glow of lamps. It was their voices that grated on his nerves. Raucous and conflicting, the tumbled whole of the words making less sense than the sum of the parts. He gripped the edge of the basin, knuckles white.

"Would you all just shut up?" Indris's quiet voice sliced across the room. He watched as heads snapped in his direction, expressions ranging from con-trition to fury. He breathed deeply and slowly to calm his nerves, eyes drawn to a crescent of blood under his fingernail. "Screaming at each other isn't going to change what's happened."

"They tried to kill my cousin!" Martūm joined in, ever the dutiful relative.

Bensaharēn shot Martūm a withering glance that cut off any further words from Martūm. The armoured Knight-General Maselane was at his side. Rosha had wasted little time in gathering her senior staff. Mauntro and the best of his already elite Tau-se waited in the corridor outside. There was no sign of Danyūn or his Ishahayans, though Indris doubted they would be far away.

"We need to respond!" Rosha snapped.

"You need to keep your tongue behind your teeth and listen," Mari ground out. "You weren't there! You've no idea what happened, so your opinion on what we could've done, or what we should do now, isn't worth a lot."

"How *dare* you?" Rosha seethed.

"Mari's right," Siamak said. "We do not know what else could have been done to prevent this."

"The city is a killing field!" Nazarafine growled. "Though it is the Imperialists and the Federationists fighting, let us not fool ourselves. This is really the conflict between the Nāsarat and the Erebus."

"Are you blaming me?" Rosha's voice was steely.

"For some of it you *are* to blame," Ajo said with equanimity. "You were the one who somehow arranged for yourself to lead the Federationists. You were the one who broke the rules of sende by trying to have Corajidin assassinated."

"Doesn't matter who did what first," Neva said, scratching her head, hair flat from where it had been covered by her helmet. Her cheeks were wind burned, pale circles around her eyes from where she had worn her goggles. Her armoured flying leathers creaked as she moved. "Thankfully civilian losses have been avoided, but if people's blood rises any more, it'll become a free-for-all. You all need to leave Avānweh tonight, before innocent people are hurt."

"I'll do no such thing," Rosha growled.

"Yes," Ajo countered, "you will. As Arbiter of the Change *and* the Sayf-Avānweh, I demand you leave *my* city as soon as possible. All of you. Your presence is a liability."

"But you've cleared Belamandris and his soldiers from the streets." Rosha protested.

"They weren't the only ones fighting!" Ajo shouted. He pointed at Indris. "He and his friends turned my streets into a charnel house! I'll not stand for any more threats to the Change. You're done here, the lot of you."

"Mari is a warrior-poet," Bensaharēn said tranquilly, "and one of the best I have ever trained. Indris is a daimahjin and former Sēq General. Their friends are likewise accomplished. What should they have done, Ajo? Died pointlessly so Corajidin could have Vahineh as a prize? Perhaps we all need to see reason, neh?"

"And yet, there's little we can do here with what we have." Maselane said as he scratched the bridge of his nose thoughtfully. "The majority of the Phoenix Army is still en route from Avānweh to Narsis. We've a single company of the Lion Guard here, as well as some of Bensaharēn's students and whatever Gnostic Assassins came with Danyūn. We should withdraw to a place of strength."

"Can you get our people out of Avānweh?" Bensaharēn asked.

Maselane snorted. "My friend, I gave orders for our people to be packed and ready to go the moment the violence started."

"I didn't approve that." Rosha's hands were white-knuckled on the arms of her chair.

"No, my rahn, you didn't," Maselane replied. "But it was my job to see it done, and done it was. If we're not obstructed, I can have our people on the way to Narsis within the hour."

"I assume you will have Rahn-Roshana leave the city by other, more secretive means?" Bensaharēn asked. Maselane nodded by way of response.

"Very well," Rosha said. "Maselane, see our people safely away. I'll remain with the rahns, Indris, and his friends. Bensaharēn, you, Mauntro, and Danyūn will remain with me."

Everyone made to move, but then Neva spoke.

"There's something I need to show Indris before he goes." Mari eyed the woman, though said nothing.

Instead, it was Neva's father who protested. "You'll have to get somebody else, Neva," Ajo said firmly. "These people, along with Corajidin's trouble makers, are leaving my city."

Neva gave an exasperated sigh. "There's something happening at the ruins of the Mahsojhin. Indris is the only scholar who happens to be standing here."

"Besides," Indris said, "I don't take orders from you, Ajo. As a Sēq—"

"You *were* a Sēq," the Sky Lord's voice was flat. "Now you're a daimahjin with none of the Sēq's so-called rights or protection. I want you gone until whatever it is between the Näsarat and the Erebus is settled. Neva? Yago? Would you please escort the rahns out of Avānweh. You can take that as an order or a request, I really don't care. Just see to it."

The Sky Lord's expression was disappointed as he walked from the room, leaning heavily on his cane.

Neva gestured towards the door, her message clear, though her look said she would have it otherwise.

❈ ❈ ❈

They were on their way to the Skydock, surrounded by armed and armoured Sky Knights and a handful of green-coated kherife, when Indris felt the bubble of pent-up energy burst. He stumbled, pain blossoming in his head like a sharp-edged flower.

Femensetri's voice echoed in his mind shortly after.

"*Indris!*" she snapped. The edges to her fear were sharp in his head, leaving him reeling. "*We need you!*"

"What is it?" Mari asked, seeing him stagger. Shar frowned, a question in her eyes. Indris held up his hand for his friends to stop.

"*Femensetri, I'm here. What was—*"

"*The bloody Mahsojhin!*" she growled. "*That imbecile Corajidin has had his witches open it. But they weren't alone. I sense the hand of the Drear in this.*"

"*I smelled something on the ahm. The energy they used was—*"

"*Corrupt. I need you here. Now. I don't know if there are enough of the Sēq to hold the witches off and defend the city at the same time. Hurry!*"

"*I can't. The Federationist rahns need my protection!*"

"*If the witches are freed, all of Shrīan will need bloody protection! Think about the long game for a change!*"

"*You don't think I am? I'm staying with Mari, my friends and the rahns. This is something you'll need to do without me. The Sēq have—*"

"*I'll be coming for you.*"

"*No! I need to—*"

And with an acidic curse, she was gone.

Indris pinched the bridge of his nose between thumb and forefinger in a vain attempt to stem the rising pain. Realising the others were waiting for him, he gestured for Neva to continue on.

Indris took the keys for the *Wanderer* from the chain around his neck, and handed them to Shar. Before she could ask he said, "Something may happen to me. Take her. She's faster than anything Corajidin will have. Make sure you take the rahns and whoever else you have room for, with you. Get to Narsis. I'll meet you there, or sooner if at all possible."

"What are you planning, Indris?" Neva's question sounded more like an accusation.

"I'll go with you and your people." He looked into the night sky. Low hanging clouds obscured the stars, save for the occasional fitful pinprick of light. The moon was a blue-green smear that backlit the edges of a storm that piled up against the mountain face. Femensetri may make good on her threat, weighting the greater good against Indris's own wishes. He needed to do for the rahns what he could. "We'll take a wind-galley and I'll draw lots of attention to ourselves to keep our enemies distracted. They'll expect me to be protecting the rahns. Meanwhile, Shar will pilot the *Wanderer*, and get the rahns to safety. All we need to do—Neva, Yago—is keep their attention focussed on us."

"How do you plan on that?" Mari asked, clearly unimpressed with the plan.

"I've a few ideas," Indris said with more confidence than he felt. He saw the look on her face and shook his head. "Before you ask—no, this isn't your kind of fight. I'll do what I need to do better, if I know you're safe."

But safety was a relative thing, and before she could even reply, he felt the dissonance in the ahm as a great bubble of energy burst like a boil. Corrupted energy oozed into the world, tainted and reeking. Changeling snarled, moments before Indris was rocked by a wave of nausea and vertigo. Lightning sheeted across the sky, thunder rolling in its wake. He snapped his gaze up the mountain to where a sickly aurora flickered around the heights. Tiny figures swarmed in the air, seen during pulses of jagged brightness. The lightning flared. Focussed. Became jagged spears that lanced from the heavens amidst the repeated concussive blows of thunder too rapid, too loud, to be natural. Hoots, shrieks, and keening wails reached his ears, tattered by the winds and distance.

"Erebus on a tightrope," Mari said slowly, face slack with shock. Neva and Yago were likewise stunned, looking towards the riot of surly colour in the sky.

"You need to go." Indris grabbed Mari and Shar by the shoulders, pushing them in the direction of the stairs that led down to the Shoals. Mari looked at him as if she did not understand. Shar nodded, Hayden and Ekko following in her footsteps, as she dashed away with the rahns and their own people.

"Indris . . . I . . . What's happening?" Mari asked softly.

"Your father's will is happening." Indris spared a glance at her, noted her angry frown and the hard line of her lips. There were things he wanted to say to her in that moment. Truths, half-truths, sweet but kind lies about how everything would be better with the new day. But the words got caught behind his teeth as a great gout of flame spiralled around a tower carved from the mountain. The flame formed muscular arms, great curved horns and eyes like slits of the baleful summer sun over the desert: harsh, white, and remorseless. A crown of heat haze and smoke formed above its brow, spiralling slowly amidst fractals of superheated air and dazzling carnelian light. A jinn prince, summoned from the far reaches of the Spiritlands that bordered the ahmtesh. With a stentorian, maniacal laugh the jinn twisted the top of the tower off, the stone melting to slag in its hands. Its voice creaked and groaned like a building burning to the ground.

Swallowing a very healthy and natural fear, Indris took Mari in his arms. Indris felt the grasping of familiar mystic fingers on his Disentropic Stain. There was no time to comfort her with words that may well prove him a liar all too soon.

"We won't say our goodbyes. Not yet." He leaned in to kiss her. Her eyes closed, lips parted—

And was wrenched from her embrace by a flutter of wings and a small, violent whirlwind. Lightning crackled around, scorching the air and tingling along his nerves. He was dragged struggling into the air—

Then all the angles in the world became curves. Edges blurred, while flat planes sharpened and stretched. The world disassembled itself about him and he screamed as he was dragged away and flung across the narrow rift of time and space to stand amongst—

Chaos.

"Stay here!" The Stormbringer ordered him. "We'll call for you when it's time."

And with that she wove a cat's cradle of lightning that arced outward into the night. It lit the world with a clean, brief, flare of pallid light as it struck witches from the sky. It illuminated the faces of the scholars who stood nearby on toppled columns, scattered about a weed-strewn forum. Their faces were creased in frowns, weapons drawn and Scholar's Crooks glowing bright with witchfire. It licked at the faces of the witches who flung themselves through it. Her skin shining like a lantern, bright against the black of armour and it's tracery of witchfire, the Stormbringer launched herself into the fray.

Scholars hurled the products of their minds, sweeping colours and shapes of energy, into the sky. The Stormbringer hurled lightning, boiling the air around her. Arcane fire licked across the edges of coal-dark coats, almost faint compared to the incandescent lamps the crooning, wailing, screaming, chanting scholars had become. Other Sēq were likewise engaged, from different ranks of the Order, including a powerful-looking Sēq Executioner who scythed through the enemies like a farmer reaping wheat.

Around him there was what looked to be a century of Sēq Knights, supported by some nervous looking Librarians. A Master loitered here and there, observing, or recovering, or ordering scholars into battle.

Limned by a brilliant flash, one of the nearby scholars turned to him, face backlit by an incredible power. Supernatural and beautiful she shone, eyes incredibly bright like the glare of backlit summer clouds. Her long storm-hued hair flailed in the ripping wind and she levelled her power at the witches even as she smiled her ravage-me smile and he felt his head spin as his throat constricted around one of the hardest words for him to say—

"Anj?"

23

"NOTHING IS SO VALUABLE TO US AS IT IS ON THE DAY WE LOSE IT."

—Karisa of the Ijalian, troubadour and poet to Asrahn-Selassin fa Vashne
(493rd Year of the Shrīanese Federation)

DAY 358 OF THE 495TH YEAR OF

THE SHRĪANESE FEDERATION

Mari reeled in the tempest, losing her footing and falling to the ground as leaves, dirt, and gravel spiralled around her. The fine hairs on her arms and the back of her neck stood on end from the static. Small arcs of lightning danced across her skin, leaving pinhead burns that caused her muscles to twitch.

The Sky Knights with her had been tumbled from their feet. They lay supine and groaning in a litter of limbs, weapons, and armour.

One moment Indris had been there, so close she could feel his breath on her lips and tongue. The next he was wrenched away into the sky amidst a maelstrom of crackling light and ragged, shrieking wind.

Neva leaned down and extended a hand to help Mari to her feet. Mari looked at it for a few moments longer than was polite, before taking it. Both women craned their necks for some sign of Indris. Nothing.

"Femensetri," Mari guessed out loud, not bothering to mask her anger. She looked down the stairs to where Shar was leading rahns and their protectors towards the *Wanderer*. Mari knew she was supposed go with them, though doubted Roshana or Nazarafine would welcome her presence. But that was not what mattered. Mari's friends would need her help.

"What are you going to do?" Neva asked as if reading her mind.

"Pretty much what you'd think," Mari said resignedly. Yago joined them while the gathered Sky Knights looked upward, clearly not keen to take to the air. "What about you?"

"Well Indris's plan is pretty much defunct now." Yago observed. "I dare say you'd be better off with us escorting you out of here like we originally planned."

"We've a couple of skiffs," Neva added, "a galley and two squads of gryphons. Should be enough to keep most things at bay."

"It's what it won't keep at bay that bothers me," Yago said dryly.

There came a colossal crack as the air split, high above them. A whirling vortex of spinning darkness with a tornado for a torso, lightning-traced eagle's head and rangy, almost skeletal arms tore into the world. It gave a piercing cry that echoed across the heavens before it was struck by whirling arcs and tumbling geometric prisms of jewel-hued light. The spirit shrieked again, before going on the attack.

"We're really going to fly in this?" Mari asked nervously.

"Fly yes," Neva muttered. She jerked her chin at the sky. "In that? Not on your life. We'll take it low, fast, and safe. South across the Lakes of the Sky, then we'll turn west once I think we're far enough away. Hopefully nobody will know we're gone."

"And the decoy Indris wanted?"

"Yeah, that's not going to happen," Yago muttered. "Grandfather wouldn't abide by us throwing lives away, not with the sky being so eventful and all."

"I hear you," Mari said. She doubted whether Indris would want anybody risking their lives so recklessly. Unless it was him. "The *Wanderer* is down in the Shoals. Grab what you need and we'll see you down there."

Neva and Yago looked at the sky with narrowed eyes, assessing the danger. Finally Neva nodded to herself. "Give us about thirty minutes. If we're late, don't wait up."

A final look at the roiling conflict in the sky and Mari did not need to be convinced further. "Count on it."

❋ ❋ ❋

The streets were almost deserted as Mari sprinted towards the Shoals. Doors were closed and almost all the windows shuttered, except for the occasional brave or foolhardy soul whose curiosity overwhelmed their common sense.

From time to time, she heard battle cries and the clash of metal, before rounding a corner to see soldiers in the various colours of the Imperialist houses fighting Federationists. The conflict had spread well beyond a battle between the Näsarat and the Erebus. Bodies were left lying on the streets, dead and dying, while grim-faced warriors—their eyes a lurid white in the reflected light from flaring sky—sought to add to the tally of both. There was no sign of the rahns, or Indris's friends. Mari assumed they had found safer paths than she.

All the while the conflict in the sky raged on in a terrifying play of light and discordant sound, the vibrations of which drummed on her skin. The air was filled with the cacophony of another battle. She came to a sliding halt at the next corner. Poking her head around she saw the pitched battle occurring in the middle of the street.

Between her and the street she needed to take. *A whole damned city to fight in, and you have to be here. Once in a while it would be nice to do the things the easy way.*

Soldiers in the colours of the Imperialist sayfs—with a handful of Anlūki cutting a swathe about themselves—were fighting against retainers in the blue and gold of the Näsarat. There were a small number of Siamak's marsh-knights helping them, scarecrow thin dervishes who seemed untouchable as they danced in the storm of metal, threadbare coats flapping around lean, tanned limbs.

Furtive movement nearby caught her attention. A thin, unsavoury looking man with long greasy hair and a sallow complexion edged forward. His eyes were bright in deeply shadowed orbits. His long fingered hands manipulated a metallic pyramid, like an expensive child's puzzle box. Mari rested her palm on her Sûnblade's hilt and stepped towards him.

"Nix of the Maladhi! Put whatever it is you have there down, and step away from it." Mari rolled onto the balls of her feet, fingers curled on her sword, ready to draw.

"Hoo! I don't think so, love," Nix giggled. He gave a piercing whistle and two of the Anlūki looked at her. "I think I'll get a nice little something from your father for bringing you in. You've been a very bad girl, but it's time to put such childish things behind you. Just come with the nice men and me, eh?"

The Anlūki ended the lives of the retainers they were fighting and started towards her. Nix hooted with joy, until an improbably tall, awkward looking marsh-knight stepped up to them. He seemed to do little more than tap them with his two-handed shamshir, but they both collapsed to the ground in sprays of blood. The man, who in repose looked made of bamboo wands, flicked his long hair from his brow.

Nix seemed less pleased with himself.

"Now—" Mari started to say when Nix began to rapidly work on the puzzle box. The marsh-knight strode forward, just in time for Nix to throw the metal box at the knight's face. He swayed away, the little pyramid bouncing among the feet of the combatants, giving off high-pitched musical notes that gained in volume as pieces of the puzzle box continued to move by themselves.

Nix gambolled around and ducked through the melee on quick feet, blades never finding his skin. The surviving Anlūki saw Nix leaving, disengaged and turned to follow him at a run, leaving the remaining soldiers to their own devices.

Tempted as she was to give chase to Nix, there was something about the box that put her on edge. Sword drawn she waded into the melee, fending off the wild blows of friend and foe with a fraction of her attention, trying to find the box. She had almost reached it when it was kicked away. Then again. The noise had increased in volume so that the fighting ceased in pockets as warriors turned to look.

The music stopped.

There came a series of loud clicks. Mari found the puzzle box from the way those near it backed away. Sense overrode her curiosity and she, too, took rapid strides away, towards the street she needed to get back to the rahns and her friends.

A bell chimed. Too loud for such a little toy.

Then the stones of the road and the bricks of the houses seemed to drop away, a shift in perspective as if she were standing on the edge of a deep hole that stretched in almost every direction. Those closer to the puzzle box seemed to hover in midair for a moment, before coils of shadow, thick as tree trunks, speared upward. They branched, then branched again, latching on to the walls and roofs of surrounding buildings. The air became thick with the reek of mouldering vegetation and decay.

A titanic figure dragged itself into the world from wherever it had come. Tall as a clock tower it loomed, great curved horns sweeping the sky as it turned its austere, sharp-featured head. The face was beautiful in its way, hard and angular as a statue, yet streaked and whorled like bark. Deep-set eyes were carved into that face and they looked at the world with a terrible longing. The torso was that of a bare-breasted woman, skin dotted here and there with corrupt-looking blooms, nipples leaking a noisome sap that dripped to the ground far below, forming quivering black pools. Its—her—legs were those of a goat, black furred with cloven ebon hooves. Mari felt a cold sweat down her spine. She trembled. Her mouth went dry at the same moment as she wet herself.

Bruise-hued flowers grew at her hooves. Tendrils on the walls and ground sprouted, spread, anchoring themselves before releasing rank spores onto the hesitant winds that panted through the streets.

For a fraction of a second the giant satyress looked straight at Mari. Terrified beyond anything in her memory, Mari watched as it stamped one enormous hoof, crushing a handful of soldiers beneath it. The ground trembled and any glass facing the street cracked. Throwing back its head the satyress bellowed, a basso sound that seemed to fill the spaces around it. Windows shattered. Dust puffed from buildings. Tiles slid to fall and shatter on the ground. Mari cringed, covering her ears, head ringing.

From the pools of sap grew bizarre treelings that staggered, then stood firm on a quartet of thick roots. Supple branches, the fusion of fern and tentacle, grew upward. The bark was scored with shapes that looked like faces, with slack jaws and mismatched slashes for eyes. The monsters—for Mari had no other name for them—flailed their branches like a forest in a hurricane. Soldiers attacked them. Where the monsters wrapped their fern-like fronds around a soldier, the victim shrieked and thrashed, trying vainly to escape as their flesh turned necrotic. Within seconds the soldier would turn grey, drying, skin cracking as the monsters fed on them. One of the monsters, taller than those around it, threw the desiccated corpse into the air. It fell to the ground with the sound of a bag of twigs wrapped in a leather bag.

A handful of the monsters began to move in Mari's direction, their limbs creaking and branches whistling as they thrashed the air.

Mari's Sûnblade flared to life in her hands. She was soothed by the light and the warmth of it. Part of the horror that froze her began to thaw. The sudden brightness caused the tree-monsters to halt. The many mouths on their trunks opened and began a hissing, like the sound of the wind through pine needles. The cold sound chilled Mari's blood. The cracks-for-eyes widened, glowing with baleful putrescence.

She planted herself and sought for the aipsé, but her mind would not cooperate. Rather than no-mind, she was assailed by distractions and the fear that continued to gnaw at her. The monster's hissing, the way one and then another would edge forward, the almost hypnotic waving of their branches and the hazy shine of what passed for their eyes . . .

Something black swept through the monster's ranks, scattering a good many of them. Mari swore as she rolled backwards, narrowly missing the cart-sized hoof that bludgeoned the air in its passage. The hoof crashed into a building, raining down a shower of ruined brick. There was a faint crack and a lot of pain as pieces of debris slammed into her chest. The air was forced from her lungs. Mari tumbled across the ground, sword clutched resolutely in her fist.

Rising to her feet, it was difficult to breathe. She winced, leaning to her left around the pain. More contusions than Indris had healed, opened in her skin. Blood flowed sluggishly across her skin.

Then the light from her sword went out. The largest of the monsters stepped forward cautiously. Within seconds, the others followed.

Mari looked at the sword in her hand. At the waving ranks of monsters that approached her. Gingerly she twisted at the waist and felt agony spear through her from what she thought was at least one broken rib.

Don't be an idiot, she thought to herself. Slowly at first, then more rapidly, she backed away.

The monsters gained pace.

Sword drawn, she was prepared to make a run for it when a column of silver-white light speared down from the clouds. It struck the ground with a titanic boom. The monsters caught in the light were blasted to tattered rags of dark matter that puffed away in the breeze. Those nearby were hurled sideways to slam against walls, their legs wavering.

Shining figures streaked downward, trailing liquid light behind them. The Sēq, in their black coat and iridescent *kirion* armour. Their weapons flickering with witchfire. One of the Sēq spat on the ground, his face already streaked with blood and smoke. His old eyes in his young face looked weary, the lantern of his flesh little more than a wan spark. Yet he planted his feet squarely and started to croon into the cold, dark air.

One of the scholar knights saw Mari and nodded towards the street at her back.

"I'd run, were I you." He then turned his attention to the malignant brood mother who gave a deafening, hooting bellow. She was so massive her horns seem to shred the clouds above her.

The Sēq, wrapped in tumbling sigils of light, flung blazing geometries and spinning fractal polygons at the satyress, throwing themselves at her like too few candles trying to burn down an oak tree.

I'd run, were I you.

And she did.

❋ ❋ ❋

Mari was gasping, hand held to her side, as she made her way past Mauntro and his squad of Tau-se, then up the boarding ramp of the *Wanderer*. The Tempest Wheels and Disentropy Spools were already spinning, cracking, and snarling, giving off smaller versions of the pyrotechnic show above. She felt the vibrations through the soles of her boots.

"What kept you?" Shar asked, eying Mari as she came aboard. "Looks like you took a tougher road than we did."

"Oh, you know. My life is one adventure after another," Mari winced around the words as she took a seat. She tried to control her breathing and failed to ignore the pain. There came the sound of detonations from the city. Buildings were surrounded by brilliant coronas. A deafening bellow made Mari duck her head. She had taken longer than expected and Neva, Yago, and their comrades had not arrived. "We should get a move on, I think."

"Know anything about that?" Hayden jerked his chin in the direction of the city.

"Can we just go?"

Shar called out urgently to Mauntro and his Tau-se. Once the last of them was aboard, she lifted off from the Shoals. All the *ilhen* lamps on the *Wanderer* had been hooded, so she ran dark as Shar turned her prow south and away from the city.

Hayden and Ekko stood watchfully at the stern, the old drover with his storm-rifle cradled in this arms, Ekko with his powerful bow in one massive, furred hand. The giant lion-man looked at the battle that raged over Star Crown Mountain with wide hazel eyes, pupils round as saucers.

The rahns stood towards the prow, talking amongst themselves. Siamak had none of his people with him, Nazarafine had only Navid, her nephew. The Saidani-sûk warrior-poet looked the worse for wear, face bleeding and a long gash on his arm, blood pooling in the palm of his hand. Bensaharēn stood beside Roshana, wiping his sword blade with a length of silk, his face as calm as it ever was. There were flecks of blood on his armour and in his hair, though Mari strongly doubted any of it was his own.

"Where's Martūm?" Mari asked of nobody in particular.

"We were separated when we were attacked by some huqdi flying the Erebus colours," said a soft voice. Danyūn seemed to coalesce from the shadows. Those who stood behind him were equally quiet, the hilts of their weapons rearing like scorpion tails over their shoulders.

"You didn't try to find him?"

The blond man shrugged disinterestedly.

"I've more urgent tasks for Danyūn and his crew than chasing that wastrel, Martūm." Roshana's voice was uncompromising. "Besides, we have Vahineh and she is the only Selassin left of any importance. She's in one of the cabins below with the Wraith Knight."

"Did Indris leave with Neva and the Sky Knights?" Siamak asked.

"Hmmm?" Mari stood and looked out towards the receding bulk of Avānweh. Lightning flared in vivid colours through swirling cloud. The moon tinted everything with a faint wash of blue green. There were the other silhouettes of flying ships that had taken to the air, tiny things like midges that swarmed for a moment, then broke into dotted lines that moved east and west from the city. Some of the ships formed an amorphous blob, which Mari assumed were those who headed south.

"Siamak asked you a question!" Roshana snapped. She came to stand next to Mari, jaw set and square. "Now I'm asking it. Is Indris going to provide the distraction we need to survive?"

"You're quite a selfish bitch, you know," Mari said conversationally. Roshana flushed and raised her hand, which Mari responded to with a raised eyebrow. Danyūn stepped up and Mari flicked a bored glance in his direction.

"It won't end well," Mari warned. A possibly hollow threat given her broken ribs, but she had had just about enough of Roshana to last a lifetime. Bensaharēn came to Mari's aid, shaking his head at Danyūn and his Gnostic Assassins. Mari eyed Roshana with distaste. "All you care about is your own miserable agenda," she said. "You couldn't care less about Indris, other than what he can do for you."

"I'm the rahn of the Great House of Näsarat, Mari." Roshana's voice was frigid. "And you've no concept of what I do or don't care about, let alone what I will or won't do for my Great House."

"Like trying to marry Indris off to Neva?"

"At the very least," Roshana said with equanimity. With quicker hands than Mari would have credited her, Roshana gave Mari a stinging slap in the face. "Now do as you're told and answer my—"

Mari struck Roshana with *Blade Hand*, straight to the temple. Roshana did not utter a sound as she collapsed, Danyūn catching her and lowering her to the deck.

"You'll die for that," he said. The assassin looked at her from lowered brows, his face still deceptively placid.

"Don't think so, lad," Hayden said. He and Ekko stood with their weapons pointed at the assassins. Bensaharēn remained where he was, a faint smile tugging at his lips. The old warrior-poet shrugged when Danyūn looked at him for support. Mauntro and the Lion Guard stood silently, eyes narrowed and tails sweeping the deck, muscles bunching beneath their fur.

"I hate to break up this moment of camaraderie you've all got going on," Shar called out over the whistling wind, "but we've got something strange up ahead."

"What is it?" Mari asked, moving to stand by Shar.

"*Roje faruqti cha!*" Shar rolled her eyes. "If I knew, I'd have said."

"Sweet Erebus, you've a mouth on you."

"Wouldn't need it if people didn't—"

"Fine," Mari held up her hands in surrender. She looked forward, joined by Ekko and Mauntro. "I can't see a damned thing."

"There," Ekko pointed to where there was a disturbance over the water.

"That doesn't help much, you know," Mari said caustically.

"Of course, Pah-Mariam." Ekko nodded his apology. "It resembles a waterspout, moving rapidly in our direction."

"Before you ask, I've changed course twice and it's still trying to intercept us," Shar said sweetly.

"And we are being followed," Mauntro added. "Wind-galleys and what appear to be people flying. I thought Indris said this ship was faster than anything our enemies would have?"

"I do believe he did say that, yes," Ekko agreed.

"Could it be the way the Seethe is flying?" Mauntro asked politely, casting a critical eye at Shar. "If she continues to fly so slowly, we will have a fight on our hands."

"Shame," Ekko said.

"Hmmm," Mauntro nodded sagely.

"*Faruq yaha sodden,*" Shar told the Tau-se. "The *Wanderer* is faster than anything that bastard Corajidin should have. No offence, Mari."

"None taken. I'm way ahead of you there," Mari said. "But it doesn't explain exactly what, by Erebus's burned bones, we're dealing with."

"Little ill trickles of moonlight and mist," Omen said from the doorway to the lower decks. The Wraith Knight picked his way across the deck. "Spirits and witches with hate on their lips—"

"We've no time for your nonsense words, Omen," Hayden said tensely.

After a long pause where the others all looked at Omen, then at Hayden, then at Omen, Hayden finally sighed. "I meant I wanted you to just say it. Y'know, like a normal person would."

"Oh. Very well. Whoever follows us is using disentropy. And lots of it. I can feel it from here and see the shapes of the witches and the wind-corsairs, and fell-summoned daemons, light in their flight as they dance upon—"

"Balls," Mari sighed.

"They are definitely getting closer," Mauntro observed.

"And Rahn-Roshana is quite skilled with a blade," Ekko added. "We probably could have used her awake right about now."

Mari threw both Tau-se an obscene hand gesture, regretting it as pain lanced her ribs.

✳ ✳ ✳

"I broke through their cordon once," Shar said tersely, "but they're not giving me any room to move now. We're being herded southward, further from Avānweh."

"You can't break through again?"

Shar levelled a flat glare at Mari, who shrugged and took a step back.

Mari looked forward to where the shadows of the Mar Ejir rose like blackened sword points off the port rail. Avānweh was built at the narrows where the Lakes of the Sky met, as well as the mountain ranges of the Mar Jihara and the Mar Ejir. As far as Mari knew, the Ejiri mountain tribes had little to do with the Great Houses, though a couple were sayfs on the Teshri, neutral voters who sold their support in return for whatever they needed. The kind of flexible and mercantile loyalties her father made abundant use of.

"What are you going to do?" Siamak asked as he joined them.

"Make a run for Dalour," Shar said, tone dubious, "then try to head northwest for Qeme. That puts us in Näsarat Prefecture."

"And if that is not possible?" Nazarafine's voice was panicked.

Mari pursed her lips. She knew her father wanted to take Vahineh, but to capture the Federationist rahns would be an added bonus. Out here, where there were no witnesses, anything could happen and any story told to justify the sudden loss of three heads of the Great Houses.

"If I can't," Shar said rigidly, "then I can't. I think we need to face facts we're going to have a fight on our hands before this is over."

"How do you propose to combat the witches?" Bensaharēn asked. Mari scowled at her former teacher, though admitted to herself he was right. If she closed her eyes she could still see the satyress and her brood of walking, murderous trees. She thought on the shame of her fear and in that moment thought of Indris and he would be facing such things, or worse, even now. Sadly there was no way of levelling the playing field . . .

"The Näq Yetesh," Mari whispered. Then, more loudly, "The Dead Flat!"

"I know what it is," Shar said, "but you do realize the *Wanderer* needs disentropy to, oh, I don't know, stay in the air?"

"No more so than witches need disentropy to use their Arcanum, or to keep their summoned spirits bound."

Bensaharēn smiled. "A powerless witch is just another person in a robe. It would go some way towards levelling the odds."

"Are you sure, Pah-Mariam?" Ekko asked.

"On the first part, yes. On the second, not so much, but it stands to reason. Indris told me the witches use an . . . what did he call it . . . an Excreting Precept—"

"Extrinsic Precept," Shar laughed, then sobered as she tried to keep the wind-galley level in a sudden crosswind.

"Whatever. Anyway he said their powers come from outside themselves. If they don't have that power . . ."

"I hear you." Shar pulled levers around her pilot's chair and the vessel angled further southward. Mari could see the flickering lamps of Dalour in the distance, then beyond it an expanse of moonlit emptiness, as uncompromising as an anvil. Shar spared a glance for Mari. "You'd better tell everybody to hold on to something. I'll try to land us on the edge of the flat and hope great Tyen-to-wo of the Laughing Wind isn't inclined to make fools of us all."

"Do what you can, Shar."

"And then what?"

"If I'm right, our fight becomes slightly less than impossible."

"What if you're wrong?"

"Just hope I'm not."

24

"IT IS ONLY WHEN WE FREE OURSELVES OF THE DILEMMAS OF MEDIOCRITY, AND BY VIEWING OURSELVES THROUGH THE LENS OF ANOTHER'S PERCEPTIONS, THAT WE CAN KNOW GREATNESS."

—Asrahn-Erebus fa Basyrandin (473rd Year of the Shrīanese Federation)

DAY 358 OF THE 495TH YEAR OF

THE SHRĪANESE FEDERATION

Corajidin watched with sick wonder as the sky burned.

Standing at the prow of his wind-skiff, Corajidin was close enough to Mahsojhin to hear the individual voices of the mystics as they exhorted nature to do their bidding. Witches in their diverse Aspects soared through the air, or stood firm in the ruins of their once great university with their elemental daemons at their sides, while the armoured Sēq strode the sky in their crow-dark coats, or entered the battle on foot, meeting the witches blow for horrendous, arcane blow. The mountainside roared as pieces of stone were shorn from it. Lightning flashed, striking witches and scholars from the air. Brilliantly lit geometries spun, tumbled and whirled, exploding, slicing, and searing all they touched. With every passing moment it seemed more witches and more scholars joined the fray.

Somehow the Sēq had been prepared, though from the signs of the battle it made little difference.

A witch in the Aspect of a giant albino wyrm, with luminous wing and tail feathers, undulated across the sky. It coiled about the diamond octahedron shielding a scholar. The scholar sang his canto, while the wyrm screeched and bit and constricted, the two tumbling towards the ground as they fought. On the mountainside below a prodigious ape, its back sprouting long phosphorescent quills, held a scholar above its head and dashed her brains out on the rocks. Fantastical, terrifying shapes flickered in and out of existence across the remaining shelf of the Mahsojhin, or the air above it. He had to close his eyes against the sudden brightness of the energies that were summoned, focussed and thrown with devastating effect. From behind his closed eyelids he still saw an insane afterimage of squiggly lines that seemed burned into his vision. He blinked a few times to regain his sight.

Kasraman leaned on the rail, his face intent, eyes shining like lamps even as his outline wavered with a horrific, daemonic shape that never quite settled. Wolfram stood firm, his remaining protective wards tinged a brick red. The others had been seared away in the furious exchange of energies between the witches and the Sēq.

"Has anybody seen the Emissary?" Corajidin asked. She had clearly done her part in opening the Mahsojhin, though had not been seen since. Corajidin wondered whether she was on some dark mission for her darker masters.

"No. But I've news from Igreal, one of the witches sent with Belamandris," Kasraman said. "Martūm's intelligence was correct. They took Vahineh aboard the *Wanderer* and tried to escape. Belamandris is confident they will run them down soon. Tahj-Shaheh's wind-corsairs are much faster than we gave her credit for, particularly when helped along by the witches. Indris, Mari, Vahineh, and anybody with them will soon be in our custody."

"Excellent! Martūm may be a self-serving little insect," Corajidin nodded, "but he is *my* self-serving little insect. I doubt I can trust him further than I can see him, but he has proven useful."

"You'll make him the Rahn-Selassin, Your Majesty?" Wolfram said distractedly. He had his hand on Kimiya's shoulder, channelling her energy into their defences. The young woman looked wan, skin pale against her leather collar and the sheer, partially opened coat that fell from one shoulder.

Corajidin stumbled sideways as the wind-skiff lurched drunkenly. Wolfram's wards cracked like glass, turning an angry red. Kimiya whimpered as Wolfram drew more energy from her to repair them.

"What in—"

The skiff was struck again, a resounding thunderclap rolling over them. Corajidin saw a blur of witchfire and *kirion*, wreathed in sparks, as it flew back into Femensetri's hand some distance below. It was a large spear, bright as lightning forged into metal. A sapphire-scaled gauntlet covered her entire arm, the rest of her sheathed in an ancient style of armour, each scale and lace limned in light. The Stormbringer held out her other hand. Lightning speared down. She grasped the flickering bolt and rose into the sky.

"Best move us away," Corajidin suggested. "Now, if you please."

"I'll not argue," Wolfram gasped as the spear struck them once again, before returning to the Stormbringer's hand. Her smile was a wild thing. She was about to throw again when a handful of witches in their nightmare Aspects bore down on her. Nima turned the skiff and put some distance between Corajidin, Mahsojhin, and the Stormbringer.

"So the Sēq lied about Femensetri, too," Corajidin mused. "My ancestor, Zadjinn, has proven to be something of a disappointment. There's nothing I can do here. The Sēq and the witches seem to be keeping each other busy as planned. Nima, take us over the city."

Nima guided the skiff away from the battle, over a saddle between the mountains and dropped gently down the sloping shadows between Skyspear and World Blood mountains.

Corajidin leaned over the rail to watch the madness below. Several fires had started in the city, though he doubted they would make the kind of demonstration he wanted. What point in stepping in to be the hand of mercy, when there was not enough suffering to make people truly thankful? Even so, Nix's elemental daemons—the ones the Sēq had not banished, destroyed, or imprisoned—had wrought the kind of destruction only ever heard about in histories and legends. The other beauty of the powerful spirits was that for each one released from a Dilemma Box, it drew a handful of Sēq away from the Mahsojhin each time, thinning their numbers further.

There came a great screeching sound as yet another of Nix's Dilemma Boxes was opened. A monstrosity stuttered into existence, tentacles thick as oak trees, batlike wings stretched wide, and rainbow-coloured beak protruding beneath a cluster of coal-spark eyes. Within moments smaller shapes appeared from bubbles of melted air—more Sēq, drawn away from their battle with the witches to defend the city. Corajidin smiled to himself.

"Has there been any sign of Jhem, or Nadir?" he asked.

"Nothing I'm aware of," Kasraman replied. His eyes lost focus for a moment and Corajidin saw once more, if only for a second, the shadow of his son's Aspect: a muscular and daemonic thing, wide-shouldered, long-horned, a face all sharp planes scored with tattoos of fire around deep angular eyes with slitted pupils, and the galleon sail wings with their feathers of indigo and smoking shadows—then it was gone and only his son remained. Though he wondered from what he had seen of the other witches, which was Kasraman's real face? "Apologies, Father. Sanojé, Elonie, Ikedion, and those they've chosen are ready whenever you are."

Corajidin took another look at the chaos he had sanctioned. Yes, many would see what happened tonight, but few civilians would die. The elemental daemons would kill some—such was the way of these things. Others would be slain in some tragic fight, which they could have avoided had they simply stayed in doors. And this was despite the fact that no small number of the witches had avoided the fight with the Sēq altogether, preferring to raze parts of the city instead, still thinking they fought a Scholar War against people mostly three centuries dead.

"It is time," Corajidin told his son. "Nima, take me to the Tyr-Jahavān. I will address the Teshri. Then together we will show the people of Avānweh how much we care, our outrage at their plight, and then liberate them from the evil scourge that assails them."

❊ ❊ ❊

"But how do we stop it?" Padishin asked, fists clenched around the sheath of his dionesqa. The Secretary-Marshall was smudged with soot and there was the spray of dried blood on this clothing and in his hair. Ha had taken the time to don a leather hauberk, studded with rivets that gleamed in the infernal light from the city below. It, too, was speckled with blood. "I care less—for now—where these things came from as I do preventing them from causing further harm."

"This reeks of Humans—" an elderly sayf said tremulously.

"Yes!" Another stood, fist slamming into palm. "The Humans! They've been killing people in the streets and summoning dark spirits from—"

"Then let's act!" Rahn-Narseh's voice cracked across the mostly-empty Tyr-Jahavān, as she slammed the butt of her long-hafted pickaxe onto the stone floor. "The Sēq seem inadequate to the task. We are the ones who should be defending our people!"

"There's no evidence it's the Humans," Ajomandyan said, only to be hissed and shouted down. The Sky Lord eyed his opponents darkly. "Shut it, the lot of you! Doesn't it seem convenient the Humans would attack us at the time the militant Imperialist faction is about to assume control of the State and Crown?" More hissing and shouts, even from some of the Federationists.

Corajidin hid his smile and made a great show of looking around the Tyr-Jahavān. He did not have to hide his disappointment at how many of the sayfs were missing, Imperialist and Federationist alike. He gave special attention to where Roshana, Nazarafine, Siamak, and Vahineh should have been seated, as well as the empty space the Scholar-Marshall should have filled.

Ajomandyan was flanked by his grandchildren, Neva and Yago. Both wore their flying leathers and armour, looking like the young and doomed heroes one read about in serialised adventure novels. Both were bloodied, and somehow seemed enhanced by their wounds and dirt rather than diminished by them. Corajidin gave Neva a frank appraisal, causing the statuesque beauty to blush, but she never looked away. Yes! This was the kind of woman Belamandris needed, and an alliance between the Erebus and the Näsaré would bring some definite advantages. Ajomandyan scowled at Corajidin, his eagle eyes fierce. The Sky Lord leaned forward on his gryphon-headed cane, his expression one of disdain. Corajidin ignored it, standing up to address the Teshri.

"I agree with Rahn-Narseh in that we need to take the defence of the city into our own hands," Corajidin said. "But will we have enough? I have my own soldiers, as do Rahn-Narseh and those brave enough, caring enough, to be here. But against . . . whatever it is . . . we are facing?"

"If I may speak?" Sanojé sounded as lost and innocent as she looked, her massive brown eyes wide in her doll-like face. "My name is Pah-Chepherundi op Sanojé, one of the last daughters of the once Great House of Chepherundi. We have seen things like this in Tanis, fought them, in the Conflicted Cities. These things are daemon elementals, much stronger than the creature released by the Humans in your beautiful city only days ago. They are notoriously difficult to banish, or destroy. The Humans use them as often as they use Nomads, ghuls, spectres, and vampires."

"Are you saying you think the Humans summoned these things?" Corajidin asked.

"Yes, Rahn-Corajidin," Sanojé replied earnestly. "The witches of the Golden Kingdom of Manté are most skilled in that regard . . . as you saw here recently. I've also heard of the many brutal murders in Avânweh since the Assembly began. These, too, are common in Manté and other parts of the Iron League, such as Angoth and Jiom. They believe in sacrifices, in the binding of souls—"

"We don't *know* it was the Humans," Ajomandyan shouted over the tumult. "Though they do become a remarkably useful villain, don't they, Rahn-Corajidin?"

"Ajo, please!" Padishin said. "Now is not the time. Pah-Sanojé, how do we deal with these things?"

"Of late there seems to be little time for looking into the causes of things," the Sky Lord replied before Sanojé could speak. "We seem to spend our time putting out fires, never finding out who really caused them."

"There will be time enough for blame, Sayf-Ajomandyan," Narseh almost shouted in her parade-ground bellow. "But it is neither here, nor now."

"Blame?" Corajidin mused into the dwindling echoes of Narseh's voice. "I could lay blame at the feet of Roshana for trying to kill me under a banner of truce. But I do not. I could lay blame at her people for the carnage they wrought in denying me the ability to arrest Vahineh, which resulted in the murder of Ravenet of the Delfineh. But I do not. I could even lay blame on Roshana, Nazarafine, and Siamak for not even bothering to—"

"And now is not the time for your grandstanding either, Rahn-Corajidin," Padishin cut him off with a shake of his head. "People are dying in Avânweh, during the time of year we should be celebrating peace. I won't stand for it, and neither should any of you. Now, if you'll let Pah-Sanojé speak, perhaps we can save some lives?"

"Thank you, Secretary-Marshall," Sanojé bowed, golden rings and strings of sapphires and emeralds glittering against her dusky skin. "We learned that might of arms is useful to a degree, but what you need is an arcane solution to a supernatural problem. Otherwise, the death toll will be high."

"But the Sēq—" one of the sayfs began, only to be cut off by Kasraman.

"With respect, the Sēq have done little to help." Kasraman walked to the centre of the floor, where he looked even the most belligerent of the sayfs in the eye. "They've done little since the Scholar Wars, other than to live on past glories and abuse laws that have little relevance to us in modern times."

"And you can do better, I suppose?" Ajo asked sourly. There came a hair-raising shriek from outside and the snapping of great leathery wings. A dark shape flashed past the gaps between the tall columns of the Tyr-Jahavan. It was brutish, vast, and wreathed in flame. Pungent smoke oozed between the columns, smelling like burned fat. Those sayfs who smelled it retreated, pale faced and shaking.

"I certainly can't do worse," Kasraman said into the stunned silence.

A score of voices broke into panicked argument. Ajo tried to keep the peace, while Padishin sat heavily on one of the cold, uncomfortable spheres. The one-time soldier rubbed his face with one hand, while the other firmly held his sword.

Kasraman came to stand beside Corajidin and Sanojé. He leaned close, though his caution was hardly necessary given the background noise.

"Father, we'll need them to make a decision soon. If Nix keeps opening his bloody Dilemma Boxes, we may have a fight on our hands we can't win."

"How many of the damned things does he have?" Sanojé asked. "And I have to ask how he came by so many."

"The Maladhi made much of their fortune as traders," Corajidin said, "and perhaps more as adventurers, stealing treasures from ancient cultures we have barely even heard of. And so, to answer your first question: I have no idea how many he has. It does make me wonder what else they have managed to hide from the rest of us, though."

"Nix may be your mad dog for now, Father, but soon or later he'll need to be put down."

"True enough, and in time." Corajidin cast a glance over the squawking flock of his distressed peers. "But not until he has served his purpose."

He then stepped forward and held up his hands for silence. In truth he had no idea what the sayfs had been saying, though their high colour told him they had not agreed on anything.

"We are not all of us friends, that much I will admit." This produced as many chuckles as there were snorts and shaking heads. "But we can all agree we need to act together to save the people of Avānweh—the people of Shrīan— as there's no telling where the Humans and their mystics may strike next."

Ajo went to object, but Padishin waved him down irritably. The Secretary-Marshall stood. "What do you propose?"

"The Avān are a proud people. A warrior people who conquered half a world before the Humans—the Starborn as they remember themselves from antiquity—betrayed us. I say we should look to the strength of our roots, before we allow time, apathy, and—dare I say it—fear to rule us."

"Talk of empire again, Corajidin?" Kiraj, the Arbiter-Marshall, said wearily. "Don't you think—"

"I am not talking of empire, Arbiter-Marshall," Corajidin interrupted smoothly, "rather of our most ancient traditions. We were conquerors before we were politicians and warriors before we were conquerors.

"And we were witches, before we were scholars."

"You can't seriously be suggesting we turn to witches for help?" Ajo looked like he was about to laugh, but the look in Corajidin's eyes forestalled him. "You are! Is there no depth to which you won't sink?"

Kasraman and Sanojé bristled. Corajidin gestured for them to be calm.

Ajo looked at his peers in the Teshri, then back to Corajidin. "It's no secret you've trained Kasraman as a witch, Corajidin." There were a few muttered outbursts. Even one or two sayfs who rose to their feet in surprise. Ajo gave a false cough. "Well, at least not a secret to all of us. You know the law against a witch becoming a rahn—"

"A Sēq law!" Corajidin shouted. "A law that—"

"A law that was drafted because of the insane century we remember as the Scholar Wars." Ajo looked at the two Erebus men with some pity. "The same war that took your Ancestor's life, Corajidin. Even *she* tried to stop it! But it's a law, regardless of who originated it and it's a law for good reason."

"And if Indris had been awakened as the Rahn-Näsarat?" Kasraman asked reasonably. "What then? There is little difference between witches and scholars, truth be told, save that a witch is reviled for something that happened centuries ago, while people have conveniently forgotten it was a Mahjirahn—a trained Sēq Scholar—who sank the Seethe beneath the sea to end the Petal Empire. A double standard, don't you think?"

"What do you propose?" Padishin asked again, looking at Kasraman with renewed interest.

"Give my son and his witches a chance to prove they can do for you what the Sēq will not," Corajidin said plainly. "If he fails we are no worse off, save me who will have lost his heir. None of you risk half so much as I."

The room remained quiet for a while, before handfuls of conversations broke out. Groups converged, hands gesticulated as voices were raised and lowered, backs were turned, and jaws set. Padishin and Ajo moved amongst them, listening, speaking, moving on.

After almost ten minutes Padishin and Ajo approached Corajidin, their faces set and grim.

"We will give you your chance," Padishin said. "But if we find you've done anything to manipulate us into this, Corajidin, you'll regret ever letting the words escape from between your teeth."

"You'll not regret this," Kasraman said proudly.

Ajo fixed Corajidin with his eagle's stare. "For the sake and future of your Great House, you'd best hope not."

❋ ❋ ❋

Corajidin, Kasraman and Sanojé met Wolfram, Elonie, and Ikedion on the steps outside the Tyr-Jahavān. The witches looked at the sky speculatively.

"I hope you've good news, Your Majesty," Wolfram said. "Because at the moment it's going to be hard to end this without getting ourselves too badly burned."

"Then we will need to get burned," Corajidin snapped. "But however we do this, we do whatever is necessary to succeed. Do I make myself clear?"

The witches nodded their assent.

"Then find Nix and get him to stop with the Dilemma Boxes," Corajidin said. "He's done a lot more than was asked of him—"

"He's a mad little bastard—"

"Thank you for the observation, Ikedion. I suggest you focus your attention on the brethren of yours you will need to reign in. If there were witches who caused havoc in the city, show them no mercy. No survivors. No witnesses. No confessions. Make sure you kill enough of your Human brethren to sell the drama and make sure there is no connection with the Mahsojhin. Take no chances. All our futures rest on this."

Elonie and Ikedion nodded, then rose into the sky amid a snarling gale. Soon they were lost to sight, shooting away in the direction of the valley behind the Mahsojhin where their chosen army, the most powerful and promising witches they could trust of all those they freed, sat waiting for their chance.

"Sanojé, your liches understand what must be done?" Corajidin was hesitant to use the liches, though Sanojé had assured him they were the best weapons against the daemon elementals.

"They know what is at stake and the future here you offer them. They will do as they are bid, Rahn-Corajidin."

"Then go. But remember, none must ever know we have used Nomads! We are undone if there is so much as a hint of their involvement. If one your liches is killed, it must be shown to have come from Manté."

Sanojé bowed and like the witches before her, took to the sky.

Only Wolfram and Kasraman remained. Corajidin gave them both a long look, then rested his hand on Kasraman's shoulder.

"This is another step on the journey, my son. Show those weaklings in the Tyr-Jahavān what it means to be an Erebus and a witch. Set them an example they will not forget, for when the time comes for you to rule them all."

25

"ANY HEART THAT KNOWS THE JOY OF TRUE LOVE IS UNLIKELY TO FORGET, REGARDLESS OF THE TRAGEDY THAT MAY COME OF IT."

—From *The Nilvedic Maxims*

DAY 358 OF THE 495TH YEAR OF

THE SHRĪANESE FEDERATION

"Anj?"

Indris felt his chest constrict, and the blood seemed to drain from his face. His mouth was suddenly dry. He wanted to speak, but no words rose from the panicked, joyous, confused, wounded, and stunned miasma of his mind.

"It's me," she reached out a tentative hand to touch his cheek. His flinch was involuntary, as was the hurt in her whiteless, sapphire eyes. "It's me, Indris."

"But . . . how?" A witch flew howling overhead, long comet tail trailing behind her gargoyle Aspect, until she ploughed face first into the ground nearby, and was still.

"*That* is a very long story, and one I doubt I'll have the time to tell here. But I've missed you, hero," Anj said breathlessly, gaze flicking between his eyes and Changeling, as if the sword was going to unsheathe itself and strike her. Indris reached out to wipe away the dirt smudging Anj's cheek, only to find himself rubbing his thumb from her lips to the edge of her jaw. Yet there was something odd, a sensation of static. Did he imagine it, or did his skin feel oily with her so close? He stared at her, trying to see past the faint blurring of her face to fathom the miasma around and through her Disentropic Stain. Changeling moaned uncertainly, sending fingers of worry into Indris's mind.

Time had changed her. *More than seven years . . .* She had always been slender, but now was lean as bamboo. Her hair, in all its glory, still reminded him of a storm but looked wilder than he remembered. There was a scar at the corner of one brilliant sapphire eye, a pale line that extended to her hairline and across one long, upswept ear. She wore Sēq armour, but his eyes lingered for a moment on her sword: shaped like a Seethe weapon, slender and straight, sheathed in carved jade-hued *serill*. Its pommel was unusual, a blackened onyx octopus with its tentacles wrapped around the top of the hilt. Indris felt a chill on his Disentropic Stain when he looked at the weapon. When he looked at her. As if believing was not quite seeing.

She was looking at him expectantly, the beginning of a worried frown starting to appear. Indris forced a smile as he took her into his arms, where she relaxed into him. Anj smelled of leather and the faint char of recently used ahm.

"I looked for you—"

"And I for you," she cut him off, but would not let him go. Anj shifted so she could look into his eyes. "But none of that matters now. We're here, in the same place, together."

Together. Anj. *Mari.* Mari, who if he closed his eyes he could still smell, aloe and honey and not the smell of burned disentropy. The same Mari he had spent the day defending his friends with, protecting Vahineh. But, this was Anj.

"It's time!" A Sēq Master bellowed. "Knights to the front, flank your Masters. Librarians, stay in the rear and focus your attention on your Wards! No mistakes! Now go!"

Around them, the Sēq who had been held in reserve joined the battle.

"Anj . . ." *I think I've fallen in love with somebody else—*

But she lay a chip-nailed finger, where it protruded from a worn old leather gauntlet, against his lips. "There'll be plenty of time to talk later. For now, we've some red work ahead of us."

Indris saw fire blaze behind his long-missing wife. A witch in the Aspect of a burning corpse in molten armour charged her. The ahmsah told him the Aspect was all illusion, showing him the shape of the portly witch beneath. Indris threw up a quick Ward and rushed forward. He grabbed the man's wrist and upper arm, spun, and—rolling his shoulders—threw the witch head first into a stone wall. The Aspect stuttered once, then went out as the witch fell unconscious.

"Thanks, husband," she grinned. And with that she turned and threw herself into the battle. There came the dry rattle of leather and metal, and a dark shape plummeted from the sky with a thunderous boom. Lightning crackled around her limbs and in her hair. Indris looked at the Stormbringer, whose expression was a warning in itself.

"You can ask questions and make cow-eyes later, boy!" The Stormbringer gripped her lightning-bright spear in gauntleted hands. Farstrike was brilliant with arcs of lightning that danced from the weapon and up her scaled gauntlet. Her armour was dented, some scales almost melted with laces burned away; others smoked in the flashing light of the battle around them. She drew back her arm and hurled Farstrike at a giant flayed wolf with volcanic eyes and tentacles growing from its shoulders. The Aspect gave a brief unwolf-like yell of pain, before it flopped to the ground as a red-robed old man, the side of his head and a long strip down his throat seared and smouldering. Farstrike soared back to the Stormbringer, clanging as it slammed into her armoured palm.

"I don't know how, or why, but she's here." The Stormbringer spat into the dust, then cast a dark glance at Anj, who fought amongst the other Sēq against the witches. The air smelled of scorched earth. The sound of the battle was so loud it vibrated against Indris's skin. "There's no denying we can use her help . . . and it was she who warned us what was about to happen here."

"How did she know?"

"We'll be asking her that. Amongst other things. But she's right. It'll all be moot if we don't survive this. And there are some *faruqen* questions I'll be asking that little *sherde*, Zadjinn. Sneaky bastard showed up here with your wifey in tow, calm as you bloody please."

Zadjinn? Anj? What in the Ancestors' names is happening?

The energies expended by the warring Ilhennim ripped the night. Indris reached out with the ahmsah. The Mahsojhin and the area about it was dotted with black stars, light-devouring holes in the ahm. So much energy had already been used in the local area there was little left. There was a mechanism drawing massive amounts of energy at the doorway of what had once been the Hearthall. With his arcane sight, whatever it was looked like the spinning tumblers on a complex lock, interspersed with rotating cogs and bright glyphs, all circling a shadowy vortex. The machine powered the rift allowing the witches into the world. It also drew masses of power, freeing more witches who would draw on even more disentropy, an outward spiral of energy use. If it drew enough energy away, the arcane seal laid down by the Sēq centuries ago could well crumble of their own accord. Cinders of spent ahm already drifted like volcanic ash, eddying around half-seen, half-sensed geysers of sickly yellow green as tainted Drear energies oozed into the world. He felt the ahm currents pull on him, trying to draw on the energy his body produced. With an irritated frown Indris hardened his Disentropic Stain, becoming an obdurate rock in the flow, saving himself for himself.

"You're using too much energy!" Indris shouted above the din. "You'll kill as many of your own as you do of them if you keep this up."

"What choice is there?" the Stormbringer yelled. "Do we let them go, only to fight them again when they're even stronger? Did you know there's some bastard out there in the city, releasing daemon elementals? We've had to destroy a few of them here, misbegotten imbecile things driven mad by who knows how long in captivity. In the name of every evil Ancestor who ever died—"

Memories of the Maladhi-sûk and the litter of spent puzzle boxes. "It's Nix of the Maladhi. He was hoarding spent Dilemma Boxes and now I know why. They were practice."

"And you didn't see fit to tell me?" Surges of lightning arced along Farstrike, so bright Indris had to narrow his eyes. Changeling growled at the other weapon, which sizzled and rumbled in return. Indris opened his mouth to speak, but the Stormbringer just shook her head slowly. He took the warning.

"Now you're here—" she started.

"You dragged me here—"

"—you may as well make yourself useful, boy." She stepped aside and once more called down lightning, which sheathed her in coruscating brilliance, before unleashing it at her enemies.

Indris cast a critical eye over the battle. The Sēq were outnumbered, but not outpowered. The witches clung staunchly to their individuality, rarely fighting in groups and only doing so when overmatched by the Exalted Names of the Sēq.

The mystics fought extravagantly. Indris realized he had taken a few steps forward, his hand curled around Changeling's hilt, before he stopped himself. There were voices in his head, slithering words that flexed like tentacles in his mind, urging him to let go of restraint. It was a siren song that at once cajoled and seduced, promising the joy of union with the soul of the world. The feeling of majestic power in his limbs. His mind becoming a beacon, burning hot enough to rival the sun and melt mountains to slag with a thought, even as he reached out to push islands beneath the oceans and raise ranges from the sea with the touch of his—

Indris reeled, hands going to his head. Changeling poured energy into him, igniting the potentials in his mind that were as addictive as black lotus seeds. He centred himself behind his Inner Fortress, feeling his hearts slow as the temptation faded away.

"Stop it," he said irritably to Changeling, who still tried to fill him with the clean, warm energy that could fuel the fires to destroy worlds. In his dreams he had seen it. In his near Awakening he had felt it. Now he feared it more than ever.

Once more the fragments of words sung across the outer layers of his mind, coaxing him to relinquish his self-control. Indris shook his head to clear it, then fortified his mind with additional crystalline barriers and illusory paths to confound any who sought entry. But something worked with a dire purpose, urging the mystics to burn themselves out. It was happening all around him as both scholars and witches used more of their vital energies to sing their lethal cantos. Beside him a Sēq Knight suddenly stopped in midsong. The fire behind the knight's skin guttered, then faded as they fell, unconscious and drooling, to the dirt. A witch closed with Indris, his vulture-headed gibbon Aspect flickering before it faded away to reveal a young blond man with a suddenly confused expression. He looked down at the scythe in his hands as if wondering why it was there. A Sēq Knight beheaded him, took a few steps, then vomited bile. A witch in the Aspect of a rimed scorpion stabbed at the Sēq with pincers and tail. Indris drew his storm-pistol and shot the witch until it stopped. He did not need to inspect the ruined mass of the scholar to know he, too, was dead.

But they would not stop, even when mystics started falling from the sky like sparking hail. Others reeled as if drunk. Some of the mystics seemed aged. A few hobbled, lame from the damage done by the energy feedback in their bodies. Some looked about with wide, white eyes, obviously blind. Others, unconscious, were gripped by seizures as the mindstorms took them.

Indris gestured for nearby Sēq Knights to join him. They were breathing heavily and grimed with sweat and blood, but not badly wounded. He swept his arm to encompass the scores of battles happening in, around and above the Mahsojhin. "Be wary! There's something trying to make us use too much energy. Remember your physical training and use it first. Now come with me. We're going to shut down the rift!"

With Changeling in one hand and storm-pistol in the other, Indris and his small group of knights headed towards the yawning doorway of the Hearthall. A large number of witches in their Aspects stood guarding the rift, helping their brethren as they emerged, disoriented. But those witches who tried to stop Indris and his Sēq were reeling from too much arcane work. And while Indris tried his best to not take life, the Sēq with him had no such compunction. One of the Sēq Knights used the ahmsah to send a sizzling cloud of fractals at the witches. Then again. And again, despite Indris shouting for him to stop. The knight's eyes were fever-bright and his lips were stretched in the idiot grin of ahm-stroke. As the knight stood on wavering legs, still trying to use more of their vital energy, Indris slipped behind him. He placed the knight in a chokehold, his resistance feeble as a child, and gently lowered the man to the ground as he passed out. Even behind the walls of his Inner Fortress, the temptation to let loose with his mystic energies was almost overwhelming.

Anj emerged from the carnage to grip his arm. "Don't! There are too many of them, even for you."

"But not for us." He winced at how easily the words had come. As if the two of them had not been apart. Old jokes and well-loved quotes were forced back where they belonged, to a world where Anj was not a flesh and blood enigma, wrapped in painful questions and terrible supposition. But it was so easy to forget—

"Too dangerous for any of us, my beautiful man." She tugged at his arm even as Changeling tried to draw him back to where he was headed. "We need you in the fight."

"What I'm about to do will help stop it quicker, with fewer lives lost. Come on!"

"Fight with me, like we used to."

"It's less about the lives we take, as the lives we save."

Anj smiled sadly as she slapped his cheek harder than was playful. From the corner of his eye it looked as if the tentacles of the squid on the pommel of her sword writhed in the uncertain light. "Suit yourself, but I've got things to do. Keep your skin whole, husband."

You too, wife, he almost said, but the words were replaced by a sharp nod as he turned awkwardly away. His thoughts turned to Mari, who by now should be long gone from Avānweh. To his friends and family who were with her. Where he should—would—prefer to be.

Shaking the thoughts from his mind, Indris moved forward, he and his Sēq entering the Hearthall. Pressure built in his head, became a focused pain on the crest of a bubble that grew in his forehead. Words trickled into his brain, the susurrus of the minds around him, adding to the deafening cacophony of battle. It felt as if he could hear all the fears and regrets, angers and hatreds and sorrows of those around him. Changeling almost purred as if she, too, sensed the rise in Indris of the power he could not control. And was somehow gratified.

The Aspects of the witches were all but gone. Confused and weary, they stared at Indris for a moment, then seemed to be transfixed by something only they could hear, or see. Indris dashed between the witches as the knights engaged them in battle. It was with a sigh of relief that he stopped beside an ornate device, a step-pyramid frame with many lenses, moving wheels and a still pendulum. It was not so large as he had thought—coming no higher than his waist, and that due to the tripod—seeming bigger at a distance because of the corona of energy that magnified its contours. This close Indris felt the tug on his Disentropic Stain, as if the mechanism was trying to siphon off his energy. He inspected the artefact, looking for some means of deactivating it. There was nothing obvious.

A red-robed witch walked through a seam in the air, eyes unfocussed. Indris rapped her on the temple with his storm-pistol and she fell to the ground, unconscious.

Plagued by the feeling he was being watched, Indris turned to see Anj fighting not far away. She struck witches down left and right, spurring the other Sēq on. Her eyes rested on him, then the device. She shook her head in warning.

For lack of a better idea, and pressed for time, Indris turned and kicked the mechanism over.

The beam of light that pieced the clouds above disappeared. The wavering tear between here, now, and then vanished. *Huh. That was easier than expected.*

He picked up the mechanism, and moved towards the exit. Outside the Hearthall, on the far side of the forum, he saw Femensetri and some of the Exalted Names had taken position on a decrepit gazebo, an old folly that looked to be as much mould and rust as it was marble and iron. He gathered the Sēq Knights with him on the way out, though two of them needed to be carried by their friends.

Without thinking, Indris reached out with his mind and one hand, and picked up the Sēq he had rendered unconscious. His companions looked at him, ahm-drunk and bewildered, yet said nothing.

The remaining Sēq were converged around the old gazebo, its verdigris dome badly canted where the stone had collapsed and the supporting ironwork rusted away. The ground around it was strewn with fallen columns, fallen stones and fallen people. The air was redolent with blood and burned skin and hair, mingling with rotting flowers and mulch. Some of the Exalted Names remained. Some had gone to help the city. So few. A very pitiful few Sēq Masters and Knights remained; hollow eyed, breathing like wheezing bellows.

Most of the mystics were too exhausted to fight. The sky was empty except for a handful of very powerful witches and scholars, yet even they were drifting to the ground. Most of the people around Indris looked like they were ready to collapse, their energy spent. The ahm in the Mahsojhin was almost spent—only a fitful lapping of tepid energy touched his Disentropic Stain.

Indris carefully set the mechanism on the ground, but as he did, frenetic motion caught his eye. Anj was a dervish, her sword shimmering greener than witchfire as it hummed and sliced. Witch Aspects guttered out like candle flames as she struck.

A powerfully built young man in a badly torn red robe struck Anj on the shoulder with his heavy-looking club. Indris heard the crack as the weapon made impact. Saw the agony written on Anj's dirt- and blood-smeared face. Indris took aim with his pistol and fired.

Nothing. He was out of ammunition.

He moved without thinking, away from the gazebo and towards his wife. Light footed, he covered the distance at speed, Changeling held low and trailing behind him like a snarling tail. The witch raised his club again as Anj surged to her feet, her own sword a whistling arc of emerald in shadow. A second witch narrowed the distance. A third, fourth, and fifth. On one knee, Anj parried and cut, her left arm curled against the ruined armour on her chest.

Indris sliced one witch from shoulder to hip. Pivoted on one foot. Windmilled his arm and cut another's throat. By the time he had turned, Anj was making an end of the final witch, who slumped to the ground.

Indris offered Anj a shoulder to lean on, which she took. She kissed him, her lips feather light where his earlobe met his jaw.

"You're so good to me," she murmured, voice muzzy with pain, but she carried her own weight and only used him for support over the rough areas. Her amenesqa, with its disconcerting octopus pommel, was clutched in one hand, while with the other she took his. Indris looked down at the familiar gesture, conflicting feelings fluttering in his chest.

The exhausted witches and the Sēq glared at each other impotently across the killing field, stones and dirt soaked with wet, dark stains that glistened in the moonlight. Each faction had suffered heavy losses, the survivors leaning on their weapons, or each other, for support. It took Indris nowhere near as long as it should have to count those scholars who survived.

"It was like this the first night of the Scholar War," Femensetri said as she came to stand by Indris's side. Her voice was even rougher than the angular croak he had come to know. "We fought each other until we could barely stand. We had almost nothing left."

"How did it get worse?" Indris asked quietly.

Femensetri scratched some dried blood from Farstrike. She inspected her nail from different angles, as if the rust-hued flakes somehow contained the mysteries of the living condition. With a grunt she flicked them into the breeze.

"How did it get worse?" she mused absently. When she spoke next her voice was filled with something Indris thought might have been shame. "We both wanted to be the power that held the crown in our greedy hands, is how. It's amazing what can happen when power is the reward."

"Seems not much has changed."

✳ ✳ ✳

Indris sat sprawled on a couch, Changeling almost purring in his lap. The chambers of the Suret Council in Avānweh were close to the last place he wanted to be, yet there had been little choice. The Exalted Names had taken possession of what they called the Emphis Mechanism, then brought Anj and he here.

Towering natural limestone columns marched around the room, each carved with the solemn faces of the Sēq Masters and Magnates who had come before. Femensetri's likeness was up there somewhere, carved during the time of the Awakened Empire. *Ilhen* lamps shone up each column, bright ivory beams soon lost to the jagged darkness of the cave ceiling overhead. The walls, too, were rough stone in as many places as they were polished smooth, a jigsaw of nature versus craft. Jade radiance washed the room, reflected from the brilliant and different curves of the crooks held by the Masters.

Anj stood at the centre of a stone table that dominated the chamber, wincing as she shifted her weight, her shoulder recently healed but still tender. The Masters sat in their high-backed chairs around the sweeping curve of the table—which resembled a crook—while high-ranking Sēq Knights and Inquisitors, those fit enough to attend, were seated along the straight edge. There was a chair there for Indris, which he had politely declined.

Zadjinn smiled politely at Indris, nodding his head in greeting. His gaze, when it settled on Anj, was not one of surprise or revulsion, as was the case with the others. No, Zadjinn *expected* Anj to be there.

"I didn't abandon the Order, sahai-Femensetri—"

"I'm no longer your teacher, girl!" Femensetri looked at Anj across the ridge of her knuckles, long dirty fingers interlaced. "You'll address me the same as any other Master here and not presume on any fondness I certainly don't feel."

"As you wish," Anj inclined her head politely. "I didn't leave the Order, jhah-Femensetri. I was tasked with a mission by a sect within the Sēq, who understood my need to bring back my husband after he was abandoned by the Order."

"I would be careful of your tone, young one," He-Who-Watches said, his eyes clear as backlit glass. The man's nimble fingers toyed with the greyed edges of the taloub he wore about his head. "And remind you that you are responsible for the consequences of both your words and actions. Falsehood will not be tolerated."

Two of the Inquisitors rested their hands on their dauls, expressions cold as if Anj were nothing more than a puzzle box to be opened.

"Of this I'm well aware" Anj said tightly, "but it doesn't change the facts of how I came to do what I did. I was sent to follow Indris's path. It happened these orders coincided very much with my desires. There was no way I was going to refuse, and those who approached me knew it."

Indris leaned forward in the couch, almost at the same time as Femensetri. He could hear Femensetri's voice in his head, clear as if she actually spoke. Her inner voice gave truth to her expression. Indris felt he owed his sahai an apology. *You didn't know! All these years you've resented Anj, and all this time she's been faithful.* Zadjinn likewise gave himself away. Leaning back in his chair, face too calm to be natural, with no hint of surprise. *You, on the other hand, knew all too well.*

"Enlighten us, please, Anj-el-din shel Näsarat," Aumh said in a voice as small as her body, at odds with her mind and her strength. A tiny blue butterfly rested on one of the flowers that grew in the Y'arrow woman's green-brown hair. Indris pursed his lips at the use of Anj's full name and the guilt he felt at abandoning his quest to find her rose new in him. For two years he had searched for his missing wife, after he had been away from home for more than five. Everybody had assured him she was dead, or gone so far away in the world she was unlikely to return. Even those who knew better and could have told him the truth . . . "Who were these mysterious benefactors who found such an elegant and timely way of satisfying the best interests of yourself, your husband, and the Sēq Order of Scholars, all at the same time?"

Anj remained quiet for a few seconds, before saying in a strong voice, "I'm unable to answer that question for you, jhah."

"Unable, or unwilling?"

"Does it matter?"

"Yes it matters!" Femensetri shouted, her voice cracking around the room. Arcs of lightning jumped between her fingers and her mindstone blazed an angry black. Indris jumped a little in his seat. "This isn't a bloody game, girl, and you shouldn't be feeling so satisfied with yourself! There's something . . . wrong . . . about you. About this. No matter what your orders were, you've a tale to tell and we'll have it from you. We'll soon see how unable, or unwilling, you really are."

Anj's face contorted into a snarl, quickly overcome. Femensetri and the Waterdancer looked back at her from beneath raised brows, He-Who-Watches tapping his forefinger against his chin, the nail reflecting the light.

"So," He-Who-Watches murmured, "part of the mask slips and what I see is dark and cold, something coiled around the deepest parts of the world and something we have long thought anathema. The end, child, does not always justify the means."

"I've done what I've for—" Anj began, only to be stopped by Zadjinn. The Erebus.

"There's no need for fear, Anj-el-din," Zadjinn interrupted urbanely. "If you've done what was asked of you."

"Oh, that I have, jhah."

Indris tried to relax and let the bubble that swelled in his mind burst. Voices lapped at his consciousness like sluggish little waves, strewn with the flotsam and jetsam of thoughts. He picked at them, but they all looked and sounded similar, too difficult to tell where their journeys had started.

He let the spoken voices in the room drift away, focusing on his breathing and eliminating sounds one by one. First the voices. Then the metronomic dripping of water down the limestone columns. The creak of people moving in their seats. The faint sizzle as the air burned where it touched the witchfire of the Scholar's Crooks. Changeling's contented purr. The beating of his own hearts and then finally the sound of his own breath until there was only the colour and shape of the voices in his head.

Eyes open, he looked at Femensetri. One of the voices bobbing in his mind became clearer, its shape, weight, texture, and timbre more defined. Femensetri stared at him. Unless he was mistaken, there was a satisfied look in her opal-coloured eyes. *Does she know I can do this? Was she waiting for this?* Within moments her voice in his head faded to nothing. He opened his mind further, to hear the others at the table. When Indris opened his mind, voices from all across Amer-Mahjin crashed over him. He clamped his teeth shut around a groan. It was like trying to listen to different singers in a massed choir, all singing different songs in different tempos and keys. Indris concentrated on the people he could see, narrowing in on each voice as it was coloured by its unique signature timbre. It was hard, but he found he could match a face to a voice—

Until he came to Anj.

Her mind was hidden behind complex defences that baffled Indris. They were a confusion of writhing thoughts, cool and slick, coiled about each other and constantly flexing, slithering, and changing. But there was something there, a flicker in the depths of her mind, gone almost as quickly as it appeared.

She was sent to find me!

As if knowing her thoughts had been heard, Anj revealed her purpose. "I was sent to find Indris by the Dhar Gsenni. They had learned it was Sedefke who left instructions across the centuries for Indris to travel to the Spines," She looked at Zadjinn, who sat in his chair looking betrayed. Anj gave the man a look devoid of sympathy. "The same as it was the Dhar Gsenni who asked me to follow him. And the Dhar Gsenni who wanted me to find whatever secrets Sedefke had hidden, investigate them, then bring them back in secret.

"And it's this same sect who knows Indris found signs of the Founder."

"He *what?*" Femensetri stared at Indris, who looked back in shock. She turned her attention back to Anj. "How could you know that?"

"Because when I found Indris on the Spines, he told me. Why do you think he went to Sorochel in the first place? It was to continue the search. It seems the Founder is alive after all."

"But why did you not return to . . . us?" Zadjinn's voice was plaintive, though his mien was aloof. "We thought you had betrayed the Order. We sent Knights, Inquisitors, and even an Executioner, to find you."

"I know. They weren't very good."

Indris shuddered at the offhanded way she dismissed some of the most skilled hunters and killers the Sēq could produce. *She killed a Sēq Executioner? Sweet Näsarat!* But then, she was one of the Eight.

"So why return now, child?" He-Who-Watches asked, his gaze keen.

"Because my task is done." Anj turned to Indris, her smile warm, tears making luminous sapphires of her large eyes. "My husband has returned, and locked in his head are the secrets Sedefke tried so hard to hide from you all."

26

"IF A HAPPY ENDING IS WHAT YOU'RE AFTER, STOP THE STORY WHERE IT
MAKES YOU SMILE, OR CRY FOR LAUGHTER. IN LIFE, IT'S THE RARE
SWEETNESS TO HAVE TEARS OF JOY, OR PAINLESS ENDINGS. PEOPLE FEEL.
IT'S WHAT THEY KNOW, AND IT'S WHY I WRITE."

—Nasri of the Elay-At, Shrīanese dramatist (495th Year of the Shrīanese
Federation)

DAY 358 OF THE 495TH YEAR OF

THE SHRĪANESE FEDERATION

Behind the *Wanderer* the shapes of their pursuers were quite clear, brilliant points of lanterns picking out the lean, predatory shapes of the corsairs. The witches and their spirits were close enough to be blurs in the darkness. Shar had tried on a few occasions to turn them northwest, yet each time they had been hemmed in and driven southward.

The ship crossed over the white sands of the Dead Flat. There was no discernable difference in the *Wanderer*, but Hayden had warned them that would change soon enough. The mountains of the Mar Ejir were a jagged shadow to the east, a long wall down the Dead Flat all the way to the borders of Erebus Prefecture, about the last place Mari wanted to go.

The first of the corsairs crossed the boundaries of the flat a few minutes after, her sister ship not far behind. While the corsairs made a smooth transition, the same could not be said for the witches who flew beside them. Mari smiled with grim satisfaction as the barely perceived shapes of the witches dropped from the sky. There were flashes in the air like diamond dust under lamplight, which Mari assumed meant the release of the bound spirits. From what she could see, the witches enjoyed neither a soft, nor elegant landing. The way they bounced along the sand looked painful. The trailing corsair turned back, then settled into the sand where the witches had fallen.

"How will they get their ship out?" Bensaharēn asked. The Poet Master of the Näsarat stood easily on the rocking deck though. "Come to think of it, how will we get *this* ship out?"

Hayden squinted at the ship, which had landed, then shrugged. "Ain't going to be easy. If they's smart, I reckon an enterprising person'd take the smallest couple of Disentropy Spools and head out of the Flat. Let them store up energy, then walk them back in."

"Sounds like fun."

"Ha!" the old driver laughed, then coughed. Mari frowned at the rattle in Hayden's lungs. When he recovered from his coughing he patted the deck and said, "It'll be worse for us when we come back for our girl here. We'll be a lot further into the Flat, so it's a much longer walk."

The *Wanderer* shuddered. The hum and spark of the Tempest Wheels lowered in pitch and Mari felt her stomach rise into her throat as the ship dropped a metre or so. Hayden patted the rail, as if soothing the *Wanderer*.

Ahead of them, rearing out of the rippled blanket of sand, was the outline of a rounded ziggurat set in the middle of a reaching spiral of columns. Mari pointed it out, and Shar angled the *Wanderer* in that direction.

The *Wanderer* dropped again, in time with the sound of the Tempest Wheels slowing.

"Figure we're just about done flying," Hayden said. "Best bring our girl down soft as you can, young miss."

It wasn't a crash. Nor was it a landing. The *Wanderer* was still travelling at a reasonable speed when her landing legs hit the ground. There came a groan of distressed metal. The grinding and snapping of wood. Then the ship canted sharply and slid, almost turning to face the pursuing corsair. It, too, came to a landing only a hundred metres or so away, though far more elegantly than Shar's attempt.

"Why could you not have done that?" Mauntro asked.

Shar flipped him a rude hand gesture.

"We may have violence in our immediate future," Ekko said with what Mari was sure was enthusiasm. The lion-man pointed to where a score or more of shapes were disembarking from the corsair. Mauntro and his handful of Tau-se escorted Roshana on deck. The woman gave Mari a vengeful glare, holding one hand up to her temple. Danyūn and his Ishahayans lurked not far behind. Nazarafine and Navid stood close together, Siamak towering over them. Omen was true to his nature, standing wraith-like in his pale Shroud behind Vahineh with her expression of childlike innocence in her patchwork face. She clutched a fold of Omen's Shroud in her hand, as if it were the favoured blanket of a babe.

"There's the remains of a building and some columns up ahead," Mari nodded to where several columns stretched from the sand like the stiffened fingers of a drowning man. "It'll give us some cover."

"What disaster have you led us into, Mari?" Roshana asked scathingly as she looked about the rippled expanse of the Dead Flat, harsh under moonlight. "We should've been in Qeme by now if you—"

"There was no choice, my rahn," Bensarahēn said.

"Danyūn," Roshana said, "can you get us away from here without being seen?"

The Master of Spies surveyed the world around him placidly, though quickly. He looked to his Ishahayans, whose fingers flickered quickly in the low light. Danyūn nodded, looked at Nazarafine, Navid, and Vahineh for a second, then to Roshana.

"Not all of us, my rahn," was his quiet response. Roshana took his meaning, her glance at Nazarafine, Navid, and Vahineh was calculating. It was like watching a farmer deciding what animals to cull and it made Mari uneasy to see.

"May I suggest, my rahn, the Lion Guard and the Ishahayans take to the sand to slow pursuit." Mauntro inspected his powerful recurved bow and counted arrows. "It will give us the opportunity to even the numbers some-what."

"Do it." Roshana chewed her lip, hands clutched around the hilt of her own well-used shamshir. "Kill what you can, then regroup with us at the top of the ziggurat."

Mauntro and Danyūn nodded, then led their warriors silently off the grounded ship. Vahineh remained where she was, crouched in the folds of Omen's Shroud. The Wraith Knight stood still, seemingly impervious to what was happening around him.

I don't know if I can trust him, but I need him. We are too few, against too many, and our chances are slim at best.

"Vahineh seems to have taken a liking to you, Omen." Mari went to touch the young woman's hair, but she ducked and buried her face in the folds of the Omen's Shroud. "We need you to take care of her, no matter what. Can you do that for us?"

Omen did nothing for a long while. He just stood there, head angled away, staring at the ruins in the desert. Mari was about to speak again, to get some response, when Omen leaned down and picked Vahineh up like a child. She wrapped her arms around his shoulders and her legs around his hips, face buried in the hard angle of his neck and shoulder. Holding her tightly, Omen ran stork-like and at speed for the ziggurat.

Mari, her friends and the rahns dashed after Omen. Roshana outdis-tanced her peers, leaving Siamak to help the portly and wheezing Nazarafine. The outer ring of stones—hundreds of them like broken teeth—was not much taller than she was, yet wide enough she did not think she could span one with her arms. They had been worn smooth by storms of wind, rain, and sand. The wind wheezed across the stone, rising and falling, like an old man trying to catch his breath. Mari cringed at the sound, glancing this way and that as if she were about to be set upon by soul-stealing Nomads at any time. There were legends of ghuls roaming the Dead Flat, preying on merchant caravans and travellers who strayed too far from the roads. Or worse, vampires who could change shape into desert lights and lure the unwary into their withering embrace. Mari drew her Sûnblade and moved on more cautiously, ashamed at herself for being afraid of childhood stories, but aware all such stories had a dark and terrible truth to them.

On quick feet they raced through the columns, made spectral in the moonlight and drifting clouds of sand. At what she took to be the centre of the place the rounded ziggurat rose from the sand. It looked to be almost forty metres across, with twenty or so tiers to the top, each tier as tall as her chest. She wondered how much of the ziggurat had been buried under centuries of sand in the fallout of the Scholar Wars. Some of the ancient shrines her people had built were hundreds of metres tall. She didn't dwell on it long, however, for soon Ekko found a narrow stair that they used to scale the ancient ruin.

The top of the ziggurat was almost ten metres across, and had several heavy blocks of stone curved along the top like a saddle, surrounding a broad, dark pit. *Sacrificial altars*, Mari thought with some distaste. She knew her people had a barbaric past, but seeing it was different. Mari looked away, wishing there was somewhere else they could seek cover, but they had what they had. Wooden poles leaned awry, bleached as old bone under centuries of summers. Dark granite statues were set in a circle around the platform, their cruel, angular features dulled by time. The carved plates of their armour were worn, as were the sweeping folds of their coat that merged into the stone of the platform. She chanced a look into the pit but could see nothing save the sands that drifted downward before being lost to sight in the sharp-edged shadows.

Her comrades waited in the lee of the statues, out of the wind. The rahns stayed together, whispering among themselves. Roshana crouched sullenly with her back against a statue, the bare blade of her heavy shamshir across her knees. Siamak leaned on a long-hafted battleaxe. Nazarafine's only weapon was her wounded nephew, who sat silently nearby. Hayden held his storm-rifle at the ready, Ekko had a thumb-thick arrow to the string of his bow. Shar was rubbing at her recently healed arm, sword unsheathed, while Bensaharēn knelt facing the stairs, eyes closed, face peaceful, hands like old oak resting on his thighs. Omen was so still he may as well have been another statue. Vahineh crouched at his feet with a length of the Wraith-Knight's Shroud wrapped around her head. The broken woman rocked back and forth, fingers splayed on the stone to either side of her.

Distant screams carried on the wind. Fierce roars and the sound of metal on metal. The Tau-se and the Ishahayans were culling the enemy. One group fierce, proud, and loud; giving voice to their prowess. The other as silent as a man dying alone and surprised.

Nazarafine approached Mari, hands fidgeting. "Mari? Can you come and have a look at Navid? His wound looks more serious than I thought."

Navid sat with his head back, eyes closed, hand clenched around his wounded arm. Bloodstains made deep shadows between his fingers. Mari stepped across her friends and crouched beside the Saidani-sûk warrior poet. The air smelled of mould from the pit, mingling with the metallic scent of Navid's blood. His skin was clammy and he barely opened his eyes when she touched him. His pulse was slow and weak. She took a knife from her boot and sliced the man's sleeve open, then covered her mouth with her hand at what she saw. The wound was long and ragged, a divot of flesh missing, exposing muscle and the hint of bone. She swore. The sounds of combat and shouting lingered on the wind. *They're getting closer. It won't be long now and Navid will be no use to us at all.*

"Why didn't you tell anybody your wound was this bad?"

"You suffered worse at Amnon and still killed fifty Iphyri with a broken amenesqa." He barely moved as she poured water across the wound to clean it. *He can't feel pain in his wound. Not a good sign.* "All the stories say so."

"Don't believe everything you hear. I'll bind this as best I can, but—"

"Out here this wound will be the end of me and we both know it," Navid said with a bitter smile. "My fate was sealed the moment we were forced into the Dead Flat. At least I can make my end worthy of remembering. If any of us escape, that is."

"If any of us escape."

Mari tightly bound the wound in strips torn from her own coat, though they began to stain with blood soon after she knotted them in place. She noticed Ekko, Shar, and Hayden tense, and reached for her weapon. Then her friends relaxed as Mauntro and Danyūn joined them. They were both bloodied and breathing heavily.

"Report," Roshana said grimly.

"Baniq is dead," Danyūn said with equanimity. "Zoer and Fyra will continue to hamper our enemies as best they can. From what I could see there are a very great number of trained warriors on that ship that followed us. The wind-corsair is the *Skywolf*, Tahj-Shaheh's flagship. The Marble Sea corsairs aboard will be her elite crew. There are at least four squads of Anlūki here also."

"That'll be trouble and a half," Mari said. She hesitated, afraid to ask the question Danyūn answered for her anyway.

"Yes. Belamandris the Widowmaker leads them. It was he who slew Baniq and took his head."

"Don't suppose you could ask your brother to let us go, young miss?" Hayden asked, rubbing sand from his eye. "'Cause I really ain't inclined to fight his lot. Amnon was eventful and all, but it ain't something I'm in a hurry to repeat."

"Anani, Furu and Kofo, Nsay and Samu, have also gone to their rest," Mauntro growled. He plucked an arrow from the meat of his upper arm, snapping it before throwing it away. "We are badly outnumbered and our enemies are right behind us. Perhaps, Rahn-Roshana, you should—"

"Mari!" Belam shouted. Mari peered over the edge of the platform to see her brother at the foot of the stairs. Roshana shot Mari a hate-filled look, teeth preternaturally bright in the moonlight, but Belam's voice cut off any chance for Mari to care about that. "Please come out and talk with me, before anybody else gets hurt. You're outnumbered and there's really no other logical choice but to surrender."

Before Mari could draw breath to warn the others to stay silent, Roshana cried out.

"Pah-Erebus fa Belamandris! This is Rahn-Näsarat fe Roshana. I'll parley with you, if I have your word you'll treat with us fairly."

After a brief pause, Belam yelled back. "As you like. But please understand my trust in you is no big thing, not after the stunt you tried against my father at The Twelveway. If I suspect you of any treachery, I'll end you."

"Agreed." Roshana shared a few terse words with Nazarafine and Siamak. Then she whispered something to Danyūn and Mauntro before walking down the stairs towards Belam, her head held high.

Mari looked to the bottom of the ziggurat to see the lean, blood-hued streak that was her brother. His outline was snagged in the shifting sands as he prowled silently, waiting for Roshana to come to him. His soldiers were nowhere to be seen.

Mari turned to her companions and spoke to them quietly. "Belam will be sending people to flank us, so keep your eyes peeled. We've the high ground and they can only come at us in small numbers. If we stay calm, we can survive this."

Ekko ran his thumb along a fortune-coin plaited into his mane, lion's face as calm as it always was. "I hear you, Mariam."

Shar took a feather from her dawn-toned quills and whispered into it, banishing ill-omen, before casting it into the wind. It fluttered for a while, then was snagged and carried swiftly away to the west. Shar swore to herself. In answer to Mari's look she grinned weakly and said, "*Makhar-hawana-yé*. The west is the place where shadows and ill-omens are born."

Mari flicked her Sûnblade with her thumbnail. "She will chase the shadows down and end them, Shar. We are all of us in the best of company here. We can come out of this alive."

"I wonder where Indris is?" Hayden mused before coughing, almost doubling over. Shar was soon at his side, supporting him. The fit lasted an uncomfortably long time, his loud coughs cracking across the wailing wind. When he finished he looked up, eyes glazed with pain, fist pressed to his chest. He spoke, though, as if nothing had happened. "He usually swoops in like some hero from the sagas, Changeling afire and crooning, scaring our enemies so much their stones creep up into their bellies. Reckon he'll be sorry he missed this."

"No doubt you'll tell him yourself," Shar murmured.

"Oh, I've no doubt of that at all, young miss."

Belam was still alone when Roshana joined him. Her brother made the Second Obeisance, true to the tenets of sende, while Roshana stood imperious and unmoving. No sound drifted up from where they stood, though Mari cautiously watched their hand gestures, her eyes darting to any imagined motion amongst the stones. Belam and Roshana spoke for several minutes before the two of them headed up the stairs.

"There's no need for everybody to die here," Roshana said as she reached the top. Belamandris lingered behind her, a gentle smile on his beautiful golden face. Roshana looked to each of the companions in turn. "No need. I'm sure we can agree on that."

"What do you suggest?" Nazarafine asked cautiously.

"None of you really know me, save Mari," Belam nodded to his sister, smile turning melancholy for a moment. But like the sun coming from behind clouds he brightened. "And some of her friends, of course, from our little difference of opinion in the Rōmarq. But I'm a honorable man and I don't want any more deaths. Right now we can agree to some simple terms, and go our separate ways."

"What are your terms?" Siamak asked. Danyūn sauntered to the edge of the platform and looked down. His frown caught Mari's attention. The sand was littered with soldiers who had emerged from the surrounding stone circle. Nadir and Jhem were among them. There were the severed heads of the two Ishahayans and five Tau-se at their feet. Mari looked at her brother, who shrugged indifferently.

"I want Vahineh," Belam said. It took him a while to see her, hidden behind Omen as she was. Omen remained still as the statues around him and Mari's heart lifted when Belam seemed not to recognise Omen for what he was. Belam then looked at Mari. "And Mari returns with me. Though Father wants the rest of you, I know the trouble it would cause, even if he refuses to admit it. So, for all I care you can leave here unharmed."

"And if we are tiresome about the whole affair and refuse?" Bensaharēn had not risen from his knees, or even opened his eyes. Belam looked at the old man.

"It will end quite badly, Poet Master."

"But for you first, I think." Bensaharēn finally opened his eyes and smiled. Belam took a step back and reached for Tragedy.

"I accept your terms," Roshana said quickly. She looked at Nazarafine, who nodded even as she flushed in shame. Siamak stepped away from the other rahns, his face like stone. Roshana looked imploringly at the huge man, though he would not see her. The Rahn-Näsarat said to Belam, "You promise safe passage for us?"

"I promise you'll leave this heap of rocks alive. How you fare once you've gone from here is another question. Live. Die. I don't much care. Just know, Roshana, my father will have such vengeance as to make you wish I'd ended you here. I'm doing you no favours by letting you go. Think of it more as a head start."

Belam turned to face Mari. He took a hesitant step. Raised a hand shyly, which seemed to not know what to do with itself before finding comfort once again by Belam's side. "Mari? Father won't hurt you. He's angry, but he'll cool down. I need you to come with me. It will save the lives of your friends and perhaps your presence can be a calming influence on Father. He's surrounded himself with . . . people of questionable character. But first, where's Indris? He and I have business I'd settle."

"He's not here." Mari took a step back from her brother, who looked pained at the gesture. She hunched down, chilled more by the thought of returning to her father, than she was by the wind. "And what do you—?"

"Then where in Erebus's shadow is he?" Belam growled, reaching for her but stopping as she moved another step away.

"He never left Avānweh. He's with the Sēq, as far as I know."

Belam swore profusely as he walked to the edge of the platform, angrily kicking sand over the side. He gestured to his soldiers and a goodly number of them started to climb the stairs. Belam turned towards her, eyes haunted. "It makes no matter. He'll come to find you, I'm sure. This just delays the inevitable."

Roshana came to Siamak's side and started speaking with him urgently. Nazarafine joined her. They spoke for a long while before Siamak gave a great sigh, then nodded. The three rahns took to the stairs without looking back. Danyūn and Mauntro picked up the groaning, feebly struggling Navid between them and carried him off. *Looks like he won't have an end worthy of remembering after all,* Mari thought. Bensaharēn was the last to leave.

"I am proud of you Mari, as if you were my own daughter," he said, holding her tight. "Remember what I taught you about there being times for everything? This is the time for patience."

"I didn't agree to return to my Father." Mari tensed in her old teacher's arms. "I don't . . . I don't even know who my Father is anymore."

"But what of the lives of these others?" Bensaharēn said gently. "A warrior-poet fights, we sacrifice, so others don't have to. You know what you must do. Besides, the girl, Vahineh, will need you. Patience, Mari. The world reveals to us the time to act."

"I understand." Mari did not want to let the old man go. When he left the circle of her arms, the warmth of him was whistled away too quickly by the cold wind.

Shar, Hayden, and Ekko approached Mari. The three said nothing, simply stood in her orbit. She smiled at them. "Today is the day we count ourselves lucky to survive."

"Indris always jokes about times like this," Shar whispered into Mari's ear as she held her hand. "He says, *It's less about winning than being able to walk away afterwards.*"

"And you need to walk away and find him for me," Mari whispered back. "I'll be waiting for him. But not too long. He'll regret it if I have to come looking for him because he kept me waiting."

"We'll tell him, young miss." Hayden said, his lips grazing her forehead as he pulled her down for a farewell kiss. "Figure we'll get the *Wanderer* back in the air where she belongs, get Indris, then come looking for you. That's if it ain't too much trouble for you to wait a bit."

"Only for a bit." She smiled warmly at the group that had become her friends. "I'll keep a light on."

And with that they walked back to the other side of the platform, toward Omen and Vahineh.

Belam kept the distance between them. "Thank you for doing the right thing, Mari. I know your hearts, sweet sister. The same as I know my own. Neither of us would willingly endanger the ones we care for. It's why I made the offer in the first place. But you've said goodbye to your friends, Mari. It's time we were going."

Several Anlūki reached the platform, along with as many Marble Sea corsairs in their mismatched armour and finery. There was an attractive, rangy woman with them whose hungry gaze settled on Belam, before she looked at Mari. Pinpoints of metal gleamed at her fingers and earlobes. There was a small chip of diamond on her brow and gems plaited into her dark hair. She stood with the casual grace of a seasoned killer. The woman started barking orders in dayeshi, the patois of nahdi and pirates. *So, you are Tahj-Shaheh, the great reaver who now serves my father. I'll remember you, pretty lady. If my father relies on you, it's really best I plant you in ashes.*

The corsairs were looking at Shar and laughing amongst themselves, while eyeing Ekko with trepidation. Hayden looked miserable, his hands clenching and unclenching around his storm-rifle.

Four of the Anlūki went to take Vahineh from behind Omen . . .

And that is when things went wrong.

* * *

Mari was stunned by Omen's sudden burst of activity.

"Omen!" she yelled. "No!"

He had kicked one of the Anlūki square in the stones. The man gasped, face red, then stumbled back with his hands to his groin. One step too far and then he was gone, screaming as he fell into the pit.

Omen drew his blade and cut the throat of another. On the back swing he hacked the jaw off another Anlūki who fell in a gout of blood, clutching uselessly at part of his face no longer there.

Hayden shot the last Anlūki in the head.

"Kill them all!" somebody screamed.

Vahineh cowered behind Omen as more soldiers advanced. Hayden was an automaton, aiming and firing, aiming and firing, every shot killing its target. More soldiers bustled on to the platform.

"Keep Mari and Vahineh alive!" Belamandris yelled. The Widowmaker was quick as a cat, using the statues as cover from Hayden as he circled around to engage Omen. Bolts rang from the granite statues as the old drover tried to bring the Widowmaker down, without success.

Trusting in her friends, Mari chased her brother. She spared a glance for where Ekko and Shar wove a deadly net of *serill* and steel. The powerful lion-man's roar was deafening, causing his enemies to quail. Shar sang her war chants, her voice seeming to send despondency and fear into those she fought. The Tau-se and the Seethe reaped like farmers at harvest.

Omen used his ceramic arm as both shield and a weapon. The enamel was scratched, chips of it flying, his fire-hardened and onyx-sheathed nails tearing through the soft-tissue of a corsair's throat. All the while Vahineh looked on, screaming silently, saliva forming glistening bars between her slack lips, and her nails digging runnels in her cheeks.

Mari used the sheath of her Sûnblade to trip her brother. Belam turned the fall into a roll, came up facing Mari and sent a warning stroke her way, which she skipped away from. The two eyed each other.

"Don't test me on this, Mari," Belam said. "Your friends could've walked away and never seen us again. But no! The bloody Wraith Knight had to go and ruin it all. I felt a little sorry the first time, when I burned his body down. This time I think I'm going to enjoy putting a permanent end to the filthy Nomad."

"I don't want to fight you, big brother."

"And I don't want to fight you, either."

"Then we're at an impasse."

"Not so much."

Mari saw the warning flicker in Belam's eyes and threw herself sideways. Sheathed swords clubbed the air where she had stood. Mari swore, then turned to face the handful of soldiers who tried to subdue her.

More and more soldiers came for her, until it was all she could do to dodge, duck and weave through the complex net of blunt weapons that tried to hit her. Her vision was filled with frenetic activity, set against the tattered banners of sand-filled wind. Moonlight shone from armour. Eyes and wide-open mouths made hollow pools of darkness. Teeth became darkened with blood. The clamour of battle was a deafening counterpoint to the fluting wind. She hammered her fist into a man's face. Lips split and teeth came free. A corsair took a blow from her elbow across his unarmoured collarbone, snapping it. Another she kicked in the groin, then kneed in the face, sending he and the two he grabbed screaming on their journey to the bottom of the pit.

She took a pummelling as the minutes wore on. A cut opened up over her eye, another at the corner of her lip and across one cheek. Somebody had stamped on her foot and she suspected at least one of her fingers was broken. Mari felt the familiar burn of fatigue and knew time was against her.

From the corner of her eye she saw Ekko and Shar in the fray. Both were spattered with gore, their weapons slick. Hayden's face was florid, his lips slack and trembling. The man was wheezing and looked barely strong enough to lift his storm-rifle.

Belam aimed a whistling cut at Omen, who caught the blade in his hand and twisted it down. The small finger of his hand flew away. Omen stabbed at Belam, who in turn bent at the waist and the Wraith Knight's shamshir skidded across the ruby scales of Belam's armour. Belam twisted and disengaged, Omen following.

The two men ranged back and forth, meeting form for form and style for style. Some of the combatants stopped to watch, mesmerised by the display of skill. Belam fought as a man at the height of his youth and power. A man who was passionate, his stance and cut changes showing wit and sensitivity. His execution of Swallow's Wing almost made Mari's hearts ache for the beauty of it—even as she caved in the chest of a pirate who tried to bludgeon her.

Omen duelled like a teacher seeing the world outside his academy for the first time. He took the theory of swordcraft to the point a living person could not go to for fear of their flesh. The Wraith Knight bore stingless cuts that did not bleed, across his limbs, torso, and face.

Mari felt a blow on her back and stumbled forward, breath driven from her lungs. Memories of Avānweh crashed in as she saw a roundhead arrow—a resign ball on a shaft, used to incapacitate, not kill—roll past her toe.

She turned to see Nadir putting another roundhead arrow to the string. *Cowardly bastard!* There were other archers stepping to his side, similarly armed, and Tahj-Shaheh smiling like a cat as she looked on.

Belam forced Omen away from Vahineh and the young woman became hysterical. Jhem slid like an oil slick from the shadow of a statue, taking the squirming young woman in his arms. She shrieked for help, eyes wide with terror.

We need you to take care of her, no matter what. Can you do that for us?

At Vahineh's cries, Omen turned his back on Belam.

The Wraith Knight reached out to grasp Jhem's throat, and squeezed. Jhem released Vahineh, even as Omen moved forward to grip Jhem's sword hand. There came a dull snap as Omen broke Jhem's wrist.

Belam hacked into Omen's ceramic torso. Omen stepped forward, still crushing the life from Jhem. He tried to parry Belam and lost his limb for the trouble. His ceramic arm and sword clattered to the ground. Omen threw Jhem towards the pit, the Blacksnake scrabbling at the edge to avoid going over. The Wraith Knight turned and stood over Vahineh, using his one good arm to defend her.

"No!" Mari croaked as more soldiers surrounded Omen, hacking his body until it was latticed with deep cuts.

More roundhead arrows struck Mari. One hit her thigh, dropping her to her knees. She looked around, dazed, seeing the end of those people she had come to call her friends.

Indris's friends.

I've killed you all, she thought. She tried to muster the thoughts to form a Lament for them, but each time a phrase formed, it was pounded from her mind by another blunt arrow. Warriors approached her warily, clubs ready, circling like jackals around a wounded lion.

Hayden had slung his rifle and flailed with his broadsword. His skin was ashen, face slack. There was a lot of blood on his buckskins, much of which Mari thought was his own. Hayden ran an Anlūki through, his sword getting stuck. Another of the Anlūki stepped in and cut Hayden from shoulder to hip. The old drover's buckskins opening like a split fruit, bright and pulpy. He fell face first to the ground and neither moved, nor made a sound.

Shar screamed, reaching for her fallen friend.

Ekko pounded the Anlūki who had struck Hayden to the ground, then grabbed Shar in one massive arm. He looked at Mari, sizing up his chances of rescuing her, too. But she shook her head, and gestured for him to flee. The indomitable Tau-se stood there a moment as his enemies formed ranks. Eyes wide, tail slashing with his agitation even as Shar struggled and screamed and reached for Hayden, Ekko gave a deafening roar and pounced through a gap in the enemy lines, down the stairs, and out of sight.

Shar yelled all the while for him to let her go, until her voice faded in the din.

Mari looked across to Hayden, who lay where he fell, eyes wide, mouth working slowly. She felt a tingling in her nose and a heat in her eyes as the tears started to form—of loss, of frustration, and of guilt.

I'm so sorry.

Mari got to one knee. An arrow struck her ribs, her arm. One struck her cheek and she heard the bone crack. Pain flashed through her body, then she felt nothing as her nerves overloaded. On faltering legs she stumbled toward Hayden, though she was distracted by Belam's triumphant shout.

Her brother reached in to Omen's torso and tore free the gleaming jade and gold Wraith Jar. Omen's shattered body stopped moving. Belam held Omen's Wraith Jar close, examining it, face lit by the play of brilliant light from within.

Then with an expression of disgust he hurled it at the ground, smashing it to pieces. There was a brilliant flash of gelid light, gone as quickly as it came. The soldiers cheered, then heaved Omen's ruined form into the pit.

Reeling, shocked and empty, Mari barely had the time to turn as Nadir, contempt in his eyes, shot her in the chest.

She struck her head on the stone as she fell backward.

And welcome darkness took her in its arms and rocked her away.

27

"ONE CAN ONLY TRUST THE PEOPLE ONE IS INDEBTED TO, FOR THEY ARE THE ONES IN WHOSE BEST INTERESTS IT IS THAT YOU SUCCEED."

—Sayf-Rayz of the Maladhi, Master of Assassins to Erebus fa Basyrandin
(471st Year of the Shrīanese Federation)

DAY 358 OF THE 495TH YEAR OF

THE SHRĪANESE FEDERATION

Corajidin returned to the Qadir Erebus with Nima and his Anlūki, there to marshal what forces he may in his public defence of the city. As he marched the long, sombre corridors of the qadir he felt the first twinges of fear and a strange sense of isolation. There was none of Belamandris's comforting, golden, beautiful presence. No Wolfram either, tall, gaunt, and so seemingly frail in his callipers, yet tough as an old oak blasted and blasted by lightning until the dark core remained. Kasraman, too, was absent.

The two witches were out there in the streets of Avānweh, fighting to secure the future of the Great House of Erebus as the eminent family of the Avān. But unlike his Ancestors, Corajidin would not allow himself to fall. No matter the price. He had come so far, and sacrificed so much of what he believed in, that everything he did now had the purity of new beginnings. True, the day would come when Corajidin would be planted in ashes—his body rendered to the nothing sende demanded so his spirit was not, should not be, conflicted between this world and the next—and Kasraman would rise in his place.

Kasraman, the son his father, Basyrandin, had chosen as Corajidin's heir. Kasraman, the one to rule a new and stronger Shrīan, capable of retaking the world. Not that Kasraman's presence brought much comfort these days. Memories of what he had seen of Kasraman's Aspect knotted his guts with trepidation. The halcyon days of the witches had ended with the Scholar Wars, much as it had for the Sēq—though they still clung to their existence with the desperation of those to whom an end was near. The truly great mystics, barring a few exceptions, were the pitiful few who remained. Those who had learned during the high watermark of their arcane science, not as newer generations had done by scrabbling through recovered books of other people's wisdom, with minimal understanding and less subtlety. But what was Kasraman? The Mahsojhin witches had no fear of Corajidin, that much he knew. Yet they saw something in Kasraman that weakened them at the knees. What, exactly, had he fathered?

There had been the usual japes when his first child had been born. Had Corajidin actually fathered him at all? Kasraman bore no resemblance to Corajidin, taking almost entirely after his mother's dark line. There were stories of wild storms and Nomads walking from the frigid southern ocean, witches soaring through scudding clouds, the night Kasraman had been born. Yet the contemplative, courteous child had grown to be the same in adulthood. He had believed the stories of Kasraman being the vessel for darker forces as nothing more than a rumour started by the enemies of the Great House of Erebus.

But now Kasraman's Aspect lent some truth to those fears.

Corajidin paused for a moment, halfway across the Hearthall. *Ilhen* lamps burned behind horse-heads of ruby crystal. The carved limestone columns, stalactites and stalagmites glowed a faint pink in their light. The air was gently scented with vanilla and orchid, two of Yashamin's favourite scents. The walls sparked with the shapes of gold-plated skulls, generations of enemies kept around for mockery and memory. He looked up to see Ariskander's gilded skull grinning down. *You think you will have the last laugh, my enemy of enemies. Though I do not have your soul in a box, it is* you, *for all your noble blood as the Great House of the Phoenix, who hangs on my wall.*

"My rahn?" Nima asked, concerned. "Uncle? Are you well?"

"Pardon?" Corajidin snapped out of his reverie. His nephew stood waiting a few paces ahead. Corajidin smiled. Nima was a much better man than Farouk in all respects. A relative who could almost be trusted, and who had not yet proven to be a disappointment. He resembled Belamandris, to a degree, though brazen rather than golden, a man made of lesser materials who worked hard to shine as bright. "All is well, Nima. Come, help me with my armour. It has been a long while since I have been a warrior-rahn, like my forebears."

Corajidin strode to his chambers, Nima a pace behind. The two men entered Corajidin's private armoury, where the various suits of armour he had worn, from childhood to adulthood, were arrayed on mannequins of red and yellow gold. A vast array of weapons were laid upon glittering jewelled racks. Everything in the room shone to a high gleam under *ilhen* light, unwavering and perfect, without a hint of shadow anywhere.

For I have gathered enough shadows in my life, without them clinging to my lethal instruments. He slid a finger along the elegant curves of his first amenesqa. It was a weapon he had shown little skill with, yet the Petal Empire antique of the Great House of Bey was coveted by others, so it meant something to Corajidin. It was not alone, at rest with a dozen others, all equally valuable because it had once been precious to somebody else.

"I'll take the crimson silk gambeson and trousers," Corajidin said, pointing to the items as he named them, "the black suede hauberk with the golden laces and the gold-chased black scale hauberk."

"And your weapon, my rahn?"

"Ah, there is only one real choice for me, nephew." Corajidin took a baroque watered-steel shamshir from its case, furnished in gold and rubies, beautiful and deadly. "Not as hard to use as an amenesqa, this is the weapon of the common people, yet made for a leader of them."

Nima bathed Corajidin with hot water, rubbing a blend of myrrh and aloe vera into his skin with a silk cloth. Then he helped Corajidin into his armour, which was much heavier than Corajidin remembered. Nima took the time to fit it properly, adjusting the laces, straps, and buckles as Corajidin checked his range of movement. There were times when the light shone from

Nima's blond hair, and Corajidin was reminded of Belamandris, who had done this for his father on many occasions. Corajidin smiled and rested his hands on Nima's head, pretending he was the son he loved above all other people, except for—

"Me, my heart of hearts," Yashamin's voice tickled his nerves. Eyes closed, he felt her breath across his ear, which sent tremors through his chest. Corajidin opened his eyes, yet could not see her anywhere. He took a stuttering breath in disappointment.

"Is that too tight, my rahn?" Nima asked, concerned.

"No. You have done well."

"You are the great Golden Stallion, my husband." It sounded like Yashamin knelt before him. He imagined he felt her hands on his thighs. *"Soon, you will trample your enemies beneath your hooves. Soon, all things will be in your grasp. Perhaps even me."*

Corajidin's breath caught in his throat. He looked down to where Nima was fastening the thick leather weapon belt over Corajidin's sash. "Never mind, Nima. I can finish this. Gather the Anlūki and four squads of the Horse Guard, and meet me in the courtyard in thirty minutes. Also, send a message to Feyd of the Jiharim. Tell him to come to Avānweh with as many of his Jihari as he can bring."

Nima bowed, then hurried away.

"Finally! We are alone," Corajidin sighed.

"You're never alone, Jidi," she said against his chest. He could hear her and feel her, but not see her. *"It's the light, my love. I love the light, but it loves not me."*

Corajidin hastily shrouded the *ilhen* lamps. As the room darkened to that of a late afternoon overcast, Yashamin's gauzy form materialised like a sculpture of jade and black smoke. She was naked, her long hair as dark as night, beads of jade as pale as milk around her throat, wrists, and ankles. This was how he loved her best—how she had loved herself best.

He tried to embrace her, but her form boiled around him like smoke. Tears of frustration and loss formed at the corners of his eyes, hastily wiped away.

"We stand on the brink, my love," he said to her. "Everything we planned for, fought for, bled for—"

"Died for . . ."

"Is about to come to fruition. I will be crowned Asrahn and join the august ranks of the Ancestors who have come before me. No longer will I need to fear the shame of disappointing them."

"And I'll be with you, Jidi." She paused, then drifted away on a boiling cushion of fragmented light, like dust in the breeze. *"But it won't be as it should've been."*

"If I could bring you back—" he choked, realising he meant what he said. He stepped back, aghast. What was he saying?"

"What are you saying?" It was as if she could read his mind! *"It is our souls that speak, Jidi. You can not lie to the dead."*

There were so many things he had believed in over the years. A construct of morality, such as it was, and principles, such as they were, which had guided him since childhood. Over the years he learned the flexibility of necessity, allowing many of his tenets to bend to the breaking point, while justifying them for his greater personal good and the good of his House. But since his illness and the virtual walking death he had endured, principle had become a luxury he could afford less and less.

The Emissary had given him a sharp education in the fragility of principle when he had succumbed to her and Wolfram's advice. He had trafficked with Nomads. Kept his son from finishing his sacred journey to the Well of Souls. Murdered, extorted, and lied. And what of freeing the witches from Mahsojhin? The litany of his transgressions was long, yet still he walked and in two days' time would be rewarded for his relentless pursuit of power. Everything he had done, he had done for the glory of his House, and his Ancestors in their turn had been witches, scholars, rahns, Asrahns, and even Mahjs! And traitors. And heretics. The road of the Erebus had been long, with as many hills and mountains as there had been valleys. History was written by the victors. Rules and laws were made by those who dared face the uncertainty of change with a keen eye and unshaking resolve. Such people *took* what they wanted, and asked neither forgiveness, nor permission.

So how was bringing back his murdered wife any worse than what he— or others like him— had already done? How was it worse than what he was yet prepared to do?

"*It is not, my love,*" Yasha melted into him, firing his nerves as she had always known how to do. His body trembled in response. He was brought to the brink of release, before she passed through him and out the other side. He turned to face her, hungry for her caress. "*You know what you need to do, Jidi.*"

"I do."

"*Yes! A thousand times, a million times, yes! Everything will be well when we're together again.*"

"It will, my Yashamin."

"*Now drink your medicine, Jidi. You need to be stronger tonight than you've ever been before.*"

✳ ✳ ✳

Corajidin and his soldiery made a grand spectacle as they rode through the streets of Avānweh. It would have been better if there were Iphyri in their number, as the powerful horsemen always made an impression. But the Assembly was a time of peace and there was no way he could justify the deadly shock-troops as his personal guard. Besides, the Anlūki were deadly enough and the Second Company of the Erebus Horse Guard were seasoned veterans all.

He spared a glance for his warriors and his spirits lifted. By now the witches and liches would be in place, facing the worst of the danger represented by the daemon elementals. He hoped somebody had gotten to Nix and stopped the unstable little man from releasing more.

The small army clattered into a large empty forum, dominated by four towering statues standing back-to-back, Scholar's Crooks with their sharp hooks looming over all below. Bird droppings stained the carved folds in the dark stone and along the arms, mixed with centuries of wear by the rain. Waiting for them were Kasraman, Wolfram, Kimi, and Nix.

"Father," Kasraman bowed formally. When he looked up his smile warmed the glacial blue of his eyes.

"News?"

"Mostly good. We lost all but one of the witches sent on the *Skywolf.* Igrael reports that Belamandris has secured Vahineh and Mari."

"What about the Federationist rahns?"

"They escaped into the desert, but he's sent soldiers after them." Kasraman chuckled to himself. "I'm assuming it was Mari's idea, but they made a run for the Näq Yetesh, no doubt to neutralise the witches. All but one of the witches we sent with Belam was killed when they crossed into the Dead Flat and speared into the sand. A painful end, one would think."

"It's not bloody funny," Wolfram growled through his beard. His sinewy hand tightened on Kimiya's arm and she winced.

"It's a little funny," Kasraman insisted, his expression unreadable as he looked at Kimiya. He turned to his father. "Belam confirmed the deaths of the Wraith Knight, Sassomon-Omen, and the Human rifleman, Hayden Goode."

"And Indris?"

"He wasn't there. Apparently he's with the Sēq."

Corajidin's jaw clenched in fury. The man was slipperier than a greased snake! What did it take to kill one man, for the love of Erebus? He strangled his reins until the anger passed.

"And my sister is badly battered, but well." Kasraman added into the silence. "In case you were—"

"Thank you, Kasraman," Corajidin said, cutting off that line of thought. "And how fares our fight against invaders?"

"Sanojé and her liches have done all we asked of them," Wolfram replied, "as have Elonie, Ikedion, and those they chose to help. Even where the Sēq were fighting, the witches lent assistance until the daemon elemental was bound."

"I'd like them back, if you don't mind," Nix said, gnawing at his thumbnail. "There was considerable expense involved in faking your Human invasion, Rahn-Corajidin."

"We'll return the ones we can, Nix. Some of what you released took more than a little convincing to behave, and had to be destroyed. I'm sorry if our need to actually survive this confrontation has inconvenienced you in any way." Kasraman's smile belied his words, and Nix's mocking bow did not hide the flash of malignant rage in his expression. Kasraman continued, "Once or twice the Sēq tried to attack the witches, but they only defended themselves until the Sēq left the field. All in all, a good first step, Father."

"And now?" Corajidin asked, hearts swelling in his chest at the thought of action. He had taken a massive dose of the Emissary's Font potion and it infused his body with a strength he did not remember having in his prime. "I would have the people see me in action, and remember."

"Then come, Father, and taste the victory long in the making."

※ ※ ※

The great mass of the daemon elemental's bilious tentacle curled around the shrieking warriors, before lifting them high and throwing them to the ground where one of them burst like a watermelon. Gibbets of flesh landed on Corajidin's armour. His horse reared, and screamed, spraying foam everywhere. Corajidin tumbled from the saddle. His horse bucked and kicked, then thundered insane and out of control until a massive tentacle flattened it.

Corajidin edged back along the bloody stones, voice frozen with terror, as the betentacled elemental swept a dozen or so men from their feet in front of him.

The daemon elemental was a bloated, toad-like thing almost seven metres tall, with a wide gash for a mouth filled with a jagged fence of teeth. Tentacles sprouted from its shoulders and coral grew in a razor sharp fan down its back. Its breath smelled the same as a dirty fishery in high summer. When it talked, or what passed for it talking, it was a burbling, wet sound that made Corajidin want to vomit.

Corajidin gained his feet and joined Kasraman, Wolfram, and the other witches on the assumption it was the safest place to be. The Anlūki and the Horse Guard were proving ineffective—the ones the daemon elemental had not eaten were strewn about like rag dolls on the ground.

The elemental lurched sideways, causing a high wall to collapse. Stones rained down, killing some, wounding some, and burying others.

"Kill it!" Corajidin's voice was high-pitched with fear. He went to clutch his son's arm, but Kasraman was burning hotter than a furnace. Even hovering centimetres above the ground, the stone beneath his feet had turned to molten slag. Corajidin could feel the skin of his face drying and his armour heating up. "Kasraman! You must kill it or this will all be for naught!"

The Aspect of the Daemon Prince faced Corajidin, who quailed and soiled himself. It was Kasraman's face, made hard and sharp, geometric patterns shining on his skin. His eyes burned white as glaciers under the sun and two massive horns curved from his brow.

"This is our future, Father," the Aspect said in a voice that was many voices at once. "This is the door you've opened and the one I'll have to close one day. But today we need these witches if any of us are to live."

Corajidin dropped to the ground. Kasraman, Wolfram, and the other witches filled the air with their chants and songs. Kimiya knelt at Wolfram's feet, eyes rolled back into her head, skin like wax, and lips slack. "Not this. How could I have forgotten this—" the rahn murmured.

And the curtains of the past whipped away and he was Asrahn-Erebus fe Amerata, the Red Queen, whose world was falling apart around her. The witches had betrayed her! She had agreed to give them power in return for their assistance in cutting the final tethers that held Shrīan to the sinking corpse of the Awakened Empire—the Sēq. Betrayed, after giving them the idea and planning the coup, which should have led her people to freedom and assured the dominance of the Great House of Erebus as the one and only line of Asrahns down the ages. She could not breathe, the air was so hot it shimmered and sparkled, plants withering before her eyes. The sky was super charged, lightning bounced from cloud to cloud, causing the hairs on her arms and scalp to lift. Flame licked at the mountains. The city echoed with the symphony of fear as the witches unleashed their power on the people who had always reviled them. Witches wheeled screaming in the sky, surrounded by the shimmering forms of their half-seen spirits, their Aspects flickering. She cried for her loss. Not the loss of her people. The people were fickle and easy to replace. No, she cried for the loss of her dream—

It felt as if the layers of Corajidin's mind were peeling away. Waves of malign intent washed over him from the elemental, while the yawning, spinning, impossible vortex of his Ancestors' voices and wants and needs clattered about in his head like pigeons caught in the room and he could see their mouths opening and closing as they all tried to be heard and they all wanted the chance to live his life for death was not the—

Corajidin scrambled backwards sobbing, only to be pierced by Kasraman's sharp gaze. He heard his son's voice in his head, clear as a bell.

"I see what you see, Father. But your mind is not up to this task, and will never be. So let the nightmares go, Father. Forget what you've seen and know only you've saved your people. Forget now—"

❋ ❋ ❋

"Say something, Father," Kasraman urged.

Corajidin started at the sound of cheering. He stood in the Tyr-Jahavān and Kasraman was patting him on the shoulder, his grin wide. Corajidin found his mask and let his face fall into it. The old smile, which crinkled the corners and stretched his lips, without baring his fangs. Kasraman helped his father to his feet, then continued the applause along with the others.

Corajidin still wore his armour, which was smeared with blood, some of the laces snapped and buckles broken. Many of the scales had come off his cuirass. He looked down at his hands to see them sheathed in leather and steel and caked with gore.

Kasraman was battered and bruised, nose bloodied and long clotted cuts fresh on his neck. Wolfram leaned on his staff, which bent under his weight while Kimiya sat listlessly by. Nima had his right arm in a sling and his face was mottled with bruising.

Standing there mute, Corajidin had only the vaguest memory of his part in the battle. He had no recollection of coming to the Tyr-Jahavān. Kasraman smiled wearily at his father, then turned to those assembled.

"Counsellors of the Teshri. May I present to you Rahn-Erebus fa Basyrandin fa Corajidin, the man whose vision, and trust in our old ways, today saved the lives of thousands in Avānweh. My Father.

"Your next Asrahn, and most deservedly so!"

Their cheers were deafening. Imperialists and Federationists alike showed their respect and Corajidin flushed with pride. Even the old Sky Lord and his grandchildren, the both of them much the worse for wear, rose to their feet in respect.

Kasraman was the first to make the First Obeisance. In ones and twos others followed his son. Then in handfuls, until eventually Corajidin was the only man on his feet. He looked out over the assembled leaders of Shrīan, gaining his first true understanding of what it would be like as Asrahn for the next five years. He felt giddy and there were tingles up and down his spine. He felt taller, stronger, a man of steel only wrapped in the veneer of crude flesh, rather than it being the truth of him.

The change in light drew his attention and Corajidin saw the first crescent of the sun burn over the mountain, a glaring crescent above the hard saw-blade of the mountain shadow. The snows shone preternaturally bright. The morning sun caught in Kasraman's eyes as blinding as a glacier, lit by the fires of his soul, beacons set amidst the cursive patterns writ on his face—

His body spasmed and Corajidin averted his eyes. People looked at him strangely for a moment, including Kasraman, who was just Kasraman. Masking his discomfiture, Corajidin gave a self-deprecating laugh and the panderers joined in.

Corajidin gestured for people to be seated. Once the noise had settled to a low murmur, he looked about the chamber, nodding slowly.

"I see many changed faces here," he said. "Unsurprising, given what we've gone through and survived together. Yes, together. Everybody who remained in Avānweh took part in saving us, whether they were rahn, sayf or mystic, warrior, worrier or writer. Last night, the near razing of Avānweh by . . . as yet unknown assailants, is something we all survived together.

"But credit where credit is due. It was my son and heir, Kasraman, and those brave witches such as Wolfram of Angoth and Kimiya of the Delfineh, Chepherundi op Sanojé, Elonie of Nienna and Ikedion of Corene, and many others, who did what the Sēq would not—no, *could not*—do: stand up for our people. It was my second son, golden Belamandris, who chased dangerous traitors out of Avānweh at grave risk to his own life. It was Narseh and her warriors, Ajomandyan and Neva and Yago and the Sky Knights, my nephew, Nima and the warriors he so ably led, who deserve your praise more than I."

Corajidin paused as their adulation rang out across the high-domed chamber and into the air outside. Let the common people hear them cheer.

"So let me ask you, friends and fellow survivors, are the witches something to be feared, or friends and allies to be respected?"

Shouts of encouragement and thanks clattered from the walls. Corajidin spared a glance for Kasraman and Wolfram, whose lips were curved in proud smiles.

"Then if you agree that these people are worthy of more than your suspicion, let us embrace them and learn from their wisdom from this day forward!"

Corajidin let the people talk. He felt the eddies of discontent and mistrust, though they were soon dried up as the majority grew bigger, until almost all of the counsellors of the Teshri spoke with a common voice and said *yes.*

"Thank you," Corajidin said. "And now, who would like once more to have a Lore Master supporting their Great House, or Family, such as has not been done since the Sēq turned their backs on you so long ago?"

✻ ✻ ✻

"How many?" Corajidin asked later.

"There were forty-three of the hundred sayfs in attendance," Kasraman said. "Thirty nine of them have asked for a witch to join their household as a Lore Master. And Narseh has also requested one."

Corajidin clapped his hands together, entwining the fingers to stop them from shaking. "So many, so soon!"

"There'll be more," Wolfram added.

"If it was not for you two . . . You and yours did a superlative job, but we are not done yet."

"Your orders, Father?"

"I want you and Wolfram to hand select the witches. Kasraman, all the witches will report to you and I want you to ensure they understand their job is much more than being Lore Masters to imbecile sayfs who panicked at the first sign of trouble. Make sure they feed you intelligence on what each sayf—and Narseh—is doing."

"As you will, Father."

Corajidin watched as Kasraman and Wolfram left, the sense of euphoria making him light headed. He clasped his hands behind his back, as much to look stately, as to stop their shaking. The sayfs and their attendants smiled and laughed, drank, and ate. The vaulted chamber with its tall, crystal columns seemed warmer than it had, the colours of the dome mosaic brighter.

Tonight he had used means anathema to his people to win a battle that did not really exist, in a fictional war. And his people loved him for it. The

Ancestors had not boiled shrieking from the Well of Souls to strike him down, nor had the Teshri questioned his methods. They revelled in their good fortune, perhaps happier being ignorant, and not asking the awkward questions Roshana or her Federationists may have posed. No, the people loyal to him outnumbered those who were not, and his finest gift to them was the fiction they now enjoyed. Almost all was as he had hoped it would be, but he would need to remain vigilant until all his plans had returned on their investment.

He had Belamandris.

He had his throne.

Now it was time to speak to the Emissary about his third and final need, and to bring Yashamin out from the shadows.

28

"OUR MEMORIES ARE OFTEN THE SUGAR-COATED SWEETNESS OF A MORE BITTER REALITY."

—Madesashti, the Prime of Amajoram, the Cloud Palace of the House of Pearl in Avānweh (276th Year of the Shrīanese Federation)

DAY 359 OF THE 495TH YEAR OF

THE SHRĪANESE FEDERATION

Indris leaned back in his chair with his eyes closed, trying unsuccessfully to relax and enjoy the sun on his face where it streamed through the high, narrow window. A small alabaster bowl of incense burned in a wall niche, filling the air with the scents of sand and sea. Bowls of fruits, dips, and bread sat half-eaten on the dining table. Blue and yellow lotus flowers floated in a glazed porcelain dish and the *ilhen* lamps sent faint beams of radiance across the obsidian ceiling. Changeling lay across an ornate weapon rack, brooding and silent. She, too, seemed bored.

There were no visitors save the silent Sēq Major who brought his food, water and wine. There was no news, only the building pressure on Indris's senses of something happening about him and to him, rather than *with* him.

He was alerted by the part of his consciousness set aside to feel for the subtle changes in the Restraining Ward pattern, which had kept Indris confined—body and mind—to his sprawling guest chamber ever since Anj's revelations to the Avānweh Suret yesterday. The Sēq Colonels who brought his food and drink would not talk to him and the lack of information about what was happening in the world was making him anxious. With the change in the fabric of the Ward, it was time once more for Indris to climb the ladder of his consciousness, and try to reach out with his psé to see whether Mari and his friends—and the rahns—were safe. As well as to learn anything else he could of Anj, or what was happening in Avānweh.

Physical eyes focussed on the light that reflected from the corner of a crystal prism, Indris made it the centre of his universe. He was ready and waiting in the upper reaches of his mind when the scholars began to relinquish their control of the old Ward, in favour of the new. Using the ahmsah, Indris watched as the new pattern merged with the last, like blending two brightly coloured rugs with different weaves together, the new pattern being set by a different mind with a different life of experiences, observations, and context. Indris's mind tagged along, light as a dust mote, following the mystic fireflies that defined the rules of the new Ward.

The first layer was a fluid circuit of tumbling phosphorescent prisms that flowed across and through walls, floor and ceiling. It was an elegant thing of deceptively straight intersecting bars, a lattice of radiant mystic code that changed direction and speed at intervals. There was little physical danger, though any contact with the chameleon-like traps would result in a shock to his nerves and an alarm being set off, as he learned to his earlier chagrin. He dropped his ahm probe into the flow of the Ward, using his previous twenty or so attempts to quickly locate the vortex of fractals that served as the tumblers in the lock that would let him through to the second layer of the Ward.

The box outside the box was comprised of shining glyphs, which streamed in circles, curves, and lazy spirals, continually expanding and contracting. Characters and symbols tumbled around and through each other, turning from strings of nonsense to lines of text and back again. Learning from his last battering by the second layer of the Ward, Indris paused. Good thing, too—he had mistakenly followed the first strings of text, until he realized he should have been following the keys given in the Pashrean dialect behind it. *There*! A quote by Marak-ban, a Sēq Knight serving the Sussain. *We have only this moment in which to make a difference.*

Indris spoke the words in his mind and flew outwards with a dislocating sense of speed into the third layer of the Ward. This was a maelstrom of abstraction and analogy, images forming from fractals as tiny as the head of a pin, flowing together like storm clouds to be blown away again. Each fractal changed colour and shape, ripples sent out across a mental landscape that was seemingly infinite. But trapped in the confines of a set space, Indris knew this, too, was an illusion. The last time he had focused on scanning the rapidly changing images, too close to see the whole, ended in his failure for the seventh time. This time he overcame his fascination with the minutiae and allowed his ahm-probe to soar away. Between the second and third layers of the Ward, Indris hovered close enough for the second layer to be a dizzying race of illuminated nonsense words. Yet it was here he found the answer he was looking for and saw that what appeared to be thousands of smaller images were nothing but the weft and woof of an integrated whole. It was an image all novice scholars knew from history, The Rise of the Phoenix. In it, Näsarat, the progenitor of his Great House, was being trained by Sedefke at Isenandar. Erebus was there, along with Chepherundi, Bey, Selassin, Sûn and their peers, along with other disciples. But what was the key? Without knowing who had architected the Ward, Indris had no idea what would turn the lock. He watched for what seemed an eternity as the image broke apart, reformed, showed only parts of the whole, fused into a single complete image, then washed away like sea foam only to start again. Taking a gamble he said a single word.

"*Näsé.*" The High Avān word for phoenix.

Mystic pain inducers lashed the parts of his mind that told him to feel pain. And he did. A lot of it. He barely had time to howl a profanity before his ahm-probe disintegrated and he plummeted back into his agonised body. Within moments his door opened and an elderly black-cassocked Master he did not recognise, politely, if sternly, asked he not do that again. Indris lay on the ground, body twitching, and told the Master exactly what he could do with his suggestion.

The sun had crossed the sky and was well into the west when the door to his chamber opened again. Femensetri and He-Who-Watches entered without being bid, and sat themselves down. Femensetri scooped dip on to her fingers, sticking the pasty food in her mouth, before doing it to another bowl. Indris gestured at the food.

"Help yourself, sahai. I'm sure you know where your mouth has been."

"Not kissing the Teshri's—"

"Apologies for our long silence, General Indris." He-Who-Watches was one of the orjini, an ancient tribe of people who dwelled along the Mar Ejir and in the depths of the Näq Yetesh. His skin was like polished mahogany and marked around his temples with orange and yellow dots, his hair a mass of loose curls dark as goat fur, making his colourless eyes more striking. "We've been otherwise engaged and not had the leisure of speaking with you until now."

Indris probed the Restraining Ward and found it still present. He gestured casually at the room around them. "I take it then you've something you want to ask me, that you don't want prying ears to hear or eyes to see?"

He-Who-Watches laughed. It was a deep and musical sound. He turned to Femensetri, teeth a startling white as he smiled. "I see why you like this one. His reputation may prove true, a refreshing surprise after so many flawed heroes. Yes, General—"

"With respect, jhah, I've no right to that title. I'm not in service to the Sēq, as well you know."

"That might need to change, boy," Femensetri said.

"Not bloody likely," Indris countered. "The Sēq have already used all the goodwill I might have had and moved straight into the territory of me really not being interested—with possible prejudice."

"Indris,"—He-Who-Watches continued—"I apologise for what may seem like our rough handling of you. But we were desperate. We still are! So please, is there anything you remember about your time on the Spines? I've wrung the story from Zadjinn as to his attempts on you. But Anj-el-din has made some . . . remarkable claims. We'd have answers."

"What bothers you more," Indris asked quietly, "that the Founder of our arcane science may actually be dead and gone, or that he's not and he just won't talk to you?"

"Watch your mouth, boy," Femensetri warned, her voice hard, flat and edged with the misery she could inflict. "You were sent on a mission—of which I had no knowledge—and you never returned. Anj-el-din, the woman you married against our wishes, followed you and likewise didn't come back. I'm sure you can appreciate why we'd be bloody curious as to directly what, by the Ancestors' ashes, happened."

"I didn't return because somehow I ended up in Manté, in the slave pits of Sorochel, with no memory of how, what, when, or why, where you bloody well left me to rot!"

"It is important we know the truth, Indris," He-Who-Watches said calmly. "We live in perilous times and there are forces moving in the world that we are ill-prepared to face. Yes, the Sēq in Shrīan have grown complacent without a Mahj to serve. We've watched and waited and pondered, yet done little to live up to our promise to our people. We know there are forces at work we've not seen for centuries and more. Fenlings, malegangers, dholes, and worse are rampant not just in the Rōmarq anymore. The Soul Traders are more brazen, buying, selling, and stealing the dead. The Golden Kingdom of Manté digs deeper into things best left alone and the Conflicted Cities are on the verge of falling to the Iron League, Tanis right along with them.

"Knowing whether the Founder is alive, being able to question and learn from the man who penned much of what we've lost over the centuries since his disappearance, would be of great value to us. The Sēq, along with the rest of the world, aren't what they were."

"The Scholar Wars destroyed the Sēq almost as much as it did the witches of Mahsojhin," Indris replied. "So many of you were lost that you don't know who or what you are anymore."

"It wasn't our proudest moment, Indris." Femensetri rose from her chair and stretched, groaning. Indris heard the faint popping noises coming from her joints. The ancient scholar stalked the chamber, scowling. "But we've darker times ahead of us and need to make some drastic decisions if our scholastic traditions are to survive."

Indris sat back in his chair and studied the two jhahs. Both had served the Order for longer than Indris cared to contemplate, Femensetri since the Order was founded almost two millennia ago. She was one of the very few Avāndhin, the Firstborn, who still lived, made on an island far over the Great Salt by the Seethe and their Torque Spindles. He was a nomadic tribesman, at least centuries-old, who had somehow come to have a terrifying power—and grasp of it—despite being born in a desert where no disentropy flowed. Both had done something Indris could not: they had given themselves over completely to the service of something so vast it terrified him. Despite the disappointing hammer blows of the centuries, both had remained steadfast in their belief in something greater than themselves.

In the shallow hours of morning, when sleep would not come and the many sins of his past rose to choke him with their accusations, Indris often had wondered whether it was a deficiency in himself that would not allow such blind faith. Had he ever believed, as the others believe? He did not remember doing so. During his childhood years it had not mattered because he did not understand his indifference. During his teen years and into adulthood, he started to see the way the others looked at him, so secure in his independence and ability.

But he never understood how people could simply rely on the works of one enigmatic man who had simply vanished without a word, as if all he had done and all he was to others, meant less than the time it said to say farewell. It was still one of the questions taught to scholars during their novitiate: *who was Sedefke, where did he come from, and where did he go?*

And the Sēq—Sedefke's greatest students, including many who had sat at the Master's very feet—still saw Sedefke as the greatest Avān who had ever lived. Witch and scholar. Philosopher and inventor. Teacher, poet, and warrior, Sedefke's works were prized above all others and his work was the foundation upon which the Sēq Order had been made. Old shoes following worn paths and wondering why everything was so familiar.

But despite what Femensetri and He-Who-Watches may have hoped, Indris had no answers for them.

"There's nothing, I'm sorry," he told them honestly. In that moment he felt like he was drowning in the mountain-lake depths of He-Who-Watches's eyes. The clarity of them opened and Indris imagined he saw right through, to the incandescent brain beneath, striated and coiled upon itself like some serpent eating its own tail, knowledge consuming while always being consumed. The man's flesh burned away into motes of light, then the skull with it, until all that remained was a burning brain that sent beams of edged light through Indris, pinning him, holding him fast and illuminating all the thoughts and secrets that—

Indris wrestled his gaze away, sweating heavily. He-Who-Watches grunted in surprise. "Well done, young man. There are few who can escape the power of my jhi. There are depths to you that I think even we, who have watched you closely, may be unaware."

"He's full of surprises," Femensetri said dryly. "But then again, he and his classmates were supposed to be that way, remember?"

"The great work?" He-Who-Watches mused. "One is unlikely to forget it was the great failure. Of the Eight, born of carefully nurtured generations, you've lost all but three. And one of them is highly dubious, to say the least."

"So I take it you've spoken with Anj, then?" Indris cursed himself for how quickly he spoke, his discomfort with the turn of the conversation overcoming his control. It was no great surprise who He-Who-Watches was referring to. Of the Eight, there were but three who remained: Indris, Saroyyin—who Femensetri had mentioned once when Indris was healing in Amnon, but never since—and . . . *Anj*. Her name tasted good in his mouth, like a spice he had not savoured in too long. Then visions of Mari rose in his mind, filling him with guilt, and Indris pushed thoughts of both women away. "Is it possible she's lying?"

"If you'll excuse me, Indris," He-Who-Watches said, cleary not willing to enter this discussion. He flicked Femensetri a quick glance. "There are things that need my urgent attention. I'll leave you with your former sahai. It was a pleasure, and thank you for your help at the Mahsojhin. Press-ganged or not, you made a difference and it will not be forgotten."

Femensetri waited for the other scholar to leave before she sat and faced Indris. Her expression grave.

"Tell me the truth, boy. Have you been in contact with Anj since she vanished?"

"No! Why?" *Best Femensetri never learn the truth of how Anj helped me escape. I may need Anj again if this goes badly.*

"The Council is having trouble believing it, but I've convinced them you'd naught to do with her. There's something *wrong* about her," Femensetri muttered. "Something dark and cold and malign, which wasn't there before. We know she's hiding something, but we don't know what. He-Who-Watches couldn't sense any falsehood in her, but there are powers in the world older and more cunning than—"

"You think Anj is a servant of the Drear?" Indris said the words before he thought about them, and regretted them instantly. It was not the kind of thing one asked about anybody, for fear of an answer you did not want to hear. "Can you prove it, though?"

"Yes. And no." Femensetri pincered a slice of blood orange between thumb and forefinger and ate it quietly, staining her teeth and lips red. She spat a seed into the corner of the room, where Indris heard it bounce before it was finally still. His former teacher started shovelling food in to her mouth. Realising he had all the answer he was going to get, Indris asked the other questions that weighed on his mind.

"What happened with the rahns? And my friends?"

"No idea," Femensetri said around a mouthful of food. She swallowed loudly. "I know Maselane led a large force out of Avānweh. There were reports of the *Wanderer* heading south. I assumed it was your friends."

"With the rahns."

"What? Why didn't you tell me?"

"I tried to! But as usual, you had your own interests on your mind."

"You should've told me earlier what you had planned. If anything happens to them because of this, it'll be a bloody disaster!"

"If you'd not snatched me away for tea and cake with the witches, then locked me here for a day without any contact, then maybe I bloody well could've told you. Better yet, if you'd left me alone, I could've done what I planned and gotten the rahns to safety. Sweet Näsarat, I wish some of you would own up and take some accountability for something, rather than dumping your woes and mistakes at my—"

"Watch it!"

"Face it. You locked me down and shut me down. For the second time in a few days, first Zadjinn, then the Suret. I take it from your outrage—which you should aim at yourself, rather than me—there's been no sign of the Federationist rahns?"

"No. Neva and Yago remained in the city, helping defend the people along with Corajidin, Narseh, and the sayfs. I thought the Federationists had gone into hiding, which would've been no bad thing."

"You say Corajidin defended the people? That's out of character."

"He used the attack on the city to have his witches get rid of the daemon elementals. Of course he's blamed the attacks on the Humans. From what I hear, that dusky little bitch Sanojé talked like Corajidin's trained parrot to the Teshri, revealing what she knew of the Golden Kingdom of Manté, the Humans, and their doings. So while we were trying to stop the madness at Mahsojhin, Corajidin was out playing warrior-rahn with his new witchy friends. And doing a fine job." Her tone was especially bitter, her look melancholy.

"What happened?" *Is this another question I don't want an answer to?*

"Corajidin not only convinced the Teshri to repeal the law against witches, he's also petitioned the Teshri to remove the caste-freedoms associated with the Sēq. We'll no longer be of a higher caste than the Asrahn, rahns, or sayfs. We'll serve the petty whims of weak, self-serving leaders, or leave Shrīan. Corajidin will have no power above him. He's already offering witches as advocates and advisors to the rahns and sayfs."

Indris's chest tightened. His mouth was dry and his throat felt tight. The roots, trunk, and branches of the Possibility Tree lit in his mind. Witches and scholars without a true sense of community, beholden to the whims of different leaders. Each rahn or sayf would use—or abuse—their newfound power for their own ends. It would not start so, but over time the temptation would grow too strong, and as soon as one leader misused the power granted them, then others would soon follow. A nation of leaders with the power in their hands to destroy the nation, led by a man who heard only the echoes of empire. Unless . . . and another Possibility Tree superimposed itself over the other, this time showing a more frightening and likely story.

"Corajidin isn't a fool," Indris said. "He'll control them all, though the rahns and sayfs won't know it. The illusion of freedom, while every mystic will be an extension of his will."

"A Mahj-by-proxy," Femensetri nodded. "The vote hasn't been taken, but with Rosha, Nazarafine, and Siamak out of the way, we've little doubt of the outcome. So we're preparing for the worst."

"We know it wasn't the Humans who released the daemon elementals in Avānweh," Indris said. Femensetri looked at him, then her eyes widened. Indris nodded as she followed the breadcrumbs to the answer.

"Nix of the Maladhi, that odious little turd." She pursed her lips as she drummed jagged, dirty fingernails on the black and white marble table. "We can use this, if we can get proof. It should give the sayfs pause."

"I'd send some veteran Sēq to the Maladhi-sûk," Indris suggested. He saw the question in Femensetri's eyes. "No, not me. If there's going to be evidence anywhere—other than what I've seen with my own eyes, which is far from incriminating—it'll be there. But you need to let me go so I can find out what happened to my friends."

"We'll find out what we can and let you know. Until then, you'll remain our guest."

"You mean your prisoner. And no, I won't."

Femensetri looked surprised at the surety in his voice. "Do you really think you can escape here? The Suret are quite comfortable with you back in custody."

"All this, because you think I've spoken with the Founder? Anj could be lying."

"That, and other things. No doubt she is lying about a lot of things, and we'll learn the truth in time. But if she's telling the truth, she presents opportunities that require examination." Femensetri spat on the floor, scratching her belly through her cassock. "Nobody has spoken with Sedefke for almost six hundred years. We thought—I thought—he died during the Insurrection! He was my sahai, Indris. Kemenchromis and I . . . we . . . sweet Ancestors on a stick, he was like a father to us. And you may have all the answers trapped in that head of yours. So no, Indris, you're not going anywhere."

"Do you really think you can hold me?" Indris took in the room with a gesture.

"Yes."

"Do you want that much blood on your hands?" Indris's voice was low and hard. He felt the iron in his expression. Changeling growled from where she laid, a serpentine shadow, menacing even at rest. "I am what you made me, Femensetri. And you've been warned what will happen."

"If you defy us, you'll regret it."

"More than I already do? Hard to imagine." His laugh was dark and hollow. "You need me alive if you're going to get the answers you want. If you hurt anybody I know, or put them in danger, you'll get nothing from me other than my gift to you of wondering, until the mountains are nothing but sand on a beach, what secrets I may have had."

Femensetri was silent as she walked to the door. She opened it and stood there, looking out into the bustling corridor. Indris caught sight of the four Sēq Captains guarding his door, all armed and armoured. Without turning she said, "I advise you to caution, Indris. By nightfall you'll be in Amarqa-in-the-Snows. You'd best be prepared to give the Suret, and the Inquisition, the answers they're after."

"And what about the answers I'm after?"

"Do you think there's any other place else you'll get them, boy?"

❈ ❈ ❈

Femensetri was with the two Inquisitors, a full squad of hard-bitten Sēq Knights and jhah-Aumh when they came for him. The tiny Y'arrow woman seemed almost embarrassed by the proceeding, the butterflies in her hair fanning their wings rapidly.

"You're resolved to do this, then?" Indris asked. He watched sourly as one of the knights packed Indris's satchel, storm-pistol, and dragon-tooth knife into a chest. Changeling growled as she was handled gingerly, like an adder, and put into an ornate case of jade-patterned *kirion*. "My personal freedoms, your promise of release from service to the Sēq— your word of honour!—mean nothing to you?"

"All things change. It is a constant in the world." Femensetri rested a hand on the cool obsidian-sheathed wall. She was sober for a moment, tinged with sadness, though it lasted only a moment. "Corajidin has made it clear we serve, or we leave. We, who have defended our people with our lives, have dedicated the long span of our existence to studying the past, serving the present and preparing for the future, have walked paths which would shred the minds of the people we protect, are to be discarded because we're inconvenient. So our answer was clear and uncompromising. Amer-Mahjin is a place. There are other places. Your freedom, or the illusion of it, is just as transitory. Remember what I told you. The Sēq love in the abstract, and the absolute. Subjective bonds have no hold, so we don't fall prey to attachment to places, or things."

"Or people." Indris did not care how bitter he sounded.

"Mostly, no," Femensetri nodded. "But rest assured we'll leave nothing behind that our enemies could use against us. We may need to come back here one day."

"Do we need to restrain you, General Indris, or will you come willingly?" Aumh asked gently. "There is no need for this to be more unpleasant than it already is."

"We wouldn't want that now, would we?"

Aumh gestured for Indris to follow as she left the room, Femensetri by her side. The knights took station, two in front of Indris and two behind. The Inquisitors trailed behind, hands on their dauls.

The corridors of Amer-Mahjin teemed with scholars. Cases, trunks, chests, and bags were being carted along. Indris watched as works of art were taken down from the obsidian-sheathed walls, books were catalogued and boxed, ornaments and other treasures carefully packed. Even *ilhen* crystals were removed from their mountings.

Indris felt the pinpoint flares as layers of different Wards were tapped into natural currents of disentropy, powering them forever. There was a static buildup on his skin and when he looked, his own Disentropic Stain looked so compressed to be little more than a tight, wavering blur of darkness around his body. There were so many defences being invoked, Indris felt the weight of them on his body, mind, and soul. Femensetri saw his look.

"We're setting layer upon layer of Wards"—she said—"from the heart of the mountain outward, until everything in Amer-Mahjin will be held inviolate for so long as Ïajen-mar stands. Only a small number of us can come and go. Anybody else who tries won't have the chance to regret it . . . their minds will be caught within so many illusion loops, they'll never understand they've failed."

"The *Elhas Shion* and the Water of Life?"

"The heart of the mountain will be sealed off. As for the Water of Life, we can't stop Ïa from being what it is, nor would we," she said. "But we can make it so as nobody ever tastes of the Water of Life again, until we say otherwise."

There was another question he wanted to ask. He was sure Femensetri could see it in him as he paused by the door, mouth open, breath held for longer than was necessary without purpose.

"Forget her, Indris. She's not the woman you loved and she's not the woman we knew."

"What will you do with her?"

"What I'm told," Femensetri spat on the ground, wiping her mouth with the sleeve of her cassock. "She gets to go free. At least for now. We don't know enough about why she's returned, and don't want to alarm whomever sent her. No doubt they'll suspect we're watching. But if she's out in the world we can learn more about who she's working with, and why. With you in our custody, I've little doubt she'll wander far."

They led Indris away from the docks, deeper into the mountain. He frowned, trepidation rising. They went down dimly lit, sweeping flights of stairs carved into natural fissures in the rock so deep Indris could not see the bottom. There was a vibration through his boots and the distant rumble of water, even as the air became heavy with damp. Other scholars passed them, as purposeful as ants, carrying burdens of various shapes and sizes.

When they reached the vaulted chamber at the foot of the stairs, Indris was escorted through a jagged cave entrance. A deep, wet grinding sound made conversation impossible. Flurries of water swirled in the air, lit to tiny rainbows by jagged petals of *ilhen* that grew from the rough stone walls. At the far end of the large cave, already half filled by scholars and cargo, was a carved arch leading to a short corridor. The far wall of the corridor was moving, sluiced with water that sprayed everything nearby.

The Pivot was a massive, threaded tower built in the depths of the mountain and cushioned by water. It held the Sēq's greatest treasures, and could only be accessed at certain times every hour—when the doors in the Pivot aligned with two walkways from the rest of Amer-Mahjin. Only a few amongst the Suret had the combination to disable the arcane locks and allow access. Nestled at the centre of the Pivot were the great vaults, and a series of ancient Weavegates.

Indris took a nervous breath at the thought of travelling by Weavegate. The Weaveway made by the Time Masters was a treacherous road to take when one was being subtle and travelling alone. But to travel en masse, with scholars as powerful as some of the Masters were, would most certainly draw the attention of some of the creatures that lurked in the Drear. Indris looked at Femensetri, who simply shrugged and turned away.

Soon after, the sliding wall at the far end of the corridor became an open space. Indris was hurried forward, and the Sēq formed a dense line behind him as they moved double-time through the falling curtain of cold water and into the Pivot itself. There was a moment to adjust to the speed of the moving floor, then Indris was ushered down more stairs and into a cylindrical room with five galleries, each gallery featuring dozens of gazebos with verdigris and rust stained domes, held aloft by lace-patterned diorite columns.

Auhm muttered a few words and the columns and dome of the nearest gazebo rippled with green hued light. The texture of the space inside the gazebo changed, edges softening, curves deepening and flat planes stretching away into forever in every direction. Aumn walked through first, her butterflies fleeing her hair, with the two Inquisitors in tow.

Femensetri gestured for Indris to follow.

"And what about the answers I'm after?" he had asked. He remembered her answer. *"Do you think there's any other place else you'll get them, boy?"*

Calming his mind, he stepped into the Weavegate.

29

"FREEDOM CAN SOMETIMES BE AS MUCH A CAGE AS CAPTIVITY."

—From *The Common Illusion*, seventh volume of the Zienni Doctrines

DAY 359 OF THE 495TH YEAR OF

THE SHRĪANESE FEDERATION

Mari was blinded by latticed sunlight.

She groaned. Pain bludgeoned her as she tried to roll over. She could not move her hands. Through one slitted eye—she could not open the other—she saw the ropes tied around her wrists and trailing off the edge of the bed. Her skin felt gritty. Throat swollen and mouth dry, Mari inhaled the old lavender-and-salt smell from the sheets on which she lay, and let herself be lulled back to sleep, away from agony, by the swinging of the bed and the sizzle of the Tempest Wheels.

❈ ❈ ❈

Hands jerked her awake, forcing water down her throat.

Mari looked up to see a man whose face had been weathered to old shoe leather, eyes set amidst deep creases from staring out across sun-dappled seas for too long. His breath reeked of decaying teeth and cheap tobacco. His skin of sweat and brine.

His hands wandered across her torso even as he poured water over her mouth, then her throat and across her chest. His eyes became fixed and staring. The tip of his tongue lingered on a browned tooth. He looked to the door furtively—

Mari swung her legs up and wrapped them around his throat. A twist of her thighs and his neck snapped.

She was using her teeth to undo the knotted ropes around her wrists when another corsair came into the room and beat her back into unconsciousness.

❋ ❋ ❋

The next man who came to feed her and bring her water seemed nice enough. A young man, he neither spoke nor leered nor tried to fondle her. Yet she remembered him as one who had helped bring Omen down.

As the young man turned away, the sunlight flared from the pearl that hung from his ear and the beads in the tousled mass of his hair. The bright glare of lighted squares that was her window plunged the remainder of the room into shadow, save for where long streaks of white painted the enamelled wooden beams of the ceiling. He would be almost as blind as she, oblivious of everything outside the glare.

Mari flexed her abdomen at the same time as she curled her legs. She made it to her knees and got her tied hands over his head and down to his neck.

He struggled . . . for a while. Eventually his breathing stopped, as did his spasming muscles. She kicked him away as he soiled himself.

She did not struggle as the guards who arrived shortly afterwards beat her down once more, only this time she just pretended to pass out, waiting for them to leave.

Now she had hours before she would be interrupted again, and went back to freeing herself from her bonds.

❋ ❋ ❋

Mari's hearing turned suddenly flat and she vomited bile. There was a sense of dislocation. Hard angles turned to soft curves and the planes of the walls, floor and ceiling seemed to stretch forever in every direction. The light in the window flickered blue green, as if she were underwater, and there came a dreadful shrieking sound that grated on her nerves. She clutched both hands to her ears but the sound was inside her head and there was no way she could drown it out no matter how loud she screamed. Maybe if she stuck a needle in her ears she could make it all stop but—

The world snapped back into place abruptly, leaving her reeling. She dragged herself wretchedly from the floor, wiping the sputum from her slack, sore lips. She gasped for air, breath steaming, noting how cold it had suddenly become. The angle of the light from the window had shifted along the wall, as if the wind-corsair had turned. Had she passed out? Had she missed her chance to escape?

She wrapped her arms around herself and rubbed her torso. The thin tunic and trousers she wore were little protection against the cold. With chilled fingers she grabbed the sheet and wrapped it around herself to keep warm.

Mari tried the door. It was locked. She searched the cabin, trying to find something to use as a weapon. The cabin had been stripped of anything useful—even the metal brackets for the lanterns had been taken away, the wood pale in their absence. Needing a weapon, Mari tore a strip from the sheet, twisting and knotting it into a makeshift whip and garrote.

Hidden in the shadows, allowing the glare to be her ally, Mari looped the knotted sheet around the female corsair's neck as she entered the cabin. Turning, Mari and the other woman were back to back. With a sharp jerk of her arms and shoulders, Mari broke the woman's neck. Carefully, quietly, she dragged the corsair to the bed and laid her on it. It was the work of moments to take the dead woman's loose hooded over-robe and taloub, which she wrapped around her lower face. Mari swore quietly and thoroughly when there were no weapons to be found. So she worked the buckles off the woman's boots, trousers, and over-robe, threading them on the end of her improvised weapon. It was not perfect, but was better than nothing. She covered the dead woman with the sheet and wolfed down some food before she left the cabin, locking it behind her.

Conversation and laughter drifted along the corridor. There were a number of doors to the left and right, stairs both up and down. The wind moaned through the cracks in the door at the top of the stairs. Mari went up the stairs two at a time, coming out into the harsh glare of a cloudless sky so pale it was almost white. A freezing wind scoured the deck and the few crewmen present were stamping their feet against the cold. As casually as she could, Mari went to the rail to see if she could get her bearings.

There was the vista of white-capped ocean, waters darker than wine, far below but drawing closer. Jagged islands reared their hoary backs out of the sea, stretching south towards mist-shrouded isles. With a lump in her throat she recognised those islands: Kaasgard. The land of savage barbarians, rhyme-bearded giants and monsters that should only exist in books and fables.

Which meant the islands directly below were somewhere much worse, with horrors of a different kind. She had not been here since she was a child, though still held the awful memories of a cruel and domineering grandam, long dark halls slick with hoarfrost, and the painful recollection of bloody family feuds that seemed seeped into every stone, joint, and crevice of Tamerlan—the place where the children of Erebus went until they could once more be of use to their Great House.

Had she been a prisoner for days? How had they managed to cross most of Shrīan so quickly? Mari started to hyperventilate. Better to be sent to Maladûr gaol, or Exiled from Shrīan, than to spend even a single night in the Ancestors-forsaken fortress of Tamerlan, with its black stone walls and towers that reared from steep mountains like broken old teeth. She controlled her breathing, forcing herself to think. To re-evaluate her means of escape and how far she would need to travel to find allies.

"Mari," Nadir said from behind her. "If you behave, you'll not be harmed. Much."

She turned from the rail to see Nadir and Jhem standing there, as well as a tall, plain woman in a baroque red over-robe standing beside them amongst a handful of raggedy corsairs. Jhem's throat was badly bruised, as was Nadir's face. Mari unwound the taloub from her face.

"Surprised at our destination?" Nadir said. He made a small gesture to the woman in red. "Witches. Awfully useful for so many things, if you take the leash off. Turned almost a week of travel into hours."

"Where is Belam?" she asked, surprised at a calm in her voice she did not feel. "I need to speak with him. Now."

"The time for you giving orders is past, girl." Jhem lisped. "The Widow-maker is with your father in Avānweh, preparing for the coronation. You're far away and near forgotten, trusted to my and Nadir's tender mercies."

Mari swung her improvised weapon in a slow circle, allowing her ankles, knees, thighs and hips to absorb the swaying of the wind-corsair. She scanned the deck and saw none of the Anlūki, only common reavers who would not be difficult to best.

Nadir laughed. "What? Do you seriously think you can escape from this? Enjoy being the guest of your beloved grandam, Khurshad. I'm sure it'll be a touching reunion."

Mari tried not to think of the malignant old crone, Khurshad, who sat in her nest of misery, pain, and secrets. *No! I'll be good! The whistle of the rod as it tore into her flesh. The claustrophobic box of a room with its miserable bed and tiny, mean fireplace. The too small, too dark, too cold cell she had been locked in, for not eating her food, or eating too much, or wanting to be other than what her House had decreed for her*— Khurshad barely knew the meaning of restraint. Mari had been unable to walk for almost two days after having the soles of her feet caned for not making obeisance rapidly enough. The Dowager-rahn had a reputation for the darkness of her entertainments. Mari would kill everybody in Tamerlan if it meant escaping Khurshad's idea of instruction.

"Good luck making that happen," Mari growled, spinning her weapon till it hummed in the cold air. "All I see are two failed upper-caste criminals, a pasty bitch in a tacky red robe and a handful of mangy bottom feeders. Hardly what I'd call impossible odds. I could win this fight in my sleep. I'll be off this crate and on the way home before you have the time to pick your teeth up off the deck."

"And what about Vahineh, who you went to such lengths to protect?" Nadir clapped his hands. The forecastle door opened and a bedraggled, whimpering Vahineh was rudely pushed on to the deck by a gaunt, scabrous man in a hooded scarlet robe, stained around the hems with filth. His skeletal hand was fixed like a vulture's claw on Vahineh's shoulder. "Would you abandon this poor little waif, after so much effort?"

"Vahineh!" Mari cried in shock. *I thought Father would keep her close and make an end of it. But no. If Father has sent us to Tamerlan, he means for his punishment to be lingering.* "If you harm her—"

"Vahineh is of use to us yet. As are you," Jhem whispered in his ruined voice. He looked at Mari with his ophidian eyes and she stared back, until she felt tendrils creeping through her brain, the suggestion to put down her weapon, to give herself over, to forget herself and live only to please—

"No!" Mari shook her head vehemently as she launched herself from the rail. She swung her weapon, knotted with metal buckles, and struck Jhem in the mouth. There was a spray of blood and teeth as she sidestepped towards the corsairs. Even as Jhem fell, choking on blood and pain, Mari caught sight of the knives that flicked into his hands.

The nearest corsair stood, gaping. Mari slammed the heel of her hand into his face, gripping the hilt of the corsair's shamshir with her other hand. As the man fell, the weapon unsheathed itself. She turned, blade whistling, to the sound of a voice cracking across the deck.

"Stop!" Nadir took a couple of steps forward, hands far away from the twin knives thrust through the sash at his waist. He gripped his father's arm, Jhem's breath bubbling blood through the ruin of his mouth. "Mari, just stop. There's nowhere for you to go. Why do you think we brought you here? There's no escape. There's no rescue. Nobody other than your father and us even know you're here."

She gestured to the rail with her chin. "I could jump and kill myself."

"Yes," Nadir smiled, "but you won't. You'd rather kill a thousand people, with the slimmest chance you'd survive, than face the surety of taking your own life. I know you, Mari."

"You *knew* me, Nadir."

"Drop the weapon, Mari. Or it's Vahineh we hurt, not you. How much pain do you think she can stand? She's already been through so much . . . "

"Kill her and she'll just Awaken somebody else. Go ahead! You'd be doing her a favour." Mari realized as she said the words that she actually meant them—Vahineh would be better off dead and free of the Awakening that had nearly killed her. But was she still even Awakened? Indris had never said whether his Severance had been successful. Could Jhem still compel Vahineh to Awaken who her father chose? The possibility made her feel sick.

"Drop the weapons, Mari." Nadir moved closer. Other corsairs were moving to surround her. Faced with little choice, Mari opened her fist and let the sword clatter to the deck. Her improvised weapon joined it. "Good choice. Bind her tightly!"

The corsairs dragged her arms behind her back and tied her securely, hobbling her ankles and tying everything to a makeshift noose that would choke her if she tried to move her arms too far. They were not taking any chances.

Jhem and Nadir watched the proceedings calmly. As three of the corsairs escorted her past, her steps short because of the ropes, Nadir leaned in close.

"And don't think I've forgotten it was you who killed my sister," Nadir hissed in her ear. He took her arm, digging his thumb into her already bruised flesh. "You broke my heart, shamed yourself with the Näsarat, and then spurned me. We've much to talk about."

Mari spat in his eye. He punched her in the mouth, knocking her to her knees. Mari felt the blood trickle down her chin, but she looked up at Nadir with what she hoped was a ghastly smile, bloodied and broken. Nadir wiped the spittle off. When he spoke his voice was as cold and soft as the wind.

"Get used to it, Mari. You've much to atone for, and I'm sure Khurshad won't tell anybody if I play with you a little."

"You're dead men" Mari promised.

They dragged her away, her arms burning with the pain.

Rather than a cabin, they locked her in a narrow cupboard that was too small, too cold, and too dark. But she was not a little girl anymore.

30

"I AM, I DO, AND MAKE NEITHER APOLOGY NOR COMPROMISE, FOR I AM
THE EMPEROR OF THE KNOWN WORLD AND NONE STAND ABOVE ME."

—Vane-ro-men of the Men-da Troupe, last of the Petal Emperors (2235th
Year of the Petal Empire)

DAY 360 OF THE 495TH YEAR OF

THE SHRĪANESE FEDERATION

Corajidin looked at himself in the mirror. The lines around his eyes
made him look tired, where Vashne had seemed both intelligent and wise.
The grey in his hair made him look old, where on Ariskander it had looked
distinguished and noble. The layers of his clothing, in ruby and gold stitched
red and black damask, made him look haughty, where his father had looked
a ruler of the world.

The time had almost come for him to take that for which he had fought,
lied, and murdered. But the prospect of how much he still had to do, to guide
his nation to where he needed it to be, seemed such a long and perilous road.
More so than the one he had followed to get here.

He was reminded of the vision he had been granted in Wolfram's quarters, where the ancient spirit trapped in a mystic carpet had said, *You will know power, though for the children there will be naught . . .*

Corajidin stole a glance at Kasraman, who was joking with Belamandris while Wolfram smiled his secretive smile behind his jagged beard. Despite his success, doubt weighed on him like a rusted old anchor being dragged through the mud. Was this a mistake? Was he doomed to fail and be toppled by another, just as he had toppled those who came before him?

"You're better than all of them, Jidi," Yashamin's voice hummed across his soul.

"I do this for us, my love," Corajidin said.

"Father?" Belamandris asked, puzzlement on his face. His golden son leaned elegantly against the wall, the darker Kasraman seeming somehow cruder by comparison, as if the light loved and lingered on the younger, while merely touching the elder, of his sons.

"The light shines on them the same as your love does," Yashamin murmured from nowhere and everywhere. *"I loved the way it shone on me."*

"We've not much time, Father," Kasraman said urgently, "if we're to meet the Emissary at the sycamore grove before the Coronation."

"Yes . . . the Coronation," Corajidin drew the words out. The past two days had been chaotic with rumours of secret meetings of political cabals. Ajomandyan had been evasive, the Arbiter of the Change giving only the most perfunctory of attention to what should have been the most splendid day of the past five years. "Did she explain to you where she was, when we needed her most?"

"She was at the Mahsojhin, Father," Kasraman assured. "Some of the details she provided, when I questioned her about it, were too accurate for her not to have been there. The Emissary was true to your cause. She freed the witches—"

"Not all of them," Wolfram said tiredly, still recovering from the energies he had used in binding the daemon elementals. Kimiya had fared worse, barely able to rise from her bed until an hour ago. She curled at Wolfram's feet, wan, with circles under her eyes vivid as bruises. "There are still hundreds trapped, and after the fight with the Sēq we don't have the energy to open another rift. And the Sēq took the Emphis Mechanism, too."

"Then we'll work with what we have." Kasraman rested his hand on Wolfram's shoulder in a way he had never done with his father. Corajidin scowled at the intimacy of the gesture, then let his pique go when he looked at Belamandris, thankful his golden son was with him.

But it was Belamandris who frowned, clearly considering his words before he spoke.

"Father, are you sure this is the . . . right, thing to do?" Belamandris sounded hesitant, frightened, and apprehensive. Kasraman and Wolfram remained silent, watching. "Our people vilified the Empress-in-Shadows for interfering with the hallowed dead, and you're going to do the same. Please, take the time to think about this! The truth is—"

"Truth and fact. Justice and law. Morals and ethics. One is subjective and the other objective. Our behaviour is driven by society, upbringing and history. But what of our nature, as opposed to nurture? There have been many truths tested of late, my son. Perhaps others should also be challenged?

"Besides, a great leader sets the tone others would follow."

"But to start your reign as Asrahn with this . . ." Belamandris shook his head.

"You would deny Father this?" Kasraman folded his arms across his chest as he looked down at his half-brother. Corajidin was surprised and touched by Kasraman's support. "Belam, she was taken away from Father before her time. And given what we've experienced of late, the alliances we've made and the help we've received, perhaps we need to rethink our notions?"

"This is an abomination!" Belamandris's voice sounded strangled. "Our revered dead dwell in the love of those who have gone before, content in the Well of Souls. It's always been this way! Father, please, let her go and don't become that which you've always held in contempt."

"I wouldn't expect you to understand," Kasraman said. "How could you?"

"Understand?" Belamandris glared at Kasraman. When he spoke his voice was very soft. "I understand full well what it's like to be wrenched away from the peace of my Ancestors, brother. Not so long ago, I lingered on the lip of the Well and, truth be told, would've been content to fall in. But I was brought back, whether I would or not. Now, you are going to wrench her away from somewhere she is no doubt happy, and safe. Please. Leave her be."

Corajidin came forward and embraced his son, holding him close.

"Enough of such talk!" Corajidin said gently. "We are a family and it was the power of our love for you that kept you tied to the land of the living. You must have wanted to live, too, or else I would have lost you. The times are changing. If we are to set an example, we need to change with them."

"But is it the right example you're setting?"

Corajidin steepled his fingers, looking across the peaks of his fingertips at his sons. "Belamandris, I do what I do because I think it's time we challenged some of that which has gone on faith. Take for example our blind acceptance of Sēq superiority? Did we not disprove that myth? As for the hallowed dead? It seems to me, my sons, that they are no more, or no less, kind or malevolent than any living person.

"So *is* this the right example?"—Corajidin smiled, though it did not feel like it had the enthusiasm, or belief, that such a momentous event deserved— "I think so. I *hope* so."

"Then is your doubt not enough?" Belamandris asked quietly, his gaze searching. "Father, so much has happened to our nation. To our people. Perhaps a little more caution, a little more reserve, may not go astray?"

"Leave him be, Belam!" Kasraman's voice was stern, but not unkind. "We've neither experienced the loss, nor the challenges, that Father has. Let him have this, and trust in he who has guided us this far."

Corajidin took both his sons in an embrace, and held them close. He kissed them both on the cheek, fuelled for the first time by pride in them both.

"Forget your quarrel and remember you are brothers. Now, escort me to the sycamore grove of the Mahsojin so the Emissary can do what needs to be done."

❋ ❋ ❋

"Father,"—Belamandris gripped Corajidin's arm in a painful grip— "don't." Clearly he had not been swayed by Corajidin's words earlier. "This can't be what you want for the future. Or for her."

"*Tell them Jidi!*" Yashamin urged. "*When the Emissary asked, you said you wanted it all. I was so proud of you. Now you can have it. The world is ours, my heart of hearts. I would feel again.*"

"It is," Corajidin said, hoping his voice didn't betray his apprehension.

"Then let's begin," the Emissary said in her rusted croak. Hood thrown back, her once austere beauty pallid and cold, marred by blackened veins across her skin. Her mindstone was dull, a flat thumbprint the colour of moss on her brow. She waved and three tiny figures began leading a taller fourth, her body barely concealed by her light robe of burgundy gossamer, sparkling with blood stones.

Corajidin leaned back in his weathered camp throne, trepidation weighing his limbs. They were on a hill overlooking the Mahsojhin. Giant sycamores clattered and creaked, crotchety old men complaining of age. Beams of almost coherent light made pillars under the canopy, igniting pollen and spiralling leaves as they fell. It made ever-changing patterns on the mulchy ground. The swollen, humid air sheathed him in sweat. The odour of rot was almost overwhelming.

On the truncated cliff below, the Mahsojhin seemed more forlorn than it had been. Some of the buildings that had survived the centuries had been flattened by the Sēq. Red-robed bodies lay fallen like autumn leaves between stiff fronds of yellowed grass. Small clouds of flies swarmed, their buzzing a distant, somnolent drone. Where the three crones walked, the flies fell from the air to land still, like so many pieces of gravel.

The creaking of callipers became louder than the creaking of branches. The faint scent of musk, iron, and leather. Corajidin watched tall Wolfram emerge from the shadows, as he so often seemed to do. He bowed his head, causing his matted fringe to sway. His old stave, which had seen much better days, groaned and bent under his weight.

"Was it not the Imrean philosopher, Atticus Sorigo, who wrote, *Tell a lie large enough and all the world will believe?*" the witch asked musingly. "And you've made the lie large indeed, Asrahn."

"And told the world." A thrill went through Corajidin at the name. *Asrahn.* "But for how long will they believe, Wolfram? How long before the jackals start to pick apart the body and find the taste of the lies not to their liking?"

Wolfram stared down through his brindle fringe, eyes burning a fierce yellowed hazel. The witch smiled, a tear in the iron-grey matt of his beard. His teeth and lips were moist with spittle. "Once you've a crown on your head, what does the warhorse need to fear of carrion dogs?"

"Were it only so simple," he murmured, transfixed as the three tiny crones shuffled past, eyes stitched closed, twisted nails clicking together like insect mandibles. A fine yellow dust clouded their skin and swirled in the air around them. Through the translucent robe and hood, the woman they led was a work of art, a burnished treasure that made Corajidin's hearts pound.

The Emissary stood before Corajidin. "You understand the consequences of what you're about to do?"

"Who is she?" he asked, staring at the woman.

"Until this moment, nobody of consequence." She snapped her fingers, bringing him back to attention. "Corajidin, you must answer me. Do you understand the consequences?"Corajidin swallowed and nodded.

"No! Aloud, so Ïa and the powers I serve can bear witness."

"Yes," he whispered. At the disdainful turn of her lip he said more loudly, "Yes! I understand the consequences of what I'm about to do."

"You're asking ancient powers for their help," Wolfram reminded. "You've asked of them before. But they get . . . hungrier, more demanding, each time. You must sacrifice this time."

"Can not another . . ." Corajidin's skin crawled at the thought of what he would endure, a litany of horrors in the absence of fact.

The Emissary's laugh sounded like rusty nails being rattled in a jar. "It's the webs of your own life you want changed. Scataqra, the Weaver of Fates, demands something from you—not another. If you're unwilling—"

"Erebus curse you!" Corajidin spat. *Scataqra*. The name chilled him . . . but he was too close. "I'll do what you want."

"Of course you will." Her voice was flat. "It's always been thus. You just needed to admit it."

The Emissary walked into the shadows of the sycamores, Corajidin, his sons, and Wolfram following. With each step, Corajidin found it harder and harder to breathe, as if the ancient boles of the sycamores were stealing the air from his lungs. He looked upward, his eyes dazzled by the glitter of a too-bright sun in a too-distant sky, where it poked its face from behind waving leaf shadows.

The Emissary wove this way and that between the dark trunks. Figs, fallen from the trees like dull orange jewels, had gone rotten in the light-starved grasses and leaf mulch. Soon, the sunlight world beyond the trees was a memory. Replaced by something older. Something darker, unrepentant, and glowering.

Without a word, the Emissary stopped. Before them was a tree whose trunk was psoriatic, discoloured with dried gold sap turned red as rust. The lower branches looked frail, their creaking little more than the whispers of a dying matriarch too long in her bed. Spiderwebs hung like gauze curtains, their silk desiccated, dotted with the remains of generations of previous inhabitants and the cracked ivory of bleached egg sacs.

Wolfram poked at the dry earth with the jagged butt of his staff. The soil lifted in pathetic, listless clouds before falling back to the ground. He kept digging at the earth until he had hollowed out a deep bowl in the dirt.

"Kneel here, Asrahn," Wolfram said, pointing at the ground in front of the hole he had dug. Corajidin felt a protest rise to his lips, yet there was something in the witch's tone that accepted neither argument, nor excuse. Sharp twigs and pieces of stone dug into his knees as he lowered himself to the ground.

A knife was dropped on the ground in front of him. A long silver blade curved nearly to the point of being a sickle. It had an ivory hilt carved with leaves and flowers, stained black. Wolfram knelt beside him. He hissed with pain as he forced his ruined legs to bend in the confines of the callipers, but there was no hesitation in his movements. Reaching into a robe, which had seen better times, the witch removed a small crystal vial of the Emissary's potion. He unstoppered the vial and held it out to Corajidin, who took it with a strong hand. Now that he had embarked on this course of action, Corajidin would not be unmanned.

The crones guided the unknown woman to her knees. She swayed, her expression dreamy, the veil over her face billowing gently with her breath.

"What you ask for is not unnatural, though your people believe otherwise," the Emissary said, crouching in the dirt beside Corajidin. Belamandris swore, kicking a small cloud of mulch into the air. The Emissary looked up at the changing patterns of the leaves, head cocked to one side, as if listening to something only she could hear. "The web that is woven links every soul, every mind, and every dream. All things are connected, then, now, and forever. The vessels we inhabit are crude things, easily broken. Why not as easily replaced? If the Weaver and her children do not discriminate, what gives mortals the right?"

Corajidin nodded. He raised the vial to his lips. He could smell nothing more than summer rain and the scent of sunshine on a cat's fur. Downing the draught in one gulp, the rahn gasped as the fluid filled him with rapturous energy.

"Cut!" the Emissary thundered.

Before he knew what he was doing, Corajidin had taken the knife and sliced deeply across his forearms. Blood coursed down his arms, black in the strangled light of the sycamores. It trickled from Corajidin's fingers, into the bowl of hollowed earth at his knees. Belamandris muttered a curse. Kasraman's expression remained closed, his gaze intent.

The pain of the wounds was excruciating. Worse than any battle wound, the cuts scalded as if they bled acid. Corajidin was about to pull his arms back when Wolfram held them in place. He struggled in the other man's grip.

When Corajidin looked up, the Emissary's eyes shone with madness. Her mindstone flared into emerald life.

"Not yet! More—you must give more!" she whispered urgently.

Corajidin choked back a cry of anguish. The pain was too much! He could feel the blood scalding his skin. Could hear his own hearts labouring with the strain of his agony, his pulse hammering in his ears. Could feel the sweat beading his brow, before it trickled hot down his face. He threw his head back, breath hissing between his teeth.

When he opened his eyes, he saw other silhouettes crawling across the bright places between the leaves and limbs of the sycamores. At first he thought they were walking across thin air. His eyes adjusted, and he saw in fact that they were making their way across fine threads. They moved with lazy purpose, deliberate and precise. Their bodies were lean and hungry. Their legs long and barbed. From time to time sunlight would lance through the canopy, reflecting from the clusters of their beaded eyes.

Their grotesque march spiralled inwards towards the twisted trunk of the decrepit sycamore.

Down.

Down.

Down they came to crawl amongst the whorls of bark and the exposed roots of the old tree until they crept—silently, terrifyingly—in their scores to where Corajidin knelt.

"Do nothing!" Wolfram warned the others. Spiders crawled across him. Through his hair. Along his beard. Over the swollen knuckles of his long-fingered hands.

En masse they crawled to the edge of the blood-filled bowl to drink their fill. They scuttled atop each other, legs waving. A seething, furred mass of fangs and bodies. Corajidin wanted to retch. From the corner of his eye he saw Belamandris, poised, hand caressing Tragedy's hilt, while Kasraman stood apart, taking everything in.

Their thirst sated, the weavers made their way—bloated—back to the sycamore. They heaved their rounded bodies upward, vanishing amongst the waving leaves and torn curtains of web.

Corajidin felt faint from blood loss. His vision contracted. Light, shadow, all else faded into the stark contrast. Time contracted. It felt as if moments disappeared, or were stolen. Time stuttered. Became seemingly haphazard, scattered, rather than serial moments, one after another.

Then stopped altogether.

A single spider, much larger than the others, descended on the end of a web as thick as Corajidin's little finger. It was a beautiful monster, so pale as to be translucent, shining with a swirling blue-white light at its heart, which resembled a face seen through mist. Corajidin looked around, but his companions seemed frozen in their moment.

The giant arachnid landed on the gossamer-clad woman, whose face was spread in a euphoric smile, her teeth improbably white against full, darkly painted lips. The light from the spider shone on her burnished skin, reflected like stars in her eyes. Legs spanning the woman's torso, it reared . . . then plunged glass-needle fangs into her chest.

Corajidin wanted to cry out, but could not. The spider pulsed, each flare of light getting fainter, radiant filaments pouring into the woman who remained rooted to the spot.

The light in her eyes faded, leaving them little better than dull beads.

They remained so for what may have been a second, or an eternity, before they shone brightly, backlit by thousands of flickering candles.

Then the spider fell to the ground and shattered. The crystal fragments of its body broke apart into a fine cloud of diamond dust, rainbow hued with refracted light. There came a resounding chime like the sounding of the great bell.

And time started once more. The light poured across the world, like molasses at first, then quickening till it filled the bowl of Corajidin's world. It was darker now. *How much time had passed?*

Corajidin fell sideways, head bouncing on the dead leaves and dried twigs. He lay there, light-headed and gasping, only the barest sensation in his fingertips as if his hands had fallen asleep.

Everybody stuttered into movement. Belamandris and Kasraman rushed to Corajidin's side. The woman in red gossamer fell backwards into the mulch like she had been poleaxed. The three crones fussed about her, pierced grey tongues working in their dark mouths, long-nailed hands prodding and probing the supine form. The Emissary stood, heedless of the stains on her clothes, and watched with fixed determination while her crones worked.

The gold spout of a wine skin was placed against Corajidin's lips. Liquor, sweet as honey, gushed across his tongue. Kasraman bound his wounds, chanting over them. The pain rapidly dwindled to a pleasant tingling. For several moments he sat there, head lolling, before he felt a sense of gentle lassitude sweep over him.

Belamandris helped his father to his feet. Corajidin staggered, but soon found his footing. His eyes were drawn to the woman in red gossamer, who had not moved since she had fallen.

The Emissary crossed to where her crones worked, twigs snapping beneath her split-toed boots. She spoke in a guttural, phlegmatic language, which the crones answered in, their voices high-pitched like a branch scratching glass.

"Father," Kasraman said. "We need to go. Now!"

"Your Coronation—" Belamandris began.

"Can wait!" Corajidin snapped, head light and feeling dizzy. "I'm sorry, my sons, but this . . ."

"Is something people may hear of in the fullness of time," Kasraman said sharply. "But your Coronation is something thousands are already in attendance to see."

"Your boy is right," the Emissary said over her shoulder. "Go. Put a golden hat on your head. We'll do what needs be done here."

"But—"

"Just go. This is the day you've plotted and schemed for." The Emissary patted the woman in gossamer's cheek. "Enjoy it so there's at least some recompense for the price you'll pay."

※ ※ ※

Hours of ceremony all for one Imperialist rahn and a score of loyal sayfs to attend. Kasraman's estimate of thousands had been somewhat inflated.

Where was everybody?

Ajomandyan as Arbiter of the Change—the man supposed to crown the new Asrahn—was absent. They had waited until Corajidin had finally demanded Narseh perform the ceremony, and the old Knight-Marshal bellowed the oaths across a Tyr-Jahavān, which may as well have been a ghost town.

Roshana, Nazarafine, and Siamak were not present. None of the Federationist sayfs made an appearance and even some of the Imperialists were missing. Kiraj, the Arbiter-Marshall and Padishin, the Secretary-Marshall, spent the entire ceremony talking quietly to each other. Ziaire and a goodly number of her courtesans were present, though Corajidin doubted their attendance was anything more than business.

Corajidin had learned that the Sēq were gone, Amenankher closed fast behind them. The witches were unable to navigate the complex Wards left to secure the Sēq's mountain fortress. The Emissary laughed when Corajidin demanded she break them. All the Sēq treasures, their weapons, plus the source of the Water of Life, were locked away and useless to him.

Time oozed on as he slouched on his cold, uncomfortable sphere in the Tyr-Jahavān. His thighs began to cramp and his head to ache, along with a sense of foreboding that the Emissary's most recent task had failed. Around him people talked and danced and laughed their brittle laughs. They whispered, looking at him over their bowls of wine. The mixed scents of grilled meats, vegetables, dips, and spices made him nauseated. And everywhere were the ones who asked for favours in return for their support. *You promised me.* Promised.

Promises.

Promise.

It was Ziaire, not Corajidin, who declared the evening at an end when she made her vague and enthusiastic farewell, much more enthusiastic than her greeting. No sooner had the courtesans left than the others began to trickle away, the chamber becoming a ludicrous place of vast and silent emptiness between small, quiet conversations.

He left as soon as it was seemly to do so, his fury barely contained by the way he throttled the crown in his hands.

❈ ❈ ❈

Corajidin tossed and turned on his wide bed. The stars outside the window tracked slowly across the black night sky and the streets outside were silent. At regular intervals the Anlūki could be heard, their armoured tread loud in the stillness of the early morning.

A play of light and shadow at the door to his chamber caught his attention. Figures stood there, limned in the radiance of *ilhen* lamps. Three were short and hunched, holding a golden chain attached to a tall figure in red gossamer. The fifth spoke.

"We've done what you asked, Corajidin," the Emissary said. "Your new bride is prepared, and not without cost."

"I paid—"

"We need more." She held up her hand to forestall his protest. "And you'll give us what we ask, without complaint, when the time comes."

"Or what?" he sneered, sick and tired of the Emissary's haughty attitude.

"Or what was given can be taken away." The crones tugged on the chain so the woman in gossamer was forced to bend double. Her eyes were panicked, but her mouth remained closed. One of the crones extended a yellowed claw against the woman's long neck. "But the price will be paid for services rendered, regardless. You swore you knew the consequences of your actions to the powers that are. They don't give second chances, Corajidin.

"So . . . will you do as you're told, or do we destroy this magnificent specimen right here?"

The woman in chains clearly heard what was being said yet did not speak. There was a mixture of defiance and fear in her eyes, a look he recognised. If only he could be sure! But the Emissary was leaving him little choice.

"Very well. What do you want?"

The Emissary smiled, rubbing her thumb along the squid carved on to the pommel of her sword. "I understand you've sent your daughter to Tamerlan, to learn from the whip and rod, coal and pincer of the Dowager-Asrahn, your mother-in-law. I want Mari shielded at all times, so no mystic can ever find her. And I want her to remain there, freezing and alone, until I say otherwise."

"But she's my daughter!"

"Be thankful I've not asked for her head. *Yet.* Indris needs to be kept from distractions, and your daughter is nothing if not a distraction to him. I need my husband back."

He started at the emphasis in her voice on the word, *need.* "Why?"

The crone dug her nail into the chained woman's throat. The Emissary stared at Corajidin. "Will you do it?"

"Yes! Ancestors, yes. I'd rather Mari not be in contact with the man who led her astray."

"Ha!" The Emissary barked a laugh. "Your daughter strayed long before she met my husband." Before he could respond to that, she said, "And there's something more we would have, for all we've done for you."

"What?" he asked nervously.

"The Sēq are by no means broken, Corajidin. And there is the matter of the Empress-in-Shadows who stands in . . . your . . . way. My Masters would have you unite the Avān sooner, rather than later, and there can not be two Mahjs of the one people."

"You want me to—"

"Destroy Pashrea and the Sēq powerbase, yes. How else can you help deliver the world my Masters need?"

She clapped her hands and the crones pushed the woman in gossamer and chains into Corajidin's chamber. She stumbled and he caught her. When he looked up, the Emissary and her crones were gone.

Corajidin removed the collar and chain from around the woman in gossamer's neck.

"Thank you," the woman said in a voice like smoke on brandy.

"You can speak?"

"Oh, at least," she purred. She looked at him candidly, appraisingly. She walked about the room, touching things, seemingly oblivious to the way her robe parted as she walked. Her gestures were so familiar it pained him as much as aroused him. She ran her fingers over silk sheets, almost shuddering with the sensation. The woman picked up a scent vial and delicately dabbed behind her ears, the inside of her wrists and between her breasts, the last with a shy smile that was all artistry. *Yashamin's favourite scent.*

"My name is Corajidin."

"Jidi." His hearts rapped against the cage of his ribs. *Was it really her?*

She walked around the bed, to where several of his most treasured items were. She lay her long fingers on them, slowly, sensually, her eyes lit with the reflection of precious metals and jewels. She stopped in front of Yashamin's funeral mask and picked it up.

"What is your name?" he asked, afraid of the answer. *The body is different the face is different but the way she moves and talks surely it must be her?* He felt lightheaded, his desire threatening to overwhelm him. Corajidin staggered forward a step. Then another, and another. He wet his lips with his tongue as she settled on the bed to lay, supple and exposed, her robe parting to reveal new lands for him to conquer.

She put Yashamin's mask over her face.

"What would you call me?"

31

"SOME CONSIDER IT IRONIC WHEN WE SAY THAT WE FIGHT IN THE NAME OF PEACE."

—from The Values, quotes by Kemenchromis, Sēq Magnate and
Arch-Scholar (Third Year of the Awakened Empire)

DAY 5 OF THE 496TH YEAR OF

THE SHRĪANESE FEDERATION

Sitting cross-legged on a broad balcony at Amarqa-in-the-Snows, Indris closed his eyes against the reflected light from the harsh white vista of the Mar Silin. The towering peaks of the Mountains of the Moon stretched in an achromatic line, stark against the cloud-streaked sky, which seemed all the more blue in contrast. There came the distant rumble of the Anqorat River where it burst forth in sheets of glistening spume, the start of its journey to the Marble Sea almost fifteen hundred kilometres away. The air was crisp, redolent with eucalyptus. A sharp cracking sound echoed across the many-tined valley below, as another tree exploded in the cold.

He had come here every day since his arrival, in order to nurture his bruised psyche from the none-too-gentle caresses of the Suret and the Inquisition. Taqrit had been a rank amateur by comparison, though at least Indris's current interrogators were not trying to be deliberately cruel and, thus far, there had not been a daul in sight. But escape was necessary, even if it was fleeting, like this current retreat.

There were few people out. Some Sēq novices trained with their wooden swords, spears, and knives, while others were given rigorous training in unarmed combat. From a distance they looked like a murder of crows flapping about, beaks stabbing for food. A lone librarian sat at an open window, her face beatific in the sun. A black-hulled wind-galley, bright with flashes of lightning from its Tempest Wheels and Disentropy Spools, made its way home. All was at peace. If all one did was look at the surface.

Invisible to the untrained eye, the ahmsah was incandescent with patterns of energy that overlapped and intersected with each other. Wards, barriers, and mystic filters covered the valley in an umbrella of power and illusion, monitored at all hours for anything untoward. Not even a rabbit could enter the Amarqa valley without the Sēq knowing about it.

Indris climbed to the top of his consciousness and watched the circuits flowing around his world. While it was true the Sēq had protected themselves, they also needed to view what transpired beyond their walls—more so now than before, given the chapterhouses of Irabiyat and Avānweh were lost. It had taken four days for Indris to isolate the gaps in the pattern, quantums of nothing like pinpricks in a sky-sized sheet. The gaps moved along in the wake of several ahm dense states, where the sheer volume of energies could not be perfectly merged. After several hours Indris had mapped his way through and was finally able to access the ahmtesh, where the souls of the dead moved, spoke, danced, and dreamed with little care for the troubles of the world they left behind.

Almost immediately he saw two bright stars rocket his way from the luminous thunderhead that was a gathering of souls. They spiralled around each other, firefly bright, leaving fading trails behind them. Indris fortified his kaj, in case these two meant him harm. He waited tensely; ready to slide back down the ladder of his states of existence and shelter within his physical body.

"Indris!" Chaiya said. As she closed, the star transformed into the features of his friend, her jade and ink etched form beaming. Beside her was another shape, which swung and spiralled behind her as if it were a kite on a string. *"We've been looking for you. Where have you been?"*

"*I'm in Amarqa-in-the-Snows, and I don't have much time, not if I want to keep my soul excursion a secret. I'm sorry to rush you, but can you tell me what happened to my friends? To Mari and Shar? Hayden, Omen, and Ekko?*"

"*Oh, Indris!*" He quailed at the remorse in her voice. Tiny diamonds lit on her cheeks, the analogy of her memories of sorrow.

"*Tell me, please.*"

"*Death is truly not the end,*" —the other soul pulsed—"*with naught to fear, nor heart to rend. One wonders now, with all that's here, what it was I came to fear.*"

"*Omen?*" Indris choked the name.

And the figure transformed, slowly at first, then more rapidly, into a tall, slender man in a fine over-robe, long coat, loose trousers and boots with the toes curled up. The face had high cheekbones and deep-set eyes, set between a long straight nose and thick eyebrows. The face turned into a small cloud of swirling jade smoke, before it settled again into a gentle smile.

"*Do not be sad, my intrepid friend, for we can still speak, now and then.*"

"*What happened?*"

Omen recounted the events of the Dead Flat, of his and Hayden's deaths and of Vahineh and Mari being taken. He spoke of the deal Roshana made with Belamandris and how Ekko had managed to spirit Shar away before they, too, were killed. Indris listened to it all with growing sorrow, mixed with a rising anger and frustration.

"*This happened because of me,*" Indris said. "*You and Hayden. Mari. This is on me.*"

"*Don't be foolish, Indris,*" Chaiya wrapped her soul around Indris's and held him close. "*You carry the weight of too much that is not your fault. Don't add this to your burdens. They're happy here.*"

"*They?*"

"*Hayden,*" Omen smiled. "*Along with his wife and daughters. It seems we do all come to the one place when we die, the same place all our souls come from. I even found an old cat of mine, one who had shared my life for almost twenty years. He had been waiting a long time, as relaxed and proud in death as he ever was in life. But as to Hayden. He told me to tell you, if we spoke, that he is happy, and that he finally managed to make it home.*"

Indris felt his soul shine with bittersweet melancholy. Movement from the corner of his eye caused him to turn. A shimmering curtain was drifting their way, vertical lines and streaks of grey similar to approaching rain. The Sēq.

"I need to go"

"What will you do about Mari?" Omen asked.

"I'll find her and bring her back," Indris said. *"But she's gone for now, and there are other friends to whom I must make amends. But there are things I must do here, first."*

"And once you're done here?" Chaiya's face floated in front of Indris's.

"I'll call upon some friends, old and new, for what will come next."

The rain-grey curtain was much closer now. Indris bid his friends farewell and plummeted back to his body.

Indris stood and wiped the snow from his over-robe. The tears of grief he kept.

He turned and walked into the vastness of Amarqa. The time would come when he would pay back his debts in full, as there would be a time he would exact his price from those who had wronged him, and caused those he loved to suffer.

But for now, this is where he needed to be if he were ever to find the answers he needed, to the questions he was only now learning to ask.

CAST OF CHARACTERS

Indris	Avān. Pahmahjin-Näsarat fa Amonindris, formerly a knight of the Sēq Order of Scholars and now a daimahjin, a mercenary warrior-mage. Once commanded the Immortal Companions' nahdi company. Also known as Dragon-Eyed Indris; Indris, Tamer of Ghosts; and Indris, the Prince of Diamonds. Bears the mind blade, Changeling.
Shar-fer-rayn	Seethe. War-chanter of the Rayn-ma troupe, reputed to be the last surviving member of her family. Met Indris in the slave pits of Sorochel, from which they escaped together. Now travels with Indris.
Hayden Goode	Human. A drover turned adventurer and once a skirmisher for the Immortal Companions. Expert rifleman. Now travels with Indris.
Sassomon-Omen	Nomad. Became a Wraith Knight in the collapse of the Awakened Empire. Formerly an artist and philosopher, he became an infantryman with the Immortal Companions. Now travels with Indris.
Ekko	Tau-se. Former Knight-Colonel of the Lion Guard First Company. Commanded the expedition to retrieve Far-ad-din after his escape. Now a kombe, travels with Indris.

GREAT HOUSE OF NÄSARAT

Roshana	Avān. Federationist. Rahn-Näsarat of Näsarat Prefecture, and Prefect of Narsis.
Ariskander	*Avān. Deceased. Avān. Former Rahn of Näsarat Prefecture and Prefect of Narsis.*
Nehrun	Avān. Pah-Näsarat, once Ariskander's rahn-elect but now incarcerated at the Shrine of the Vanities.
Tajaddin	Avān. Pah-Näsarat and Ariskander's third child.
Bensaharēn	Avān. Poet Master of the Näsé-sûk, the Phoenix School, in Narsis. Poet Master of the Great House of Näsarat. Also the Sayf-Näsarin, distant cousins to the Great House of Näsarat. Called the Waterdancer. Bears the amenesqa, Rain.
Danyūn	Human. Member of the Ishahayans, and Master of Spies for the Great House of Näsarat.
Maselane	Human. Sayf of the Family Ashour and Master of Arms for the Great House of Näsarat. Also Knight-General of the Näsarat Phoenix Armies.
Mauntro	Tau-se. Knight-Colonel of the Lion Guard.
Anani	Tau-se. Lion Guard.
Baniq	Human. Gnostic Assassin.
Furu	Tau-se. Lion Guard.

Fyra	Human. Gnostic Assassin.
GREAT HOUSE OF NĀSARAT (CONT.)	
Kofo	Tau-se Lion Guard.
Nsay	Tau-se Lion Guard.
Samu	Tau-se Lion Guard.
Zoer	Avān. Gnostic Assassin.
GREAT HOUSE OF NĀSARAT (PASHREA)	
Malde-ran	Avān. Mahjirahn of Pashrea and Mahj of the Shadow Empire. Also known as the Empress-in-Shadows. Prefect of Mediin.
Kemenchromis	Avān. Sēq Master Magnate and Arch-Scholar. Twin brother of Femensetri. Lore Master and rajir to the Empress-in-Shadows.
GREAT HOUSE OF EREBUS	
Corajidin	Avān. Imperialist. Rahn-Erebus of Erebus Prefecture and Prefect of Erebesq.
Yashamin	*Deceased. Avān. Corajidin's third wife and former nemhoureh of the House of Pearl.*
Kasraman	Avān. Imperialist. Pah-Erebus and Corajidin's rahn-elect. Trained as an Angothic Witch by Wolfram. Son of Corajidin's first wife, Laleh of the Ars-Izrel.
Belamandris	Avān. Imperialist. Pah-Erebus, called the Widowmaker and leader of the Anlūki. Corajidin's second son. Born to Corajidin's second wife, Farha of the Dahrain. Bears the amenesqa, Tragedy.
Mariam	Avān. Federationist. Pah-Erebus, called the Queen of Swords. Former member of the Feyassin. Born to Corajidin's second wife, Farha of the Dahrain.
Nima	Avān. Imperialist. Corajidin's nephew and warrior of the Anlūki.
Basyrandin	*Deceased. Avān. Imperialist. Corajidin's late father and four-time Asrahn of Shrīan.*
Khurshad	Avān. Imperialist. Widow of the late Basyrandin, Corajidin's mother and the Dowager-Asrahn. Khurshad is currently the Sayf-Tamerlan.
Qarnassus	*Deceased. Avān. Imperialist. Corajidin's grandfather and five-time Asrahn of Shrīan.*
Armal	*Deceased. Avān. Imperialist. Thufan's son.*
Brede	*Deceased. Human. Formerly a Sēq librarian captured and turned by the Angothic Witches. Now Wolfram's former apprentice.*
Farouk	*Deceased. Avān. Imperialist. Corajidin's nephew and adjutant.*
Feyd	Exile. Avān. Imperialist. Leader of the Jiharim. Corajidin's Master of Arms.

Jhem	Exile. Avān. Imperialist. Sayf-Delfineh and Corajidin's Master of Assassins. Known as the Blacknake.

GREAT HOUSE OF EREBUS (CONT.)	
Kimiya	Exile. Avān. Imperialist. Youngest daughter of Jhem, and Wolfram's apprentice.
Nadir	Exile. Avān. Imperialist. Son and eldest child of Jhem. Before his Exile, Nadir was Mari's lover, and a former student of the Näsé-súk.
Nix	Exile. Avān. Imperialist. Sayf-Malahdi and son of Rayz, the Ironweb.
Ravenet	Exile. Avān. Imperialist. Oldest daughter of Jhem.
Sanojé	Exile. Avān. Imperialist. Pah-Chepherundi. A Tanisian witch.
Tahj-Shaheh	Exile. Avān. Imperialist. Marble Sea corsair and daughter of Hatoub, the late Sayf-Näs-Sayyin. Corajidin's Sky Master and Master of the Fleet.
Thufan	*Deceased. Avān. Imperialist. Sayf-Charamin and Corajidin's Kherife-General and Spymaster. Prefect of Jafke.*
Wolfram	Human. Angothic Witch and Corajidin's Lore Master, and rajir. Originally took service with Corajidin's grandfather, Rahn-Erebus fa Qarnassus. Corajidin's close friend and adviser. Kasraman's teacher in the arcane.
Yotep	Avān. Warrior of the Anlūki.

GREAT HOUSE OF SELASSIN	
Vashne	*Deceased. Avān. Rahn-Selassin and Asrahn of Shrīan. Prefect of Qeme.*
Afareen	*Deceased. Avān. Rahn-Selassin and wife of Vashne.*
Daniush	*Deceased. Avān. Pah-Selassin and Vashne's rahn-elect.*
Hamejin	*Deceased. Avān. Pah-Selassin and Vashne's second son.*
Vahineh	Avān. Rahn-Selassin and Vashne's only daughter. Third child of Vashne and Afareen.
Martūm	Avān. Pah-Selassin and Vashne's cousin.
Sadra	*Deceased. Human. Vahineh's weapon-master.*
Chelapa	*Deceased. Avān. Knight-Colonel of the Feyassin.*
Qamran	Avān. Knight-Major of the Feyassin.
Mehran	Avān. Knight-Lieutenant of the Feyassin.

GREAT HOUSE OF SÛN	
Nazarafine	Avān. Rahn-Sûn of the Sûn Isles and Speaker for the People. Prefect of Qom Riyadh.

GREAT HOUSE OF SÛN (CONT.)	
Navid	Avān. Pah-Sûn and Nazarafine's nephew. Warrior-poet of the Saidani-sûk, the 'Four Blades School.' Navid is the commander of Nazarafine's Sûnguard.
Jarrah	Avān. Poet Master of the Saidani-sûk, the Four Blades School, in Saidani. Poet Master of the Great House of Sûn.
GREAT HOUSE OF KADARIN	
Narseh	Avān. Imperialist. Rahn-Kadarin and Knight-Marshal of Shrīan. Prefect of Kadariat.
Anankil	Avān. Federationist. Pah-Kadarin and Narseh's heir. Knight-General of the Yourdin, the elite Kadarin heavy infantry.
Nirén	Avān. Poet Master of the Habron-sûk, the Heron School, in Avānweh. Poet Master of the Great House of Kadarin.
GREAT HOUSE OF BEY	
Siamak	Avān. Federationist. Rahn-Bey of Bey Prefecture and Prefect of Beyjan and Amnon.
Vasanya	Avān. Federationist. Rahn-Bey and wife of Siamak. Formerly of Tanis.
Umna	Avān. Federationist. Pah-Bey, Siamak's eldest daughter, and rahn-elect.
Harish	Avān. Federationist. Pah-Bey and Siamak's eldest son. Prefect of Ifqe, Master of Arms to the Great House of Bey, and leader of the Marmûn, the elite warriors of the Rōmarq and Bey Prefecture.
Indera	Avān. Federationist. Poet Master of the Marmûn-sûk, and Poet Master to the Great House of Bey.
(FORMER) GREAT HOUSE OF DIN-MA (THE SEETHE DIN-MA TROUPE)	
Far-ad-din	Exiled. Seethe. Rahn-Din-ma, deposed at the Battle of Amber Lake. Former Prefect of Amnon.
Ran-jar-din	*Deceased. Seethe. Pah-Din-ma. Far-ad-din's rahn-elect.*
Anj-el-din	Seethe. Pah-Nāsarat. Far-ad-din's daughter and Indris's once missing wife, now returned
THE HUNDRED FAMILIES	
Ajomandyan	Avān. Federationist. Sayf-Nāsiré and Prefect of Avānweh. Also referred to as the Sky Lord.
Bijan	Avān. Federationist. One of Vashne's and Ariskander's allies.
Chanq	Avān. Imperialist. Sayf-Joroccan and heavily involved in organized crime. One of Corajidin's supporters.
Hadi	Avān. Imperialist. One of Corajidin's supporters.
Iraj	Human. Federationist. One of Vashne's and Ariskander's allies.

THE HUNDRED FAMILIES (CONT.)	
Kiraj	Human. Neutral, though generally allied with the Federationists. Sayf-Masadhe and Prefect of Masadhe. Arbiter Marshal of Shrīan. One of Vashne's and Ariskander's allies.
Maroc	Avān. Imperialist. Sayf-Jayan and Prefect of Zam'Haja. Younger brother of Delfyne, the Poet Master of the Grieve.
Neva	Avān. Federationist. Ajomandyan's granddaughter and heir. Commands the Sky Knights of Avānweh, and performs in the Näsiré Flying Cirq.
Rayz	Deceased? Exile. Imperialist. Former Sayf-Malahdi, and former Master of Assassins for the Great House of Erebus.
Teymoud	Avān. Imperialist. Sayf-Saidani and Magnate of the Mercantile Guildsman and one of Corajidin's supporters.
Yago	Avān. Federationist. Ajomandyan's grandson. A senior officer of the Sky Knights of Avānweh, and performs in the Näsiré Flying Cirq.
Zendi	Avān. Imperialist. Sayf-Bajadeh. Runs bordellos in competition to the House of Pearl. One of Corajidin's supporters.
Ziaire	Avān. Federationist. Sayf-Manshira and Prime of Amajoram in Avānweh. One of the most celebrated nemhoureh of the House of Pearl.
THE SĒQ	
Ahwe	Avān. Sēq Magnate. One of the greatest of the Sēq, and one of Sedefke's first apprentices. Helped found the scholastic orders.
Aumh	Y'arrow-ti-yi. Sēq Master and member of the Suret.
Femensetri	Avān. Sēq Master and Scholar Marshal of Shrīan. Formerly Indris's teacher. Also known as the Stormbringer. Member of the Suret and one of those who helped found the scholastic orders.
He-Who-Watches	Avān. Sēq Master and member of the Suret. An orjini tribesman.
Kemenchromis	Avān. Sēq Master Magnate and Arch-Scholar. Twin brother of Femensetri. Lore Master and rajir to the Empress-in-Shadows. Prime of the Suret. Helped found the scholastic orders.
Madiset	Avān. Sēq instructor and one of Indris's teachers at Amarqa-in-the-Snows.
Sedefke	Avān. Founder of the Sēq Order of Scholars, who discovered the process of soul binding with the consciousness of Ía, otherwise known as Awakening.

THE SĒQ (CONT.)	
Taqrit	Avān. Sēq Inquisitor and one of the Eight. Childhood friend of Indris and Anj-el-din.
Yattoweh	Avān. Once, Sedefke's first and greatest disciple. Helped found the various scholastic orders.
Zadjinn	Avān. Sēq Master and member of the Great House of Erebus. Member of the Suret.
OTHERS	
Delfyne	Avān. Poet Master of the Grieve, also known as the Erebon-sûk, or the Stallion School, in Zam'Haja. Elder sister of Maroc.
Kembe	Tau-se. Patriarch of the Tau-se tribes and Protector of Taumarqan.
Navaar	Avān/Human. High Palatine of Oragon.
Tyen-to-wo	The Laughing Wind spirit of the Seethe.

GLOSSARY OF TERMS

Ahm	Also referred to as disentropy, it is the energy created by all living things. It's most powerful source is the qua, the theorised centre of all creation.
Ahmsah	The collection of disentropic effects taught to scholars. It includes the various arcane formulae, as well as the perceptions used by scholars to see entropic and disentropic effects.
Ahmtesh	The fluid space of the ahm, which connects all things together. This is where the disembodied kaj dwell, as well as a space being accessible to pséjhah, or psé-masters, where mental communication is possible over vast distances.
Ahnah-woh-te	Books of Seethe mystic teachings.
Ahoujai	Medallions, amulets, or jewelry made from salt-forged steel and the sand from burned-out arcane mandalas. Used as protection from the effects of the ahmsah.
Aipsé	The no-mind taught to warrior-poets.
Ajamensût	War of the Long-Knife.
Amenesqa	High Avān word meaning long wave. From amen (long) and esqa (wave).The traditional weapon of the Avān during the Petal Empire and the Awakened Empire. It is a long recurved sword, shaped like an elongated, flattened 's' from the pommel to the tip of the blade. The weapon has a long hilt and can be used either one handed or two handed.
Anlūki	Elite personal guard of the Rahn-Erebus. Trained and commanded by Pah-Erebus fa Belamandris.
Arbiter	A legal advocate and practitioner of the law. Generally works in conjunction with kherife, as the enforcers of the law.
Arbiter of the Change	A sayf or rahn appointed by the Magistratum and the Teshri, to oversee periods of political or military change. During the Change, this role is subservient only to the Asrahn.
Ascendants	The progenitors of the Avān Great Houses.
Ashinahdi	A warrior of the elite-caste or royal-caste who has cut the ties to their Great House or Family, to pursue a course of action which might otherwise be contrary to the best interests of the family group. A person becomes an ashinahdi generally only after some great shame, or insult to the family, which the rules of sende would otherwise forbid. The separation from family exempts the greater family group from the consequences of the ashinahdi's actions.
Aspect	Illusory form taken by witches.
Asrahn	The highest ranking rahn in Shrīan, elected through the process of Accession, held every five years in Avānweh.
Asrahn-Elect	The second-highest ranking rahn in Shrīan, elected through the process of Accession, held every five years in Avānweh.

GLOSSARY OF TERMS (CONT.)	
Avāndhim	The Firstborn of the Avān, the original generation created in the Seethe Torque Spindles on an island chain across the Eastron Divide.
Awakening	The process whereby a person is given the potential to connect with the consciousness and power of Īa, as well as gaining the ability to access the unbroken line of their Ancestors in living memory. An Awakened rahn is able to affect the weather, see and hear vast distances, increase the speed crops grow, see through the eyes of birds and beasts, etc in their Prefecture. The process is solidified, and made stable, through the drinking of the Water of Life in the Communion Ritual, and the process of Unity.
Catechism	The governing body of the witches, represented by the Mother Superiors and Father Superiors of the various covens. The Catechism works closely with the ruling class of the Golden Kingdom of Manté and is reputed to have significant influence in setting policy across the Human nations of the Iron League.
Communion Ritual	The ritual whereby a rahn, who has passed the Sēq testing for their eligibility, enters the Ancestor's Heart under World Blood Mountain and drinks the Water of Life.
Daikajé	Travelling warrior-ascetics, thinkers and monks of the various orders of philosophy across South Eastern Īa.
Daimahjin	A warrior-mage who is no longer a member of the Order that trained them. Such people have been released from service and given the freedom to exercise their skills on behalf of suitable employers, though are forbidden to pass on their teachings to others. Most are also highly sought after nahdi.
Daul	An esoteric pain amplifier and concussion weapon favoured by Sēq Inquisitors.
Dhar Gsenni	From the High Avan term for the good of all, the Dhar Gsenni are an ancient sect of Ilhennim that work within the Sēq.
Dionesqa	High Avān word meaning 'great wave.' From dion (great) and esqa (wave). The name for the Pashrean and Shrīanese recurved double-handed sword. It is a rare weapon, generally used by select members of the heavy infantry trained in its use.
Disentropic Stain	The discoloration of an Ilhennim's aura as the result of their training.
Disentropy	The power of creation, manipulated by scholars using the formulae of the ahmsah, or by witches using their own arcanum. The use of disentropy is known to cause rapid decay of those materials that it comes in contact with, including living flesh. Metals that decay slowly are generally used in the construction of arcane devices powered by disentropy.

GLOSSARY OF TERMS (CONT.)

Drear, the	The darkest and most malign depths and reaches of the ahmtesh. Source of dark desires and dreams, as well as the dwelling place of ancient beings from the old world. A place where one forgets all the good things about themselves, and sees only the dark, bitter, melancholy that pooled in the most hidden depths of the soul.
Ebrim	Nomads who take artificial simulacra in which to interact with the world.
Ephael	The purest of the Nomads, who exist as pure spirit.
Ephim	Nomads who exist symbiotically with a host.
Eshim	Nomads who take possession of others against their will.
Esoteric Doctrines	Various schools that articulate how the Ilhennim perceive and stimulate natural energy to supernatural outcomes.
Exalted Name	Famous people who have gained a name, epithet, or other title as the result of their actions.
Extrinsic Precept	Within the Esoteric Doctrines, a method of mysticism that uses external forces as a conduit. The method has little restraint, or control, and is not as reliable as the Intrinsic Precept.
Fayaadahat	Books of Sēq mystic teachings.
Font, the	Central point from which the ahm flows. Theorised by scholars to be the centre of all the worlds in space and time.
Gnostic Assassins	A group of highly trained assassins of the Mar am'a Din. Highly sought after as killers for hire, the Gnostic Assassins are taught a series of physical, mental, and other disciplines which makes them formidable spies and killers. Also known as the Ishahayans.
Grieve, the	Also known as the Erebon-sûk, or the Stallion School of warrior-poetry. Currently under the governance of Master Delfyne of the Zam'Haja.
Habron-sûk	The Heron School of warrior-poets of Avānweh. Currently under the governance of Master Nirén.
Hazhi'shi	The complex language of the Dragons.
Houreh	Versatile entertainer companions.
Huqdi	From the High Avān term, street dog. The huqdi are generally common bravos, freebooters and soldiers of fortune, sometimes criminals, without the sense of professional ethics of a nahdi.
Ilhennim	The illuminated, a general term used to describe the various types of mystic.
Intrinsic Precept	Within the Esoteric Doctrines, the way power is channelled, focussed, and exercised from within. Based on the repeatable, predictable effects of formulae.

GLOSSARY OF TERMS (CONT.)

Ishahayans	Gnostic Assassins.
Jhah	High Avān word for Master.
Jhi	The stigma which identifies the most powerful of mystics. It is a physical phenomenon which appears when their power is used to a greater degree.
Jombe	Tau-se warrior who has chosen to travel beyond the protection and guidelines of their tribe. Generally outcasts who have committed crimes of honour, in search of redemption.
Jûresqa	High Avān word meaning 'short wave.' From jûr (short) and esqa (wave). The name for the Pashrean and Shrīanese recurved short sword.
Kaj	High Avān word for soul.
Kaj-adept	A scholar who has mastered a suite of complex spiritual disciplines.
Karia, the	The elite military force of Mediin, comprised of both living and Nomad warrior-poets, warrior-mages and other soldiers.
Kherife	An enforcer of the law.
Khopesh	The long Tau-se sickle sword.
Kirion	A rare metal smelted from meteors, also called star metal. It is usually black in colour, shot through with a rainbow hue when seen in direct sunlight.
Krysesqa	High Avān word meaning 'quick wave'. From krys (quick) and esqa (wave). The name for the Pashrean and Shrīanese recurved long-knife.
Lament, the	Also referred to as the Näsé-sûk, or the Phoenix School of warrior-poets, from Narsis in Näsarat Prefecture. Currently under the governance of Master Bensaharēn of the Näsarin.
Lion Guard	The elite Tau-se companies in service to the Great House of Näsarat.
Lore Master	A mystic who has been appointed to a Great House or Family as advisor to a mahj, rahn or sayf. Traditionally Lore Masters have been members of the Sēq Order of Scholars, though it is not unheard of for Zienni Scholars, Nilvedic Scholars or witches to assume the role.
Magistratum	Senior officials who represent the holistic interests of the Crown and State, led by the various Officers Marshall. The Magistratum is a neutral body, with a number of portfolios created to represent the common good, each managed by a senior officer. Examples of portfolios in the Magistratum include education, law, the military, finance, trade, etc.

GLOSSARY OF TERMS (CONT.)

Mahj	An Awakened emperor, generally one who is a fully trained Sēq Scholar. The last Mahj was Mahj-Näsarat fe Malde-ran, currently known as the Empress-in-Shadows, in Mediin.
Mahjin	Title or honorific given to one of the Ilhennim. Usually only used by scholars.
Mahjirahn	A rahn who is also a trained mystic. These were quite common in the Awakened Empire where the Mahj was also a fully trained scholar, generally of the Sēq Order.
Mah-Psésahen	A dead school of the Esoteric Doctrines, which sought to teach higher mental functions without the need for disentropy.
Mahsayf	A Coven trained witch who is the leader of a Family.
Maladhoring	The arcane language of the Elemental Masters.
Marmûn	The elite warriors of the Rōmarq and Bey Prefecture. Most are graduates of the Marmûn-sûk.
Marmûn-sûk	The Marsh Hawk School of warrior-poets, from Bey Prefecture. Currently under the governance of Master Indera.
Master of Arms	The highest ranking military officer and strategist in a Great House or Family.
Master of Assassins	The commander of the assassins assigned to a Great House, or Family. This role will include the responsibilities of the Master of Spies.
Master of Spies	The commander of the spies assigned to a Great House, or Family. Generally used when a House or Family does not usually have assassins in their permanent employ.
Master of the Fleet	The highest ranking naval officer of a Great House, or Family.
Master of House	The role of managing all the financial , mercantile and other administrative tasks required to run a Great House, or Family. Quite often the role is also that of Secretary to a rahn, or sayf. Sometimes the role also assumes the responsibilities of a rajir.
Nahdi	From the High Avān word meaning iron dog, a nahdi is the name for a mercenary or other professional soldier unaffiliated with a Great House or Family. Nahdi generally operate with a strict code of professional ethics.
Näsé-sûk	Also known as the Lament.
Nayu-adept	A scholar who has mastered a suite of complex physical disciplines.
Nemembe	Tau-se belief that a person gets back from the world threefold what they give it, both in kindness as well as suffering.
Nemhoureh	Gold Companion of the House of Pearl. A prized courtesan and entertainer who engages only with the upper castes and the most affluent members of society.

GLOSSARY OF TERMS (CONT.)

Nomad	The Avān term for the undead.
Officers Marshall	The most senior officials in the Magiustratum. Some are representatives from the Hundred Families or the Great Houses, though many are representatives from the merchante-caste, warrior-caste or the freehold-caste which includes artisans, farmers and other trades people.
Pah	High Avān word for the child of a rahn.
Pahavān	The highest ranking members of the Avān in a country where there are no Awakened rahns.
Poet Master	The head of a Poet Master academy, teaching the ancient arts of the warrior-poet.
Prefect	The appointed ruler of a city. A Prefect is always a rahn, or sayf, where the title is inherited. Where a Great House or Family is Exiled, or otherwise removed from the roles, a new Prefect from a different House or Family will be appointed.
Psé	High Avān word for mind.
Psé-adept	A scholar who has mastered a suite of complex mental disciplines.
Psédari	High Avān word meaning mind blade. From psé (mind) and dari (blade). Used by some Sēq Knights and Sēq Masters who have the skills and disciplines for creating such weapons. A psédari can only be wielded by the person who made it.
Pséja	The marriage of minds, used by mystics to work in concert and maximise effectiveness.
Qua	Also referred to as the Font.
Rahn	Leader of one of the Great Houses. A member of the royal-caste.
Rajir	Closest advisor to a rahn, or sayf. Usually a Lore Master, Master of Arms, Master of Spies or other senior officer in a household.
Rōm	The Time Masters, a long declined civilisation which predates the Elemental Masters. They are known only through the minimal footprint of relics and ruins found on Ĩa.
Sahai	High Avān word for teacher.
Saidani-sûk	The Four Swords warrior-poet academy of Sûn Prefecture. Currently under the governance of Master Jarrah.
Sayf	Leader of one of the Hundred Families. A member of the elite-caste.
Sende	The collection of policies, codes, measures, and other behaviors that the Avān use to regulate their social interactions.
Sēq, the	Scholastic order that teaches a combination of physical, mental and spiritual disciplines.

GLOSSARY OF TERMS (CONT.)

Serill	The drake fired glass of the Seethe. *Serill* is lighter and harder than steel and can be made into almost any shape. Often coloured, *serill* is popular with the Seethe in the making of armour and weapons.
Shamshir	The typical weapon of the Avān. It is a long, single edged curved weapon with a hilt long enough to use in either one or two hands.
Shan	The unofficial title used by the heads of influential tribes or clans. Generally used by the mountain peoples of the Mar Jihara, the Mar Ejir, the Mar Siliin, the Mar am'a Din, and the Mar Shalon. It is also sometimes used by affluent families with a military tradition. Generally members of the warrior-caste.
Sifr Hazhi	The collected mystic teachings of the Dragons.
Speaker for the People	The third highest ranking person in Shrīan, elected as the voice of the State, as opposed to being a representative of the Crown. In some cases, a rahn will be elected to this role, though their mandate is to serve the will of the people.
Sûk	A school.
Teshri	The government leaders, representatives of the Crown and State. Members of the Teshri are sayfs and rahns, though senior members of influential consortiums are also appointed, such as the leaders of the House of Pearl, the Banker's House, the Mercantile Guild, Alchemists Guild, etc.
Unity	The process whereby an Awakened rahn travels their prefecture, communing with the consciousness of Ía. Successful Unity provides the Awakened rahn with the ability to share, harness and leverage from the vast natural forces of Ía.
Vayen-sûk	The Lotus School of the warrior-poets, from Myr in Selassin Prefecture. Currently under the governance of Master Tarshin.
Yourdin	The elite heavy infantry of the Great House of Kadarin.
Warrior-poet	Arguably the most dangerous weapon masters in the world, a warrior-poet is trained in various weapons, strategies, unarmed combat and military history and philosophy. They are also trained in the creative arts of writing, poetry, painting, sculpting, etc as a means to off-set the violence of their core teaching and to gain an understanding of the value of life. A warrior-poet lives according to the tenet 'the one will fight, so the many do not have to.'
Water of Life	Also known as the World Blood, the Water of Life is a rare and vital source of water, enriched with a high content of disentropy from where it has flowed through areas where the border between the physical world of Ía, and the ahmtesh, are tenuous.

GLOSSARY OF TERMS (CONT.)

Witch	The first group of the Ilhennim, mystics who are able to harness a vast array of natural forces to affect a supernatural outcome. A more dangerous, and less predictable, set of practices than those used by scholars. The first scholastic orders were created by witches.
Witchfire	A natural ore with the mineral properties to more effective channel disentropy, without being destroyed in the process. Often alloyed with *kirion* for greater strength, though can be alloyed with other metals.

CULTURES

Avān	A species originally made by the Seethe in Torque Spindles from Seethe and Human specimens, as well as samples from predatory animals. The Avān were originally used as peacekeepers in the Petal Empire, though they ros up against the Seethe. Rather than release Humanity from their servitude, the newly formed Awakened Empire kept Humanity as a vassal race for the next millennium until it was toppled as part of a Human revolt.
Dragons	One of the Elemental Masters species, Dragons are also known as the Fire Masters. They call themselves the Hazhi. Rarely seen in the modern world, they are known to spend much of their time in slumber as part of the Great Dreaming, with only a small percentage of their population awake at any one time.
Fenling	A race created by the Seethe in the Torque Spindles, the Fenling are the merger of giant tool-using rats and the Avān. They are a race of scavengers who rarely deal with non-Fenling, and are known for their cannibalism and carrying of virulent diseases.

CULTURES (CONT.)	
Feyhe	One of the Elemental Master species, the Feyhe are also known as the Sea Masters. They are capable of changing into a series of simple and complex shapes.
Herū	One of the Elemental Masters species, the Herū are also known as the Earth Masters.
Humans	Also referred to as the Starborn. The most populous species on Ía. Once a vassal race to the Petal Empire of the Seethe, as well as the Awakened Empire of the Avān, Humanity is now independent. The largest Human faction in South-Eastern Ía is the Iron League; composed of Atrea, Jiom, Imre, Manté, Ondea, and Angoth. Humans are known to live in almost every nation.
Iku	An ancient and enigmatic race of avian-like humanoids, with strong ties to the Sēq Order. They are rarely seen outside their mountain retreats, and generally people mistake their appearance for a disguise. For the most part the Iku are daikajé, travelling warrior philosophers and teachers. Sometimes associated with bad omens.
Nomads	The undying or undead. Generally, they are without physical form and need to inhabit a physical shell in order to interact with the physical world. Seen as heretics by the Ancestor-worshipping Avān.
Rōm	Also called the Time Masters, the Rōm predate the Elemental Masters. There is very little documented about the Haiyt Empire of the Time Masters. It is known the Haiyt Empire simply ceased as a result of the Time Masters vanishing from Ía.
Seethe	One of the Elemental Master species, the Seethe are also known as the Wind Masters. The founders of the now fallen Petal Empire, they are effectively immortal, though they can die via sickness and violence. As Seethe mature, they undergo a physiological change where their bones thin and they grow wings. Seethe elders are capable of flight. The Seethe live and travel in extended family units known as troupes. They can be found in many cities across South-Eastern Ía, though most dwell in the floating Sky Realms, which drift around the world, propelled by the winds.
Tau-se	The lion-folk of the Taumarq, originally made in the Torque Spindles by blending Humans and lions. They are collected into a tribe-based patriarchy, though it is the women who run businesses and households. The Tau-se are sought after as mercenaries, but they will only serve an employer they respect.
Y'arrow-te-yi	A reclusive species reputed to be descended from earth elementals.

ACKNOWLEDGMENTS

So many people are involved behind the scenes of a novel, every one of them enthusiastic about the project and supportive of it. And stories are such subjective things: one person's passion, is a another person's poison . . .

To the usual suspects of my family and friends, for the patience, the laughs, and the care.

To my agent, John Jarrold, who has been a constant source of wisdom, advice, and support. A writer could not hope for a better agent.

To David Pomerico and the 47North Author Team, for the duty of care and the guidance, where no question was ever too much trouble, and every answer was cheerfully given. You made what could have been an arduous journey feel surprisingly smooth. Thanks also for the tremendous effort in your promotion and marketing of *The Garden of Stones*, and *The Obsidian Heart*.

To Stephan Martiniere for such wonderful artwork on both *The Garden of Stones* and *The Obsidian Heart*.

To my copy editor, Wenonah Hoye, for your attention to detail, and thoughtful suggestions.

Thanks to all of you. Any success I have is shared by you.

ABOUT THE AUTHOR

Mark Barnes was born in September, 1966, in Sydney, Australia. Raised and educated in Sydney, he was a champion swimmer who also played water polo, soccer, cricket, and volleyball. Drawn to the arts at a young age, he wrote his first short story at age seven, and was active in drawing, painting, and music as well.

His career stuttered in finance, slid into advertising, then leaped into information technology, where he continues to manage a freelance organizational change consultancy. It was not until January, 2005, when Mark was selected to attend the Clarion South residential short story workshop, that he began to write with a view to making it more than a hobby. Since Clarion South 2005, Mark has published a small number of short stories, worked as a freelance script editor, and done creative consultancy for a television series. *The Obsidian Heart* is Book Two in the *Echoes of Empire* series, which began with his first novel, *The Garden of Stones*.